COLD OPEN

A SAM NORTH MYSTERY

GREG CLARKIN

Published by Telemachus Press, LLC
http://www.telemachuspress.com

Visit the author website:
http://www.gregclarkin.com

ISBN: 978-0-9993952-4-0 (paperback)
ISBN: 978-1-938135-39-2 (eBook)

Version 2012.04.16

For Rani, Sophia, Matthew, and Alex.
And Vincent and Rosemary.

Cold Open

Cold Open (noun): the opening of a newscast by jumping directly into a story without rolling the beginning or opening credits. No top-of-the-show introductions, no fancy graphics, no dramatic music, no deep-voiced narrator telling you about all the important news about to be covered.

Chapter 1

I walked into Liberty News just before four a.m., and Charlie Morris was on me like I owed him money.

"Sam ... Sam, I need to talk to you," he said.

The big, hangar-like newsroom was near empty. It was a Tuesday in August, the heart of a slow, late-summer news cycle. Anybody with any pull or money was on vacation. I wasn't.

Morris zigzagged his way through the desks, determined to ruin my morning.

"Hey, Sam, wait up."

"No," I said.

A guy needs a little personal space at this hour. Charlie was a good guy, a veteran cameraman, but there was a little code of conduct among those of us unlucky enough to be on the morning shift. It included not getting in someone's face as soon he walked in the door.

"Sam, listen," he said as he closed in.

He had played the angles nicely and was just twenty feet from me.

"I need to talk to you."

He was dressed in his summer uniform. Cargo shorts and sneakers and a black Metallica T-shirt. I was in a gray-checked light-weight suit. A Joseph Abboud and one of my favorites. I had a light blue shirt on, with my tie folded and stuffed in the pocket of the suit jacket, which I carried slung over my shoulder.

In my other hand I had a cup of takeout coffee from the Redwood Diner, the little place tucked away downstairs on Forty-ninth. I wanted to get to my desk, sit down, crack the lid on the coffee, and ease my way into the day. Charlie had other plans.

He was a few feet from me now. I had lost.

"Sam, I got to talk to you."

"You already are, Charles," I said.

We were in the middle of the newsroom on the ninth floor of the Sixth Avenue office tower. I glanced over Charlie's shoulder at the row of red digital clocks on the far wall. My eyes settled on the first one.

New York: 3:47:13 a.m.

"I'll make you a deal, Charlie," I said. "You let me sit down and have a little coffee, and you can talk to me."

He was agitated and impatient. "Yeah, sure. Whatever."

We walked across the newsroom, past the handful of producers and writers for Liberty Live, our five a.m. show. They sat with their heads down, pecking away at keyboards. Outside it was dark, except for a few scattered lights in the neighboring buildings.

We got to my desk, and I grabbed a memo that had been left on my chair, put it on the desk without looking at it, and sat down. I had some coffee because I was pretty much useless without it at this hour.

"Okay, what's so important that you had to attack me at four in the morning?" I asked as he pulled up an empty chair. "You got an intern problem or something? Maybe had a little too much to drink and—"

"No, come on, Sam. You know me better than that."

"Well, you never know."

Charlie rolled his chair closer, and our knees almost touched. He looked around to make sure no one was close.

"Just so you know," I said, "I'm not trained to hear confessions."

He smirked. "Hey, that's good."

"I mean, I can listen and all, but I can't make the stuff go away."

He turned serious. "You remember my buddy, Wade?"

"No. Is that all?" I asked.

"Guy was a shooter at Channel Four. Got fired. Now he sits in his car all night and most of the day listening to the police scanner. Lives in the damn vehicle."

"Scanner jockey, huh? Sorry to hear about it."

"Tries to be the first to the scene and shoot the footage then sell it anywhere he can." He chuckled and shook his head. "Guy lives for a good crime scene."

I had some more of the coffee and looked at him. "What's he got?"

"He's says something good, *real* good."

"Go on."

"Wade hears a call this morning around two thirty. Someone spotted a floater in the East River, off Twenty-third Street."

"Okay, but we're not really breaking any new ground here."

He leaned even closer and looked around. "He says the floater is real high profile."

"He give you a name?"

"Not a chance."

"What about a clue?"

"Nope."

"Doesn't have to be a *Jeopardy* clue, just a little one."

He shook his head.

"Jock? Actor? Actress?" I asked.

"Nope. He's not going to budge, Sam."

"How much does he want?"

"Two Gs."

"He's never going to get it."

"He says he will," Charlie said.

"You got to be kidding me."

"Nope. He wants two thousand. Cash."

"Damn well better be the president for that money."

"Doubt it. Wade is unpredictable," he said. "It could be huge, or he could be overreaching."

I sat back and looked across to the far end of the room and the cluster of desks over by the windows that looked east, out onto Sixth Avenue. It was the assignment desk, and off in the distance I could see a lone figure sitting in his char. He was a tall, skinny guy, and at the moment he was napping, chin to chest.

Blake Jennings was the early-morning assignment editor, and any and all decisions needed to go through him. Newsrooms were cheap, penny-pinching places even in the best of times and we weren't in the best of times at the moment.

"You know there's no way Blake is going to pay two thousand dollars," I said.

"I know," he said. "Plus, he's not really a big fan of Wade at the moment."

I looked at him like I didn't understand, mainly because I didn't.

"Go on," I said.

"Couple of months back Wade sold us something that didn't quite pan out," he said.

"Oh, boy."

"Yeah, said he had shots of the mayor leaving the apartment of a woman other than his wife."

"And?"

"It wasn't the mayor."

"Wade swings and misses," I said.

"Big-time. On top of that he kept the three hundred bucks. Said it was for gas and emotional stress."

"They often go hand in hand."

"Blake banned us from doing business with him. Called him a head case."

"There is that whole living-in-the car thing."

Charlie leaned closer. "Sam, I'm the first to admit Wade is a nut …"

"But you think he's got something?"

"I do. I could hear it in his voice. He says everyone will know this name."

"Not the mayor again, is it?"

Charlie ignored the crack and stayed focused. "Plus, he's already shopped it to Channel Four."

"And?"

"They didn't bite. Said they weren't going to play some game with him. They wanted to see the footage first. He said no way."

"But, now they know someone big went for a swim," I said.

"Exactly," he said. "And I'm sure they're calling every cop source they got."

"Where's Wade?" I asked.

"Downstairs. Parked in the NYP zone."

I thought about it for a moment and looked over at Jennings. He was rustling, coming out of his nap. It was August and things were slow, the silly season for assignment desks. I hadn't had a decent story in weeks, okay months. My contract was up in three months, and at forty-seven my career had stalled. The question was, Could I jump-start it?

"Why don't you give old Wade a call," I said. "See if he'll soften his stance."

"He won't."

"Just try," I said. "Tell him I'm getting the cash and we want it, we just want to see a few seconds of it."

"He's too smart to fall for that, but I'll try."

Charlie pulled out his phone and called, and I sat back and took another drink of the coffee. I grabbed the memo I had tossed on my desk. It was from Liberty's security office.

Please be advised that a large protest targeting Jack Steele's show is planned for today, August 9, at 2 p.m. in front of the building. A demonstration permit had been granted for the sidewalk of the Avenue of the Americas between 49th and 50th Streets. We ask all employees to use the side entrances of the building in order to avoid protestors and to use discretion in displaying your Liberty News identification badges when entering and exiting the building. Liberty News is working with the New York City Police Department to ensure the safety of all employees during the protest.

Chet Dixon

Director of Corporate Security

Liberty News

Jack Steele was a loudmouthed cable host, but he was our loud-mouthed cable host. Anchor of *Steele Yourself,* which aired every night at eight p.m. The man had more than three million viewers a night, or at least he had last year. Over the last six months or so, his numbers had been dropping. No one could point to a specific reason, but his audience was slowly eroding.

Network brass wasn't sounding the alarm bells just yet, but we were starting to see a few worried looks upstairs in the executive office area.

"Hey, Sam," Charlie said.

I looked over at him. He was rattled.

"You okay?" I asked.

"No go," he said.

"You don't look real good," I said.

"Something's going on here, Sam," he said. "Wade says we need to buy this. Like *us,* Liberty."

His face was paler than before.

"Charlie, what's up?"

"I don't know. He kept saying this was going to hit close to home."

Chapter 2

"There's something you need to know about Wade," Charlie said.

We were crossing the lobby of 1221 Avenue of the Americas, the office tower that Liberty News called home. There was a lot of marble, and it was dark at this hour. A security guard manned the big reception counter and waved as we headed toward the revolving doors.

"Such as?" I asked.

"He's a bit high strung, a bit edgy. Kind of out there."

"Little close to the edge of the grid, huh?"

"Yeah."

"Understandable, given his working conditions."

We pushed through the revolving door and stepped out into the hot, damp August air. Even at four in the morning the heat and humidity were on you as soon as you walked outside. The building was set back from the street, and we crossed the plaza out front and headed toward the sidewalk.

Charlie continued on like I didn't understand.

"I mean, he's pretty wound up, Sam. That's part of the reason he

hasn't been able to stick at one place for too long. It doesn't take a lot
to set him off."

"I consider myself warned."

Charlie was nervous. We didn't have the cash for Wade, and we
both knew it was going to get ugly. I wasn't quite sure what I was
going to do, but I'd figure something out.

"What are we going to do when he brings up the money?"
he asked.

"Not sure," I said.

"That's what I was afraid of."

"But we got a better crack at this if we're in standing in front of
him, right?" I asked. "Doesn't do us any good sitting up in the newsroom why he's off trying to peddle it somewhere else."

"I guess so," he said.

"Look, Wade wants to make a sale now, so someone gets it on one
of the five o'clock shows. And the longer he's with us, the less time he
has to find another buyer," I said. "So there's our plan. We try to work
the clock and force a sale, for much cheaper, of course."

"That's a plan?" he asked.

"Kind of, sort of," I said. "Which car is his?"

"He's got a tan Toyota. That's him up there," he said as he pointed
to a car parked at the curb. It was three back from the corner of Fiftieth, with the door on the driver's side open.

As we neared we both slowed down, like we were approaching
with caution. And when we stepped up to the car, I could see why.
There in the driver's seat of the compact car was Wade, sitting sideways, with his thick hairy legs extending out onto the sidewalk. He
was a bear of a man and had the hair everywhere to prove it. He was
dressed in shorts and sandals and a white tank top. His brown hair
was thick in some spots, bald in others, and gave the appearance of a
poorly kept lawn.

I stopped a foot or so away from the car, not sure of how close I
should get.

"Wade," Charlie said, "this is Sam North."

Wade extended a hand, and I didn't dare hesitate to shake,

although the thought crossed my mind. I wasn't a hygiene nut, but maybe it was something I should start thinking about.

"Wade, good to meet you," I said.

He was wired and wound up, just like Charlie said.

"Hey, yeah, I've seen you."

"Charlie tells me you're holding the winning lottery ticket," I said.

"This is big shit, Sam. You're not going to believe who they fished out of the East River," he said.

"Big name, huh?"

"Oh, yeah."

"Ballplayer? Actor? Who do we got?"

"Ah, come on, Sam, you know how this works."

"Well, how about I get a look at it first, Wade," I said.

Charlie's eyes were on me. This was where it was going to get tricky. We were three guys in the dark on a Midtown sidewalk trying to make a deal.

"Oh, sure," Wade said. "You can get a look at it. For two Gs. Then you can look at all you want."

"Look, Wade," I said, "you know how this works, too. No way Liberty or anyone is going to pay two grand for something, especially sight unseen."

"That's not my problem," he said.

"Maybe not," I said, "but you know what your problem is, Wade? How do I know what you got is real, huh? How do I know it's as big as you say?"

Charlie took a half step away from me. No sense standing next to where the bomb was going to land.

Wade looked at me like I had insulted him. I had, but it was part of the plan. I was making it up as I went, and this little tactic just kind of occurred to me.

"It's big because I say it is," he said.

"Big like the mayor leaving the apartment? That kind of big?" I asked.

"Where the fuck did that come from?" Wade said.

"Oh, Jesus," I heard Charlie mutter.

I fully expected Charlie to hail a cab and speed off. Just leave the scene while he could.

"Let's face it, Wade. Folks are a little skeptical of you after that last stunt," I said.

Wade slung his legs back into the Toyota and reached out for the door handle.

"End of conversation," he said.

Hmm. Maybe the insulting strategy wasn't the best idea.

Wade yanked the door to pull it shut, but it slammed into the back of my legs.

"Get the hell out of the way," he said.

"You need us to buy this, Wade. Don't you?"

Another yank on the door and another slam into my calves, then he looked up at me and hesitated. I actually think I had played a hunch right. There was something here that Wade wanted us to have.

"What the hell are you talking about?" he asked.

"Why else would you sit down here waiting for us? If it's as big as you say it is, you'd be out shopping it, driving all over the city to sell it."

"I've got other feelers out."

"I'm sure you do."

"My phone rings and you dicks will be sorry."

"But your phone's not going to ring, Wade," I said. "You've burned other places, and people think you're bullshitting them. Plus, you know we have to have this, right?"

Before he could answer I reached into my suit pocket, took out my wallet, removed my American Express Gold Card, then held it out to him.

"What the fuck is that?" he asked.

"Take it," I said.

"Right, like I can just swipe it through my little machine here, like I'm a frigging cashier at Best Buy or something."

"Look, buy yourself two Gs worth of stuff, okay? No one checks signatures anymore. Get a nice flat-screen TV, whatever. Just take it. It's a show of good faith."

Wade was staring at the card long and hard. That was better than his trying to close the door on my legs again.

"Gimme your ATM card," he said.

"Even better idea," I said. I didn't flinch as I handed over my Citibank card. "You let me take a look at what you got, and I'll give you the PIN. There's an ATM down on the corner of Forty-fourth. Your stuff is as good as you say, and you can go take out the money right there."

He considered it and stared straight ahead out the windshield of the car, looking up a dark and mostly empty avenue.

"Work with me here, Wade," I said. "You told Charlie this would hit close to home. I'm not sure what's going on, but you need us to have this footage, don't you?"

"Give me your driver's license, too," Wade said. "That'll be your little security deposit."

I pulled it from my wallet and handed it to him. He held the three cards like he was playing poker, examining them.

"I need a yes or no," I said.

He looked up at me. "Get in."

I raced around the front of the car and opened the door on the passenger's side. As I did I saw one of Wade's big paws sweep across the seat and clear away a pile of trash. There were McDonald's bags, cups from Dunkin' Donuts, and Diet Coke bottles all piled on the floor.

I lowered myself onto the seat and put my feet down onto the garbage. The place stunk like cigarette smoke, and I swore I got a whiff of stale beer in there as well. I felt like I had sat down in a dorm room garbage can.

Wade thrust a pair of bulky headphones at me, and I hesitated, uneasy about putting those things over my hair, let alone on my ears. He picked up on my hesitation.

"These go on your ears."

"Yes, I understand."

"That's only if you want to hear."

Wade's voice had softened now. It was as if we had gone from adversaries to business partners. Sitting in his car, I felt bad for the man. It was a hell of a way to make a living.

I adjusted the headphones and fitted them over my head, trying to keep them off my hair as much as possible. Wade had his camera on the console between the seats. It was a big old Sony. There was no fancy little model for him; he was old school all the way.

I leaned over and peered into the little viewfinder. I was nervous. I had just committed $2,000 to a large, overweight, hairy man dressed for the beach. And my career and bank account felt like they were hinging on this.

Wade hit Play, and the viewfinder sprang to life. The shot started in the dark, the kind of dark you find at two in the morning when the only people out are the ones getting into trouble and those trying to stop, catch, or help them. Wade was crossing the parking area of the little Gulf station at the end of Twenty-third Street at the East River and shooting as he was walking.

The light atop his camera was on, and up ahead in the darkness you could make out two cops standing at the guardrail at edge of the asphalt parking lot with their backs to him. The lights of their radio car flickered dully off to the side. They were looking down into the river, and Wade closed in on them like he had been invited.

One of the cops spun around. She was young, Hispanic, with a chubby but pretty face. Her partner, a young clean-scrubbed kid, wheeled around, too.

"Who the hell are you?" the young male cop asked. He looked like he had been on the job for all of two days and was anxious to take charge. He had been trained at the academy, and he was ready to go.

Wade's voice was muffled. "Press," you could hear him say.

The camera shook a bit as he waved the press badge that hung around his neck.

He moved right in alongside them without waiting for a response. "Where is it?" he asked.

"Straight down," the kid said. "Wedged in there by those posts."

Wade was leaning over and shooting straight down. It looked to be about a ten-foot drop in the black water. Could have been more, it was hard to tell. There were clusters of posts sticking straight up, some barely above the water, others a few feet higher. All had jagged tops worn down by time and weather.

The camera moved across the water, its dim light searching for the body. There was nothing, and it felt like forever. Then the light hit something. It was white, a dress shirt. You could see the body now. It was floating facedown, bobbing gently on the currents of the river. The body bumped into the maze of posts that prevented it from being swept down the river, through New York Harbor, and out to sea.

As Wade's light hit the body everyone got a better look at it.

"That is one fat son of a bitch," the kid cop said.

And he was right. The body was big and round, and the dress shirt ballooned out in the water, making the poor bastard look even fatter.

In the distance the low rumbling of an engine could be heard. It grew louder, and Wade left the body and focused out on the river, where you could see a police boat approaching. Its pilot drove it like it was his car, cutting the engines and swinging it sideways as it came close to the posts. It was an old Harbor Unit boat, and you could see the large NYPD painted on its blue side. Floodlights flashed down onto the dark waters now.

The guys in the boat jabbered with the Hispanic gal and the kid next to Wade. Fishing and swimming jokes were cracked while they got to work. Now there was the sound of a truck engine close by, and a few seconds later there was more commotion as the guys from the Emergency Service Unit arrived.

The camera jiggled as someone gave Wade a shove.

"Gonna need some room here, chief. Move over."

You could hear someone to the side asking about who the guy with the camera was, but everyone was more interested in the body.

The cops got to work, the guys on the boat using a long pole with an open circle on the end to lasso the floater and pull it to the side of the boat. They reached over and tried to hoist it up. It was a struggle.

"Geez, this guy's a fucking cow," one of them said.

The body slipped, and they grabbed at it, grappled with it, and started to pull it up again. The two cops on the boat gave a unified try to get it on board, and as they did it rolled over.

It was faceup now, like it was looking into the camera.

My body jerked from shock, and I shot back in my seat.

"Holy crap," I said.

I heard Wade from the driver's seat.

"Told you."

In the viewfinder Wade zoomed in on the face, and it was staring right back.

One of the harbor cops yelled.

"Holy shit, man."

Then the kid on shore.

"Guys, it's fucking Jack Steele."

Chapter 3

"**F**our minutes out, Sam," the voice in my earpiece crackled. It was just before five, and I stood in the dark at the edge of the parking lot of the very same Gulf station at the end of East Twenty-third Street. The East River was behind me, and it was about a ten-foot drop down into the water.

The voice in my ear belonged to Steve Townsend, the director of Liberty's morning show, and he spoke to me from back in the control room. In the background I could hear what sounded like a dozen other voices. There was screaming and tension, and I was glad I was out here.

The big stories tended to attract all the network's executives and wannabe executives to the control room. They felt like they were participating. They could get on a mic and bother you in your ear while you were trying to concentrate on what you were going to say on live TV.

"Cast of thousands in here, Sam," Townsend said in my earpiece. "This is crazy."

Charlie was in front of me, camera on his shoulder, and we were all ready to go. I was all set to break what was the biggest story I had had in years, the death of cable superstar Jack Steele. But there was one little problem at the moment: no one had officially confirmed it, and that was setting off a mad scramble in the control room.

"Sam," another voice said in my earpiece, "you got to pin this down."

The voice belonged to Blake Jennings, our napping assignment editor.

"Blake," I said, "would you please, for the fiftieth time, ask Cal to talk to Robbie Steele. Hell, she's his wife; she would probably know if the man is dead or not."

Cal Daniels was the president of Liberty News and a media big shot. He had stumbled across Jack Steele over a decade ago and created the bombastic talk-show host who had ruled the cable airwaves. I would think he would know if his cash cow was dead.

"He says he can't reach Robbie; she's not answering her phone. And no one answers Steele's cell number."

"Maybe because it's on the bottom of the river," I said. "Fish aren't tech savvy."

"Not funny, Sam."

"Listen, you saw the footage, Blake. Two of the cops recognized him. I recognized him. You recognized him. It's Steele."

"Yeah, but we can't take a chance with this, Sam," Jennings said. "What if it's, like, the fat guy from accounting somewhere? You know, the guy who everyone always said looked just like Jack Steele?"

I hated, and I mean *really* hated, to admit it, but Jennings was right. If I went on the air and said this was Steele, and it wasn't, I was done. I'd be teaching TV at some community college three miles east of nowhere.

Townsend was back in my ear.

"Three minutes out, Sam."

"Crap," I muttered.

I didn't like the feel of this. My gut told me I was right. But I needed confirmation.

Charlie poked his head out from behind the camera.

"You okay?"

"No," I said.

I had the mic in one hand and my iPhone in the other, and I felt the phone vibrate with an incoming call and glanced at the number.

Unknown.

I knew who it was. I shut off the mic and answered on the second ring.

"Pep?"

"You must want something," Detective Peppe Rinaldi said.

His voice was scratchy and dry, like this hour of the morning did not sit well with him. And he was angry, bothered that he had been bothered.

"The three calls gave it away?" I asked.

"There were four. You didn't leave a message on one."

"This is why you're a detective."

"Let me guess, this is this about a popular broadcaster?" he asked.

"More top-notch detective work."

"It's what I do."

"Was that Jack Steele they pulled out of the East River a few hours ago?"

"Jack Steele. News with a point of view. That's what the billboard on the West Side Highway says."

"So it was Steele?"

"How come you don't have a billboard, Sam?"

"Pep?"

"Yes?"

"I'm supposed to go on national TV in four minutes to either break the biggest news of my career or make an ass of myself."

"Can it be both?"

"Yes, that also is a possibility. But how about we stick to the question. Jack Steele. Dead or not dead?" I asked.

"What were the choices again?"

Townsend's voice crackled through my earpiece. "Two and a half minutes, Sam."

I gave him a thumbs-up to acknowledge him and spoke to Pep.

"Pep?"

"Not my case, Sam."

"But you know about it?"

"I do."

"And?"

"It was Steele," he said.

"So why doesn't his wife seem to know?"

"Couples just don't communicate anymore, Sam. It's a real problem. Everybody's crazy busy."

"Thank you. You do understand what little is left of my career is on the line here?"

"That's why I told you to go into police work years ago. Much less pressure and you don't have to worry about your hair."

"My hair is fine."

"Sure. If you say so."

"Last we heard from Steele's wife she said he went out last night and never came back," I said.

"Why he even went out is beyond me," he said. "You ever see her? Quite the looker. A yoga instructor. Page Six calls her the Yoga Babe."

"I need you to focus," I said.

"How come I don't have a wife like that?" he asked. "Half my age and a yoga babe."

"Has she been told yet?"

"Yup. Guys practically tripped over themselves to get uptown and break the news to her."

"Any idea what happened here?"

"Well, if I had to make a guess, I'd say Steele's lungs filled up with water."

"Thank you."

"Not a problem."

"For real now."

Rinaldi paused before speaking. "You going to protect me on this one, right?" he asked. "This is so frigging high profile, it's not funny."

Charlie caught my eye in front of me. He was gesturing like he was having a seizure, pointing to his earpiece, asking if I could hear

Jennings trying to talk to me. I could, but I was ignoring all the voices except Townsend's and Pep's. They were the only ones that mattered at the moment.

"Consider yourself protected," I said.

"From what I hear, there were no signs of a struggle or anything like that."

"Accident?"

"Yeah, maybe he tripped over his ego. Or his wallet."

"There has to be something more, Pep. Come on."

Pep was silent for a moment.

"I'm not going to screw you," I said.

Townsend was in my ear. "Ninety seconds, Sam."

Pep spoke through the phone pressed against my other ear. "Word is they found a note."

"Suicide?"

"No, a thank-you. To the cops, for pulling his fat ass out of the river."

"You got to be kidding me. Jack Steele killed himself?" I asked.

Charlie poked his head out from behind the camera and stared at me.

There was no answer from Pep, which I took as a bad sign.

"Pep, I'm going to say police found a suicide note. That works, right?"

Pep hesitated for a second. "Yeah, you're good. I haven't seen the note, but word is they found one in the apartment."

"What'd it say?"

"Good-bye, cruel world."

"He was known for his originality."

Townsend was frantic now. "One minute away, Sam. You got to turn that mic on. We need an audio check."

"I got less than a minute, Pep. Anything else? Who called it in?"

"Garbage man. Private hauler. Stopped there to take a piss in the river and saw it," he said.

"Ouch."

"Yeah, guy makes a living pissing on people and gets pissed on when he goes. Little irony for you, huh?"

Townsend and Jennings were both screaming in my earpiece as panic reigned in the control room. Pep and I finished up, and I got off the call. At thirty seconds Townsend went over the plan a last time.

"Coming to you right at five, Sam. A cold open," he said. "No anchors, no intro. Commercial ends and boom, you're up. You ready?"

"We'll find out."

"Here we go," he said.

I took a deep breath as Townsend continued in my earpiece.

"In ten ... nine ..."

It was seconds to five a.m., and my head throbbed. The sky to the east behind me was starting to lighten and it was about to get even hotter and sticker once the sun came up.

"Eight ... seven ..."

The collar on my dress shirt was damp and matted against the back of my neck. A line of sweat across my forehead was annoying me.

"Six ... five ..."

I heard the dull thumping of a traffic chopper overhead and prayed no one else was onto this.

"Four ... three ..."

I turned my head to try to loosen the tight muscles of my neck. In front of me on the elevated roadway of the FDR, cars barreled up and down the coast of Manhattan, smacking the metal plates of a construction project.

In my ear, Townsend kept going. "Two ... one ..."

I took a breath and locked on the camera as Townsend yelled in my earpiece.

"Go!"

Chapter 4

"I'm Sam North on the East Side of Manhattan with breaking news. Liberty News anchor and host of *Steele Yourself*, Jack Steele, is dead."

I paused for a beat, listening to my own words and hoping like crazy that I was right. I was a confident guy, but there was always that little voice of doubt when you were way out in front on something like this. You knew you had the goods, but maybe, just maybe, that body did belong to the fat guy in accounting somewhere.

I also paused for effect, figuring there were probably cheers in some living rooms at this news, and it would be best to let those quiet down before proceeding.

"A New York City Police Department source confirms that Steele's body was found floating in the East River here at the end of Twenty-third Street early this morning."

I turned and walked back the few steps to the edge of the parking lot, and Charlie moved with me. He went past me and shot straight down into the dark water so people could see the rotting pilings as I spoke.

"Steele's body was found floating right here in this spot among those posts you can see sticking up out of the water. The body was discovered by a private sanitation worker."

I kept a hand on Charlie's midsection as he leaned over to shoot down into the water. Figured having my cameraman plunge into the river might take a bit of the oomph out of my scoop.

Charlie came off the river, took a few steps back, and I was again on camera.

"The recovery of Steele's body was recorded by a freelance cameraman who arrived on the scene. Liberty News has obtained that footage and will air it now. Before we do, however, I want to caution viewers that it does contain graphic images."

Townsend was in my ear. "Video is up."

I spoke and allowed enough time for the video to run twice, as planned.

"A New York City Police Department Harbor Patrol unit responded, as did an Emergency Services crew. Steele's body was recovered from the river. Jack Steele was pronounced dead a short while later."

Townsend cued me. "You're back up."

I took a breath and tried to phrase this perfectly. This was the hard part, the part that could come back to bite me in the ass.

"As for the circumstances surrounding the death of Jack Steele ... a police source tells Liberty that a suicide note has been discovered in Steele's Manhattan apartment where he lived with his wife, Roberta. No further details are available at the moment."

I stood there and let it sink in. That was it. That was all I had to say. I wrapped and tossed it to the studio to the morning anchor team of Kelly Hunter and Dan Miller.

"Once again, New York City Police Department sources confirm that Liberty News anchor Jack Steele has been found dead. His body was found floating in the East River at approximately two o'clock this morning. On the East Side of Manhattan, I'm Sam North. We go now to Liberty's New York studios, where Kelly Hunter and Dan Miller are standing by."

I waited for Kelly or Dan to speak up and knew the next few

minutes were going to be like walking through a minefield. The question was, did either of them have the composure to get through this on air? Had they pulled themselves together before the show started so they could handle this?

A few seconds passed and neither spoke, all I heard in my earpiece was something that sounded like a sob off in the distance. It was awkward and uncomfortable. I maintained my serious-reporter-delivering-serious-news look the entire time. I was now in danger of looking like a display in a wax museum. Finally, Hunter broke the uncomfortable silence.

"Sam, it's Kelly. This ... this is shocking ..."

Miller chimed in from next to her on the couch back on the set. Typical morning-show stuff, a couch was supposed to make the anchors look like a family. Like they got along. Or at least tolerated each other.

"It's truly shocking ..." Miller said.

It was now had it confirmed by both anchors that Steele's death was shocking. It was safe to proceed, so Hunter sped ahead.

"This ... this ... note the police say they have, Sam. It's a suicide note?" Hunter asked.

Of all the info Rinaldi had given me, it was this little tidbit that made me the most nervous. I hadn't seen it. Rinaldi hadn't seen it. It was a rumor at this stage and a mighty big one at that. But screw it, it was my rumor.

"Kelly, as I said, a police source tells us that a note, and they are terming it a 'suicide note,' was discovered. We don't know much more at this stage."

Somewhere in the sky to my right, up by the UN, I heard that helicopter. It was now definitely headed this way, quickly. The news was out there, and the exact spot I was standing in was about to become the center ring of the circus.

Back in the studio, Miller pressed on, not satisfied with my response to Hunter.

"Any idea what specifically the note says, Sam?"

I shook my head and tried my best to not look like I thought the man was an idiot. But it was hard. Another chopper headed toward us from directly west. The rapid, dull thumping of the blades was filling the air as I spoke.

"Dan, at this point, that is all the information we have."

It was said with an edge. It was a plea to end this live shot and let me get back to work.

Hunter's voice was choked by sobs.

"I ... I just saw Jack yesterday," she said.

"Me ... me, too," Miller said, not to be outdone.

Viewers no doubt were left with the comforting impression that, yes, many of the people at Liberty did in fact see one another at work. They probably asked themselves why I had not seen Steele at work yesterday. If asked on air, I would have to admit that I hadn't see Jack yesterday. I kind of wished I had.

After a few more questions, to which I basically repeated the news I had already delivered, because that was all I had to offer, the live spot ended. I think I heard Miller call this a "tragic development," as he thanked me.

I stood there with sweat coating my forehead and waited for Townsend to clear me. My phone was vibrating like crazy as calls and texts came into it waves. Finally, after what felt like an hour but was probably ten seconds, Townsend's voice crackled through my earpiece.

"You're clear."

I could hear voices behind him in the control room; there was screaming and people barking orders, and Jennings got in my ear before I could unhook everything.

"Don't move, Sam. We're going to need you back on in sixty seconds, Kelly and Dan are sobbing on the goddamn set. You'd think they could at least pretend to be professional."

I turned off the mic so I was free to talk and looked at my phone. Seven missed calls. Three voice mails. Thirteen texts. I knew one from Liz was in there somewhere. I had called her and told her to watch.

I looked over at Charlie, who had the camera on the ground at his feet. He was shaking his head and looking both tired and shocked.

"What the f?" he asked.

"This is huge," I said.

"We're screwed, Sam. You know how much ad revenue that guy brought in?"

"A lot."

"We named the extension on our house Camp Steele. He was our gravy train," he said.

"I got to figure out now why the hell he'd go and kill himself."

Charlie shrugged. "Pressure? An affair? Drinking?"

I heard the thumping of more news choppers and looked up to see three others speeding toward us from different directions. I knew camera crews, reporters, and producers were being deployed, assignment editors screaming at them to get to Twenty-third Street. Word was out now. In a few hours the double-decker tourist buses would be swinging by to take a look.

I heard Jennings screaming in my earpiece. "Need to get you back on. Fast."

My phone vibrated again, and I looked at an incoming number I didn't recognize.

"Yeah," I answered over the din.

"Is this Sam North?"

It was a woman's voice.

"It is."

A siren blared as an ambulance off in the distance raced uptown on First Avenue.

She spoke between sobs, and her voice had an edge to it. "You're wrong," she said.

A jolt of fear raced through me, and my mind was a cluttered mess of thoughts. Was it not Jack Steele they pulled from the river? Was Steele sitting somewhere having breakfast?

I pushed the phone against my ear and struggled to hear.

"I'm wrong?" I asked, with an edge all my own.

"Yes. Jack Steele didn't kill himself."

Crap, I thought, *the damn note. Maybe it wasn't real.*

I was getting pretty worked up. I was hot and covered in a film of sweat and Blake Jennings was yelling at me in my earpiece to get into position.

"What are you talking about?" I asked.

"Jack didn't kill himself," she repeated.

She was defiant now, and I would be just as defiant.

"Look, I don't have all day; you going to tell me how you know this?"

She continued to sob, and I thought for a second that maybe I had lost her.

Jennings voice knifed through my earpiece. "Get in position now, Sam. *Now*," he screamed.

Then I called into the phone, "Look, lady, you got to tell me what you're talking about. How the hell do you know Jack didn't—"

She cut me off, and her voice was filled with anger. "Because I'm his wife," she yelled.

Chapter 5

At ten minutes to midnight I got out of a cab at the corner of Fifth Avenue and Sixty-eighth Street right across from Central Park. I felt like I had been in my clothes for a week; my shirt was wrinkled and damp with sweat, and the only thing keeping me going now was adrenaline.

I stood on the sidewalk and looked up at the white brick apartment building in the middle of the block facing the park. It was home to Jack and Roberta "Robbie" Steele. There had been camera crews out front throughout the day, but the last of the live shots were done, and the place was quiet now.

I had been on the air nonstop from five in the morning until eleven p.m., and I wouldn't have had it any other way. I lost count of the live shots after forty, but it had been a good day's work.

I stepped into the revolving door of the apartment building and stepped out into what felt like a walk-in freezer on the other side. A doorman stood in front me blocking my way, like he expected me to make a run for the elevators across the lobby.

"May I help you?" he asked.

"Geez, you could chill fish in here," I said.

That got me nothing. No response, no indication of a sense of humor. Just a blank expression from this guy. It was a toss-up as to which was colder, the doorman or the lobby.

He was dressed in a green uniform with gold braid, and he wore his doorman's cap over salt-and-pepper hair. He looked to be in his forties, but he seemed determined to act older.

"I'm here to see Robbie Steele," I said.

He stared at me like he was waiting for me to take it back, but I didn't.

"Your name?"

"Sam North."

He walked to the little doorman's desk, which was jammed in a corner right by the door, picked up the phone, and punched a few buttons. His eyes stayed on me the entire time.

"I have Mr. North here, ma'am," he said.

I was having a very tough time thinking of Robbie Steele as a "ma'am." Steele had been sixty-one, and she was thirty years younger. Most of the pictures I had seen of her were from a *New York* magazine spread on the hottest yoga instructors in the city. She was right at the top of the list, dressed in a skintight outfit that would make it virtually impossible to focus on anything else in her class. There was nothing "ma'am" about her.

"You can go up," Mr. Serious said. He seemed displeased that I had been approved. "Apartment Ten D. Take a left off the elevator. Last door on the right."

"I'll try not to break anything," I said.

I crossed the lobby and rode the elevator up to ten wondering about what I was about to walk into. I expected there would be an apartment full of comforters, a support group to help the grieving widow. Was I going to step in and be yelled at? A kind of let's-beat-up-the-messenger type thing? Or would there be some civility to it? I assumed emotions would be high and nerves raw. But my expectations were low; I was hoping only to get five minutes with Robbie Steele to hear why she was convinced that I was wrong.

I got out and followed instructions. I walked all the way down the long hallway and slowed a bit as I got to the last door on the right. I stood and listened for a moment but heard nothing: no voices, no sounds of anyone walking around. Nothing.

I knocked lightly on the door and listened. Still nothing. I rapped a bit harder and finally heard the sound of shoes on a hardwood floor, and they were coming closer.

Deadbolts were turned, the door was unlocked and opened, and there she was. Robbie Steele stood in front of me. Her sandy-blonde hair was long and straight and shiny and she wore it in a ponytail. She had a healthy tan, and it looked like she had a minimum amount of makeup on; but under it I could still see faint circles around her eyes, and her eyes themselves were a dull red, bloodshot from a day of crying.

Behind her low lights just barely illuminated the apartment, and I didn't see or hear anyone else. She extended her hand to me as I stood in the doorway, not knowing quite what to say or do.

"Robbie Steele," she said.

Her tone was businesslike and sent the message that this needn't get messy.

I grasped her hand and tried not to squeeze too firmly. He hand was soft, but she had a grip that said she was used to shaking hands.

"I'm sorry about your loss." I had no idea what else to say.

There were plenty of stories that didn't paint her in a favorable light. The one in the *Post*, "Yoga Bimbo Busts Up Steele Marriage," came to mind. But who the hell knew, maybe she actually did love the cranky cable host.

She invited me in, and I followed her out of the foyer and down a short hallway, trying not to stare. If she was making a fashion statement, it was Chic Grief. She wore black leggings and a long button-down maroon top that I'm sure sold for five times more than I could guess at some Madison Avenue boutique a few blocks over.

She was of medium height and had on low heels that still managed to show off her legs. We passed a large, open kitchen on the left, and I spotted a several empty glass and small plates on a counter, the only sign that others had been here.

She led me into the living room, which was a big, open room, with a wall of windows that looked out onto the black expanse that was Central Park. Way across the park I saw the lights of the Time Warner Center and the buildings along Central Park West.

There were sliding-glass doors that opened onto a terrace, and a baby grand piano was positioned in one corner, next to a few high bookcases that were packed with hardcovers. It was the apartment of a couple trying to make sure people knew they had a bit of culture in them.

She stood and faced me, and I figured this was when she was going to unload, to tell me why I was wrong, but she didn't.

"May I get you something to drink?" she asked.

She was observing the rules of decorum for a guest.

"No, I'm fine, thanks," I said.

She crossed the room, and sat down on the edge of the couch with her back to the windows. I took a seat on a matching leather chair across from her. We were separated by a large glass-and-chrome coffee table.

She seemed calm and collected, and I assumed it was a yoga thing. Whatever it was, it was impressive. I had merely worked a long day, and I was mess. She had lost her husband, yet she seemed to have a better handle on her emotions than I did.

"Thank you for coming to see me," she said.

She sat with perfectly straight posture and made it look easy, like someone very in tune with her body. Her legs were angled slightly, touching at the knees and lined up perfectly.

"I'm very sorry about Jack."

She nodded, and I said a few kind words about her late husband. Actually, I had only a few. He was a son of a bitch to work with, but you know how it is. There's a need to speak well of the recently departed. She thanked me again and there was an uncomfortable moment where neither of us spoke.

"So I'm wrong?" I asked.

"Yes," she said, and even from across the room, in the dim light of the apartment, I could see her eyes becoming soft and moist. "You are."

She let it hang there, so I barreled in.

"And you'll tell me why?"

"Yes, in a moment."

I was tired and exhaled a sigh; she must have seen my shoulders rise and slump because now she glared at me.

"If you don't want to hear what I have to say, I'm sure there are a hundred other reporters who would. The reason I called you was because I saw your report this morning."

"I want to hear what you have to say," I said, in as neutral a tone as I could manage.

"Jack did not kill himself," she said.

"Okay," I said.

She looked at me for a second or two before speaking. "You trying to sound like you believe me."

"Should I not believe you?"

"I know you don't. I'm not stupid," she said.

"I can tell."

"And this isn't some widow-in-denial thing," she went on. "That's what the detectives told me when I talked to them about this."

"You want to tell me what you told them?"

"Only if you agree to help me," she said.

For some reason I hadn't been expecting to sit down at a bargaining table on this visit with her, but that is exactly where I felt like I was now. And I wasn't even sure of what I was bargaining for.

"I'm not sure I can agree to help you if I'm not even sure what it is I'm agreeing to."

"I need you, or someone else, to find out who killed Jack. The detectives won't. They think it's Jack's handwriting on that damn note."

"And you dispute that?"

Now it was her turn to take in a big breath and exhale slowly, like I was just plain exasperating to deal with.

"I don't know, okay? I really don't know. They say it's his handwriting, and even I think it seems to be. It's being checked out. But ... but I don't know."

She needed a moment to gather and get control of her emotions, and I was happy to give her the time. With a graceful little motion she muffled a sniffle with the back of one hand, then looked at me like I was spoiled food.

"If you're not up to this, I can find someone who is," she said. "This could be the biggest story of your career. Unless you want someone else to have it."

I put my hands up like I was trying to slow an oncoming car.

"Whoa," I said. "What makes you think I'm not up to this?"

She didn't answer, and that gave me a moment to try to determine if she was crazy. The only thing I could decide was that I needed more time.

"Robbie ..." I said, but before I could go on, she jumped at me like I had just called her crazy.

"If you're going to tell me I'm just upset and emotional, save it."

This was getting to be like trying to drive at night with no headlights.

"Can you tell me why you have doubts about the note?"

She sat there with her posture perfect and an almost elegant bearing and shook her head at the whole idea of the note. "There's something about it that ... I ... I don't know ..."

"Let's come back to the note," I said, hoping a new line of conversation would maybe bring me some answers. "Why don't you tell me what you think happened," I said.

The word from Rinaldi was that Steele had left here just before one a.m., gotten into a cab, gone down to Thirty-fourth Street and First Avenue, then walked over to the end of Thirty-fourth by the heliport and jumped in the river.

That wasn't the way Mrs. Steele saw it.

"I think he went to meet someone," she said.

"And this someone would be?"

"I don't know," she said.

"And that's what you want me to find out?"

"Yes. He had a lot of enemies, people were always sending him

threatening e-mails," she said. "Some of things people said were so
—" She choked back a sob and tried to gather herself.

It crossed my mind that Robbie Steele, much like her late
husband, might be something of a conspiracy theory nut. Jack Steele
had built multimillion-dollar cable-TV franchise using conspiracy
theories as a key component, and it would only make sense if some of
that flowed into his home life.

She looked at me like she was waiting for me to say something,
but I didn't.

"You think I'm crazy, don't you?" she asked.

I had learned it was never good, and rarely smart, to agree with a
woman's self-assessment if it included the word *crazy*. And definitely
not to agree with any assessment that included the word *stupid*.

"Robbie ..." I said. "The police say—"

"I don't give a damn what the police say."

Her face tightened, and she wiped away a tear then began to cry. I
decided this was getting a little too nutty for me. Here I was, sitting in
Jack Steele's apartment almost in the dark, with his very attractive
widow, fewer than twenty-four hours after he killed himself.

She was becoming more unhinged by the second and asking me
to chase some wacky conspiracy theory. And if I did, I would then
become the wacky, conspiracy theory reporter. I was having enough
trouble hanging on in this business without that label.

It was now officially time for a graceful exit before she completely
broke down and I felt the need to give her a hug or something,
making this scene all the more bizarre.

So I got up and tried my best to sound comforting while at the
same time moving to leave.

"Robbie, look, I'm not so sure I can be of much help here," I said.

She got up and glared at me, then snapped, "Listen to me."

Oh boy, I thought, *I may have missed my opportunity for a graceful
exit.*

She stepped closer to me, and I wasn't quite sure whether to go to
her, to stand where I was, or just to turn and run out of the apartment.

"I am telling you that Jack did not kill himself," she said.

My attention now was focused on not making any sudden moves. "Okay," I said. "And I get that. But there's the note, in his handwriting."

"I don't know how to explain that," she said.

"Then how can you be so certain he didn't kill himself, Robbie?" I asked.

She had moved even closer, and now looked up at me, her eyes brimming with tears. I was officially uncomfortable.

"Because ..." She began to flat-out sob, and I felt like garbage for pushing her.

She took another step toward me, crying, and before I could react she pounded on my chest with the side of her fist. There was a day full of grief and anger being let loose.

She hit me again then looked up at me through tear-filled eyes.

"Because I'm pregnant."

Chapter 6

"And she hasn't shared this little nugget with anybody else?" Liz asked.

"Nope."

"Interesting."

"Guess I'm special," I said. "But you already knew that."

"Yes. Of course," she said.

We were at a table for two upstairs at the Union Tavern on Park Avenue South at Eighteenth Street. Our table, next to the metal railing, overlooked the open bar and seating area downstairs giving us a view of the mingling crowd below.

Liz Harrison was the only person I had told of my conversation with Robbie Steele. At the moment Liz was picking through her salad in search of another piece of spinach or something, but I could tell the Steele news was bugging her.

"You think that's odd?" I asked. "That she told me but no one else?"

Liz put her fork down, picked up her glass of Montgras Carmenere Reserva, sat back, and took a sip of the red wine.

"Well, yes. I mean, no knock against you."

"No knock taken."

"But why not tell the police?"

"She said she didn't want it getting out in the media."

"Then telling a reporter might not be the smartest idea."

"I prefer TV personality," I said. "'Reporter' sounds so pedestrian."

"Of course," she said.

"Plus, I have a face you can trust. Look, it worked with you," I said.

Liz raised her wine glass to her lips and shot me a smile before taking a drink.

"Then I guess it's quite an honor," she said after she had a drink. "Picking you to share the big news with."

It was just after eight, and dusk was settling over the city. The place was noisy and full of drinkers and diners. Somewhere behind the conversations a gospel blues thing was playing: Mavis Staples, if I wasn't mistaken.

Liz was still dressed from work, a white blouse and a form-fitting black skirt, with heels that were tasteful yet sexy. Most of what she wore was tasteful yet sexy, and it was my feeling that she was easily the sexiest investment banker in the business.

I had a tall glass of Brooklyn Lager, and I had some of the beer and enjoyed the moment. Liz and I were about six months into our relationship, the spot where things were still novel and fresh and not a lot of work.

"Robbie said they had been trying for a long time," I said. "Said Jack had always wanted to be a dad and knew it had to be now or never."

"Scary thought," she said.

"Cable talk-show hosts are allowed to spawn like the rest of us," I said.

"Some shouldn't be allowed to."

I looked around to make sure no one was eavesdropping. A woman at the table to our right shot me a smile while the guy she was with was working on a large, messy burger.

"Worried?" Liz asked as she watched me watch others.

"A little bit."

"Would you like us to speak in hushed tones?" she asked.

"You're an investment banker; doesn't your type speak in hushed tones anyway? You know, when you're doing a deal and stuff?"

"No. Usually I speak in a normal conversational tone. Sometimes I even shout," she said. She studied me. "You're not sure whether to believe her, are you?"

I had a drink of the beer and used my nice cloth napkin to wipe the corners of my mouth. It felt very proper. "She was pretty convincing. But it doesn't help me decide whether or not she's a nut," I said.

"She certainly has a not-so-stellar reputation. You know, the whole home-wrecking thing."

"Be nice," I said.

"I am," she said.

Liz sipped her wine and looked at me over the rim of her glass.

"She's a grieving widow," I said. "Okay, a very good-looking and rich widow, but grieving nonetheless."

Liz was back to moving things around on her plate, determined to find some other vegetable to nibble on.

"Do insurance policies pay off on suicides?" she asked, looking up.

"I have no idea. But that occurred to me."

"Maybe Yoga Mama isn't getting the money she thinks she needs or is entitled to if her hubby the talker did in fact kill himself."

"It's Yoga Babe."

"Soon to be Yoga Mama—that is, if you believe her," she said.

"What do you think? You think she's making this up?" I asked.

Liz shrugged, and even that was attractive as her long silky brown hair fell easily over her shoulders.

"It would be pretty extreme for her to make it up," she said.

"Part of me thinks she's nuts."

"It's that other part of you that worries me," she said with a wink.

"Now, now. I should be able to control myself around a beautiful, vulnerable woman."

"You didn't around me."

"Yes, but only after you had given me the green light," I said.

"Funny, I don't remember flashing any signals, colored or otherwise."

"Hmm," I said, "maybe not. But it worked out for the best, don't you think?"

I had met Liz shortly after her engagement had broken off. Fast-forward, and here we were, around the corner from my Gramercy Park apartment, where Ms. Harrison was spending more and more of her time, which was fine with me.

I knocked off the last piece of my steak and followed it with some more of the Brooklyn.

"Here's the problem," I said, again checking to make sure we could talk without some busybody overhearing. "I have to decide if this is worth chasing. I mean, let's say she's not nuts. That would mean that someone killed him."

"One heck of a big story, Mr. Reporter," she said.

"But—"

"There's always a but," she said.

"If someone didn't kill him, then what?"

"Then she's a conspiracy nut like her late husband," she said.

I saw our waitress on her way to our table. She was in her mid-twenties, her blonde hair pulled back in a ponytail, and she paid more attention to me than to Liz. A busboy was with her, and he took our plates. We placed an order for coffee. Almost the entire exchange had been done with her never leaving me, and after she left Liz shot me a little smile.

"Think you have a fan. It must be so difficult being a TV personality."

"It can be a burden."

"Hah," she said.

Liz was sitting back looking very relaxed, her glass of wine raised. Under the table I felt the brush of her bare foot against my leg.

I looked down to my right at the crowd at the bar.

"Please, what about them?" I asked, nodding toward the scene below.

"I have no intention of rubbing all their legs."

"I meant, what would my public think if they saw you trying to seduce me?"

"Trying?"

Liz had some wine and seemed to enjoy my little problem of whether to get involved with Robbie Steele.

"So why you?" she asked. "Why does Ms. Steele pick *you* to confide in?"

I shrugged. "The rugged good looks, maybe?"

"Hah, again," she said. "And this time no footsie."

"Darn," I said.

"Dang."

"Drat."

"How long you want to go on for?" she asked.

"Until we run out of *d*'s," I said. "Besides, you already cheated. Dang is not a word."

"It most certainly is. I'm expressing my dissatisfaction and annoyance," she said.

"You never expressed dissatisfaction with me before."

"Until now."

Outside a horn blared, and I saw a cab angled diagonally to the corner, letting a passenger out. The guy behind him in an SUV was none too happy with the cabby's sloppy park job.

Liz sat forward and looked at me.

"Ah, to get involved with the beautiful widow or not. Tough choice to make, tough guy," she said.

"Tough guys make tough choices," I said.

My new friend the blonde waitress was back with dessert menus just in time to hear me.

"Oh, I like that," she said.

"You have my permission to use it," I said.

She gave me a little smile and walked away.

I looked over to Liz. "I may have to come back here solo some night," I said.

"Yes. So you and Barbie can discuss geopolitical events."

"I bet she's actressing to put herself through waiting school."

Liz smiled, and all felt right. I had gotten lucky, and I knew it. But I still had the Robbie Steele issue to work out.

"So what's it going to be?" Liz asked. "Work with the crazy, but gorgeous home wrecker, or be happy to capitalize on your newfound fame and return as the conquering hero to the morning shift?"

"I'm not even quite sure where to begin, if I decide to work with her. I'll have to start poking around in whatever Steele was involved in."

"That could be interesting."

"Let's not forget the cops have this thing down as a suicide, end of story."

"Hmm. I sense hesitation," she said.

I sat back let out a sigh as I thought about this. "I'm forty-seven," I said.

Liz covered her mouth in a fake gasp. "Good heavens. I thought you said you were thirty-seven when we met."

"I may have."

"I just consider you experienced, if that helps."

"It does. Especially from someone eight years younger."

"Tell me again about the seventies," she said, with a very large smile.

"When I remember them, I will. Mind if I get back on topic?"

"Please do."

"To do this right, I'm going to have to start asking a lot of questions of a lot of people, all on the premise that the New York City Police Department is wrong and Jack Steele's gold-digging wife is right."

"You'll be doing a great service to gold diggers everywhere if she's right," she said.

"Did I mention this is my career, or what's left of it, that we're talking about?"

"Not in the last thirty seconds."

I looked down on the crowd milling about the bar and thought about Robbie Steele. I was still uncertain if she was nuts, or right. I looked over at Liz, who couldn't have looked more relaxed.

"The chances of her being right are pretty damn small," I said.

"But if she is, and you pass on it and someone else nails it, how are you going to deal with that?"

"Not well."

"So you have to go for it."

"But if I go all in and there's nothing there, then I become the reporter linked to the nutty widow."

"Thus becoming nutty in the process."

"And thereby ruining what's left of my career." I tried to pull a memory up from a decade ago. "There was a guy, big name years ago, who insisted a plane had been blown up when everything pointed to a mechanical problem."

"Who?"

"Exactly," I said.

I had some more of the Brooklyn, and Liz gave me some space to figure it all out. I put the glass down, and she leaned forward.

"So, what's it going to be, tough guy?"

Chapter 7

"You want to do what?"

The question came from Calvin M. Daniels, who happened to be the president of Liberty News, which made him my boss. The man who granted contracts and decided whether or not I was worth keeping employed when my contract expired on October 25.

His tone was disbelief, and I think there's a bigger word that may work nicely here: incredulous.

"I want to take a few days and poke around to see if there's anything odd with Jack's death," I said.

I was seated in one of his visitor chairs, in his office on the floor above the Liberty newsroom. Behind him, through the floor-to-ceiling windows, you could look across Sixth Avenue to the east, and uptown as well, where the windows wrapped around the corner of the building, providing more than just a glimpse of the marquee at Radio City Music Hall and the green of Central Park beyond that.

"Say that again," he said.

"I want to look into Jack's death."

"To see ..."

"To see if there's anything odd."

"Odd?" he said.

I had worked here long enough, almost nine years, to know when a hurricane was about to hit land. And sometimes it was best just to stay down and seek shelter.

"You want to know what's odd?" he asked, his voice rising. "What's odd is my number one fucking anchor just killed himself. That's odd."

His voice climbed another octave.

"And you know what else is odd? He happened to be the goddamn biggest generator of advertising for this goddamn network, and that puts us in a pretty big hole. That's odd. You want some more odd?"

I shook my head. "No, I'm good."

He was shouting now, and I was glad the office door behind me was closed.

"What's really fucking odd is I got one of my reporters in my office asking for time off to try to figure out why my anchor killed himself. Now, that's odd."

"I'm not trying to figure out—"

"What are you, going into psychology or something?"

"Cal," I said, but it was no use.

He exhaled and shook his head. "What am I, stupid? Is there something I'm missing here?"

I glanced at the framed pictures and articles that lined the wall to my right. There was one about how he had to drop out of Harvard after sophomore year to help support his family. The man wasn't stupid.

"No, you're not stupid," I said.

"How about you just stick to being the—"

"Cal," I said, cutting him off. "I got a call from Robbie Steele."

He stopped and we were back to incredulous. "What?"

"Robbie Steele called me," I said.

"She looking to remarry?"

"She says Jack didn't kill himself."

"I'm still trying to get past that she called you."

On the wall to my left were nine small flat-screen TVs hanging in a tick-tack-toe grid. They were all on with the sound down, Liberty was on in the center one. His eyes drifted over to them. The news that Robbie Steele had called me seemed to have at least slowed him down.

"I went up to their place the other night," I said.

His eyes came back to me.

"You went to Jack's apartment? To see Robbie?" he said.

"Yes. She's convinced Jack didn't commit suicide."

"She understands he left a note, right? Or does she think that was a grocery list?"

"Pretty sure she knows it's a note," I said. "But she said she would eventually be able to explain it," I said.

"I'm sure." He exhaled a long, slow sigh. The man had just lost a close friend and his network's biggest cash machine.

"I told her I'd help her," I said.

He looked at me and shook his head. He was tired, and his ruddy, creased face reflected it. "Help her do what? Regain her sanity?"

"No, ask some questions, see if maybe something doesn't add up with Jack's death."

"We're back to that."

"We are."

He pushed himself farther into his high-backed leather executive chair and yanked at the knot of his tie. It was red and contrasted nicely with his starched white shirt.

"Look, there's something you got to understand. Robbie Steele is flat-out crazy," he said. "Drop-dead gorgeous, but nuts."

"Doesn't make her wrong."

"Please don't tell me you believe her."

"All I said was her being crazy doesn't make her wrong."

"You don't know this broad and what she's capable of," he said. "Jack was happily married, *very* happily married, before she came bursting onto the scene."

His phone rang; he glanced at the number and ignored it.

"Jack didn't stand a chance around her," he said.

"Maybe he didn't want to."

He shook his head and had the look of someone trying to teach a slow student. "Or maybe she feels guilty, like she drove him to jump in the damn river."

"Give me a few days, we'll find out for sure."

"And what, I get to play musical chairs and move reporters around to cover you on mornings while you're off chasing this?"

"Only for a few days."

"Big chance you're taking."

I knew where he was going with this, and I shrugged. "I think it's worthwhile."

"I been looking for somewhere to put Katie, see what she can do," he said.

Katie was Katie Wallace, a tall brunette and former swimsuit model who I assumed would take my or someone else's spot here once she learned to speak in complete sentences.

"That's valuable real estate on the morning show you want to give up," he said.

"I understand," I said. He was a network president, which meant he knew exactly how to play on a reporter's natural paranoia. "I just need a few days. Like I said, I'll take my chances."

If Robbie Steele's hunch was right, and if she was being honest about being pregnant, then maybe Jack hadn't jumped into the river. I shouldn't need more than a few days, maybe a week, to get a better sense of whether something had happened here.

In the meantime, I'd gamble that, despite her good looks, Katie Wallace would need more time than that to stop looking like a deer caught in the headlights when she was on TV.

Daniels gave me a little snort and shook his head.

"It's your career."

"It is."

Chapter 8

I was sitting at the bar of a place called McNeal's on Third Avenue between Nineteenth and Twentieth Streets, a few blocks from my place. I had walked by here hundreds of times and never stopped in.

Now I knew why.

The place was dark and smelled of stale beer. I nursed a bottle of Heineken and was relieved to see Rinaldi come in the door to my right.

He was dressed in a tan suit, a white shirt, and a tie that was supposed to be either a splashy pastel pattern or had Russian dressing stains on it. He carried a folded copy of the *Post* in one hand and took the barstool next to me.

"If it isn't my friend the celebrity," he said.

"Your kind of place, huh?" I asked.

"Dark and mysterious. Just the way I like my women."

"Your wife is Irish, last time I looked."

"What? Get out."

Rinaldi was what's called heavyset these days. Ten years ago he would have been overweight. Twenty years ago he would have been fat. A few years from now he'll probably be called husky. He had a thick head of jet-black hair that hadn't thinned at all since high school. As a matter of fact, he appeared to have kept the same hairstyle he'd had in high school as well.

The bartender tossed a coaster on the bar in front of him then reached below the bar and came back with a small bowl of peanuts like he had tapped a secret stash.

"Detective Rinaldi," he said, "a beer like your friend the TV star?"

Rinaldi looked at me and smiled.

"I knew you were a celebrity. Getting recognized everywhere."

"I'm not convinced it's a good thing to be recognized in a cop bar."

Rinaldi looked at my Heineken then ordered a Jameson's. It was poured, and he raised his glass.

"To my friend the TV star." He finished his drink and slid the glass onto the bar. "So you're hot shit again?"

"Thanks to your confirming things for me."

"I provide the info, you get the glory. Nice gig, this TV reporting," he said.

"An honorable profession filled with noble, hardworking individuals."

"All with perfect hair and teeth," he said.

"Amazing how I slipped through the cracks."

On a crummy sound system behind the bar, late-eighties rock was playing. It may have been Bon Jovi.

"So what else can I do to further your career?" he asked.

"I need to know about Steele."

"He's still dead," he said. He took a handful of peanuts and jiggled them around like he was about to roll dice.

"Yes, so I heard," I said.

"Glad I could help," he said before tossing nuts one at a time into his mouth.

I drank the beer and tried to decide how much I could and should tell him.

"I got a call from his wife."

"The Yoga Honey?"

"She's convinced he didn't kill himself."

Pep raised his glass and drank slowly, thinking about it. "She's new to the widow game. Give her a week or two, then she'll realize fatso went for a swim."

"She thinks he went out to meet somebody that night," I said.

"Then what, maybe jumped in the river to cool off after the big meeting?" he asked.

"You think there's a chance?"

"Yes. Slightly less than zero."

I finished my Heineken, and the bartender noticed from the far end of the bar, where he was engaged in a conversation. He made his way to us, pulled another one from the cooler below the bar, and put it in front of me.

Rinaldi turned his head a little and scanned the faces down the bar before speaking.

"I'm not a big fan of the guy who caught this," he said. "He's a pain in the ass."

"He any good?"

"We're all good. That's my point."

"So no way he missed anything?"

He finished the last peanut and turned to me and tapped the bar with a thick finger.

"We got a note. In his handwriting, at least as far as we can tell. It was found in his home office. Where he was last sitting before he went out. We got a cabbie who picked him up in front of his building, then dropped him at Thirty-fourth and First. We got easy access to the water a short walk from there. Then we got him in the water."

"Pretty convincing."

"Unless there's something we're all missing," he said. "Which I doubt."

I thought about Robbie telling me she was pregnant. I was close to sharing but decided not to. Why wouldn't she tell the cops? I was going to have to try to sort that out, but not here.

"Anything at all make you think something else could have happened?" I said.

"Not from what I've heard," he said, then took a slow pull on the

Jameson's. "I brought you a copy of the paperwork. The report and his note."

He glanced at the copy of the *Post* on the bar. "Tucked into the horoscope page. By the way, my moon is in a good house this week. I'm not sure what that means."

"Think it means it's your lucky week."

"Then why am I sitting here with you?" he said.

"My winning personality, maybe."

"Maybe."

"You think Robbie Steele is just being emotional and in denial?" I asked.

"Yes."

"And she'll eventually realize there were some subtle signs she was missing all along about her husband's mental state?"

"Probably," he said.

"She's determined to find out what really happened."

"Fatso Steele snapped," he said.

"What's his note say?"

"Pressure. The weight of the world. Something about drinking. All the usual, woe-is-me stuff."

I drank a bit of my Heineken and again wondered if I was wasting my time. And ruining what was left of my career.

Chapter 9

I was in the lobby of Carnegie Court, scanning the big glass-encased board on one of the dark marble walls. The narrow office building was nestled in among the bigger, flashier buildings on the south side of Fifty-seventh between Sixth and Seventh Avenues.

The lobby was dark and cool, with kind of a hip, futuristic feel to it. Not a lot of tenants in the place, but I found the one I was looking for right away.

"Webber Sizemore Associates: Suite 6F"

"Healing Strategies & Health Alternatives"

According to the police report Rinaldi had given me, Dr. Alan Webber was one of the last people to speak to Jack Steele. The report referred to him as Steele's therapist and business associate. I was going to bet he was either a high-end shrink, specializing in substance-abuse treatment, or a charlatan, specializing in bilking his well-to-do clients.

I was on my way to the elevator bank at the far end of the lobby when a young black guy behind the security desk looked up from his book as I passed.

"Excuse me," he said.

I broke stride when it was apparent I wasn't going to make it past him unchecked. His book was a big, meaty paperback, not the usual pass-the-time-on-a-boring-job book.

"And where might I direct you today, sir?"

"Actually, I am a bit self-directed today," I said.

"And that is all well and good, but the building staff likes to know the comings and goings of our guests."

"Well," I said, "if you have to know."

"I do."

"Of course. I will be going to see Dr. Andrew Webber. I'm in desperate need of a healing strategy, or quite possibly a health alternative."

"I understand fully," he said.

"I knew you would."

He punched a few keys on his computer then tapped an open binder on the counter.

"Please sign in," he said.

I did, and he gave me a look of vague recognition when I glanced up. I got that a lot. He kind of recognized me, or the name. He wasn't sure from where. He checked his computer screen, saw my name, and approved me.

"All set," he said.

"So I'm cleared to embark on my coming and goings in the building now?"

"You are indeed," he said.

I got off the elevator on the sixth floor and approached the double wood doors at the end of the hall with the gold lettering that read "Webber Sizemore."

I opened it and stepped in and was greeted with a glare from a stern-looking young woman behind a desk to my left. She was skinny and seemed to stick straight up from the desk. It seemed as though whatever healing or health program she was on may have gone a bit too far.

"Mr. North?" she said.

"That would be me."

She rose and came around the desk and extended a hand. Not only was she tall and skinny, she had on heels. It was like greeting a large two-by-four with arms and legs.

"My name is Grace. Andrew is expecting you," she said.

"That is exactly what I wanted to hear."

"Can I ask the nature of your visit?"

"You just did."

"Very nice," she said,

"Strictly informational."

"Of course," she said.

She took a manila folder off her desk that had my name on a label across the tab. She opened it and studied a sheet of paper inside. "And you were recommended by Jack Steele?"

She looked at me and I nodded and answered in a somber tone. "Yes."

"A horrible tragedy," Grace said.

"I know of no other kind."

Grace chose to ignore my wit.

"As a matter of fact, I saw your reports that morning," she said.

The image of Grace in the kitchen fixing her breakfast of four raisins danced through my mind.

"Tough morning," I said.

"I can only imagine. You two were close?" she said.

"In a way."

Grace didn't need to know I had never said more than a half-dozen words to the man.

"Well, I can tell you that we have many, many high-profile patients here, and their privacy is our number one priority," she said.

"I'm so glad to hear that," I said.

"Whatever treatment you require, I assure you will remain strictly confidential," she said.

"Thank you," I said.

When I called to set up an appointment, the officious young man who took the call had assumed I was looking for a counseling session. I mentioned it was in reference to Steele, and he took that as my having been recommended by Steele; I did nothing to change his thinking.

And here I was, in front Grace the Stick on my way into see Dr. Andrew Webber, Therapist and Healer of the Stars.

Grace motioned for me to follow her down the hall.

"I'll take you right in to see Andrew," she said, and off we went.

We turned down a hallway next to Grace's desk and walked past offices on the right that looked out onto Fifty-seventh Street. On the left was a large open room with windows and a handful of cubicles. The place had a sunny, open feel to it, and a few people were pecking away at their keyboards as we passed.

Webber's office was the last one in the hallway, the corner office. Grace tapped on the door and opened it, poked her head in, and introduced me. I thanked her and stepped inside, and she closed the door on her way out.

Webber was behind his desk on the other side of the room. He rose and came out from behind it as I crossed over to him.

"Mr. North, it is so nice to meet you."

He was probably not all that much older than I was; my guess would be early fifties. He was about my height, a touch over six feet, and slim.

He was dressed in business clothing, but expensive. A striped shirt with muted greens and browns, a tie with a lot of gold and deep yellows, and olive slacks. His hair was neatly cut and parted, and he had a tasteful salt-and-pepper beard. He was well groomed and healthy looking, which I guess was a good thing if you're trying to help people straighten out their lives.

We shook hands, and I thanked him for seeing me. The office was clean and neat, Webber's desk empty except for a few small stacks of manila folders. All the desk accessories were neatly arranged like someone put great care into displaying them, or maybe he was obsessive compulsive.

"I watched you on the morning of Jack's death," he said as he took his seat behind the desk and motioned me to one of the chairs in front of it. "That must have been very difficult, I mean, knowing Jack and all."

"It was a tough morning," I said.

"I'm sure."

He moved my folder front and center and looked at my sheet, then slid a yellow legal pad in front of him. He had a pen ready to start transcribing our chat.

"Before we start, let me say that I treat many high-profile people, and we go to extraordinary lengths to protect their privacy."

"That's comforting to hear," I said as he studied my sheet.

"So it says Jack recommended you." He looked at me like he smelled something. "I treated Jack for close to three years, but I never heard him mention your name. Were you two close?"

"Not particularly."

"Oh, okay," he said.

"I'm not here for treatment."

Webber held my sheet in both hands and studied me. I spoke to save him the trouble of asking me.

"I'm here because Robbie Steele doesn't think Jack killed himself."

He took a big breath like he was running out of patience and trying to stay calm. "It's frequently hard for the spouse to accept this," he said.

"Funny, that's what the cops said, too."

"There'll be a point when she does," he said.

"Well, right now, she doesn't. She thinks he went out to meet someone that night and was killed."

"And she's asked you to ..."

"She's asked me to ask around. My background is in investigative reporting. I got a bunch of local news Emmys from years ago to prove it."

"Congratulations." Webber put the sheet of paper back in the folder and closed it. "Well, I don't see what help I can be."

"According to the police report, you and his driver were among the last people to speak to him. Aside from his wife, that is."

"And are you going to go misrepresent yourself to the driver as well?"

"Yes. I may say I need a ride somewhere when I really don't."

"Mr. North, I really don't have the time, nor the patience, to indulge your little investigation. You obviously know I spoke to Jack that evening."

"But what I don't know is what you two spoke about."

"I already told the detectives who showed up here unannounced," he said. He squirmed like the thought of someone dropping in was the worst thing that could possibly happen. I realized the good doctor was one of those neat and orderly guys; everything had to be just so.

"Mrs. Steele told me Jack called you to cancel your session. Did he say why?"

"Mr. North ..."

"Did you two normally meet at night? How unusual was that? Did he cancel a lot?"

"Mr. North," he said again. This time his tone was harsher. "In an effort to keep your little intrusion here short, I'll tell you exactly what I told the police, if that will help."

"I'm sure it will."

"Good. Jack and I met at least twice, sometimes three times a week. Most of the time it was after his show had ended. The vast majority of the time it was at my apartment. We lived only a few blocks apart. He called that night just before ten and said he was tired and not feeling well and canceled."

I nodded, taking it all in.

"There. No you can go," he said.

"That was it? I'm tired and not coming over?"

"Yes. Even if there were something else, I wouldn't tell you. Doctor-patient privilege, maybe you've heard of it?"

"Hate how that gets in the way."

He made a move for his phone. "I'll have Grace show you out."

"You surprised Jack killed himself?"

"Mr. North, really."

"You were his shrink."

He put the phone back down. "I am not a shrink. We provide a full range of services, specializing in substance-abuse treatments. This is not about someone coming in to get on the couch."

"Well, whatever it is, it obviously didn't work if you believe Jack went out and jumped in the river."

Webber gritted his teeth, and for a second I thought he might smash his desk with a fist.

"Mr. North, I work to heal people. To restore their vitality and sense of self as they battle various forms of substance abuse. Not everyone responds to our treatments in the same way."

"I worked with Jack," I said, "always heard he was battling the bottle, but it didn't seem too bad lately. Something happen that we all didn't know about?"

"I am not going to get into the specifics of—"

"Come on, Doc," I said. "This whole thing isn't exactly an advertisement for your expensive services. I mean, your treating of Jack isn't going to make your testimonial brochure after this."

Webber picked up his pen and began to turn it back and forth, end over end. He'd keep his temper in check this time. "I really don't know why you're poking around in this."

"I need to poke somewhere; it's what I do for a living. Plus, Robbie Steele asked me to poke around."

He sighed and shook his head. "Roberta Steele and reality don't always see eye to eye."

"Who does?"

He got up and moved from behind his desk. "I told you what I told the police. You can go now."

He crossed the office and went to the door; I followed right behind him and stood too close for either one of us.

"Here's something I found odd," I said.

He stiffened and raised his chin.

"The police report described you as Jack's therapist slash business associate. That's probably how Robbie described you to the cops."

"That is a private matter."

"Business been good?"

He opened the door. "Good-bye, Mr. North."

"Maybe things have been tough. Maybe you were tapping Jack for a few dollars? Maybe Jack was going to be a celebrity endorser or something? Am I close here on any of this?"

"No. Good-bye."

"Maybe there was some business deal that didn't work out."

"Jack had a lot of business interests. Last I checked, his agent and his executive producer handled them."

I had taken a step toward the open door, satisfied I had given him a hard enough time when I stopped. "What? Who handles them?"

"His agent."

"And? Who was the other one?"

"His executive producer. Marty—"

"Glover?"

"Yes. Maybe you can go waste their time."

Chapter 10

I found Marty Glover standing in Jack Steele's office.

He was behind Steele's desk, which is what I was assuming was buried under the mountains of books, papers, and files surrounding Glover.

"Waiting for the hazmat guys to come in and clean up the place?" I asked.

Marty jumped, startled by me. He had been staring off into space and may have been in deeper thought than I had realized.

"Hey, Sam," he said, like that was all he could manage at the moment.

Marty was a guy who usually had a big laugh and a sarcastic word for just about every situation, but he had been taking Jack's death hard.

"You okay?" I asked.

"Yeah, just sad. You know?" he said.

"I do."

I looked around at the office, which was cluttered with stacks of books and papers that began on the floor and rose up to your waist. There were windows that looked out onto Fiftieth Street, but most were blocked with piles of crap on the windowsills.

"You would never have known the man was such a ..."

"Slob?"

"Yeah."

"Jack preferred pack rat to slob," he said.

Glover was short but packed a lot of weight on his frame. He was dressed in khakis and a light blue dress shirt that strained to do its job of covering his wide belly. What was left of his thinning hair was going from black to gray. Around his neck was a lanyard holding his Liberty ID card, which was tucked in the breast pocket of the shirt.

"You know the amazing thing?" he asked. "Jack really did know where every piece of paper was in this mountain of crap. The man had an incredible memory."

He tapped the top of the desk, which looked like a landfill, with all the piles of folders and papers.

"I'd put his nightly research folder on a pile here, and he never once had to ask where it was," he said.

I picked up a book off the desk. It was a hardcover. *The Retaking of America.* "Oh, boy," I said.

Glover shook his head. "Jack never read any of this shit. He got more books than Amazon, but he barely cracked them. The author would come on, and he'd make it sound like he read them but he never had."

"And the guest was usually too intimidated to call him on it."

"Bingo," he said. "You knew one his little tricks."

"Maybe I could host the show."

He stared at me, not quite sure what to say.

"It's a joke," I said.

"Oh, okay. It's just that I got every freaking talk-radio-show host in the country bothering me for a tryout."

"They're all going to be the next Jack Steele. The next big super-star," I said.

"They all suck," he said. "It's a lot of work, and Jack made it look easy." He sighed and shook his head. "This goofball doing tonight's show? Hotshot talk-radio guy from Miami. Has the usual bag of tricks: anti-gay, anti-government, anti-everything rants. But you know what? He sucks on TV. He doesn't know that—he thinks he's hot shit."

"How'd he get in the door?"

"Cal is under all kinds of pressure to find someone who can at least hold the ratings steady until he discovers the next big star," I said. "Jack's been gone less than a week, and there's already squawking from some advertisers."

"You lose a guy like Jack, and all of sudden your network doesn't look so strong," I said.

"Exactly," he said. He pushed some of the papers and books back from the corner of the desk and sat on the cleared space. It was like he needed to take weight off his feet. "What are you working on?" he asked.

"Special assignment."

"Anything good?" he said.

"You know Robbie Steele at all?"

"Just from when she would call and scream at me because Jack wasn't answering his cell phone."

"She doesn't think Jack killed himself."

His eyes squinted, and he shook his head like he had trouble processing what I just said. "Huh?"

"She refuses to believe Jack killed himself."

"Oh, brother," he said. "She's a piece of work."

"She called me after I went on that morning to tell me I was wrong."

"Helloooo, the note," he said.

"Yes, that presents a problem, a hole in her theory. Although she doesn't really have a theory."

"Thank God," he said.

"She just has ... well, she has a feeling Jack didn't kill himself."

I had decided I would tell no one other than Liz of Robbie Steele's pregnancy. I'd operate on the assumption that she was being truthful, even though I had my doubts. And I'd respect her desire to keep it quiet at the moment.

"Well, if Jack didn't kill himself," he said, "that would leave an accident as cause of death. Or ..."

"Or someone killed him."

His shoulders slumped like an invisible weight had fallen on him. "Oh my God. Does she actually ..."

"Yes, she does."

"So where do you come in?" he said.

"She asked me to investigate."

"Investigate?"

"Yes, you know, ask questions and all."

He smiled, happy for even weak humor. "She paying you?"

I shrugged. "Who knows?" I said.

"Maybe you'll get to make out with her," he said.

"Depends on what I find."

"This is fucking priceless," he said.

I was still undecided on the question of whether Robbie Steele was nuts and wasting my time. I was also worried about being labeled a nut right along with her the more I told people that I was working with her on this. But it occurred to me that there was a way I could get people to speculate.

"I think she's probably trying to make sense of why Jack did what he did. You know, get some answers and bring some closure. That sort of thing."

"Whatever," he said.

"You got any theories for me, about what happened?"

"Is this part of your official investigation?"

"Yes."

He shrugged and his big, round shoulders rose. "I don't know. I'm not a shrink, but I think maybe it got to be too much for him."

"The weight of being Jack Steele?"

"Yeah, you got to remember, Jack and I were doing a radio show in Hartford when Cal stumbled on us," he said. "He was battling the bottle, trying to stay sober. I was coming out of some financial difficulties, as they say. And then, boom, fourteen years later, here we are.

He's the biggest cable personality in the country, and we got the number one show."

"But not exactly loved by everyone."

"He said some nights it felt like everybody hated him," he said.

"That's got to get to you after a while."

"Depends on if you care about it," he said.

"Did he?"

"Sometimes. I mean, you can only read so many nasty stories about yourself before it affects you." He looked past me to the windows, where you could see Sixth Avenue between the piles of crap stacked on the windowsills.

"But you know what, Sam? Those people didn't know him like I did." He looked back to me. "Let me tell you something. A few years ago my mother was very sick. I mean, real sick. Found out she had a heart condition. Jack knows my dad is gone, so what's he do? He makes sure she sees the best specialists in the city, gets the best treatments."

"Damn big of him," I said.

"And that's not all. She needs surgery, right? Frigging insurance barely covers the bill for the room. Jack has me send him the bills, and he takes care of them. He took care of everything."

"The benevolent Jack Steele."

"The man did some nice things. Things people didn't know about. Things he didn't want people to know about."

"How was he the last few weeks? Any signs that maybe he was unraveling?"

"He seemed to be unraveling most every night."

"So nothing unusual?"

"He was getting nuts about the numbers."

"Lose twenty percent of your audience in six months, and I'd get nuts, too," I said.

"What about that new strategy, the 'attack the fat cats of Corporate America'; that pay off at all?"

"Hah. What a load of bullshit."

"I'll take that as a no."

"You know who it paid off for?" he asked. "It paid off for the consultant Cal brought in who came up with that half-assed idea."

He was worked up now. Once the ratings of *Steele Yourself* began to slide, Daniels had pushed for the consultants to come in and make it all better. They rarely did.

"It's always the executive producer's fault when the numbers drop, you ever notice that, Sam?" he asked. "It's never the anchor's fault. Always the EP."

"That's why you get the big bucks."

"Not as big as that asshole Jerry Drake. He comes in and has Jack go after Corporate America, and the numbers get even worse. And you know who's left to clean up his mess?"

"Marty Glover," I said.

"No F-ing kidding," he said.

He got up off the corner of the desk but did so slowly, like he was hesitant to put too much weight on his feet.

"Maybe you go talk to him," he said.

"Jerry Drake, right?"

"Yeah, you know what he calls his little know-nothing operation?"

"Can't say I do."

"The Show Doctor," he said.

"Catchy."

"Yeah, like he can fix things."

"Maybe we can sue for malpractice."

"That guy caused me a shit load of trouble and worry, Sam."

"He still working with us?"

"No, thank God. Jack got pissed at him and told him to get lost. Told Drake he didn't care what agreement he had with Daniels, it was his show and he called the shots."

"Can't imagine the Show Doc was happy with that."

"With any luck, maybe it put him out of business."

Chapter 11

Liz and I ran on the sidewalk up University Place heading toward Union Square. It was early Saturday morning, and the city was quiet.

Some people went out for a Saturday-morning jog. Liz went for a Saturday-morning run. At this point, I would have preferred the jog.

"Sprint to the corner," I said as we crossed Twelfth Street.

"Loser buys coffee," she said.

"Hope you brought money."

My lead was slim and, I knew, short-lived, and within a few steps she had pulled even with me. I caught a glimpse of her long legs chewing up sidewalk as she raced ahead.

I tried to find my afterburners, but there were none. I got my knees up high, kept my body erect, just like the Olympic sprinters. I looked good, but that was about it.

Liz pulled away, her brown ponytail swaying back and forth. I gave it one last shot and pulled close to even.

"Got ya," I said.

"Not quite."

She took off again and reached the corner a foot ahead of me. We slowed, and she walked with her hands on her hips and seemed like she could do it all again. Sweat trickled down her tan cheeks, but she barely seemed winded.

"Did I win?" I asked.

"Of course. You always win."

"That's what I thought."

"You were a bit closer this week," she said.

"It's the little victories that make the difference."

"Yes. Especially when they're all you have," she said.

We walked up to Fourteenth Street, and I tried to slow my breathing.

"So tell me again why you insist on trying to beat me." she said.

"I need to make a statement."

"The 'I can beat a girl who was on her high school track team,' statement?"

"That's the one."

"And how's that working out for you?"

"So far, great. I actually think I may get a date with her." I turned and gave her a kiss on the cheek while we waited at the corner of Fourteenth for a truck to rattle past us on its way west across Manhattan. "I let you win," I said as we crossed into Union Square.

"Of course you did," she said. She reached over and slapped my butt. "That'll teach you to challenge a younger woman."

We walked along the western edge of Union Square and into the big open area at the north end, where farmers from as far away as Syracuse and Pennsylvania were unloading trucks for the farmers market.

Metal poles clanged on the asphalt as tables and tents were set up. In a few hours the crowd would be thick here, but right now it was a few dozen farmers and us. The only ones out on an August Saturday when you felt like you had the city to yourself.

We crossed Park Avenue South at Seventeenth Street and walked over to Irving Place, then turned north toward Gramercy Park. My apartment was around the corner, and this was my neighborhood. The buildings along Irving Place weren't tall, and there was a quaint, unhurried feel to the street and the handful of restaurants that lined it.

We got to the front of Gramercy Grounds, Liz stretched out her hand and snapped her fingers.

"Fork over the buckeroos."

"Going to hold me to it, huh?"

"A race is a race."

I gave her a ten and took a seat at one of the little tables out front and waited. It was hot and humid, and sweat dripped from my forehead. It was Saturday, four days since Jack Steele was discovered floating in the East River. Four days since I had taken a flyer and told Robbie Steele I'd help her, and it felt like I had nothing.

Liz was back with the coffees. She took the plastic lid off hers, raised the cup toward her nose and breathed in the aroma.

"I make just as good at home you know," I said.

"Not like this you don't," she said.

I had a little of mine. "Bold with a hint of something or another," I said.

"Bold is the new strong," she said.

"So mild is the new weak?"

"Yes, and you don't want to be described as mild," she said.

I had a litle more and saw Liz studying me as I drank. "May I help you?" I asked.

"You already have," she said.

"Why the look? Do I have a pimple I don't know about or something?"

"You're perplexed."

"I am."

"The Widow Steele?"

"Yup."

"You still don't know what to make of her."

"I lied my way in to see Jack's therapist and pissed him off, and I'm sure I came across as a nut in the process."

"He's a shrink; he's used to nuts."

"Then I told Marty about her little theory, and he looked at me like I'm insane."

"I don't think you're crazy, if that helps."

She smiled one of her megawatt smiles that showed off a small dimple on her left cheek. It's always nice to be able to remind yourself of how lucky you are, and I was.

"Let's not forget I told Cal Daniels, one of the most powerful TV execs in the business, that I was okay with taking my mug off TV for a few days to chase this. *I'm* beginning to wonder if I'm nuts." I had more coffee and hoped it would give me some insight or clarity or whatever the hell it was that was needed right now. "But you want to know the crazy thing?" I asked.

"Who doesn't?"

A young woman in shorts and a T-shirt walked past with her shades on and headed for the door of the coffee shop. I waited until she was inside before continuing.

"My gut tells me there's something here. I don't know what it is," I said, looking around to make sure no one was nearby, "but I think she may be right."

"And the note?"

"I don't know. But maybe something will eventually explain it."

Liz took a drink of coffee, and there was something about her demeanor that changed. I saw her stare off across the street like she was lost in thought.

"Hello?" I said.

She snapped back and looked at me.

"Solving a world problem?" I asked. "Maybe the whole Middle East thing?"

She shook her head and was serious, very serious. It wasn't a place she went to that often, at least not in the months I'd known her. Her sense of humor and playfulness were irresistible, and when she became serious there was usually something wrong.

"I'm worried," she said, looking right at me.

I knew what she was talking about before she explained.

"If she's right, and your gut is right," she said. She uncrossed her legs and sat forward over the table so she was closer to me. "Then someone really did ..."

Her voice drifted off and I nodded, knowing where she was going with this.

"I know," I said. "I've had the same thought."

"It could get dangerous if you start to figure it out. Someone is going to realize it and—"

"I know, Liz. I know," I said.

It was all I could manage at the moment, but the fact that I was aware of the potential danger did little to comfort her.

"I don't even want to think about ..." She shook her head.

I leaned forward over the table and put my hand over hers. "Liz, let's just say she's right. That means there is somebody out there that did this. And as of now, they've gotten away with it."

She nodded.

"Because no one, including the police, sees any reason to investigate this, because no one besides Robbie Steele, and possibly me, thinks anything happened here."

"And you have what, a strong sense of justice?" she said.

There was a bite to her tone. "You could say that," I said.

She had some more of her coffee and studied me, then said, "Or, is it that you're just dying for a good story to help your career?"

I dawned on me that Liz Harrison knew me even better than I realized.

Chapter 12

L iz's words had stayed with me all weekend. Was I willing to put myself in danger for a story?

The answer was yes.

And so here I was at a few minutes to ten on Monday morning, walking to the offices of the Show Doctor, hoping Jerry Drake could hand me a lead and help me figure out what happened to Jack Steele.

The Show Doctor was located on a bland strip of Fifth Avenue at Thirty-first Street, a few blocks south of the Empire State Building. The company was on the third floor of a squat, ugly building five floors high. A Korean grocer had the first floor. What looked to be a combination nail shop and palm reader had the second. The fourth and fifth floors showed no signs of commerce or life.

I hit the little button on the panel next to the steel-gray door marked "#3: Show Doctor." The door buzzed, and I walked in. I rode the slow-moving elevator to the third floor. The car creaked and groaned its way higher, and I thought it might just get there and then die.

The elevator door opened into a sunny room with a battleship-gray metal desk a few feet in front of me. An attractive young woman with shoulder-length black hair that matched her black-framed librarian glasses greeted me. She looked entirely out of place behind the drab desk.

"Well, hello," she said with a wide smile.

I checked behind me, thinking maybe Brad Pitt had also stepped off the elevator. He hadn't.

"Well, hello to you, too," I said.

Off to my right was a small seating area with windows that looked down onto Fifth. To my left was a wall with a door that I guessed led back to the examining rooms of the Show Doctor.

The wall looked as if Jerry, or maybe a brother-in-law who was supposed to be handy, had slapped it up. It barely reached the ceiling in some spots and seemed like a good solid wind would take it out.

"I know you," the young lady said. She was brimming with energy. "You're on Channel Four."

It was my guess she didn't get many visitors during the day, and she was determined to make the most of this one.

"Oh, no I'm not," I said.

"Channel Five?"

"Uh, no." I extended a hand to prevent her from marching up the channel list. "Sam North, with Liberty News."

"Oh, yes. Liberty. I'm Sherri," she said.

"Sherri," I said, "I don't have an appointment, but I was hoping the Show Doctor could see me. It's an emergency."

She kind of smiled, but I could tell she wasn't quite sure why. She picked up a pen and had a small note pad ready to go. "Okay, and this is in reference to what show?"

"I don't have a specific show. It's more of a personal visit. Jerry does a lot of work for Liberty."

"Yes, he does," she said.

"I have something I need to talk to him about."

She stood up, and dressed in a tight beige dress with a belt I had a feeling I knew why Drake had hired her. You can tell a lot about a small, independent businessman by his receptionist or assistant.

"Let me see if Mr. Drake is free."

I suspected Mr. Drake was always free when it came to Sherri. I went over to the windows that looked down onto Fifth and saw a double-decker tourist bus stopped at the light. Faces scanned the buildings like they were on safari.

"Mr. Drake is available," Sherri said from behind me.

"Imagine that," I said.

She led me to the door and showed me in and closed it behind me. I stepped into a windowless room that took up the rest of the floor. Drake's desk was against the exposed brick wall to my right. There were two Chinese screens set up in the corners opposite him, with empty desks behind them.

Either everyone was at lunch at ten in the morning, or the Show Doctor was experiencing a drop-off in patients.

Drake was seated behind his desk and got up to greet me.

"Hey, Sam," he said, "nice to see you. I'm a fan."

He came around to me and we shook hands, and he put a hand on my arm as he did.

He was of medium build and on the skinny side with not much in the way of shoulders. He wore wrinkled tan dress slacks with a blue-and-white-striped dress shirt open at the collar. There was no sign of a T-shirt, so I was treated to a view of his chest hair.

He went back behind his desk, and I took a seat on the only other place to sit, a beat-up brown leather couch to the side of his desk. I sat on the edge of it for fear this was where the doctor may have performed some examinations on the office staff.

Drake caught me looking around the office.

"We're moving. This is just a temporary office. Until the work is finished on the new place," he said.

"Of course."

"You did a real nice job out there, Sam," he said.

"Thanks."

He was sitting alert and attentive, and one hand fiddled with a pencil while he tried to figure out just what the hell it was that I wanted.

"So what do I owe this visit?" he said.

He asked his question with a little smirk on his face, a little fake smile that gave you the impression he was happy with everything.

"You know Robbie Steele?" I asked.

"No, but I'd like to," he said.

Again, the little smirk, this time cementing the impression he was a sleaze.

"She asked me to look into the circumstances surrounding Jack's death. You know, see what it was that drove him to—"

"Throw himself into the river?" he said.

"Yes. That."

"Hmm," he said, like he was giving this some deep thought to try and help me out.

"I think it's one of those closure things," I said.

"Why you?" he said.

"Lucky, I guess."

"So what can I tell you?" he asked.

"I'm trying to see what Jack's state of mind was. I know the show had been causing a lot of angst."

"That ain't the half of it," he said.

"Marty Glover said all the changes and new strategy hadn't really paid off."

He slapped his desk and let out a loud "Hah" as he did. "Oh, that's rich. That is so fucking rich. Sounds like something Marty would say."

"Why?"

"Why? Because he screws up the show and I try to clean up his mess, and now he's criticizing me?"

"Is he wrong?"

Drake put his pencil down to focus on defending his good name. "You got to understand something, Sam, guys like Marty hate guys like me."

"Interlopers."

"Exactly. But the thing you got to remember is that I'm only being called into a shop because guys like Marty aren't doing their job," he said. "There has to be a patient before the doctor is called."

"Ain't that the truth."

He shook his head like it was a painful experience. "There was just so much F-ing resistance to change on that show," he said.

"From Marty?"

"Not just him. That asshole Ron Marshall always had to chime in," he said.

"The superagent."

"Super*jerk* is more like it," he said. "Pompous ass."

"So you got Glover, who doesn't want you meddling with his anchor. And Ron Marshall, who doesn't want you meddling with his prized client. Sounds like a no-win situation."

"It wasn't one my finer moments," he said. "You remember that *Times* article?"

"I do."

The *Times* had written a page-one story with a nice big color photo of Jack with the headline "Man of Steele's Ratings Drop Worries Liberty."

"Unfortunately," Drake said, "the reporter failed to mention that Glover and Marshall were blocking me and keeping the show from being fixed."

Drake knew the article well enough to have it memorized.

"The article said, 'Even the hiring of outside consultants failed to slow the defection of viewers. TV consultant Jerry Drake was brought in to help, but his strategy of targeting Corporate America has thus far failed to produce a rise in the ratings,'" he said. He sat back in his chair and looked hurt.

"Not something you'll use in your promotional materials," I said.

"It wasn't a good day, Sam. I can tell you that," he said. "And if really affected office morale. Think of poor Sherri."

"Okay."

Then Drake shot forward and slapped the desk and I jumped, thinking I might have to defend myself.

"But," he said, "and it's a big but, notice how the reporter said 'thus far.' Right?"

I was now hoping he would stay calm.

"Has *thus far* failed to produce a rise in the ratings," he said.

"Got it."

"Meaning it was about to turn around," he said. "See what I'm saying?"

Only a TV consultant could take the phrase 'has thus far failed to produce a rise in ratings' and read it to mean things were about to change.

"You were on the brink," I said.

"Damn straight, big fella."

He bolted from his chair and raced back to an old-style, light brown file cabinet and pulled open the top drawer. He reached in and yanked out a folder then came back over and thrust it toward me.

"Get a load of this shit, Sam," he said.

I opened the folder to see printouts of e-mails. I read the To and From lines and saw Jack.Steele@Libertynews.com and Stuart.Ripley@ite.com.

"Those are the e-mails from Operation Outrage," Drake said.

"Which was?"

"That was the code name for my strategy of attacking the fat cats," he said. "I wanted to brand the segments with that name but Marty didn't go for it. He kept saying, 'Let's see how it goes first.' Mr. Take It Slow and Easy."

"Not your style."

"Freaking Rome is burning, my friend. The numbers are sliding, and he's worried about slow and easy. Slow and easy got them in the mess in the first place."

There had to be at least twenty e-mails in the folder. Across the tab of the folder there was scrawled in ink, Op. Outrage—July.

"These are just the e-mails from July?" I asked.

"Oh, yeah. Got a file for August, too," he said. "We were ramping it up, Sam."

"Who's Ripley?"

"The corporate communications weenie for IT&E," Drake said.

"Interesting title," I said.

"This guy is Mr. Protective. Anybody says a word about IT&E or Buck McConnell, and he hits the roof."

International Technology & Energy was a Fortune 500 company, one of the largest oil and exploration companies in the country, which also happened to manufacture equipment used for oil and natural gas production and a mess of other industrial purposes.

I read the first e-mail in the file. It was dated July 11 and was from Ripley to Jack.

Your report on the Iran story is completely false and absent of facts. There are at least six outright lies in your story, and you have done irreparable damage to Buck McConnell and the IT&E brand. That you would, on national TV, accuse Mr. McConnell and our company of selling equipment in Iran, and imply selling eqipment to the Syrians, is simply outrageous and reckless. IT&E legal counsel is exploring what options we have available, and you can expect to hear from us shortly.

I looked at Drake, who had been watching me read it. He had a smile on his face like he was a kid showing off a test with a good grade.

"Pretty good, huh?" he said.

"He does sound like a weenie."

"Big time putz, Sam," he said, pointing at the e-mail. "And that was just the beginning. That e-mail was from the first report Jack did on IT&E. And there were other companies right smack in the middle of our crosshairs."

"But you never got to pull the trigger?"

He shook his head.

"Nope. Marty was always right there with the stop sign. Then Jack would go to Marshall for advice, and he'd side with Marty, and Op Outrage would get shelved for a week or two. Marty would say, 'We need more proof if we're going to go after these companies.' Then I'd see a report about IT&E on a Web site or blog or somewhere, tell Jack, and he'd start screaming, 'Why aren't we covering this?' So we would get it in the show and get a little traction, but then it would go nowhere again. I was always fighting an uphill battle with Marty."

"Why?"

He shrugged. "He's a baby, Sam. He's not like you and me. He's not a man of action. He was afraid it was going to backfire and the ratings would slide even more. And he was afraid he was going to get shit-canned if that happened."

"Why'd Marshall push back?"

"Because he's an ass. I told Jack he should dump him. Get a younger agent—someone in tune with a hipper audience," he said.

"And?"

"Nothing. End of the day, Jack wasn't going to make a radical move. Not unless everything really fell apart," he said.

"Guys like Marshall have a lot of infleunce," I said.

"Don't you know it," he said, shaking his head and sighing. "We were so close, Sam. The public wants this stuff. Mr. and Mrs. Front Porch are tired of seeing fat cat CEOs and their mansions and million-dollar yachts."

"I know I am."

"And the idiots at these companies like Ripley aren't used to having a guy like Jack attack them," he said. "The business reporters don't ask any tough questions, No one says, 'Hey, so why is your equipment showing up in Iran?'"

"But you wanted to," I said.

"I did. But I'm only one man, Sam. There was only so much I could do," he said.

I opened the folder and thumbed through the e-mails. "You think I can get copies of all the e-mails you have from Operation Outrage?"

"Sure, Sherri can take care of that for you," he said.

I stood up and thanked him and we shook hands and he caught me looking around the office.

"Like I said, these are temporary quarters, Sam. While the new place if being finished. You'll have to come by sometime," he said.

"I can't wait."

Chapter 13

I stopped in the big Starbucks on the corner of Thirty-third and Fifth for a cup of coffee. The place was quiet, with tourists sitting at tables going over subway and street maps and figuring out what sight to see.

I ordered my coffee and didn't think much of the individual behind me, who seemed to be unaware of the concept of personal space. The guy was right behind me, and I mean *right* behind me, anxious to get his coffee.

I ordered mine and stopped at the little station by the door where you add your milk and sugar when the same guy moved in next to me with his cup.

"So what are you finding out?" he asked.

I was grabbing a napkin from the dispenser and stopped in midmotion to look at him. He was my height, maybe a touch taller, and built like a beer keg with a barrel chest and thick arms. He was dressed in a stylish summer outfit of white slacks and a short-sleeved, navy-blue shirt. The outfit was topped off with a straw fedora. His face was reddened like he had seen too much sun over the years and there were deep creases at the corners of his blue eyes. A goatee of silver hair matched the ring of hair under the fedora.

"You got a thing with personal space, huh?" I asked.

He gave a little snort like a laugh and shook his head.

"Yeah. Ever since I was a kid. Been an issue of mine. I like to get close to people. What can I say?" He looked at my coffee. "How do you drink that black? Must be awfully bitter," he said.

"You get used to it."

"I suppose," he said.

I took a half step back and tried to find a little space. I had my coffee in one hand and the file with the e-mails from Drake in the other, and all of a sudden I found myself wishing one of my hands was free, just in case.

"What's in the file?" he asked.

"None of your business. Who are you?"

"An interested party," he said.

"Interested in what?"

"Interested in whatever it is you're finding out in your little investigation."

A woman moved in behind me to grab a packet of sweetener and forced me to edge closer to him again. When she left I stepped back and took a drink of the coffee.

He was right, it was a bit on the bitter side, but it didn't bother me.

He took two packets Equal, held them at the ends, and shook them vigorously.

"That's a lot of sweetener," I said.

He shrugged as he poured them in his cup. "I'm weak, what can I say?"

He stared at me, and I had an uneasy feeling. He was enjoying letting me know that he had been following me, for how long and why I didn't know, but he wanted to let me know he was onto me.

"You're asking a lot of questions about your late colleague," he said.

A couple speaking what sounded like German came up behind me, and I stepped away from the little station and he moved with me.

"What do you want?" I asked.

"Here's a piece of unsolicited advice," he said. "You need to be very careful. You're asking people questions about something you don't know anything about."

"Hopefully, the more questions I ask, the more I'll learn. That's generally how it works."

His little eyes darted to a point over my shoulder and made me nervous. I wondered if there was someone else back there.

"Listen, you have a great day, okay," I said, and walked to the wide glass doors on my left.

I had the coffee and folder in one hand and pushed open the door with the other. I was on the sidewalk of Fifth Avenue when I heard him again.

"It's extremely rude to walk away from someone like that," he said from behind me.

I turned, and he was in my face again.

"I wasn't done talking to you," he said.

We were standing in the middle of the sidewalk, which was thick with knots of tourists.

"Listen," I said, "I'm walking to the curb and getting a cab. I don't know who you are or what you're after, but—"

"I'm not after anything."

"Good, then leave me alone."

"You need to stop bothering people."

"It's what I do for a living," I said.

"Maybe you need to go back to being the morning-feature guy, you know?"

"Thanks for the career advice."

"You look like you could use it."

The engine of a double-decker bus rumbled to life and the bus left the curb packed with sightseers just a few feet away from us.

"Last shot to tell me who you are, or do you not have the balls to say?" I asked.

"Let's just say I'm here to confirm what New York's finest have determined regarding the unfortunate death of Jack Steele," he said.

I turned to leave, and as I did I felt his hand on my arm, right at the bicep.

"You're in way over your head with this thing, my friend."

"I'll take my chances," I said.

He tightened his grip on my arm.

"This will be the last time I'm this gentle," he said.

Chapter 14

"What was that supposed to be about?" I asked.

We were walking up the steps out of the basement of what at one time was a Polish community center down on Avenue A in the East Village. Back when the neighborhood was full of immigrants. Today a sign identified the building as the "New Filmmakers Institute." A smaller sign was below that one. "Dedicated to the Development and Enrichment of the Next Generation of Film Artists."

The girlfriend of one of Liz's banker colleagues was a film artist and had just premiered her independent film, *Taxi Man*. That was how the two of us came to be part of this privileged group this evening.

Liz took too long to answer my question.

"Well?" I said.

"I think it was supposed to be about man's struggle for recognition," Liz said. "You know, the battle to make your way in the world and persevere in the face of the sometimes daunting odds the world presents. And really about developing and listening to your inner voice."

We climbed the steps to the first-floor hallway along with the rest of the maybe eighty or so people unfortunate enough to have sat through the world premier of *Taxi Man*.

"Oh," I said as we reached the front doors and stepped outside. "I thought it was about a guy trying to hail a cab."

"It may have been," she said.

"I know it was," I said.

And I was certain it was. All fifty-seven minutes of it to be exact. Shot from a handful of angles. A scruffy, thirtysomething guy with a suitcase that couldn't get a cab in midtown at rush hour.

"But I think there was something deeper there," Liz said. "Didn't you see the looks he got from people passing by?" she said. "Or how about when those cabs, obviously empty, passed him by?"

"Why didn't he take the F train or something? It was right there, like a block away."

"I think you missed the broader point," Liz said.

"Yes, I think I did. You think her uncle who put up the twenty-three Gs to make it got the broader point?" I said.

We walked over to First Avenue and crossed Ninth Street. It was after ten and the sidewalks were as crowded as midtown at noon. It felt like the neighborhood was just getting going and chances are, it was going to go for a while.

Liz wrapped her arm around mine and we walked on, me wondering how long I could avoid the obvious topic.

"After movie drink?" I asked.

"You don't really think you're going to get off that easy, do you?" she said.

"You mean we have to talk more about *Taxi Man*?"

"I was thinking of another film. Maybe we call it the Fat Man with the Hat," she said.

"I'd rather discuss *Taxi Man*. I now see how his inability to get a cab was part of a larger societal issue."

"Nice try," she said.

"What if I said I identify with the guy in *Taxi Man*?" I said.

Liz didn't answer and I pulled her closer. I had told her about my encounter with the fedora-wearing coffee drinker on our way to the world premier, which really didn't feel like a world premier so much as a punishment.

"We need to talk," she said after a few moments.

"Would you feel better if I told you I'm going to take every precaution I can?"

She took her time before answering. "This is all kind of new for me," she said.

"It's actually been a while for me, too," I said. "I mean, I've had people threaten me, but that was years ago, back when I actually had a career and worked stories that mattered."

"And you don't know who this guy was?" she asked.

"No, I don't. Didn't recognize him, and he wouldn't give me any clue."

"But he knows what you've been up to?" she said.

"He seemed to, or at least that was the impression he wanted to give me."

Somewhere behind us, down First, a siren wailed then faded.

"He's been following you?" she asked.

I shrugged.

"Maybe. Maybe not. I think he heard from someone that I was asking questions about Steele's death."

"But someone would only care if …"

"If they didn't want me to find something out," I said.

We reached the corner of Fourteenth Street and waited for traffic to clear or the light to change. Liz looked at me and took in a big breath, like she was trying to calm herself down.

"I think we both knew this was a possibility if Robbie Steele was right," I said. "That if I started asking questions and pissing people off, someone eventually was going to want me to stop."

"But this seems so much, so much more real," she said.

"It is."

We crossed Fourteenth and she was quiet again, lost in thought.

"But there's the note," she said after a moment. "So, if someone is keeping track of you, maybe that means the note isn't real after all."

"Exactly what I'm thinking," I said. "If someone wants me to stop asking questions, then maybe Robbie is right about the note."

"But the police said it was his handwriting," she said.

"I don't know how to explain it. Sometimes you have to ignore the obvious signs and just trust it will make sense at some point."

She leaned over and put her head on my shoulder as we walked. This story had fast-forwarded our relationship, taking it from the giddy everything-is-great phase to another level entirely. And it was going to help us discover real fast if the two of us were going to work out.

"When this thing started, I thought Robbie Steele was crazy," I said.

"But you agreed to help her."

"I did. Partly because she seemed so damn sure of it. Plus, she tells me she's pregnant and that Jack always wanted to be a dad—so why would he jump in the river?"

"But the pregnancy hasn't been verified. You're not even certain of that," she said.

"She'd have to be pretty warped to make that up, don't you think?"

"Maybe," she said.

"Let's assume she's telling the truth," I said. "I go out and start asking questions, and look what happens. Some guy threatens me. That right there tells me there's something going on."

She pulled away and stiffened and she seemed to want some space, like she had to work it all out. It wasn't like we were twenty-something kids, we both had plenty of experience in the relationship department, but this was a new twist and was going to require some careful navigation for both of us.

We turned onto Eighteenth Street and walked west. The block was quiet and empty. Lights were on inside apartments and it all seemed like what passes for a run of the mill evening. The quiet of the street added the silence between us and all this quiet was killing me.

"Am I going to have to choose?" I asked.

Liz turned and looked at me and I hoped I wasn't going to regret asking.

"Choose?" she said.

"Between the story and my fabulous girlfriend?"

"I'm not so sure I want to hear the answer," she said.

"You're going to make me sweat a bit," I said.

"Having someone you care about being threatened is serious, Sam," she said.

"I get that."

"You start turning over rocks and look what happens," she said. "Someone tells you to leave it alone. We both know the deeper you get in the more dangerous it's going to get."

"So, I have to choose?" I said.

That brought the quiet back in a big way. We walked on, up to Third Avenue where we took a right and walked north. Things felt pretty icy at the moment.

"If forced," I said, "I'd have to choose the fabulous new girlfriend."

Liz looked over and in the glow of the lights around us I saw her face relax and a smile appear and I could see her dimple.

"A wise choice," she said.

We were getting there, little by little.

"You'd know I'd never ask you to choose. At least not yet," she said.

"Such a banker move."

"What?" she said.

"The whole, never, at-least-not-yet thing. Trying to hang on to the option."

"A girl's got to keep her options open," she said.

I pulled her to me and wrapped her in a hug.

"If it's any consolation," I said, "I'm going to call someone I know to kind of work with me on this. You know, so I'm not roaming around asking questions by myself."

"You mean, like, some muscle?" she asked.

"Yeah, I know a guy who knows a guy who's going to help me out," I said.

"Will you be referring to me as a broad when you talk to the muscle?"

"Whatever you like," I said, leaning over to kiss her.

Chapter 15

I stood waiting in what felt like the lobby of an upscale hotel. Lots of light, gleaming wood and a few huge circular tables, upon which sat big oversize pots containing flowers and plants that appeared to be very well tended.

And as far as waiting goes, this was not a bad place to have to pass a few minutes. Young women walked by in short-shorts or workout leggings with tight-fitting tank tops, their hair in ponytails, on their way either to or from a workout.

As far as gyms go, this was a scene. And most likely that was what the owners of The Club in the Time Warner Center on Columbus Circle had in mind when they conceived of it.

I was more of a down-and-dirty, bare-bones-gym kind of guy, but sitting here watching this scene made me question that.

Off in the distance I saw a guy walking toward me. He went about six two and wore sleek back sweats and a matching sleeveless workout shirt that showed off his biceps. He made his way across the lobby, smiling and glad-handing just about everyone, from the young things ready for a workout to the guy pushing a cart of drinks into the juice bar area.

I stood up as he approached and shook my head.

"Absolutely disgusting," I said.

"How the hell did you get past the front desk?" Freddie Sanchez asked.

"Charm and good looks."

"Unlikely."

We shook hands and did the bro-hug thing, but then Freddie did the bro-hug thing with everybody, whether he knew you for a dozen years or a half hour.

I shook my head and looked him over. "A street-savvy shooter now training the beautiful people. What's happened to you?" I ask.

"Funny, I was going to ask you the same thing. Look like crap. But you still got the nice suits."

"It's important at least to look good," I said.

"Feel good, being a big-shot reporter again after that Steele story?"

"Nice to get a win every once in a while."

"I know the dude you bought it off, Wade. Crazier than my first wife."

After a minute or two more of small talk, I got down to business.

"Got a place we can talk?" I asked.

He glanced toward the juice bar, which was the size of a restaurant. We took a small table in the rear corner, kind of tucked to the side of the counter and out of earshot of the handful of others scattered around the room.

Freddie got up before we started and went to a large glass-fronted refrigerator and took out two containers of juice.

"Orange guava," he said, handing one to me. "Keeps you alert."

"I need all the help I can get."

"I remember," he said.

I tried my guava drink. I would have to admit it was good if asked.

Freddie eyed me, trying to figure out why I came looking him up after a year.

"I got an offer for you," I said.

"Uh-oh."

"You're going to love it, believe me."

"Like I said, uh-oh."

I waved an arm around the sleek tables of the juice bar. "It will take you away from all this ... this slickness ... and ..."

Across the juice bar in the lobby area a woman walked by in an outfit that someone had apparently painted onto her.

"And all these beautiful people," I said.

"Which could only mean I'm working with you," he said.

"There's an insult in there somewhere"

"Still sharp as ever," he said.

"Plus, it gets you back to your roots," I said.

"We going to Puerto Rico?" he asked.

"No, I mean as a cameraman."

"I'd rather go to Puerto Rico," Freddie said.

"There's some more you need to know."

"Now I'm worried," he said.

I leaned in and took a quick scan of the neighboring tables. We were clear to speak. I filled Freddie in on the call from Robbie Steele and my little stops by Dr. Webber's and the office of the Show Doctor.

"You come uptown to fill me in on this goose chase?"

"It gets better," I said.

"I hope so, because so far all we got is you running around because Yoga Babe made eyes at you."

"That's what I was afraid of, at first. Until ..."

"Until what?"

I told him the story of my encounter with Fedora. Freddie sat back and had some of his orange guava drink, and I had some more of mine as well. I was feeling more alert already.

"So you think you're onto something?" he asked.

"This doesn't go beyond this table?"

"I ever mess with you before?" he said.

"Nope. That's why I came to you."

"Then no reason to worry," he said.

"I'm onto something. I don't know what it is. It could be big, or it might not be. But I got a feeling."

"Yeah, I remember what that was like. Always meant I was driving somewhere and shooting someone who preferred not to be on camera."

"And loving every second of it, right?"

Freddie smirked. "If you say so."

"You in?"

Freddie looked past me to the open lobby area of the club. "Hmm, let's see, the boring, middle-aged white guy, or the lovelies at The Club. Who do I want to spend my time with?"

"I'm not middle-aged," I said.

"Fifty is middle-aged."

"I'm mid-forties. You can say 'on the cusp of middle age,'" I said.

"Whatever."

"This may be a chance for some excitement," I said.

"Lack of excitement ain't exactly a problem these days." Freddie knocked off the last of the orange guava mix. "How you doing this and keeping a regular reporting gig?" he asked.

"Actually, that's been a bit of an issue. Daniels gave me some time to chase it and see what I come up with."

"When you go to report back?"

"Soon."

"You think you got enough to keep going?" he asked.

"You betcha, big guy."

"Unless of course somebody shoots you or something."

"That would certainly present a change in plans. But that's why I need you."

"Which is what I'm afraid of."

"Someone's got to step in front of me and take a bullet," I said.

"Oh, boy," he said.

Chapter 16

I walked into the lobby of 1730 Broadway a day later while Freddie stayed in his car, an older-model Jeep Grand Cherokee, out front. The high-rise was home to the offices of Ronald Marshall and his prestigious RCM Talent Management. Marshall was also known as Jack Steele's agent.

RCM was the premier management firm for TV newspeople, representing pretty much every big name at the networks and a lot of the pretty faces on cable news. If the firm signed a young reporter or anchor, it was an indication that person's career was moving to another level.

I wasn't represented by RCM.

I'm not quite sure I could even get in the door of the place unless I lied, which is what I had done to set up this little meeting with Marshall.

The building was a newer high-rise on Broadway in the fifties, above Times Square. It had a sleek, open lobby, with lots of steel and big windows looking out onto the street.

I cleared security and rode the elevator to the tenth floor, to the offices of RCM Talent Management. I stepped off the elevator and spotted the dark wooden doors at the end of the hallway to my left.

They were imposing, with "RCM Talent Management, Inc.," in gold lettering.

When I stepped inside, I was greeted by a young woman behind a desk. She was in her mid-thirties and serious, like this was a career and not a job. I introduced myself and she made a call, then looked at me the way receptionists always do when they need to lie to you.

"Mr. Marshall is running a few minutes late," she said.

"Of course."

I now officially did not feel bad about BS-ing my way into this meeting.

"I'll show you to his office, and you can wait there. He'll be with you shortly."

I liked the strategy. Marshall would let me soak in his office for a few so I would be impressed and awed to be in the presence of the Great Man when he strode in.

I followed the career woman down a hallway and past a row of offices. I looked into one as I passed and caught a glimpse of the back of someone I was pretty sure was Marshall. He was sitting on a couch talking to a young blonde at her desk.

Seconds later I was in a big office that was stuffed with shelves of photos and awards and all kinds of TV memorabilia, like old-time big microphones. It was like being in a mini Cooperstown for broadcasting.

"May I get you something to drink?" the receptionist asked as we stepped inside.

"Is that a camera?" I pointed toward the corner of the office, to where a big, bulky camera from a TV studio of decades ago was sitting.

"Yes. It's vintage National Broadcasting Corporation."

"This is like a TV Cooperstown, or something," I said. "Do I need to pay admission?"

I turned, and she had the same blank expression I used to get when looking at a calculus problem on the chalkboard. She was still waiting for my drink order.

"I don't need anything," I said, and she disappeared, closing the door on her way out.

Now it felt like I had been left behind in the museum after hours. So I walked around and admired the memorabilia. There was every award conceivable that an agent could win, including something called the Reppy, given out by some bogus-sounding TV trade group to the top agent representative. There were lots of photos of Marshall with the elite: presidents, Hollywood types, and of course all of broadcasting's beautiful people. There was the prerequisite photo of Marshall with Bono. Anybody who was close to being somebody in the business had a picture with Bono.

I didn't.

A few seconds later I heard the door open behind me.

"Ahh, Mr. North."

I turned and saw the distinguished Mr. Marshall.

"Ahh, Mr. Marshall," I said.

I spoke with the same smart-aleck tone that used to get me in trouble in high school with the Jesuits. Except they had witty retorts for me. Marshall seemed to be at a loss.

He crossed the office and extended his hand. He was a few inches shorter than me and trim for a guy in his mid-sixties. And very well dressed, in a crisp navy suit and one of those Wall Street shirts, light blue with a white collar and cuffs. I was never quite sure if or when those shirts were back in style.

"I apologize for the delay. My wife just got my ear and, well, you know how it is. It's hard to break away," he said.

That was lie number one. No way the little blonde chippie he had been talking to was his wife. But I smiled and tried my best to be polite.

"I understand."

I took a seat in one of the comfy leather chairs facing his desk, which I had just realized was shaped like a set. A TV news set. Kind of crescent-moon shaped, with him right smack in the middle behind it.

"You got everything in here," I said.

"I am a bit of a TV news buff," he said.

His demeanor was heavy and serious, and I had no way of knowing if he was like that every day, or if it was because he had lost one of his biggest clients last week. I wanted to give him the benefit of the doubt, but something told me it had been a while since this guy was the office clown.

"Before we get down to the purpose of this meeting," he said, "let me say you did a very nice job the morning of Jack's death."

"Nice to hear."

He put on a pair of reading glasses that had been sitting on the set —I mean his desk—and slid a yellow legal pad in front of him. I expected him to check a box or something.

Compliment guest on work. Check.

"Now, I understand you wanted to talk about representation. Is that what brought you here to RMC today?" he asked.

"No, it was a Jeep. A friend's Grand Cherokee," I said.

He frowned like he didn't get it, and I realized he didn't.

"Ill-fated attempt at humor," I said. "Bit of an ice breaker."

"I see," he said.

"I'll consider the ice unbroken."

"Mr. North," he said. Now he was impatient.

"I'm not looking for you to represent me," I said, "so you can relax."

"Okay."

"I thought I'd save you the stress of trying to figure out how to say no to me."

"Indeed."

"Besides, I'm semihappy with my agent at the moment," I said.

"I'm glad it's working out for you," he said.

"Well, working out is being kind."

Marshall put his pen down and folded his hands on his desk. Everything was neat and clean around him, and now I understood how the man won those whopping contracts for his clients. He was calm, steady, in control.

"Would you care to tell me why you're here?" he asked.

"Robbie Steele doesn't think Jack killed himself." I watched for a reaction, but there really wasn't one. "That's about as good as I got," I said. "You don't react to that, I don't know what it's going to take."

"You're serious about this?" he asked. "Roberta Steele doesn't believe Jack committed suicide?"

"She thinks he was killed by someone," I said.

"Interesting."

"And she's asked me to look into it."

"So you're investigating the death of Jack Steele?" he asked.

"Yes," I said.

"Investigating?" he asked again.

"Yes. I think it means 'to look into.'"

"Haven't the professionals—the police—already done so?"

"They have. That's what we pay them for. You know, our tax dollars and all that," I said.

"Yet Roberta thinks they, the people who do this for a living, missed something?" he asked.

"You're pulling this all together very nicely," I said, and gave him my best I'm-proud-of-you smile.

"Does Roberta have an explanation for the note? The suicide note?"

"No, she doesn't."

"So we should just ignore that?"

"For the moment."

He reached for a bottle of Poland Spring on the side of his desk. With slow, precise movements he opened it, took a drink, put the cap back on, and turned his attention back to me.

"I suspect this ... this investigation of yours may end up being a waste of everyone's time, Mr. North," he said. He took a breath and leaned forward, and I prepared for some words of wisdom. "Mr. North ..."

"Yes."

"As you'll no doubt learn, Roberta Steele is very good at manipulating people, but not so good at being smart."

I thought about it for a second. "You're saying she's not bright?"

"She's an aerobics instructor," he said.

"Yoga."

"Whatever."

"Here's the odd thing," I said. "I start asking people about this—guys like Jerry Drake, Andrew Webber—and all of a sudden some guy appears and tells me to stop asking questions."

"And this has emboldened you to push onward?"

"Absolutely. Heck, what kind of reporter would I be if I didn't?"

He gave me a small smile and shook his head at my foolishness. "You spoke to Jerry Drake"—he made little air quotes with his fingers —"the Show Doctor?"

"You know Jerry? Great guy," I said.

"The man is a menace to the industry, and himself," he said.

"I don't know, he seemed to have some nice ideas for Jack's show. Says you kept blocking him."

Marshall removed his reading glasses and placed them on his desk, then rubbed his eyes, like he found this whole discussion was tiring. Finally, he shook his head, sighed, and tried to talk some sense into me.

"Mr. North."

"Mr. Marshall."

"You seemed to have gotten yourself tangled up with two people who don't exactly have good reputations," he said. "I suggest, if you'd like to capitalize on the goodwill you gained by your work last week, that you distance yourself from people like Roberta Steele and Jerry Drake."

"Thank you for the advice."

"You're welcome."

"Drake says you didn't want Jack going after CEOs. That you didn't like his Operation Outrage strategy."

He shook his head again and sighed. I was wearing him down, all part of my plan.

"Look," he said, "Jerry Drake is not the brightest guy around, understand?"

"Kind of."

"His little Operation Outrage was cute and catchy, but it was an idea, not a strategy. A strategy implies a well-thought-out plan of attack. This was merely an idea, and an ill-conceived one at that."

"How?"

"Because after Jack goes after the second or third CEO, they are all going to sound the same to the viewer, Mr. North. So even if the ratings get a little pop at first, eventually we would have been back in the same boat."

"Possibly."

"And then the stories would have made us sound desperate. Trying everything and anything to get the numbers up."

"Us?"

"I beg your pardon."

"Us. You said the stories would have made 'us' sound desperate? Were you involved in all the show decisions?"

"I went back a very long way with Jack," he said. "I was his first TV agent when he came to New York and Liberty."

"So you take some credit for how successful Jack became?"

That got me another shake of his head.

"I don't see the point of—"

"Drake says Jack was thinking of dumping you," I said.

He showed no emotion. Zero. He just sat there and stared at me, and it was yet another example of how this guy negotiated with TV execs. My agent couldn't keep his mouth shut for two seconds. This guy had a poker face and an I'll-call-your-bluff manner that was unnerving.

"Yes ... no?" I asked.

He smiled, and I almost jumped out of my chair. Emotion. How about that?

"Oh, now it all makes sense," he said.

"Thank goodness."

"You think maybe I ... I killed Jack, right? Because he was going to switch agents or something?"

I held up my hand to slow him down. "Whoa, whoa, I'm not so sure of that," I said.

"And Roberta has told you that maybe I had a secret meeting with him that night?"

"Hmm, I hadn't thought of that, but—"

"And let's just keep going," he said, clearly enjoying this. "Maybe I, what, push Jack into the river and then speed off in a waiting car?"

"Okay," I said, "now this is getting a little creepy."

He took a deep breath and got himself back together.

"Mr. North, you need to be very clear on something."

"I'll try."

"Roberta Hopkins was the worst thing that ever happened to Jack," he said.

"Hopkins?"

"Her maiden name."

"I'm starting to get the impression you don't like her."

"You have to make your own decision, but I certainly wouldn't risk my career on something she told me." He paused and then made sure I got it. "You risk damaging your reputation," he said.

"I'll remember that."

"You start chasing after conspiracy theories, and you may hit a point of no return."

"I appreciate the advice," I said. "But I got to be realistic here. My career was stuck in neutral before all this started."

"Maybe," he said, "but just remember that reporters have second, third, even fourth acts in this business."

"I'll be sure to keep that in mind."

"My point to you is that if you get yourself tangled up any more with Roberta Steele, you may find you'll have a very tough time bouncing back," he said.

Chapter 17

I walked through the lobby and looked out onto Broadway. There was no sign of Freddie—or the Cherokee—out front where I left him. Just as I pushed through the revolving door, my phone rang. I recognized his number. "That's it? The partnership is over?" I asked. "Didn't even last a day."

"You done?" he said.

"For now."

"Walk down to Fifty-fifth and turn the corner."

I walked down the block to the corner, turned right, and saw the back of the Cherokee parked three spaces in, next to a hydrant.

"You get chased by a traffic cop?" I asked as I got in.

Freddie held out his phone for me. On it was a picture.

"Holy crap," I said as I stared at it.

"That the guy?"

On the phone was a picture of my friend Fedora. He was walking to the revolving doors of the building I just came out of.

"Go to the next shot," he said.

I did. It was a picture of Fedora pushing through the revolving door.

"Walked in about five minutes after you did," he said.

"How'd you spot him? He spot you?" I said.

"I saw some round guy with a hat coming down the street in my side-view mirror," he said. "Remembered how you described the guy."

"He make you?"

"Can't say for sure. Don't know if he followed you here, or maybe he knew you were coming here."

"That's a lot of yous in there," I said. "I prefer 'us.' You know, maybe he followed 'us.'"

"I prefer you. Maybe we keep my ass out of this."

"Too late, champ," I said.

"Great, now I got to worry about some doughy-looking white guy with a bad hat."

"I kinda like the hat," I said.

"Figures."

I stared at a third photo of Fedora leaving the building through the revolving door.

"You got him leaving, too, huh?"

"Yup. I drove around the corner here just to confuse him in case he was looking for the Jeep. Went into the Citibank ATM there on the corner and pretended to be taking care of business but kept an eye on the doors."

"You're good at this," I said. "I may have to make you a full partner."

"Notice something about him in that shot?" he asked.

I stared at the picture. Fedora was coming out of the revolving doors, but he kind of looked like he did yesterday, with one exception.

"The sharp-looking sports coat?"

"Uh-huh."

"And he's wearing a light blue shirt, not the navy one. So he changed his shirt and went with a jacket. Looks like the same tie."

"If you say so."

"Jacket is kind of odd, being that's it's about ninety out."

"You wore yours into your meeting," he said.

"But mine is a nice lightweight gray plaid," I said. "He's got the basic navy-blue thing going."

"Okay, let's forget the whole fashion debate," he said. "Just look at the jacket."

"I am."

Freddie looked over at me like I was dense. "How'd you get to be on TV, man?"

"Don't need to be licensed, you know."

He looked at the phone. "Tap the screen to zoom in."

I did and the picture zoomed up, and I was tight on Fedora as he went through the door. His hand was on the bar of the revolving door, and his jacket was slightly askew as he pushed.

"Is that a ..."

"Now you see why he's wearing a jacket, right?" he asked.

"Yeah, to hide the gun," I said.

Chapter 18

It was close to three in the afternoon on Thursday when Daniels sent word that he could see me.

Word came via his secretary, Susan, who made the trip down from the floor above and walked over to my desk. I was reading a story on the *Journal's* Web site about the deep hole Liberty News was in now that it didn't have its number one star, Jack Steele.

There were many quotes talking about how Steele solidified the prime-time lineup and brought in more ad dollars than the next two highest-rated shows combined.

"The king will see you now," Susan said.

I looked up from the computer screen to see her standing next to me.

"Would that make you the queen?"

"Please, never speaketh that way again."

"I like it," I said, getting up. "Would it be all right if I called you fair maiden, Susan?"

"You can call me anything you like, so long as you call."

I walked through the newsroom with her. As the long-time assistant to Daniels, she probably knew more about what was going on here than anyone else. She was in her mid-forties, with a husband

and kid out on the Island, and was flirty by nature and able to put up with the demands for working for Daniels.

"And what type of mood will I find the boss man in when I go in there?" I asked.

"If I had to choose between say horrible, lousy, and downright hostile, I'd go with hostile," she said.

It didn't make me feel great. My few days to poke around were gone and Daniels was in a cranky mood. At this rate I'd be back on the mornings doing fluffy features in no time.

"Would you like to know one of the reasons I came down to get you instead of calling?" she asked as we reached the big exposed stairway that led up to the floor with the offices.

"I just assumed it was to share a few quality minutes with me," I said.

"My idea of quality minutes with you doesn't involve walking through the newsroom," she said.

"I'm flattered."

"You should be," she said as we got to the top of the stairs. "You are penciled in the number one spot on his shit list at the moment."

"It's good to shoot for the top," I said.

"I'm not kidding, Sam. He's in a pissy mood to start with, but he's saved an extra-special dose of nastiness for you," she said.

"I feel special."

"What'd you say to Ron Marshall?" she asked.

"Uh-oh."

"He called before. He sounded all bent out of shape about something, and I heard your name come up."

"Maybe he told Cal I need a super-big contract, and he wants to negotiate it for me even though he's not my agent."

"Speaking of which," she said.

"My agent?"

"If that's what you call him," she said.

"Kenny Slattery, the premier TV news agent. That's how his Web site refers to him."

"Cal keeps blowing him off," she said.

"He's used to it."

"He called twice in last few days, and Cal hasn't gotten back to him," she said.

We were upstairs now, walking down the hall toward Daniels's office.

"Hmm."

"Just giving you a heads-up on what you're walking into," she said.

I thanked Susan, and she went back behind her desk, I rapped on the closed office door and walked in to see Daniels at his desk, with the nice view of Sixth Avenue behind him.

He had his reading glasses on the end of his nose and was looking over some paperwork as I walked in.

"I'm here for my checkup," I said.

He never looked up from the paperwork as he spoke. "Pretty chipper for a guy who's pissing everyone off," he said.

"It's what I do well."

"Maybe a little too well," he said as he pushed the papers to the side of his desk. "Sit."

I took my usual spot in one of the visitor chairs facing his desk.

"I'm going to give you a chance to beg for your spot on the morning show back," he said.

"I'll pass."

"Not a wise move. Kate Wallace is doing a hell of a job. She's got good chemistry with Kelly and Dan."

"Maybe she can do her spots in a swimsuit to really boost the chemistry."

"It's been suggested," he said.

"By her, I'm sure."

He drank some coffee from his black mug with the red Liberty logo on it, then put it back down on his desk and stared at me. He shook his head as he spoke. "You don't get this, do you?"

"Depends on what you're talking about."

"Your career," he said. "Are you trying to wreck it?"

"I haven't even told you what I got," I said.

"You haven't got shit," he said. "You know how I know that?

Because I just got a call from Ron Marshall asking me what the hell you're doing. Says you lied your way into a meeting with him and started implying all kinds of crazy things about Jack's death."

"I just had a few questions," I said.

"And Marty tells me the same thing. You're going around trying to find out if anyone had a reason to kill the man."

"Just due diligence, that's all," I said. "I told you what Robbie Steele told me, about how she thinks something may have happened to him. And you said take some time and see what you find."

"Well, time's up, and this stops. Now."

Daniels was hot, and I knew I had Marshall to thank. I had pissed the man off, and he had called to complain; when Ron Marshall called to complain, TV execs listened.

Daniels glanced over at the wall of TVs to see what Liberty was doing versus the competition. After a few seconds his attention returned to me, and he was still hot. He shook his head as he repeated my offenses.

"Ron Marshall is the single most influential agent in the business, and you go and lie your way in to see him and then start interrogating him about Jack's death. That alone would get you fired at most places."

"I didn't interrogate him," I said.

"It's one thing to sniff around a bit to see if Robbie Steele's onto something, or simply delusional, as most of us believe, but it's another thing to go around accusing people."

"I didn't accuse anyone," I said.

"That's what Marshall said."

"He's wrong. Plus, you gave me the green light, remember?"

"Yes, I gave you some time, which as we said, is up."

"I need some more," I said.

He looked at me like I had lost my mind. "What?"

"I need more time. Just a bit."

"You don't have it," he said.

"Just a few days."

"No."

"I think there's something here," I said.

"You're making an ass out of yourself and damaging the reputation of this network. This ends now."

"I think Robbie is right," I said.

He balled up his fist and slammed the desk.

"Damn it, Sam. Don't be an ass. I'm giving you a chance here. When I got off the phone with Marshall, you were done. I had every intention of calling you in here to tell you I wasn't going to renew you."

"What?"

"Yeah, I was going to fire you right now. But you know what, you did a hell of a job the day Jack died, and I felt like I owed you at least something for that," he said.

"Well, thanks."

"So I was going to give you another chance. I'd mistakenly assumed you were going to tell me the only thing you discovered in your little investigation was that Robbie Steele was nuts and that you'd love to resume your duties on the morning show," he said. "But no, you come in asking for even more of this network's time to waste on this."

"You want to know why I need more time?"

"No, I really don't—"

"Because somebody doesn't want me asking around." I spoke before he had a chance to say anything else.

"What on earth are you talking about?"

"Some guy has either been following me or knows exactly who I've been going to see. He came up to me in a Starbucks yesterday and told me to back off."

Daniels seemed to calm down and was interested now. "Who was he?"

I shook my head. "I don't know. It's not like we traded IDs."

"Go on."

"He told me I needed to be careful. Then he told me if I kept bothering people, he wasn't going to be so diplomatic next time."

"And you have no idea who this was?"

"None."

"You think it's related to something with the show?"

"Don't know," I said. "All I've found out is that IT&E was pretty pissed with Jack."

"Should be, the way he went after them."

"Buck McConnell's flack spent a lot of time shooting off nasty e-mails every time Jack mentioned the company," I said.

He exhaled and glanced at the monitors and muttered. "Son of a bitch. This is the last frigging thing I need."

"That's why I want more time."

He looked back at me, and I could see the stress on his face. "It took me ten minutes to convince Ron Marshall that you weren't insane and at one point were actually a pretty good reporter."

"Thanks for the endorsement."

He sat back and exhaled a long, tired breath and fiddled with a pen in one hand.

"I damn near promised Marshall I was going to let you go. He told me you were a menace, and honestly, I didn't need a lot of convincing."

"I don't get threatened if there's nothing to find out," I said.

"That's what worries me," he said.

"What? That I was threatened, or that Robbie Steele could be right?"

"Both."

Chapter 19

I had spoken to four people at this point, Dr. Webber, Marty, Jerry Drake, and Ron Marshall. I had come close to being fired, and I guess the only reason I wasn't was because of my friend Fedora.

His appearance had been enough to convince me that there may very well be something here. Just what, I couldn't say, but maybe Robbie Steele wasn't as delusional as everyone made her out to be. Or maybe she was.

Either way, I was hoping to find out more in a few minutes.

Freddie and I were in the Cherokee driving up Park to Robbie's place. It was Friday morning, and the traffic around Manhattan was light.

I had bought myself a few more days from Daniels, but I was on a short leash. I had a bit more time to figure things out, but I also had the impression a misstep could very well lead to the end of this chapter of my TV career.

"So far, I'm not liking this arrangement," Freddie said as we crossed Fifty-seventh Street.

"What's not to like? You get to hang around with me and have a little adventure at the same time," I said.

"All I'm getting to do is wait in my car," he said. "You get to go up and have some fun bothering Ron Marshal, and I wait in the car. And now—"

"Oh, I see what this is all about," I said. "You want to meet the Yoga Babe."

"Damn straight."

"Then why didn't you just come and say it?"

"I just did."

"No, you didn't," I said. "You got all grumpy and grouchy is what you did."

"I want to meet Yoga Babe. How's that?"

"Better, but the answer is still no."

He slammed on the breaks midblock and yelled, "Out."

"Okay, okay, you can meet her."

"Now you're talking," he said, as he accelerated again.

"Some other time."

He hit the brakes again, and I tried to wiggle out of this mess.

"Look, she's a little nutty and kind of unhinged. And something tells me she was like that before Jack died. I really don't think my showing up there with a guest unannounced is the best idea."

"Then announce me."

"Some other time."

"Not liking this partnership," he said. "Not liking this at all."

"Besides, let's say you come up with me. Who's going to be watching to see if Fatty Fedora shows up?"

We drove on in silence, cutting west over to Fifth Avenue. When we got within a block, he finally spoke up.

"I see this SOB, I'm going to go for it," he said.

"Meaning?"

"Meaning, go right up to his ass and ask him what the hell he's doing and who the hell he is. I don't get some answers, maybe it gets ugly."

I didn't really have a preference whether we confronted this guy or not, so I left it up to Freddie and went inside. A few minutes later, after clearing the doorman and being announced, I was again knocking on the door to the Steele apartment on the tenth floor.

Robbie opened it wearing a lightweight gray-and-black summer dress that hit above her knees and was pulled tight at the waist with a black belt. She wore her hair down and looked made up like she was going out somewhere.

As she greeted me, her manner was serious and businesslike, and she showed me to the table just outside the kitchen. We sat down opposite each other, and it felt more like a business meeting than our first get-together the night of Jack's death.

"What have you found?" she asked before I could open my mouth.

We had spoken twice since last week, and I had asked for this meeting, hoping to get a few questions answered. I took out my reporter's pad and opened to the page with notes from my interviews.

"I found everyone I spoke to has a strong opinion about you," I said.

"I'm that type of woman," she said. "Jack's inner circle was threatened by me."

"Their opinions weren't all favorable," I said.

"I'd expect nothing less from them. Care to tell me who you saw?"

"Dr. Alan Webber."

"A sleaze. He actually hit on me once."

"Marty Glover."

"A buffoon who wouldn't last a minute in a job other than the one Jack gave him as executive producer. Incompetent and inept."

"Jerry Drake."

"A talentless clown."

"And Ronald Marshall."

"A nasty, nasty man. A piranha."

"Was Jack going to dump him?"

"Who told you that?"

"Marty mentioned he was considering a change," I said.

"It wasn't definite, but yes, Jack was thinking it might be time for some fresh thinking about his career."

"Did Jack arrive at that conclusion on his own, or with your help?"

"I suggested it," she said.

"That would explain Marshall's negative feeling about you," I said.

"They all needed to be tossed as far as I'm concerned."

"I'm glad I only got to four of them," I said.

Robbie got up and walked to the kitchen. "What would you like to drink?" she asked.

She was much more in control today than she had been last week, and I got the feeling that her way of dealing with something like this was to stay in control at all costs.

I asked for water, and she came back with that and iced tea for herself. She set the glasses down on the table.

"I don't know if you realized it, but all four of those men made a lot of money off of Jack," she said. "They were all part of this little universe of parasites that benefited from his success, and generosity."

"The Jack Steele gravy train," I said.

"Do you think any of these four men are involved in Jack's death?" she asked.

I had some water to buy a few seconds, then answered with my best unequivocally maybe response.

"I don't know. It's really too early to say."

"I thought you were checking all of this out," she said.

"I have been."

"And you haven't found out much of anything."

"You didn't exactly give me a lot to work with," I said.

"I gave you everything," she said. "I called you and handed you the biggest story you'll ever see."

"No, you handed me a hunch you had."

"Have," she said.

"Okay, a hunch you *have*."

"I was hoping you'd be able to put it together by now," she said.

I realized she was mad that I didn't have this thing locked down and all figured out. And whether she realized it or not, she was playing on a very big fear of mine: that there might be a gigantic story here and I might not be the one to break it.

As I got deeper into this and more convinced that maybe she was right, that maybe someone had killed Steele, I was starting to get real anxious about someone else putting it together before I could. His or her career would take off, and I'd be back at the starting gate, known forever as the guy who broke the big news, then dropped the ball.

Career over.

"I know you think I'm crazy," she said.

"No, I don't."

"Yes, you do. I can tell."

I was sitting with my back to the living room and the windows with the great view, facing instead the kitchen and the foyer. So there really wasn't anywhere else to look but right at her. The problem was, she was so wound up I didn't know if staring at her was going to help or hurt.

"Honestly, I don't give a damn what you, or any of the others, think," she said. "If all these men think I'm crazy, I couldn't care less. They all thought I was some evil bitch for falling in love with Jack and for him falling in love with me."

I said nothing for a moment because it seemed that was the only way I could avoid throwing gasoline on this fire. When it seemed like she had cooled off I flipped to the next page of my notebook and looked at the three things I had wanted to ask about.

"Jerry Drake showed me some of the e-mails Jack got when he started going after companies. Any chance you have copies of others? Even the ones from run-of-the-mill lunatics?"

"Yes. He called it his Wacko file. Most of them were shown to Chet Dixon, in Liberty's security office, and some were shown to the police. But Jack kept copies around just in case. Nothing ever came of them."

"It would help to take a look. See if there's anything in there worth following up on."

"I can give you those," she said.

It felt like she was back in my camp and no longer wondering why I hadn't figured this all out already. Crisis averted. Maybe.

"I read the police report," I said. "I'm going to need to talk to his driver, Manny Torres."

"I can take care of that," she said.

"What happened with Webber that night? Why'd Jack cancel?"

"He said he was exhausted," she said.

"But you don't buy it?"

"No. At the time I did, I mean, I had no reason to think otherwise. But I think he went out to meet someone," she said.

"And still no guesses on who that would be?"

"No. That's why you're here," she said.

"Of course."

She drank a bit of her iced tea and I brought up the note.

"I also saw a copy of the suicide note."

She put down her glass and didn't say a word.

"It felt ... generic," I said.

She nodded. "It is," she said.

"I can't pretend to know what you would put in there, but this read like boilerplate language," I said.

"I'm having the handwriting analyzed independently," she said.

"I'm assuming you'll let me know how that turns out."

"As soon as I know, you'll know," she said.

I glanced at the last item on my list: *drinking*.

I stared at it for a second and debated whether it was the brightest idea to pursue this at the moment.

"Why was Jack seeing Dr. Webber in the first place?" I said.

"I think you know," she said.

"Webber is a substance-abuse specialist," I said. "I know about Jack's drinking. Is there another substance involved?" I asked.

She shook her head. "No. Not now at least. Way, way back, before we met, I knew he had a recreational drug problem."

"Meaning coke?" I asked.

She nodded. "But that was fifteen, probably twenty years ago."

Steele was a well-know mostly success story for his ability to keep his drinking in check. But even now there were infrequent, but embarrassing, slips. The last one being back in December at the holidays. It involved a very intoxicated Steele sucking face with a twenty-four-year-old Liberty News production assistant at the holiday party. The episode went from an office scandal to a video sensation when some fool posted a video of it on YouTube.

"And the drinking hadn't been a problem for a while, right?" I asked.

She looked straight at me and I could see the hurt in her eyes as memory of it came back.

"If you're asking if Jack had slipped since the night he made out with the little PA, the answer is no. And if you're thinking the drinking maybe had something to do with his death, I doubt it very much," she said.

"Why?"

She sat straight up and appeared almost elegant as she put a hand on her belly, which really wasn't a belly, but was where a belly would be. She took a deep breath. "I know there is no way Jack would have done anything to miss being a father," she said.

The problem with having twenty-five years of reporting experience is that sometimes your face is saying skeptical even when you don't know it is. This was one of those times.

"It's fine if you don't believe me," she said.

"I didn't say that I didn't."

"You didn't have to."

There was still a tiny part of me that didn't believe her, and I knew at some point she was going to prove me wrong. She'd pull out a sonogram or something down the road and make me feel like a fool.

"Robbie," I said, "I believe you."

"But not fully," she said.

"No, but enough to go around asking questions and getting people angry and jeopardizing my career. I believe you enough to trust you're telling me the truth."

"Have you told anyone about my being pregnant?" she said.

I had a feeling right now that the expression on my face read, Oh, crap.

I had told Liz, and I tried to figure out how to play this one. Tell her I had mentioned it to someone and risk her blowing up, or maybe even telling me to get lost, was one option. Flat-out lying and saying I hadn't told anyone was the other option. Neither was good.

She looked at me from across the table, waiting for a response.

"I mentioned it to my girlfriend, who, by the way, I trust completely not to repeat it," I said.

Robbie's face never changed expression, and I took that as a good sign. She didn't appear to be getting angry.

After what felt like minutes, she spoke. "You're single?"

It dawned on me that she probably already knew that, given my lack of a wedding ring.

"I am."

"What does she do?"

"Investment banker."

"And you're certain she hasn't repeated it?"

"Yes."

"Why'd you tell her?"

I took a moment to put an answer together. "I tell her everything. I bounce ideas off her, look for her input and opinion on things."

"What was her opinion of me?"

"That you needed help."

She smiled.

"Not that kind of help," I said. "Help in piecing this together."

"Sounds like a nice relationship," Robbie said.

"It is."

Chapter 20

Freddie and I were sitting on one of the benches along the walkway in Union Square Park when he spotted him.

"That's him right there," he said, looking at a big guy with a tan complexion walking alongside a line of preschoolers on their way to one of the playgrounds.

The guy was dressed in a shirt with a splashy maroon pattern, kind of a dressy Hawaiian shirt look, and shorts. He was carrying on an animated conversation with one of the teachers, an attractive Hispanic woman.

The gal was trying to split her attention between Casanova and the kids. At the moment Casanova was winning.

"Guy knows everybody," Freddie said.

"More people than you?"

"By far. Plus, the son of a bitch could talk a dog off a meat truck," he said. "I'd bet you a paycheck he gets her number, except I ain't getting paid."

"That still bugging you?"

"Damn straight it is," he said.

A minute later the big guy peeled off as the preschoolers toddled past screeching and laughing. He said something in Spanish to the woman, and she laughed and said something back in Spanish. It seemed like they had known each other for years.

A second later he walked to us. Freddie got up and they hugged, and then he introduced him to me. We shook hands, and Victor took a seat on the bench.

"You guys are cousins?" I asked.

Victor threw his head back and let loose a big laugh like there was some inside joke going on that I wasn't a part of. "Hah," he said, "we all cousins."

"Vic is cousins with everybody, especially the ladies," Freddie said.

"Ain't that the truth," Vic said.

We watched two young women walk by the busy pathway, and Victor couldn't stop himself.

"Afternoon, ladies. Looking good," he said.

The brunette looked over, lowered her shades, and said something to him in Spanish. He said something back, and there were laughs all around as they walked off.

"Did they ask who your handsome white friend is?" I asked.

"If that's what you want to hear," he said.

"Believe me, that's what he wants to hear," Freddie said.

Vic pulled a slip of paper out of his shirt pocket and handed it to Freddie, who unfolded it while he spoke.

"Here's your man," Victor said.

"Charles T. Bulger," Freddie said, passing the paper to me.

I looked at it like there was some other secret information on it that Freddie had missed. There wasn't.

"This is great, Vic," I said. "But you got to give me a little more. Like, who this guy is."

"Pushy TV type," Freddie said.

"Always take, take, take with those guys," Vic said.

"You guys done?" I asked.

"Hardly," Freddie said.

"Just starting," Vic said.

"So Charles Bulger is my fedora-wearing friend?" I asked.

"You got it. Age fifty-three," Vic said. "Was in the military out of high school. Regular army. Got out and promptly got himself arrested for assault in a bar fight—twice. Second time he served two years. He got out and got himself into the security game. Did the bodyguard thing for celebrities in L.A. for a while, then came home to Jersey and started his own security contracting firm."

"Another American success story," I said.

"And seventeen years later he's driving a black Mercedes CL550," Vic said. "That's what's been tailing you all over the place. Not every-where, but a lot of places. Not sure how he's picking and choosing," Vic said.

"And you know all of this how?" I asked.

"Because I'm that good," he said.

"Yes, I've gathered as much. But I mean, how do you know he's been following me?"

"Because I've been following you."

I looked at Freddie next to me, but he was preoccupied with a blonde woman walking toward us. It was hot, and it seemed to be requirement that every woman out today had to be dressed in a sleeveless top.

"You authorize this?" I asked.

"Sure," he said, but his mind was elsewhere.

"Wow," I said.

"My thoughts exactly," Freddie said, still staring at the woman.

"I meant, wow, someone has been following me," I said.

"And last night you and a very pretty young lady, brunette, went out for a cocktail over at a little place on Twenty-third, corner of Third Avenue," Vic said.

"That would be Liz," Freddie said, "although we've never been introduced."

The blonde gal had passed, and Freddie was back with us.

"What'd I have?" I asked.

"Draft of something, couldn't see which one. Looked like an ale of some sort."

"Wow, again," I said.

"I asked Victor to watch you after seeing Fedora tailing you at Ron Marshall's office," Freddie said. "Victor specializes in surveillance."

"Among other things," Vic said.

"Of course," I said. "And was this a favor?"

"Oh no, no," Victor said.

"I didn't think so," I said.

"Gets expensive to keep yourself alive," Freddie said.

"Speaking of money," Victor said, "Bulger's car, the Mercedes, you know how much that puppy runs?"

"Maybe ninety Gs?" I said.

"Try more than one ten," he said.

"Geez, how's that thing not get ripped off when he's following TV Boy over here?" Freddie asked.

"TV Man," I said. "I prefer TV Man."

"Chucky has a copilot," Victor said. "Couldn't get a good look at him, though. Just some big dude."

Freddie whistled and shook his head. "You got two dudes after you. Looks like you're in some deep crap," he said. "You on your own now."

"What happened to my trusted partner?" I asked.

"I got enough people mad at me and wanting to kick my butt. Don't need two more."

From down the walkway the Hispanic preschool teacher was strutting back with a smile on her face. She made a beeline to Victor and slipped him a piece of paper, said something in Spanish, laughed with him, then turned and left.

Freddie watched her walk away. "No justice in the world, man. No justice."

"She say to give that to me?" I asked.

"Hah," Victor said. "You got bigger problems right now, pal."

"Meaning?" I asked.

"Meaning Bulger and his sidekick. What's that Mercedes he be driving tell you about him?" he asked.

"That he has nice taste in cars," Freddie said.

"Or that he's getting paid very well or there are some deep pockets supporting him," I said.

"Bingo," Victor said.

"Which is it?" I asked.

"You ever hear of Bergen Security Services?" Victor asked.

"Nope," I said.

"No reason to, right? But Chuck Bulger owns it."

"Okay," I said.

"And guess who their main client is? And as far as I can tell, might be their *only* client," he said.

"You got me," I said.

"Gulfway Energy," Vic said.

"Never heard of it," I said.

"Not surprising. It's a little subsidiary of IT&E," he said. "That I know you heard of."

"Yes, I have."

"So, Bergen Security is following Sam," Freddie said, "and being paid by Gulfway."

"And Gulfway is part of IT&E," I said.

"Meaning IT&E is paying someone to watch Sam," Freddie said.

"Meaning Buck McConnell is paying Chuck Bulger to watch me," I said.

Chapter 21

After lunch we drove uptown to Third Avenue and Fifty-second Street. Neither one of us saw a black Mercedes following us. Freddie parked on Third, and I got out and went into the office tower that filled the block on the west side of the street between Fifty-second and Fifty-third.

There was a police precinct a block down and around the corner, so at least in theory we should be safe. Freddie stayed in the Cherokee, and I rode the elevator up to the twenty-first floor to the offices of ShorePoint Investments.

Doug Lee met me in reception. He was geared up and smiling when I walked in.

"Whoa, ho," he yelled, loud enough for the people down the hall in the cubicle farm to hear.

"We got us a big old celebrity sighting, right here in little old ShorePoint," he said.

"I see the advanced ball-busting training has paid off," I said.

"Any more dead anchors to tell me about, ya bastard?" he said.

"No, but I'll keep you updated."

We walked down the hall past the small trading floor with about two dozen trader types hunched over their Bloomberg screens, watching numbers flashing for the dollar, bond, metals, and Lord only knows what else.

Lee's office was big and sunny, with a view clear across the East River. In the distance a plane rose sharply as it took off from LaGuardia, banked to the right and moved on. Lee closed the door and sat behind his desk; I took a seat on a white leather couch.

"So, what the F you want now?" he asked.

"Fine, thanks. And nice to see you, too," I said.

"Like I give a crap how you're doing," he said.

"I'm hurt. But then again, I'd expect nothing less from a successful hedge fund manager."

"You make us sound callous and uncaring as a class."

"Sorry, I overlooked all of your charitable contributions."

"Yes, you did."

"To Saks, Tiffany, and the contracting community in Great Neck who built the mansion."

"Thank you. It's nice to get your due. And remember, I could have made you a gazillionaire if you had taken me up on my offer way back when."

"I was happy being a thousandaire."

"Yes, that whole do-what-makes-me-happy argument. My seventeen-year-old is giving me the same crap."

"Smart kid," I said.

"He's going to follow his heart, as he drives off in his new BMW."

"Which I'm sure he saved up for."

"Yeah, right. Working weekends or something."

Lee looked good. Successful. Trim. With neatly cut silver hair, a light blue shirt with gold cuff links, and a gold-and-blue-stripped tie. He had founded ShorePoint fifteen years ago and made a killing.

"What do you know about your old friend Buck McConnell?" I asked.

"You mean, What the Buck McConnell? Stupidest CEO in the damned country."

"And that's a crowded field."

"But he stands out. Sleazy bastard is what he is. Why you want to know about him?"

"I got handed some of Jack Steele's stories to follow up on," I said.

"The dead guy?"

"Yes, he is dead."

"What's McConnell got to do with him?"

I shrugged.

"Not sure. Maybe nothing. Jack was going after IT&E, saying they were unpatriotic because some of their crappy equipment wound up in Iran, or Syria, or somewhere."

"Anything for a buck, so to speak," he said.

"You shorted IT&E a while back," I said.

"Oh, did I ever."

"Read about it in the *Journal*."

"Made close to half a million. And that wasn't even the best part."

"Pissing off McConnell was more fun?"

"Big-time. Bastard came after me with all he had."

"And?"

Lee spread out his arms to take in the office.

"I'm still here, ain't I?"

Lee glanced at his four Bloomberg screens and tapped a few keys while talking to me. Trading seemed to be a good business for adults with ADD.

"Didn't take a genius to see how IT&E stock was going to sink," he said.

"Think you can enlighten me?"

"Geez, you TV types really are thick."

"Otherwise we'd all be traders."

"Heaven F-ing forbid. Look, IT&E is down sixteen percent on the year, was down three percent last year. Probably going to keep on falling as long as Buck is involved."

"Lousy CEO or lousy business conditions?"

"He's very good at being an idiot. Daddy and Granddaddy built him a nice business, handed him the keys. And now he's driven the damn thing off the road and into a tree," he said. "With their revenue flat, it's no wonder their crappy equipment shows up in terrorist states. A dollar is a dollar even when it's not called a dollar."

It took me a second to sort that one out.

"He under any pressure to leave?" I asked.

"Hah," he said. "The board is a bunch of daddy's buddies who aren't going to say boo. They already made a fortune from when Old Man McConnell ran things, so as long as Junior doesn't completely destroy the place they'll keep quiet."

"Even when you came along pointing out his flaws?"

He spun around in his chair to face the cabinet that ran along the wall behind his desk and grabbed a slim white binder with no markings on it. He opened it and flipped through its pages.

"'Hedge fund manager Lee shorting IT&E. Says revenue trends, mismanagement to send shares lower,'" he said, reading from a page. "That was in the *Journal*."

He flipped to another page and read again.

"'Lee calls McConnell inept, says stock has further to fall,'" he said. "That was a Bloomberg piece."

"Why'd you sugarcoat it?" I asked.

"Okay, you think maybe, just maybe, the board would wake up after headlines like that, right?"

"But no?"

"They circled the wagons. Protected Buck. Said current market conditions were unfavorable."

"But they weren't?"

Lee raised his voice to where he was almost yelling. "The sector was up seven percent at the time, for Christ sakes. How the hell could Buck be losing money when everyone else was making it?"

"Hard work and practice?"

"Exactly. You got to really work at it to lose money in that environment."

"And here you come, screaming about his being an idiot."

"And you know what old Buck does? He unloads on me like nobody's business. First his little PR man—"

"Stuart Ripley."

"That's him. King of the Weenies. He rips into the reporters writing the stories."

"Kill the messengers."

"Tells 'em I'm just a sleazy short seller trying to drive the price down."

"But you're so much more."

"I show Ripley and the reporters the top ten holdings of Shore-Point. We're long eight and short two. How do you get notorious short seller out of that?"

He was worked up now, reliving the fight.

"When Ripley couldn't handle me, he went and hired some private dick to dig up dirt on me. I come out one Saturday morning to take my youngest to soccer, and there's this asshole in a car across the street taking pictures of me."

"You don't scare easily," I said.

"Get this. Guy around the corner from me used to be the special agent in charge for the Feds in the New York office. I called him, said I needed a favor. Said there's some guy taking pictures of my twelve-year-old daughter. He calls the FBI, the locals get in on it, and a half hour later this clown finds himself surrounded by guns pointed at him."

"Scared him off?" I asked.

"Oh, yeah. Called up Ripley and said, You want to screw with me, you better be ready because I'll return fire."

"A hedge fund manager with attitude."

"Here's the thing with guys like McConnell. He's a card-carrying member of the Lucky Sperm Club. He's not used to being in a street fight. I had guys calling me up, classmates of his from Harvard, telling me they loved watching me screw with him."

"Probably wished they could."

"Exactly. He always been used to bullying or buying his way out of trouble, and if that didn't work he'd call in the heavy artillery."

"Daddy?"

"And his lawyers. Had one guy tell me he could help me take him out for good if I wanted to."

"You chose not to?"

"Why bother?"

He turned and checked the Bloomberg screens again, tapped at the keyboard some more. Screens were flashing and changing colors, and though he seemed absorbed in them, he heard every word I said.

"You still involved with IT&E?" I asked.

"Nope. Made my pile and got out. That's not to say I won't revisit if I feel like pissing them off again."

"Of course. How well you know the company?"

"Probably better than Buck, but then again he's only the CEO and busy getting ready to run for president."

"Ever hear of Gulfway Energy?"

"Nope. Should I have?"

"Little unit of IT&E."

"What does it do?"

"Not quite sure."

"If it mattered to their business, I would have discovered it. We don't miss a lot," Lee said. "If I'm going to risk big money on a stock, I like to know everything the company is up to, which is why we research these places months before we make a move."

"Is it possible they could have a subsidiary tucked away somewhere out of sight?"

Lee was slapping at the keyboard again.

"Absolutely, but only if they wanted to keep it secret."

"And the reason for that would be?"

"It was up to something they didn't want anybody to know about," he said.

Chapter 22

One of the last people to talk to Jack Steele on the last night of his life was Manny Torres.

Torres had been Jack Steele's driver for the last seven years, and he wanted to meet at the Bronx Zoo, of all places, so the Bronx Zoo it was.

It was Saturday morning and we were driving up the FDR and onto the ramp to the Robert F. Kennedy Bridge. If you were going to have a bridge named for you, this wasn't a bad one. Plus, the big one over the Hudson was already taken by that Washington fella.

"You know what really puzzles me?" I asked as we passed through the tollgate in an E-ZPass lane.

"Probably the same thing that's been bugging me," Freddie said.

"Which is?"

"What an investment banker sees in you?" he said. "Thought they were supposed to be smart and savvy."

"She is. And that's not what's bugging me," I said. "I'm wondering why you're driving this beat-up thing. What is this seven, eight years old?"

"Reliable and tough. Just like me," he said.

"I remember you having a sports car."

"Still do. Classic Porsche. Keep it garaged. It's for special people and events," he said.

"I'm offended."

"It's for the ladies. Weekend trips. You know, the romantic getaways. Type of things you should be doing with Liz. Treat her right before she drops your ass."

"Thanks for the love advice."

"Anytime."

I was quiet while Freddie took the curve onto the Bruckner Expressway too fast.

"So, why would this guy pick the zoo?" I asked.

"Maybe likes animals," he said.

"You know any of the exhibits?"

"My information sign lit up again or something?"

"Just thought you might know, that's all."

"Like I work for the city tourism department."

"You could, you know. You'd be good at it, I mean, if you cleaned up a little bit. Maybe shaved the scruffy beard."

"That's for intimidation purposes. Puts a little scare in people," he said.

"Much like your driving."

Freddie changed lanes without signaling and sped along in the left lane. We jumped onto the Bronx River Parkway, and fifteen minutes later we were pulling into the zoo's Bronx River entrance. We pulled into the big parking lot, and I got out and looked around.

It was before ten in morning and it was already blistering hot and damp, thanks to the humidity. There was a line of cars paying and making their way into the zoo, but no black Mercedes.

We paid, walked up the winding concrete pathway to the American bison area, and stood next to the waist-high fence, looking out over a dusty expanse. There were already knots of tourists on either side of us dressed in shorts and T-shirts and sneakers. I overheard German and Spanish and some French. Families with kids in strollers passed by us. Tourism was alive and well in this neck of the Bronx on a Saturday morning in August.

We stood and pretended to be watching the large mounds of brown that were the bison way off in the distance, but really we were looking for Manny.

"See him?" Freddie asked.

"Nope. He said he'd find us around the bison," I said.

There was murmuring and pointing among the crowd, and everyone looked out toward one of the large lumps of brown that rose from the ground off in the distance, in the far end of the bison's living quarters. Even from this distance the animal looked dusty and hot, its thick brown coat covered in the tan of the dirt where it had been lying.

As I was watching, I heard Freddie speaking Spanish. I turned to see him talking to a guy as big as he was but older. The guy had broad shoulders and was dressed in white dress slacks, casual brown leather loafers, and a patterned short-sleeved shirt. He may have been the snazziest dresser in the zoo.

Freddie and he spoke a bit more, and then Freddie turned to me.

"This is your guy right here," he said, introducing us.

I shook hands with what felt like a catcher's mitt, and Torres pointed toward a little area set back on the other side of the walkway. It was a shaded strip with a few benches.

"Let's sit over there," he said.

The three of us walked over, and Freddie excused himself like we had planned. He'd watch from a distance, looking for Fedora, now officially known as Chuck Bulger, or anyone else I should be worried about.

Manny's eyes scanned the area, watching people, as he spoke. He had the feel of ex-military, or maybe ex-cop. Very businesslike and serious.

"Robbie said you wanted to talk to me," he said.

"She tell you what it was about?"

"She did." He had large dark eyes that moved like they were used to doing a lot of watching.

"What do you think?" I asked.

He turned and looked me square in the eye. "I think she's right."

I looked around to make sure no one was close enough to hear. When I turned back, he was still staring at me.

"You don't think he killed himself?" I asked.

"No way."

"Then what happened?"

"What do you know about that night?"

"Just what Robbie told me."

"Which was?"

"That Jack was tired and worn out and canceled his appointment with Andrew Webber. Then sent you home. She went to bed, and sometime after eleven, Jack goes out, goes downstairs, gets a cab, and isn't seen again until the garbage man sees him floating in the water."

We were quiet as a couple moved past us speaking French. He was in cargo shorts, sneakers, and a T-shirt. She was in shorts that appeared to have been stretched for her to squeeze into them. Ditto for the little T-shirt she wore.

They examined a map, pointed a lot, and after a few seconds off they went.

"Robbie's version of events add up to you?" I asked.

"That's the way it happened."

"What do you know about this Webber guy? He legit?"

He shrugged. "Don't know. There were a lot of guys who had a piece of Jack. My job was just to drive him there and make sure he got to where he was going next safely."

"I went by his office. Didn't seem to have a lot going on."

"Who else you talk to?"

I told him about my other conversations, and he sat and listened and looked straight ahead for the most part, except when he looked up and down the pathway at the people coming and going.

"You're really poking around in this," he said.

"I am."

"And your friend, Freddie, he's watching out for you?"

"He is."

"Good idea. You keep turning over rocks, and you don't know what's going to jump out at you."

"So I'm finding."

"I'll do what I can to help you," he said.

"How about tell me about that night? Jack cancels, then what?"

"Calls me, says he's tired and just canceled his Webber session. Tells me that's a wrap and I can head home."

"So you take off?"

"Not right away."

"Why?"

He hesitated and looked off toward the crowd in front of the bison. Then he turned to me. "Wanted to see if he was going out on his own."

"He was your responsibility."

"I got paid a lot of money by Cal Daniels to make sure Jack's ass was tucked in at night."

"So you're afraid he'll pull an end run on you?"

"Again," he said.

"How many other times?"

"Once. About a month ago he pulled a stunt like this. Went out late and hopped a cab. Came back about an hour later."

"Girlfriend?"

He shook his head. "Don't think so. He and Robbie hadn't been together long enough for him to be bored. Plus, you met her. She's very ..."

"Attractive," I said.

"Yes."

"How'd you find out he took off?"

"Eddie. Overnight doorman."

"Nice of him."

"I keep him on my payroll. He gets a big Christmas tip; I get any info I need on Jack."

"What happened the other night?"

"Eddie goes on his dinner break about a half hour before Jack leaves."

"And the guy covering for him?"

"Some kid who doesn't know the drill," he said.

"All comes down to timing."

"Next thing I know, I get a call from Robbie at three in the morning," he said. "She's frantic, asking if I know where Jack is."

I looked out at the crowd that was building, coming into the park. The parade of young families and strollers had begun. They clogged the walkway between us and the dusty living quarters of the bison, getting to the zoo before it became too hot and humid.

"Wonder why Robbie never mentioned this to me," I said.

"She didn't know. Still doesn't, as far as I know."

"How'd Jack manage that?"

"She was at her mother's place out in Ohio," he said.

"You ask him about it?"

"The very next day. I said, Anything new going on? He says no. Same old."

"And you knew he was lying?"

"Yup."

"Where do you think he went?"

"No idea. Jack was a restless man at times. I tried asking again, kind of in a roundabout way for a few days, but he didn't give me anything."

"What about after that? Any more end runs?"

"Only other thing was a trip to a motel in Jersey the week before that night. One night after his show."

"Okay, hang on," I said. "I thought you said there were no girlfriends."

He shook his head. "There weren't, as far as I know. Jack said this was for a story."

"Yeah, right."

Manny turned to face me. "You want this help or not?"

"Of course I do."

"Then you got to trust that I'm leveling with you. I'm telling you what I know," he said.

I thought about it for a moment. He was right. "What was the story?" I asked.

He shook his head. "Don't know. We sat there for a bit in the parking lot of the motel and waited in front of the room he was supposed to go to, but no one showed up. Left after forty-five minutes."

I looked over at Freddie, who was standing up the pathway to my left. He was leaning against a low black railing and drinking a bottle of water, pretending to be just another zoo goer taking a break.

"So you got Jack Steele sitting in a car in the parking lot of a motel in Jersey waiting to meet a source who stands him up?" I said.

"That's the way it happened," he said.

"And you don't know what the story was or who he was supposed to meet?"

"No."

This was one of those moments when I was going to have to decide whether or not to trust Manny.

"He make any calls, e-mail anyone, text anyone, maybe, while you were out there?" I asked.

"No. He sat in the back staring across the parking lot at the door to the room. And he was looking around, trying to see what cars came and went."

"And he never followed up? Never went back out there?"

"Not that I know of."

We sat there in silence for a bit and Manny scanned the crowd heading into the zoo. The crowd in front of the bison was thick; and cameras and phones were pointed, and lots of pictures were snapped.

I looked for the fedora-wearing guy, but it was impossible to see through the crowd. There were a lot of large, okay fat, guys who shared his body shape. It was America after all.

"A story, huh?" I said out loud, but more to myself.

"Yeah," Manny said.

"You think maybe someone was setting him up? He shows up with you and they bail?" I asked.

"Then try it again a week later, the night he goes out on his own," he said.

"But something goes wrong."

"And maybe they make another run last week."

"And it all works the third time."

"That's what I've been thinking."

"What about the note?"

"That's the part I can't figure out," he said.

Chapter 23

I had the file full of e-mails that Robbie had given me. Across the tab at the top was scribbled *Wackos*. I was looking through the pages as Freddie drove us back into Midtown from the Bronx. We were driving west across Forty-ninth Street, and he was listening to some sort of slow gospel music.

"Here's one from some group called Citizens for Change," I said.

"I like it. Broad enough where it can mean anything," he said.

"They took exception to a show Jack did on immigration and securing the border with Mexico."

"They for it or against it?"

"Hard to say. President is some guy named Horton L. Sundstrom, and it sounds like he just doesn't like Jack."

"You try going through life being called Horton. See how happy you are," Freddie said.

"Once again, you have shown your ignorance and complete lack of ability to grasp the facts of a story," I said, reading from the e-mail.

"Ow," Freddie said. "Sure that wasn't supposed to be sent to you?"

We were at the corner of Fifth; the sidewalks were full of tourists, clogging Rockefeller Center and the sights around it. They looked hot. Dressed in shorts and T-shirts and sweating it out as they waited for the Walk signs.

A few minutes later Freddie pulled up outside Liberty and parked in one of the handful of open spots. It was Saturday afternoon, and there was a slower pace to things; a lot of people at Liberty were away, the weekend workers the only ones around.

Marty agreed to meet me in the newsroom and give me access to the files he and Jack had relating to the stories the show had been working on. He wasn't happy about having to drag himself into work on a Saturday, but after some arm twisting he agreed.

I left Freddie downstairs and went up to the newsroom, but there was no sign of Marty. I asked around, and someone said he had seen him, but no one was sure where he had gone.

I went upstairs to the offices and saw that Steele's door was open. Marty was sitting in the desk chair a few feet behind Jack's desk. He wore khakis and a light blue button-down shirt, essentially the same thing he wore during the week. He had a stack of manila folders on his lap and flipped through them and didn't bother looking up as I walked in.

"Nothing I enjoy more than stopping into work on a Saturday," he said.

"I'll buy you a drink. You name the place."

"Malloy's," he said.

It was the bar downstairs on Forty-ninth Street that was a second home to most of us.

"No reason to try anyplace new," I said.

"I'm a man of simple tastes," he said.

I sat down on the couch against the wall to the right of Marty, and he looked up from the folders.

"See, here's the little problem with your request," he said. "You wanted to see what stories we were working on."

"Yes."

"It's a rather broad request," he said. "As a TV show that's kind of all we did, work on stories."

"There is a certain grain-of-sand-on-the-beach feel to this," I said.

"And this would all be related to the Widow Steele's investigation?"

"It would be."

Glover looked at me and seemed to be trying to find the right way to say something. "People are talking, Sam."

"They're always talking, Marty."

"Are you ..."

He purposely let the thought sit there. He was too uncomfortable to ask about the gossip specifically, so he threw a vague reference to it out there.

"Am I what?" I asked.

"You know."

"No, Marty. I'm not sleeping with Robbie Steele, if that's what you're asking."

"It is," he said.

"It's insulting, Marty. The woman just lost her husband."

"Which makes her vulnerable," he said.

"And by the way, I happen to be seeing someone myself."

"Like that stops people," he said.

I nodded toward the folders on his lap. "Think we can talk stories now?"

"Sure. Didn't know it was a sensitive subject."

Marty opened the top folder, picked up the stack of printouts, and fanned through them. "These are the stories we ran in the last few weeks." He put the papers back in the folder and put it on Steele's desk, then took the second folder from his lap and held it up. "These are ones we were chasing for upcoming shows," he said. He put that folder on the desk and held up the third and last folder. "And these were some of the letters and e-mails we received in response to recent stories."

"Who's Stuart Ripley?" I asked.

"A very big pain in the ass," he said.

"His name came up when I spoke to Jerry Drake about Operation Outrage."

He tried to stifle a laugh but was unsuccessful; it came out like he was choking on something. "Jerry Drake," he said as he tried to compose himself. "What a waste that was."

"He's convinced he was going to turn things around," I said.

"Yes, and I'm king of f-ing England," he said.

"Ripley was pretty aggressive with Jack when you went after IT&E," I said.

"That's what these corporate flacks do, Sam. They're bitter little weenies and they get all bent out of shape every time someone mentions their company. That's their job," he said.

"Jack went after IT&E, then stopped. What happened?"

He shrugged.

"Wasn't much else there. He told me to monitor the Web sites and blogs and all those fringe guys who were talking about this stuff, but we never saw anything new."

"Too bad, seemed like a good story. Its equipment shows up in Iran and Syria. An American icon doing business with questionable governments, maybe even terrorists," I said.

"Was never really that cut and dried. Some of their equipment found its way into Iran and possibly Syria, but it wasn't like they outright sold it to those dirt bags," he said.

"That mark the end of Operation Outrage?" I asked.

"The end? Hell, it never really started," he said.

"Drake makes it sound like he was going to save the show," I said.

"Consultants always do."

I got up, and Marty handed me the three folders. I thanked him for coming in on a Saturday as we shook hands.

"I'll collect on my drink next week," he said.

"I find something in here, maybe you get two."

"Hey, by the way, I saw your boy Kenny a few nights ago. At the Overseas Press Club Awards," he said.

Kenny Slattery was my agent. Given the state of my career, I had been asking myself why.

"He must have been there with some of his younger, attractive clients," I said.

"Nancy Banks, the blonde on MSNBC," he said. "He was asking about you."

"Nice of him."

"Wanted to know where you been. Said he hadn't seen you on air much since the big story," he said.

"You tell him I've been busy?"

"He already knew. Said he's been hearing from people that you're running around chasing some conspiracy theory," he said.

"Hey, at least they're talking about me."

"I'm serious, Sam," Marty said. "I don't think you want to get in too deep with this shit. It's getting kind of nutty. People are starting to say things that can really hurt a career."

I slapped Marty on the back. "Thanks for the warning. I'll keep it in mind."

"You're too good a reporter to have your career end because of something like this."

Chapter 24

It was Sunday, and Liz and I were walking up Park Avenue South from Union Square. We were taking our time and enjoying the afternoon. It was a hot, lazy day, the kind that made you wish you were sitting on a beach somewhere.

"I owe you for this," I said.

"And I intend to collect," she said.

"Do you know what I'm referring to?" I asked.

"I have no idea. But I've found when someone tells me he owes me, it's always good to accept."

A cab on its way uptown sped through a light that just turned red, prompting a horn from a car going crosstown through the intersection. I jumped and turned to look. This whole paranoia thing was starting to wear on me.

"Soon as this is wrapped up, we're out in Montauk," I said.

"Will we be staying in the gritty-yet-quaint-old-fishing-village Montauk, or the overrun-by-the-chic-and-hip Montauk?" she asked.

"I'd prefer the gritty fishing village, if any of it still exists when we get there."

"Maybe you should work faster," she said.

"I'll try, but it takes me a while to figure things out."

"Yes, I've noticed."

I squeezed Liz's hand as we walked and occasionally looked behind us and around us to see if anyone might be taking more of an interest in us than necessary.

"Marty says people are talking about me," I said.

"I talk about you all the time," she said.

"That's nice to hear."

"But mostly to myself."

"That counts, too," I said.

"But you're worried?" she asked.

"A little."

"Why? You know you're onto something."

"I do, but there's still a few doubts."

"I thought the overweight guy in the hat working for Buck McConnell telling you to be careful took care of those."

"He did."

"But?"

"But then I remember the note. I still have no clue how to explain that."

"Maybe you don't need a clue, at this particular time, at least."

We crossed Nineteenth Street. We'd be back to the apartment in five minutes. I personally felt like blowing past the apartment to just keep on walking, holding hands, and talking with Liz. She had a very natural way of bringing me back around to what needed to be done.

It was she who suggested leaving the piles of e-mails on the table for a while and going out to eat. She seemed to know I needed a break from staring at them and trying to find a clue or a pattern. And it was Liz who suggested the Thai place on the west side of Union Square.

Both were excellent suggestions.

"I have to tell you," I said, "I sit down with Robbie Steele, and I don't think she's crazy. At first, maybe I did. But the more I talk to her, the more I realize she's trusting her gut and determined to find out what happened to her husband."

"Maybe you ought to try trusting *your* gut," she said.

"Tough when you hear your agent is worried that you've gone off the deep end."

"That's just background noise."

"And the foreground noise would be?"

"The stacks of e-mails on the table back at the apartment," she said.

We walked the last few blocks to my place, and a few minutes later we were sitting in the living room, both of us on the couch with the e-mails on the coffee table in front of us. Liz reached over and grabbed the pile of those from Stuart Ripley from IT&E and began thumbing through them.

"Mr. Ripley is quite the e-mailer," she said.

"Believe it or not," I said.

"You might have a career in entertainment if the news thing doesn't pan out."

"I already consider myself an entertainer."

"If that's what gets you through the day," she said, stopping to read one of Ripley's e-mails. "Boy, this guy seems pretty intense."

"He's a corporate guard dog."

"He sounds bitter, kind of nasty."

"Probably is," I said. "Seems like one of those guys determined to respond to any and every mention of the company Jack made during a show."

"Here's one titled 'Your Show Last Night,'" she said.

"Date?"

"July thirteenth."

"July 11 was the first day Jack went after IT&E. The e-mails from Drake have Ripley's response to that report," I said.

"So this is two days later."

"Jack did a follow-up story the night before."

"This one has a lot of official, corporate speak." Liz scanned the e-mail. "Oh, here's a keeper. 'Your report contains egregious inaccuracies that are blatantly false,'" she read.

"Wow. I got a headache just trying to keep up with that line."

"Whatever happened to 'you're wrong'?" Liz asked.

"Too easy. You'll never become a flack if you're going to keep it simple," I said.

Liz looked through the rest of the e-mails from Ripley while I flipped through the stack of threats Steele had received from various wackos and fringe groups. It seemed as though there were shows where he got under the skin of a dozen people. But then again, that was what had made *Steele Yourself* a success.

I picked up a handful of miscellaneous e-mails, ones not from Ripley but still related to Operation Outrage. There was one to Steele titled simply "IT&E." It was from the e-mail address mail@cci.com.

The only thing in the body of the e-mail was a single sentence.

Last-minute change … something came up … but more on IT&E where that came from.

That was it. No name at the end as to who wrote or sent it. It was dated July twelfth, the day after Jack's first report.

"I think maybe we file this one under cryptic," I said, handing the e-mail to Liz.

I grabbed my iPad off the coffee table and shot an e-mail to the address, asking if I could speak to someone about IT&E.

"What's *CCI* stand for?" she asked. "And what is this 'last-minute change' all about?"

"This might be where you become a reporter," I said.

"Talk about a career setback. Investment banker to reporter."

"But think about the interesting people you'll meet," I said.

Liz took her laptop off the table and searched for *CCI*; a minute later my e-mail came shooting back to me through the invisible channels of the Web.

"Undeliverable," I said. "E-mail address not found."

"Too bad for you," she said. "Looks like I made more progress on my first day as a reporter."

"I knew you'd take to the field. You're a natural."

"And to think, no training," she said.

"Whattya got, kid?" I asked.

"I like it. The crusty old city editor," she said. "A gruff-but-with-a-heart-of-gold type, who mentors me."

"And maybe you and me get together after work," I said.

"Yes, to work on grammar and usage."

I looked over Liz's shoulder as she read from the laptop.

"There doesn't seem to be any homepage or anything, but this *CCI* is mentioned in a number of places."

She double-clicked on one entry from the *Los Angeles Times* and read from it: "The initial report on IT&E's dealings in the Middle East appeared in *Corporate Corruption Investigations*, a quarterly newsletter devoted to chronicling abuses of the Foreign Corrupt Practices Act."

We scanned some of the other entries, almost all of which referred to the IT&E story from a month and a half ago.

"Aha," Liz said, after a few seconds. "Here's one from some sort of business directory with a phone number for our mysterious friends at *CCI*."

I looked over her shoulder at the entry. It was an 800 number, which was better than nothing.

"I think this is what they call a lead in the reporting business," she said.

"I think it is. Nice work, kid."

Chapter 25

"So tell me again why you're doing this?"

The question came from my agent Kenny Slattery, of the esteemed talent representation firm Slattery & Stone. It was Monday morning, and my agent was telling me people thought I was nuts, one of my worst fears coming true. And all before eleven a.m. Some guys are just lucky, I guess.

I was sitting in a cheap office chair in front of Kenny's desk. The desk was a mess of newspapers, folders, piles of papers, and Styrofoam cups. My chair had a metal frame with a plastic black seat and a matching back. Everything in the place felt cheap.

If RCM Management reeked of money and prestige, Slattery & Stone reeked of, well, stale coffee and inattention to detail.

"Why am I doing what?" I asked.

"Acting like a nut. Chasing around town pissing people off."

"It's my only skill set, Kenny," I said. "What am I going to do, go someplace and become a marketing executive or something?"

Slattery sighed and leaned forward over his desk. He was younger than me, early forties, with slicked-back black hair. I could never tell if the hair was naturally oily, or if he added some sort of gel or grease to it. Either way, it was slick.

He was dressed in the business casual uniform of dark suit, light blue shirt, no tie.

He locked his long fingers together and placed his index fingers to his lips while he stared at me. I believe he was attempting to give the impression he was in deep thought, or maybe just thought. Either way, it wasn't working. Kenny lacked the gravitas to look serious.

"I'm not going to stay if you're going to fall asleep," I said.

"I'm thinking," he said.

"Same thing."

"Look, Sam, I have a responsibility here as your agent."

"Funny how you didn't seem to have a responsibility when I was bugging you to get me a new contract from Cal. Then you were busy with the twentysomething gals you seem to specialize in these days," I said.

"They need help and guidance just like my veteran clients, Sam."

"I didn't come over here for career advice," I said.

"Excuse me for caring."

"Give me a break, Kenny."

"No, Sam, I'm being straight with you. I got people calling up asking about your behavior. I get reports of you going around questioning people on all sorts of bizarre things. Hell, I feel like maybe I should hold an intervention or something."

"Only if you invite a few of your young clients. We can make it a party."

"Joke if you want to, but you're in danger of getting labeled."

"As?"

"As the nutty conspiracy theory guy who's sleeping with Steele's widow."

"That's wrong on all accounts."

"That's what people are saying."

"The people are wrong. Plus, it's disgusting. The woman just lost her husband."

He sat back and shook his head like he was actually concerned. "Case in point. I get a call from someone Friday asking if I still represent you."

"Funny, I've asked myself the same question."

"I'll ignore that."

"Too late."

"I say, 'Sure. Sam is still with me.' It was Emily Wells, you know her?"

I shook my head.

"Works with NBC on talent," he said. "Says they'd like to consider you for a full-time spot, but it's just that, you know ... there's talk you're running around questioning people about Jack Steele's death. Some kind of special project that no one can seem to explain."

"That's because it's top secret."

"Word is Robbie Steele thinks someone killed Jack, and you're going to find out who did it."

"Crazy, huh?"

"Everyone knows she's nuts; the question is, are you even nuttier?"

"Not if she's right."

Kenny sighed a deep sigh just to let me know he was very disturbed.

"Are you deflating?" I asked.

He shook his head like he pitied me. "I even have people telling me you pissed off Ron Marshall. I mean, it's like you're *trying* to end your career."

"I appreciate your caring, Kenny. I don't know if it's worth the ten percent I pay you, but I appreciate it."

"Sam, I'm serious. This is your career we're talking about," he said.

"Which was officially dead until I got this story."

I had been with Slattery for fifteen years. He had done well for me with some contracts, but had been nonexistent during the last few lean years. I had thought about dumping him but had stayed. It was inertia or loyalty. Maybe both. At this point I couldn't tell.

"This worries me," he said.

"Stop with the, you're-screwing-up-your-life talk," I said. "Robbie

Steele called me and asked me to look into something. Daniels gave me the green light to pursue it."

"That doesn't mean you just go out and—"

"Both of those developments happened without your involvement," I said.

"Cheap shot."

"Regardless of the unfortunate and horrible event that brought them about, both developments have at least pumped a little life into my career."

The door behind me opened and I heard a women's voice. "Kenneth, don't forget, you have an eleven a.m. red."

I turned around to see Cheryl, his office manager. She was late twenties, jet-black hair and an hourglass figure that today was packed tightly into a low-cut top and jeans. As much as the woman at Marshall's place said serious professional, Cheryl said party girl who had a job so she had somewhere to go during the day.

I looked at Slattery. "Kenneth? An eleven o'clock red?"

Cheryl stepped in and held up a sheet of paper with a grid and all kinds of red and orange squares on it.

"I've color coded Kenneth's schedule so he's more efficient."

"I didn't even realize Kenneth had a schedule most days. I thought this was more like a drop-in center," I said.

"Oh, no more," she said. She gave me a little wave and walked out.

"Kenneth?" I said, looking at Slattery.

"I'm trying to foster a more businesslike atmosphere, Sam. A couple of the clients complained."

"You may want to have Cheryl wear tops that actually fit," I said.

"Baby steps, Sam. Baby steps."

"Let me get to the reason I came over here today," I said.

"I assumed it was to thank me for my years of loyal service."

"No. I want to know why I don't have the paperwork for a new contract."

"You don't have the paperwork because I don't have an offer from Cal."

"You need to get one."

"Cal won't return my calls."

"Why?"

"Might have something to do with your having lost your mind. But that's just my guess."

"You need to get me a new contract."

He rocked back in his chair and looked at me. "Let me tell you something."

"Please."

"About a week ago, I get a call from Cal."

"Nice of you to share with me, your client."

He put up a hand and tried to slow me. "Whoa, whoa, there's more."

"Always is," I said.

"We had been discussing a deal for you, no hard numbers, just a let's-sit-down-and-get-this-done kind of thing. He says to schedule something with Susan, so I do."

"This was when?"

"Day or two after you broke the big news. We were going to have lunch. You know, break some bread, talk about a deal for you. Get it all worked out."

"What happened?"

He shrugged. "Day of the lunch, Susan e-mails me to cancel, says Cal had something come up. Says we'll talk about rescheduling. I don't think anything of it."

"But?"

"But I have yet to sit down and break bread with the man. I've e-mailed him directly. Nothing. Nada. Like he doesn't own a computer or something."

"And you've called," I said.

"I have. Susan takes a message."

"She told me."

"And he doesn't call back," he said.

"She told me that as well."

He picked up his iPhone and waved it. "I'm still waiting."

"You've been an agent for a while."

"I have. Twenty glorious years," he said.

"Would this fall under the-man-is-a-bit-busy category?"

"Not to me," he said.

"That's what I was afraid of."

"This would fall under the I'm-getting-blown-off category," he said.

"And you never got a reason?"

"I think we can guess. One minute you're hot stuff. The guy who broke the big news. The next, you're the nut job racing around town asking odd questions."

"So Cal goes from hot to cold on me?"

"Exactly," he said. "Right when you start your top-secret project for Robbie Steele."

We were both silent for a moment, and I wondered if it was in honor of my career.

"I think maybe he thinks you've gone around the bend on him," he said.

"Risky move," I said.

"How so."

"When I put this together, it's going to cost him a lot more."

Slattery smirked. "I'm glad one us is confident about this."

Chapter 26

It was just past eight thirty when Freddie and I made our way across the upper level of the George Washington Bridge and into New Jersey. The sun was down, but the sky still held a little bit of light; the days were getting shorter, and evenings like this reminded you summer was nearing an end.

To our left, down along the Hudson, the lights of Manhattan twinkled.

"And you think showing up unannounced at some guy's house at nine o'clock at night is a good idea?" Freddie asked.

"Nine is the new eight," I said. "Used to be you'd find people home at eight, you know, after dinner, maybe watching a little TV. Now you got to wait until nine. Everybody's busy, busy, busy."

"Show up at my house at nine, and I'm going to beat your ass."

"You're going to be that hostile neighbor, aren't you? The guy with the anger-management issues."

"That'd be me."

We drove down I-95 and jumped onto Route 4 west and headed toward the town of Teaneck, New Jersey, and the home of Herman Bindagi, the publisher of the *Corporate Corruption Investigation* newsletter. Freddie had run the number by another one of his so-called cousins and come up with the address.

"What if your cousin gave us the wrong address?" I asked.

"Oh, ye of little faith."

"What if we show up at residence of Mr. and Mrs. Front Porch instead of at the Bindagi residence?"

He sighed and signaled to get into the right lane for the exit up ahead. "Freddie's cousins don't make mistakes," he said. "I ask for info, I get info. That's how it works."

"He a cop or something?"

"Who said it's a he?"

"He or she a cop?"

"Let's just say 'loosely connected to the law enforcement field.' That's all I can say."

"Okay, no more questions."

"That would be best."

Freddie steered the Cherokee off Route 4, and we drove on using the GPS, winding through a short shopping district with a Stop & Shop and a pizzeria. A quarter mile away was a McDonald's and a small row of stores, including a florist.

A few minutes later we were in a working-class neighborhood with small single-family houses. The Bindagi residence was 119 Sherman Lane. We drove past it slowly at first and then stopped down the street at the next open parking spot.

The house sat on a bit of a hill, up about a dozen steps from the sidewalk, and looked as if yard work and basic maintenance were not a priority for its owner.

There was a dim porch light on, but the blinds were down in the front windows, and there was no outward appearance that anyone was home.

There were two reasons I needed to speak to Herman Bindagi: One was to find out if *CCI* was the source of Steele's info on IT&E and Syria. The second concerned the e-mail I had in my hands from *CCI*. I looked at the one-line message: *Last-minute change ... something came up ... but more on IT&E where that came from.*

At the zoo Manny had mentioned Steele's meeting at a Jersey motel at which he was stood up. I wondered if Jack was supposed to meet this Bindagi guy.

"You keep watch out here in case any suspicious types show up," I said to Freddie as I got out.

"I'll handle everyone with tact and gentleness," he said.

"Of course you will."

I went up the concrete steps to the front door. The house was tired and in need of a paint job, its wood sagging and rotting in places. I rang the small illuminated doorbell, stepped back, and waited.

No one answered. I rang again. This time I saw the corner of the blinds in one front window lift, and someone peered out. The door was unlocked and opened a crack. A chain lock prevented it from opening farther.

Inside was a guy with a dark complexion and head full of curly black hair that ran off in all directions.

"Yes?" he asked.

"Hi, Sam North, with Liberty News."

"I thought I recognized you."

It was a start.

"Can we speak?"

"You have ID? Just in case."

I held up my NYPD press credential, and he stared at it through the door.

"What do you want to talk about?" he asked.

"Think maybe we could take the chain off and I could come in?"

His eyes darted to the street behind me, like maybe someone was going to rush the door. Satisfied I wasn't a threat, he removed the chain and opened the door. I stepped into a dark, enclosed porch. He stood and looked at me, not quite sure what to do next. My guess was Herman didn't get many visitors.

"You have electricity?" I asked.

He reached over and flipped a switch, and a floor lamp in the corner of the porch came on. I got my first full look at Herman

Bindagi. He was in his fifties, medium height, with broad shoulders but overweight. He was dressed in a pair of worn shorts that had lost their shape long ago and a light blue button-down oxford shirt with the sleeves rolled up to the elbows. He was barefoot, with toenails that needed some attention.

"I see you on TV."

"Glad you're watching. You publish something called *CCI*? *Corporate Corruption Investigations*?"

He took a second before responding. "Why?"

I looked past him into the house. "You think maybe we could sit down for a few minutes and I'll explain?"

"Sure," he said.

He turned and led me off of the porch and into a hallway. There were stairs on the right, and we went into a room across the hall on the left. Down the hallway at the back of the house was the kitchen.

As we moved I heard scratching coming from the kitchen. I envisioned a very large rat. I heard the low rumble of a growl, and Herman sprang to life.

"Rex," he yelled, "quiet."

"Dog?" I asked, with a hopeful tone.

"Old rottweiler. Doesn't hear real well. Takes him a while to get going, but when he does ..."

"Watch out, huh?"

"Yup. So I wouldn't try anything."

"Got it."

In the living room he flipped on the lights. There was a big recliner at one end of the room with a small table next to it. The table was littered with folded newspapers, cans of Dr Pepper, and big open bags of chips and other junk food. More empty junk-food bags and soda bottles littered the floor around the table. It looked as if a vending machine had exploded.

He went for the recliner, which seemed to be where the action was. It faced the fireplace and a modest-size flat-screen TV that hung above the mantel. The only other place to sit was a small couch against the wall to my right, so I took a seat there.

"Corporate Corruption Investigations," I said.

"Yes, the authority on cases brought under the FCPA."

"Well, that clears it up," I said.

"Good."

"Mind telling me what the FCPA is?"

"Foreign Corrupt Practices Act. It's what the Feds use to go after corporations that don't play by the rules overseas."

"What are the rules?"

"Thou shall not bribe government officials for contracts. That sort of thing," he said.

"That a big problem?"

"For the U.S. government, yes. For a lot of those countries, it's a way of life. Want that government contract to build a wireless phone network? Well, first you got to pay off the son of the neighbor to the nephew of the president to get it. Cost of doing business."

"What about the countries less than friendly to the U.S?"

"Whole other set of rules and a lot more complex," he said. "And they come from the OFAC," he said.

"I'm going to need some help again," I said.

"Office of Foreign Assets Control. Part of Treasury. They implement and enforce regulations backing up the foreign policy of the good old U. S. of A.," he said.

"Sanctions?"

"Bingo. The prez signs an executive order saying you can't do business or export anything to country X because they suck and are hostile to the U.S."

"And then nobody does business, right?"

"Hah. You'd be surprised. Some of these sleazy corporations find ways around. Maybe they get in bed with a local company, or some European company that doesn't have any restrictions. When their crap shows up floating around in Syria or wherever, they say, 'Oh, gee, we had a contact with Luigi. We didn't know Luigi was turning around and selling our junk over there. Sorry."

Herman had warmed up considerably and seemed to be enjoying the visit.

"You ever work with Jack Steele on anything?" I asked.

He went quiet on me like I had crossed some line.

I pulled the copy of the e-mail from my shirt pocket, went over and handed it to him.

"You send this?"

He took it from me and looked at it. "No."

"Who did?"

"Someone else," he said.

I sat back down and angled myself to face him.

"Herm, how about we work together on this?"

"I prefer Herman."

"Not a problem. Look, I'm following up on some of Jack's stories, and I know you sent the e-mail."

"Maybe not," he said.

"My guess is *CCI* is part of your media empire, which is run from this house, right?"

He nodded.

I looked around. "Seems to me you're a one-man operation."

"I have a reporter in DC."

"Did he or she send that e-mail?"

He didn't say anything.

"I didn't think so. Like I said, I've taken over Jack's stories, so maybe you and I can work together, okay?"

No response.

"I have a feeling you sent the e-mail, and all I want to know is why you didn't go to meet Jack?"

Herman started to tap his foot while he tried to figure out what to do. So we sat there in silence. In the kitchen a low growl came from the Rot.

"Herman," I said, "it's not a big deal. I'm just curious why you didn't go to meet Jack?"

"I ... I haven't been out of the house in a while."

"What, allergies?" I asked.

He shook his head. "No, I think someone is watching me," he said. "I'm scared to go out."

"Living on chips and Dr Pepper?"

"That's what I'm down to," he said.

I wondered if this is how a shrink feels when he realizes a patient is nuts.

"I think someone figured out I was giving Jack information," he said. "Someone related to IT&E."

"But the stuff is public—it's not like secret documents, right? You put out a newsletter."

He got up from the recliner. "Come with me."

I followed him to the kitchen, and the Rot let loose a few big barks at the stranger in the house.

"Hold on," Herman said.

I waited while he grabbed Rex by the collar and half dragged the dog across the linoleum floor to the other side by the back door. Once there, he hooked the dog's collar to a chain that ran to the metal piping of an old exposed radiator.

We went into a small room the size of a walk-in closet in the corner of the kitchen. A long wooden desk, a chair, and a small table with a printer on it took up almost every inch of the space.

Herman grabbed a letter-size brown envelope from the desktop, slid a five-by-seven picture out from it, and handed it to me.

"This stuff hasn't been made public yet," he said. "I got a whole new batch of stuff I was going to feed Jack."

The shot was taken from a distance and looked like it was at a dusty airport. There were two men, one dark-skinned and the other white. The white guy was big, dressed in tan slacks and a brownish checked-pattern button-down shirt. In his hand he held a canvas tote bag. They were on a runway or tarmac standing next to a small jet.

"That slick-looking guy in the slacks and button-down?" he said.

"Who is he?"

"The frigging key to everything," he said. "Billy Hunter."

"Should I know the name?"

"Only if you represent a corrupt government in, say, Africa or the Middle East."

"Go on."

"Hunter works for IT&E," he said. "That guy next to him is some peon from the Nigerian government. That canvas bag Hunter is holding? Guess what—it's full of cash. The naira. That's Nigerian money."

"For?"

"Who knows? Best I can tell, this was tied to some contract for IT&E to supply energy equipment at a Nigerian oil facility."

I looked at the photo, and the first thought I had was how good this would look on TV as part of a report.

"It gets better," Herman said. "The bag was just a down payment. Apparently, the rest of the cash was stuffed into the backseat of a Mercedes. IT&E was paying something like a few hundred thousand U.S. dollars for the contract. Problem is, the locals wanted it in their currency. You need more than a hundred naira to get one dollar."

"Lots of bills."

"No kidding. They stuffed it all into a car and drove it to the guy's house."

"And this is what you were going to show Jack that night you guys planned to meet?"

Herman got quiet, a little sullen even, now.

"Yeah."

There were more envelopes on his desk; he reached for another one and slipped three photos out of it. They all featured Hunter meeting people in various places. Dusty places next to buildings, around a parked car. All were taken from a distance and then blown up. In one shot there was a guy in a traditional Middle Eastern robe and headdress next to Hunter.

"How bad is this stuff for IT&E?" I asked.

"Some of it is small potatoes."

"Some big?"

"Very. Let me put it this way. When this gets out, IT&E is going to be investigated by the Feds and eventually, probably, fined hundreds of millions of dollars. That don't exactly look good for Buck McConnell or his political hopes. Try running for president while your employees are paying off third-world thugs to win contracts."

McConnell had been something of a whispered candidate for

everything from a race for a Texas senate seat to the White House, but he had never taken the plunge.

I looked at the other envelopes.

"You got more here, don't you Herman?" I asked.

He didn't say anything.

"A lot more, right?" I said.

"Maybe." He shifted a bit, like he wanted to make sure he was between me and the stuff on his desk. "But these are the ones Jack was interested in," he said, looking at the pictures of Hunter.

"So Jack knew you had all these new pictures?" I asked.

"Oh yeah. He knew I had some good stuff. I gave him a little taste a few days before he died."

"Just to show him what you had."

"Yeah, dropped a copy of one of the Hunter shots off at security at your building on Sixth."

I was starting to get a clearer picture of my new friend Herman.

"You hand delivered it?"

"Yeah, I didn't want to take any chances," he said.

"With what?"

"You know, it falling into the wrong hands. That kind of thing."

"Jack comes down to meet you?"

"Oh, no, he sends an underling. Mikey, I think."

"Marty?"

"Yeah, that guy. Fat guy."

I looked at Herman. Pot. Kettle.

"So Herman," I said. "How many people subscribe to your newsletter?"

"We haven't been audited in a while, but I'd say it's in the thousands."

"Really?"

He hesitated. "Yeah ... maybe. Maybe less."

"And your readers are?"

"Some of the business press. Guys who should be covering this stuff themselves but are too lazy or incompetent."

"Not a big audience. Must be others."

"Watchdog groups. Even a lot of corporations. They read it to see of they're showing up in it."

"How do you get your info?"

"I get calls. Tips. Been doing this a long time. People know me."

"You make a good living?" I asked.

Judging by the house, Herman was either a frugal guy or struggling to make ends meet.

"I do okay," he said.

I let his answer sit there for a moment. "You were charging Jack for this stuff, weren't you?" I asked, waving the pictures of Hunter.

He bristled and became nervous. "No ... not at all. I ... I ..."

"Herman," I said. "It's okay. I'm not here to judge you, I just want to know any arrangement you guys had, that's all."

It took him a moment to decide. "Okay," he said.

"That's why you hand delivered a picture, right? Marty probably paid you?" I said.

He nodded. "Yeah, not even sure he knew it, but he gave me an envelope with five hundred bucks."

"Not bad."

"It was a start. Figured I'd get a few thousand for the rest of them."

"And you were going to show them to Jack at the motel? See if you could work out some deal."

"Yeah. Jack wanted to see what I had."

"You spoke to him?"

"Twice," he said. "Jack said he was going to nail Buck McConnell, and good."

"Which was all good for you, since you have the evidence."

"It was good until I got spooked. But I swear, somebody was out front watching me," he said.

"So you canceled."

"I tried to reschedule with Jack, but it took a day or two for us speak," he said.

"No e-mails?"

"No, not after the one you found. Jack said he wanted to talk on the phone. He said he was putting together a huge story on McConnell that was going to force the bastard out at IT&E."

I waved the pictures. "Based on these?"

"He said he had other information, too."

"When was the last time you spoke to him?"

"Monday. The day before he died. He said to call him back later in the week. Said he had a lot going on but wanted to see what I had."

"Then he dies," I said.

"Changed everything."

"Put an even bigger scare into you," I said.

"Damn straight," he said.

Chapter 27

"We got company," Freddie said.

I looked out the window. We were sitting in bumper traffic at the toll plaza for the GWB.

"Being that we're surrounded by hundreds of cars, I think that may go without saying," I said.

"Being that it's not me they have a beef with, maybe I just kick your ass out the Jeep and let you fend for yourself in the dark out here," he said.

"That's not part of our agreement," I said.

"Might be time to rework the agreement," he said.

I looked in the side-view mirror and saw a sea of cars behind us, all jockeying and squeezing down into the lanes for E-ZPass and cash.

"Black Mercedes," he said. "He's, like, five cars back now. Getting a little panicky about staying with us."

I spotted the car in the mirror. It was a dark model, probably black. In the lights of the toll plaza that was all I could tell about it. The car was angled and trying to get into our lane.

"Think it's your new best friend, Bulger," he said.

"I thought you were my new best friend," I said.

"Crap, only thing wrong with that sentence is the word *friend*," he said.

"That hurt."

"Might as well take *best* out of there while you're at it. You're getting to be too high maintenance to be a friend of any kind. People chasing you, trying to beat you up. Probably even shoot your ass eventually."

"Don't sound so hopeful."

I looked in the side-view mirror and spotted the headlights and grille a few cars back.

"Was he with us at Herman's?" I asked.

"Nope, not that I saw at least. I kept a pretty good watch while you were inside."

"Where'd you pick him up?"

"Few miles back. Saw him keeping pace with us, then closing the gap as we got closer to the bridge. He came even with us at one point, then dropped back. Probably wants to make sure he's with us when we cross."

"Think he was checking us out?"

"Yup."

"He could have followed us out from the city," I said.

"Maybe. But I like to think I would have noticed him."

"If he did, he knows where we went."

I thought of Herman Bindagi and made a mental note to call him.

"And if he picked us up when we visited that guy," Freddie said, "means he was out at the house already, watching the dude."

We edged closer to the tollbooth where the E-ZPass would be scanned. We were in line to cross on the lower level of the bridge, and it looked like things opened up a bit as soon as you cleared the booths.

"Third possibility," I said. "Could be just another motorist crossing the bridge in an expensive car."

"Then why'd he pull even with us and drop back?" he asked.

"I don't know."

"I thought you were the brains of the operation."

"No, I got the good looks, remember?"

Freddie shook his head as we crossed through the booth. "One sure way of finding out what he's up to," he said.

The roadway onto the lower level sloped downward to the right, and as soon as we crossed through the booth Freddie punched the gas and we jerked forward.

"Let's see how desperate he is to keep up with us," he said.

The Cherokee sped ahead, Freddie hitting the gas and steering us into any little space and filling whatever gap opened up for us as we raced across the roadway high above the Hudson.

I turned around and tried to pick up the Mercedes. I saw headlights of a car way back, cutting in and out of traffic.

"Here he comes," he said.

We sped across the bridge and stayed to the left to exit down the ramps that twisted and curved around and eventually led to the Henry Hudson Parkway. The Jeep hugged the curves and we were going way too fast; it felt like were driving down a corkscrew and in danger of rolling over.

"He still back there?" Freddie asked.

"About six cars back, trying to get closer."

"Let's see about that," he said, nailing the gas once again as we came to the straightaway to merge onto the southbound Henry Hudson. Freddie cut to the left, and someone hit a horn behind us. We merged into traffic he bumped up the speed.

Out the back windshield I saw a pair of headlights slicing in and out of traffic and cutting from lane to lane and closing in on us.

"How close?" he asked.

"Four cars."

"Crap."

"You used to be a good driver," I said. "What happened?"

"Started hanging around with you. Made me soft," he said.

We sped south past the big sewage plant that sat overlooking the Hudson with the Mercedes keeping pace behind us. I saw it cut from the center to the right lane to get around a car and then jut back into the center lane.

"Two cars back," I said.

"He's really starting to annoy me," he said. "Making me use a lot of gas."

"You can put in for it on your expense report," I said.

"Like I'm being paid."

Freddie cut to the center lane and hit the gas and we sped through a gap in traffic. We had to be doing close to seventy on a road where traffic averaged fifty on its good days.

"You watching?" he asked.

There was a thud from behind, and the Cherokee lurched forward.

"We've been hit," I said.

"Guess that'd be a no on the watching," he said.

I turned and saw the headlights of the Mercedes just below the back window.

"I can confirm it's definitely a Benz. I can see the hood ornament."

We flew down the stretch where the Hudson was way too close for comfort on our right, separated only by a low guardrail and a bike path. The water was just a few feet away at times, a vast blackness dotted with the yellow lights of a tugboat every now and again.

To the left was an uphill embankment separating the northbound side of the road. We were in the center lane, but that was about to change.

I watched out the back as the Mercedes cut to the left lane.

"He's coming around your side," I said.

Freddie let off the gas, and the Mercedes flew past us, then slowed to try and draw even.

"What the ..." Freddie said.

"Maybe he wants to ask directions," I said. "Roll down your window."

We were side-by-side and going sixty-five, speeding toward the exit for the Seventy-ninth Street boar basin. It would be a quick exit to the right, but I had a feeling we were going too fast to take it at this point. Plus, we were in the center lane.

"Let's get off," I said.

Freddie glanced in the rearview mirror.

"Can't. There's some clown in the right lane. I can't get over."

I looked across Freddie and saw the tinted window of the Mercedes open.

"Oh, no," I yelled. "Take the exit. Take the exit."

"What?" Freddie yelled, slamming on the breaks.

There was a flash and the sound of metal hitting metal.

Chapter 28

It was just after ten the next morning, and Liz and I were hitting balls at the driving range at Chelsea Piers. She had suggested this as a way for her to avoid going into work on another slow weekday in vacation season.

When you've had the professional success she's had, you get to call some of the shots some of the time.

I agreed, thinking it might be a nice peaceful setting in which to break the news that someone took a shot at Freddie and me last night. Liz had been at a client dinner until after eleven, and by then I had thought of a hundred reasons not to tell her that someone tried to shoot her boyfriend.

But I knew I was going to have to at some point.

The driving range sat on the far west edge of Manhattan and looked out onto the Hudson. Go any farther and you're in the water. You hit balls onto an old pier that had been redone to look like a fairway. Netting that seemed to go a mile into the sky surrounded it.

Liz had a fluid, smooth stroke that showed what a combination of natural athleticism and lessons could result in. I was more of a weekend hacker, a product of learning the game on my own at public courses.

I hit a shot with my old driver and watched it sail far and straight for a good one hundred and seventy-five yards. Then it took a sharp right like it had a flight pattern and sailed another forty yards into the netting.

"Should at least put your directional on if you're making a turn like that," she said from the next stall over.

"I was practicing in case I encounter a tricky dogleg," I said. "Just wait until we get on a course and you'll see how prepared I am."

"Remind me to wear a hard hat," she said.

I stepped back and watched her line up a shot. She was wearing shorts and golf shoes and a T-shirt tucked in. She was lean and lithe, and with a smooth and relaxed stroke she hit a three-wood that sailed straight off toward the Hudson and landed at about the one-hundred-and-fifty-yard marker, then rolled another twenty-five or so.

"Not bad," I said. "Short, but not bad."

"Short and on the fairway as opposed to long and deep in the woods," she said. "I'll keep playing, and maybe you catch up to me when you've found your ball."

I watched her take a few more shots. All were hit flush and sailed straight.

"Again, not bad," I said.

"I know."

I stuffed my driver back in my bag and went over and sat on the bench that looked out onto the fake fairway and the Hudson. Boats bobbed in a little marina to our left, and a tug pushed a barge upriver. Overhead, helicopters cruised back and forth on sightseeing tours and business runs.

Liz came over and sat next to me and draped her arm across my shoulders. "Something's bothering you," she said. "You never told me how you made out at this newsletter guy's place in Jersey."

"He had a ton of stuff on IT&E. Pictures of one of their guys paying off bribes for contracts overseas," I said.

"The jackpot."

"Sort of. Shows IT&E is definitely dirty."

"And we're assuming that's the angle Steele was working on?"

"I am."

"But is that any reason for someone to want him dead?" she asked.

"Funny you should ask."

I turned, and she was staring right at me.

"What happened?" she asked.

"You have good instincts," I said.

"You have no idea."

I looked out at the Hudson and the boats moored next to the driving range and thought about how nice it would be to have one. Maybe cruise down the Hudson and out into New York Bay. But there were more pressing matters at the moment.

"We were driving back last night after meeting this guy who, by the way, is nutty," I said.

"Some other time," she said. "Stay on point."

"Of course. We were driving back, and Freddie noticed a car following us."

"And?"

"It followed us across the GWB. When we tried to make a run for it, it sped up and stayed with us."

"Did it follow you home?"

"No."

"Well, that's a relief," she said.

"Freddie lost him."

"Thank God."

"But not before it took a shot at us."

There was silence, and I watched a small cabin cruiser make its way up the middle of the Hudson.

"A shot?" Liz asked after a second.

I turned to see her staring at me.

"Like a gunshot? That kind of shot?" she asked.

"It was," I said.

"And this shot, did it hit anyone or anything?"

"The front of Freddie's Jeep."

She exhaled in relief and turned and looked out at the river. She sat back on the bench, and I watched her carefully. Her legs were crossed and she was looking off into the distance, but I had a feeling she was not really seeing much.

I saw her eyes well up, and I put my arm around her shoulders. She was tense and resisted for a second, which I took as a bad sign. For the first time since we met I felt like I might lose her.

She exhaled slowly and then rested her head on my shoulder; I felt like the worst had passed, at least for the moment.

"Liz," I said, "I can stop poking around in this."

"This car—the one with the person inside who shot at you—did you ever see it before?" she said.

"No. It was a black Mercedes, a sporty model."

"Was this that guy? That Bulger guy Freddie's cousin told you about?" she asked.

"One would think so. But I can't be sure. It was dark; there was no way of getting a license plate or anything."

"And what happened after it, or he, shot at you?"

"We went flying down the Seventy-ninth Street exit, by the boat basin."

"Was anyone hurt?" she said.

The Jeep had jumped the curb after Freddie cut off the guy in the right lane last night. Then we barreled down the narrow off-ramp and jumped the curb again on the right as he lost control of the vehicle. We ended up half on the road and half off, then got out of there real quick.

"No, just a little shaken up."

"I can see why."

We sat and watched the boat traffic in the Hudson and the helicopter traffic crisscrossing the river. It was a quiet, lazy morning and, under normal circumstances, the kind you learn to savor.

"What do you do now?" she asked.

"Either give up or go forward."

"Going forward would mean more danger."

"It probably would," I said.

"And giving up would be walking away knowing you're onto someone and something. Something big."

"Yes again."

"Is this the type of danger where you're going to be looking over your shoulder every time you step outside?" she asked.

"It may be. I was a bit nervous about meeting you, worried someone is watching me and seeing you."

She shuddered, and I wrapped her in a hug and pulled her closer.

"I can stop all this now," I said. "I just stop asking questions, and this probably all goes away."

We were quiet for a few moments. I watched a red tug pushing a barge up the Hudson. After a bit Liz looked up and gave me a kiss on the cheek.

"Don't stop asking questions," she said.

I looked at her. "I will if you want," I said, hoping that she wouldn't ask me to.

"No," she said. "I know what would happen. You'd agree to it and then always resent me for it."

"I like to think I'm bigger than that."

"You might be, but you are only human," she said.

"I was hoping you wouldn't notice."

She smiled. "Besides, can you imagine how you'd feel if some bimbo ended up breaking this thing and not you?"

"The thought has occurred to me."

"This is the most energized I've seen you since we've been together," she said.

"You mean I wasn't energized being the morning-feature guy?" I asked.

"You tried, especially that piece asking motorists about their summer driving plans," she said.

"Hey, I did try to look interested."

"And pulled it off most of the time. But this is you," she said.

"I know."

"You like righting wrongs," she said. "Annoying the powerful."

"It does feel good."

"I can't ask you to go back to being bored for me."

I leaned over and kissed her. "Well, then, you're going to love my next move," I said.

"Is this going to involve guns?"

"Not on my part."

"Maybe I don't want to hear about this just yet."

"There's someone else I need to talk to, some might even call it confronting."

"Uh-oh."

"Yep ... I think it's time to talk to Jack's friends at IT&E. There's no other option."

She put an arm around my shoulder, pulled me close, and kissed me. "We could go to your place and smooch," she said.

"Hmm ... we could."

"Less dangerous than annoying some oil company executives."

We kissed again.

"Or maybe not," I said.

Chapter 29

There are some looks you get from people who have a say in your future that worry you.

This was one of them.

It was from Cal Daniels, who was sitting behind his desk and staring at me as if I had gone mad.

"I don't think this is a good idea," he said.

"I didn't have to tell you my plans," I said.

"No, but you were smart enough to realize that if you didn't, and I got a phone call, then I'd kick your ass right out of here. Which I still hold as an option." Daniels sat back and fiddled with a large, gold golf tee that doubled as a paperweight.

I wanted to pursue IT&E's Buck McConnell, on the premise that someone at the company, maybe even McConnell, was tied to Jack's death.

My boss didn't see the value in that at the moment.

"I thought I made it clear when I said you were embarrassing this network," he said.

"You did."

"And now you want to ambush Buck McConnell?"

"*Ambush* is such an ugly word. I prefer *confront*."

"I prefer *no*, as in, No, you're not going to stick a mic in McConnell's face and question him about some insane conspiracy theory."

"If I'm wrong, fire me."

"It's not you I'm worried about. It's my job I'm getting concerned about. I'm starting to get questions about why I can't control my employees."

I opened my folder and pulled out a couple of the shots I got from Bindagi and slid them across the desk.

"In case you think I'm crazy," I said.

"I do."

"That's Billy Hunter, an IT&E employee. That thing in his hand is a bag full of cash. He's handing it to a representative of the Nigerian government. Three weeks later IT&E wins a billion-dollar contract to be the lead on a new energy plant there."

He put the golf tee down and picked up the pictures and studied them.

"What a coincidence, huh?" I said.

"So what, Buck McConnell is supposed to be able to comment on every one of his employees?" he challenged.

"No, just the ones bribing government officials for contracts."

He flipped through the photos. "What are the other ones?"

"Reps of other countries where IT&E does business. Brazil, Senegal. Different countries, same story. Pay cash, get contract."

"And you got this by going through Jack's stuff?"

"He didn't have the pictures."

"Who did?"

"Some guy who runs a newsletter. He follows graft, bribery, corporate corruption. Jack had been in touch with him about these, but never got them."

He studied the pictures, and I toyed with the idea of telling him someone had chased and shot at me last night. I decided against it. Daniels hears that, and the next thing I know he's calling corporate security or the cops and things become a lot more complicated.

He put the pictures down, sat back, and looked across the desk at me. "Could these"—he nodded at the photos—"be so bad as to drive McConnell, or someone, to kill Jack?"

"I don't know. The Justice Department is cracking down on this stuff big-time. I'm no executive, but my guess is you don't want to be the CEO of a company indicted for handing bribes to some shady third-world government figures," I said.

"Especially if you consider yourself White House material."

"Hard enough to run for president when your equipment is showing up in Iran," I said. "Then try dealing with pictures of one of your guys handing bags of cash to third-world thugs."

"So now you want to ambush McConnell and ask him why he's paying off thugs to get contracts?"

"That's part of it."

"What's the other part?"

"I let McConnell know someone has picked up where Jack left off. Let's see what he, they, whoever, at IT&E does next."

"You want to announce yourself."

"Every action gets a reaction. Let's see what this one is."

Terrance "Buck" McConnell had a reputation of being a nasty SOB. He apparently had that special brand of arrogance associated with men who were born into wealth but believed they were responsible for their own success.

He was the third generation of McConnells running IT&E. It had been founded by the grandfather as an oil rig company, then expanded by Buck's dad, Wilson McConnell, into a larger oil services company, snapping up smaller companies that manufactured parts and equipment for the energy business.

The thing grew like a ballplayer on steroids during the go-go eighties and was handed to Buck McConnell to run a decade ago. McConnell had become one of America's outspoken CEOs, commenting on everything from manufacturing to energy. There had been increasing talk of a Buck McConnell for President movement, but it had never taken hold.

Daniels was back to fiddling with the golf tee. "So that's why you came to me? To tell me you're going to go provoke Buck McConnell?"

"You'll probably get an angry phone call."

He gave me a hard stare. "You damn well better be sure you have something here, Sam. You're running into dangerous territory."

"I'm sure."

"And it's not some Robbie Steele stupidity?"

"Nope."

"Let me make this clear, I want you to understand that you are still a long way away, and I mean light-years away, from accusing Buck McConnell of murder. Do I make myself clear on that?" he said.

"Crystal."

"Good," he said.

"All I want to do is start with the corruption allegations, and I'll work my way from there. See what else crops up once he knows I have hard evidence," I said.

"It's one thing to have evidence of bribery. It's another to accuse a CEO of murder."

"I understand," I said. "And I'm not there yet."

"But that's where you're heading."

"Possibly," I said.

Chapter 30

An hour later we were parked in a spot on the north side of Fifty-third, around the corner from the Sheraton on Seventh Avenue. Buck McConnell was scheduled to be the keynote speaker at an energy conference for Wall Street types at the hotel.

I'd be stopping in to say hello. Freddie would be along to record McConnell's reaction and to add to the drama of the moment.

"I'm going to want the whole shebang on this," I said as he jockeyed to get closer to the curb.

"The whole shebang?" he said.

"The works. Lights blazing. Cameras rolling."

"The full in-your-face thing?"

"Yes."

"I call that the Intimidation Package," he said.

"That's what I'm paying for."

"Like I been paid. I got nada. Nothing," he said.

"Not true, you get to work with a TV personality."

"Like I said, I got zip."

We sat for a moment, and I went over my notes, checking the pictures and making sure I had a game plan.

"When we're inside, maybe we can ask someone if they know who shot my Jeep," Freddie said.

"Not sure if that would be prudent."

"You shoot my car, you pay," he said.

"I didn't shoot your car."

"You know what I mean. Someone pinged me pretty good."

"You did a masterful job of driving," I said.

"Don't be trying to change the subject."

"Calm, collected, and in control."

"Someone's got to pay for the hole in my hood," he said.

"You were steely and steady. Steady and steely."

"What the hell am I supposed to do? Go to Allstate and say someone shot my car?"

"Only if Allstate is your carrier."

We got out, walked around the back and opened the rear hatch so Freddie could check the camera to make sure everything was in working order. I flipped again through the folder I had with the pictures from Herman of Billy Hunter.

"So, after you piss 'em off, then what?" Freddie asked.

"Good question."

"But no answer."

"Not yet, at least."

"Maybe get your ass fired," he said.

"Just think of all the free time I'll have to spend with you."

He closed the back, and we started down the street toward Seventh.

"You ready for this guy?"

"The question is, Is he ready for me?"

"Oh, brother," Freddie said.

The sidewalk outside the Sheraton was busy with tourists, clustered in little groups and trying to decide whether to walk in the heat or take a cab.

We went inside, cut through the crowd, and walked all the way to the back to the escalator up to the second floor and the ballrooms. We stepped off into a mostly empty and quiet foyer area. The doors to the ballrooms were closed, and there were a few long desks set up for the event's registration. They were manned by bored-looking PR types, all busy texting and talking.

Everyone perked up as we approached, and they perked up even more as we blew past their tables and ignored their calls of "Hello, may I help you?"

Freddie had the camera on his shoulder, and the two of us looked like we were about to breach security and walk straight into the inner sanctum of the ballroom, where very important people were discussing very important topics.

A young woman in a tight dress raced toward me from my left. "Hello ... hello ... may I help you?"

A slick guy in a suit closed in on us from the right. "Whoa, whoa."

This was a major offensive by the enemy, a flat-out code red. And we had caught them flat-footed, and they were scrambling to recover.

I had just gotten a hand on the hardware of the ballroom door when the when the young gal caught up with us and tried to block me from opening it.

"I'm sorry, cameras aren't allowed inside," she said.

"I'm here to see Buck McConnell. He's expecting us," I said.

It was a good-size lie right off the bat, and it occurred to me this was no way to start a relationship. She gave me one of those skeptical looks young professionals who deal with the press are trained to deliver.

"And you are?" she said.

"Oh, that hurts," Freddie said from behind me.

I handed her my Liberty News ID and a business card as more of her peers came over, silently multiplying, as if they had been beamed in as backup.

The girl looked at me, then Freddie. He winked at her, and she blushed as she handed my ID back.

"There are no cameras allowed inside," Tight Dress said.

"Are you even registered for this event?" Slick asked from the other side.

At the far end of the lobby to my right a ballroom door was flung open and out charged a middle-aged man. Tight Dress and Slick seemed relieved. The general was on his way.

He was bald and dressed in a suit and was charging hard toward us, like he had a rocket attached to his ass. If I had to bet, I'd say this was Stuart Ripley. He had probably been alerted by one of the minions that all hell was breaking loose.

He sped toward us with a phone in one hand and a manila folder in the other. Freddie had the camera on his shoulder, the light on top blazing and recorded the guy as he steamed our way.

"Is there something I can help you with?" he yelled in a dramatic tone as he closed in on us.

"Yes, you can ask your underlings to step out of the way and stop hassling me and my cameraman," I said.

He came right up to me and stood in my face, leaving me no personal space. It was play 101 from the PR handbook. Try to intimidate the pushy reporter. I inched toward him so our noses were almost touching.

He glared at me, and I looked back at him for an uncomfortable moment.

"We're going to have to dance or kiss, chief. What's it going to be," I said.

He had a round little face that went from red to crimson. He was not amused.

"May I see some ID?" he demanded.

I handed him my ID and had to step back to make a little space to do so. "I'm here to speak to Buck McConnell," I said as he stared at it.

"I don't think so," he said, handing my ID back.

"I do think so. He's expecting us."

"Oh, really?"

"Yes, I set it up with Stuart Ripley, his PR guy," I said.

That was my first lie to Stuart, and I felt kind of bad about it. And as I expected, he assumed a look of smugness, as if it were the greatest thing that he had caught me in a lie.

"Oh, really?" he asked again.

"Yes," I said.

"Well, I'm Stuart Ripley," he said.

I stuck out my hand. "Stu, nice to meet you. Sam North, Liberty News."

He shook my hand more out of habit than desire. "You didn't set anything up," he said.

"You don't remember?" I asked.

He was shaking his head in a very disappointed schoolteacher sort of way. "Nice try," he said.

"If you say so."

"You can leave now," he said.

"Sure, after I speak with Buck."

"Mr. McConnell is not available," he said.

"But he will be, right? After he gives his little speech inside?"

"No. Wrong. And just so you understand, we as a matter of policy do not speak to, or engage with, anyone from Liberty News," he said.

"Oh, geez, that is too bad. See, I've taken over some of Jack Steele's stories, and I have all this great stuff on IT&E."

"That's nice."

"And I need to get some reaction from Buck on a few things I've dug up," I said.

"As I said, Mr. McConnell is not available," Ripley said.

"Then how am I going to get his reaction to this?" I asked, opening up my folder and flipping through the pictures of Billy Hunter. I came to the one of Hunter and the Nigerian middleman and held it up for Ripley to see.

He went to take it, and I pulled it back.

"Whoa, we don't grab," I said.

"I wasn't grabbing."

"This is the only copy I have. Something happens to it and I'm out of luck."

The PR minions had edged closer, eager to get a look at Exhibit A.

I held on to it and turned it around so Ripley could see it. The minions assembled around him to study it.

"I have no idea who these people are, or what this is about," Ripley said.

"Let me help you out, Stu. That big guy there? He's a coworker of yours. Billy Hunter."

"IT&E has more than ninety-thousand employees in the U.S. and around the world, Mr. North."

"But Hunter is the only one I'm asking about."

"You do have a point to all this, I assume," he said.

"Hunter's official title is senior VP of international market research and expansion," I said.

"I don't know about that."

"But that's an awful lot to fit on a business card, so I'd like to suggest ... bagman."

"I'm sorry, but I don't follow," Ripley said.

"Hunter is one of your guys who makes payoffs to overseas governments. Also called bribes. How's that? That clear things up for you?"

"No, not particularly."

"He's freaking IT&E's Santa Claus overseas, except no one has to sit on his lap to get what they want."

"I'm sorry, but I—"

"That guy with him in the picture? That's some lackey for the Nigerian government. That bag in Hunter's hand? The one he's about to hand to the other guy? That's filled with cash. Cold, hard naira. That's Nigerian money, Stu," I said.

He stared hard at the picture as I made it clear.

"Your guy Hunter is paying off a representative of the Nigerian government. And I got the picture to prove it," I said.

Ripley shuddered, stepped back, and took on a more detached, formal tone. "I'm sorry, but I will have to look into this and get back to you," he said.

"Hah," I said, loud enough to startle the minions. "Isn't that precious? *Now* you want some time to look into it." I flipped though my folder while I continued to speak.

"And maybe while you're at it you can check this baby out as well," I said, holding up the shot of Hunter and the guy in the Middle

Eastern dress. "Maybe tell us what country he's with and why the hell Hunter is handing him that shopping bag full of cash."

Ripley was flustered, trying to play defense as best he could. "As I said, I will look into it," he said.

"Geez, no wonder your stuff ends up in terrorist hands when you have a loose cannon like Hunter running around handing out bags of money," I said.

Ripley looked like a pipe had just burst in his head. His eyes narrowed, and the crimson returned to his skin; he sputtered as he spoke. "We ... we do not ..."

"It's Payoffs 'R' Us, Stu. That's what you should call Hunter's unit. Bribes for contracts, how do you respond to that?"

On cue, Freddie stepped in closer than was necessary and just about jammed the camera in Ripley's face. Ripley reached up to push it away.

"Turn that off," he yelled.

Freddie smacked his hand aside with a violent shove. "Don't touch the fucking camera unless you want your arm broken," he said.

Ripley pulled his hand back and stumbled backward. We had him on the ropes, and Freddie handed me the handheld mic he had been carrying. I stepped forward and jammed it under Ripley's chin.

"What is IT&E's response to these photos that clearly show an IT&E employee engaged in bribery with representatives of foreign governments, some of which are hostile to the United States?" I asked.

Ripley managed to look both terrified and enraged, like he was being attacked and couldn't figure a way out.

At the far end of the foyer one of Ripley's PR peons was racing over with a guy in a suit. He had to be security, either the Sheraton's or IT&E's.

But it was okay, I had only one more grenade to toss. I made sure the mic was right at Ripley's thin lips and let it go.

"I'll ask you again," I said, much louder than necessary, "why has Buck McConnell authorized the use of bribery to win government contracts from foreign governments, some of which are unstable and not friendly to the United States?"

Ripley's little face was all rage and he stammered. "We ... he ... Mr. McConnell has not authorized—"

"So the CEO of IT&E has no idea bribery is being used by his people?" I asked.

Ripley seemed to shut down. His mouth opened but nothing came out. He tried again and still nothing.

It was like watching a dog trying to catch flies.

A big hand came in from the side, landed on my wrist, and pulled the mic back.

"That's all," the security guy said.

"I need a response from Buck McConnell, Stu. I need it now, or I go on TV this afternoon and show off these pictures," I said.

"I ... I ..." Ripley was staggered.

I handed him a business card, which he took without thinking. "You have one hour, Stu. Then I'm on. Live. Pictures and all."

Chapter 31

It was forty-five minutes later when the call came. Freddie and I were sitting in the Cherokee, betting on whether or not Ripley would call. He did.

"Guess where we're going?" I asked.

"Penthouse," Freddie said.

"Nope. Presidential suite," I said.

"First step to being president, rent the suite."

"Twenty-first floor. Let's go rattle the cage," I said.

Less than ten minutes later we stepped into the living room of the presidential suite. A large security guard greeted us as the door, and as he eyed us I half expected to be frisked.

"I'm feeling very unwelcome," I said to Freddie.

Freddie gave the guy a hard stare back. "Poor interpersonal skills on our host's part," he said.

There was a matching security guard in what looked to be the same navy suit sitting at a little round table in the far corner of the room that looked down on Times Square to the south.

"Look, bookends," I said.

The greeter's eyes narrowed like he wanted to hit me very hard. Luckily, Ripley came over to save me.

"Mr. McConnell is in the other room on a call. He'll speak to you when he's free," he said.

"Good, because if he's going to be expensive, I don't think I can afford it," I said.

Ripley stared at me like he was new to the language.

Freddie shook his head and took a seat on the couch that had its back to the windows. "Man, humor is supposed to break the tension, not increase it," he said.

It was just the four of us in the big room, and it was tense. The kind of tense PR types get when the big boss is around and not happy and somehow or another it's their fault.

"There are some ground rules we need to go over," Ripley said.

"It's a double if a fan reaches over and touches a ball in play, right?"

Freddie snorted a half laugh from the couch. Ripley failed again to see the humor in my words.

Ripley glanced at Freddie. "No camera when you go to talk to Mr. McConnell."

"What?" I said.

"Just you and pen and pad. That's the best we can do."

I waved my folder with the pictures. "And this is the best I can do," I said. "I should just go on the air with these and say you wouldn't comment."

Ripley said nothing, but it was fine. I hadn't expected to get McConnell on camera, and it wasn't really all that important. My push back was more for effect and to give Ripley a hard time.

"Like I said, that's the best I could do," Ripley said.

I looked over at Freddie, who had helped himself to an apple from the fruit bowl on the table.

"It's okay. I can stay out here and discuss staring techniques with these two," he said, smiling at the security goons.

"And I need to hear and approve exactly how you're going to characterize Mr. McConnell's response to your presenting of these photos."

"You want to know what I'm going to say on air?"

"Yes. I'll need to approve it."

"That's not going to happen."

Ripley's face reddened. Not the crimson from downstairs, just a few shades of medium red as he worked himself up for another battle. "Then we have no agreement, and we have no interview with Mr. McConnell," he said.

I waved my folder again and was starting to like doing it. It was a nice prop to have, and it seemed to drive Ripley nuts. "And we have no Buck seeing what I got in here. I'll just say IT&E refused to comment on the photos."

I looked over at Freddie. "Come on, trusty cameraman, we're out of here."

Freddie put the half-eaten apple on the table, got up, and grabbed his camera.

"Trusty cameraman?" he said. "Hell, that's what I am now?"

He walked across the room while Ripley and I engaged in a stare down. I realized then Ripley's face was ferret-like, a little round face with a pointed nose. It had been bugging me since we met downstairs. What animal did he resemble? He was a ferret.

I turned to leave, and Freddie was with me.

"At least you didn't call me your trusty sidekick," he said.

"You're a highly skilled professional. I wanted to convey that," I said.

Ripley's voice cackled from behind me. "Okay," he said. "I can be flexible."

I turned around smiled. "I knew you would be," I said.

And I had. There was no way Ripley was going to allow me to walk out the door without McConnell getting a look at the pictures. He had told his boss about them, and they were important enough that McConnell had to see them. Ripley blows this and McConnell would be all over him.

Ripley's phone rang as we walked back into the main room. Freddie sat down and started in on his apple again; Ripley looked at me and held up a finger like the big moment was here.

He got off the call and pointed to a closed door down a hallway to my right.

"You can go into the back room. Mr. McConnell is waiting for you."

I exchanged a glance with Freddie and turned and walked down the hall, past a bathroom larger than my first Manhattan apartment, and came to the closed door. It opened into an expansive bedroom that featured windows that wrapped around and looked down on Times Square and also west so you could see the Hudson in the distance and the flatlands of Jersey beyond that.

Standing in the middle of the room was Terrance "Buck" McConnell.

He was slightly taller than me, maybe six two, with the build of an athlete. Lean and in shape. His face was red and weathered, like someone who spent a lot of time outdoors. He had to be in his early sixties but didn't look it. His hair was brown and short and so neatly styled I thought it was probably trimmed every Monday morning. It would be my guess that his nails were worked on at the same time.

He was dressed in the gray pants of a suit, with a white shirt and a red-and-blue-striped tie that was perfectly knotted. Even his teeth were perfect. Large, white, and square.

He had the appearance of a baby boomer who had it all. Health, looks, and success.

I walked to him and extended a hand. "Sam North," I said.

"Sam, nice to meet you," he lied in a businesslike tone.

"You don't have to pretend to be cordial," I said while we were still shaking hands.

I felt his grip tighten before we stopped shaking. "I don't know what you're talking about, son," he said, and you could hear the Texas in his voice.

"In case Stuart hasn't told you, I'm picking up where Jack Steele left off."

"Good for you. Let's hope the weight of being a big TV star doesn't get to you as well," he said. "Fame can be a burden, you know."

"So can reporting on your company," I said.

"I'm not quite sure I know what you mean," he said.

His eyes were hard and his face taut. I could see his jaw tightening. He was used to being in charge and didn't appreciate someone occupying such a lowly position as reporter walking up to him and getting in his face.

"I got a stack of photos here showing one of your boys running around handing out duffel bags full of cash. Same stuff Jack was going after before fame suddenly became too much for him."

I opened the folder and leafed through the pictures and handed the first one to him.

"That guy there, the one with the bag, which is full of cash, is Billy Hunter. He's one of yours. Maybe you two bumped into each other at the holiday party or something."

He looked up from the picture and gave me the stare again. "Got a pretty flip manner about you, don't you, boy?"

"From son to boy," I said. "I hate getting demoted."

That got me more of the hard stare.

"What I want to know is where Hunter gets his energy from," I said. "I mean, it's got to be exhausting running around to these third-world countries handing out millions of dollars in bribes to thugs so IT&E can score contracts."

"I don't know what you're talking about."

"I'm talking about IT&E stuffing bribes in the pockets of thugs, maybe even some enemies of America."

I showed him the rest of the photos, and he leafed through them as I spoke.

"Is Billy Hunter an IT&E employee?" I asked.

"We got a lot of employees, more than ninety thousand."

"But not all of them offer bribes, right?"

He handed me back the pictures. "Sorry, but I can't help you with this," he said.

"What's a bribery scandal going to do to your run for the White House, Buck?" I asked.

He stepped closer. "There is no bribery scandal far as I can see," he said.

"You know what people are going to say: If this is how he runs IT&E, how the hell will he run the country?"

"You need to be real careful here."

"Hell, if more of this bribery stuff starts showing up on the campaign trail, you don't make it to the first debate," I said.

"You're making a big mistake," he said. "A real big mistake."

"And hell, everyone makes it to the first debate," I said. "There's like ten guys who get invited to that one. I'll probably get a spot before you do."

He moved even closer, and I could smell the stale coffee and cigarette on his breath. It was time for some good, old-fashioned, don't-mess-with-Texas talk.

"This is probably where you want to stop yourself before you say something that could end your career," he said.

"Self-control has never been a strong suit."

"There's a surprise." He stared at me and gestured toward the folder I was holding. "Something you may want to know, it might mean something to your photos there," he said. "Year or so ago a guy —some blogger or Web site guy or something—tries to blackmail us with a picture he says was of one of our employees caught doing something illegal."

I hesitated, and Buck went for the kill.

"Turns out the idiot had pictures of a guy who was a sub-subcontractor for us trying to pay off some low-level clown of some state in India."

He had me confused, and he knew it.

"The hot shot overplayed his hand, big-time," he said. "We went straight to the Feds. Turns out the guy in the picture wasn't even contracted out to us at the time of the photo. So Mr. Whistleblower had nothing except an attempted extortion charge to show for his efforts."

"I'm not talking about then, what about this guy?" I said, gesturing with the folder. "What about Billy Hunter?"

He shook his head. "Don't know a thing about him," he said. "But

I'd be real careful about believing all of the crap that's said about my company, understand?"

"I only need to believe the part about your boy Hunter and his bribes."

"I'll tell you again. You want to be real careful here, son. Real careful."

"You telling me not to run something?"

"I'm telling you that little newsletter guy was wrong. You want to play games with me, you better know you're right."

Chapter 32

"So does Hunter work for IT&E or not?" Freddie asked.

"I have no idea," I said. "All I know is that McConnell wasn't even fazed by the pictures."

We were on Seventh Avenue stopped at the light on the corner of Fiftieth Street.

"Grace under pressure," Freddie said.

"No, it was like he knew what was coming. Ripley prepped him, and he had time to make some calls and sit down and figure out a response."

I pounded the dashboard with a fist. "Son of a bitch," I said.

"Hey, hey," Freddie said, "easy on the car. And the language. I try to run a family car service here."

"I was sure I had him. But I blew it. Gave him too much damn time to come up with a response."

"The mouth again. Watch the mouth," Freddie said.

"Should have played it differently," I said.

"And maybe check out Herman the blackmailer before taking his word," he said.

"That could be a problem."

"Could be?"

"We don't know if Herman was blackmailing him. We don't know if anyone was blackmailing him, or IT&E," I said.

"Made it up to confuse your ass," he said.

"Possibly, or to slow me down."

We drove on down Seventh, heading into Times Square. The sidewalks were thick with tourists, despite the heat and humidity.

"You ask him why he had someone shoot my car?" Freddie said.

"I forgot."

"Always thinking of yourself."

"Plus, we don't know it was him," I said.

"What the hell do we know at this point?" he asked.

"We know that Steele died a couple of weeks ago. We know he was chasing this story on IT&E. We know he was supposed to meet Herman Bindagi, but Herman got nervous and canceled. We know that IT&E was well aware of Jack's desire to nail them. Plus, we know that as soon as I picked up the ball and started asking people about what was going on in Jack's life, people started coming after me. We know the guy wearing the fedora warned me, and we know the guy wearing the fedora gets paid by IT&E," I said.

"Don't forget the car," he said.

"Yes, we know someone shot your Grand Cherokee."

"Makes it sound like the car was the intended target."

"Okay, we know that, thanks to your skillful, evasive driving skills, someone shot your Grand Cherokee when otherwise it could have been you or me. How's that?" I asked.

"Much better."

We stopped at the light at Forty-sixth, and a sea of people crossed in front of us.

"He was calm and cool and scripted when I showed him the pictures. He handed them back and just flat-out said he had no idea about any of it. It was like the pictures of one his employees handing out bribes didn't even bother him," I said.

"Maybe wasn't one of his employees," he said.

"I thought of that. But I checked Hunter out as best I could. He works there. Or worked there, at least."

"Then maybe wasn't bribes he was handing out."

"Yes, it was probably tips, for jobs well done. Or maybe their bonuses."

"Never know."

We were moving again, slowly, through Times Square.

"Only time McConnell came close to losing control was when I got in his face and said it was a good story. Said if he ran for president and this came out, people would question whether he should be running the country. That really tweaked him off."

"Tweak me off, too, you come into my presidential suite and start pissing on my presidential dreams," Freddie said.

"So he handles the question about the pictures easily, but gets nasty when I bring up the idea of this hurting a possible presidential bid. What's all this tell us?"

"That you can be annoying?"

"Keep in mind that you are easily replaceable. Lots of shooters looking for wonderful freelance opportunities like this," I said.

"Not like fortysomething male reporters are in short supply, either," he said.

We were stuck in traffic at the light at Forty-second now. To my right a couple of mounted cops had their horses on the street in front of the Reuters Building, talking to the tourists and posing for pictures.

"This tells me you need a hell of lot more if you want to bust Buck McConnell," he said.

"Yes, it does. But there has to be something we're missing here," I said.

"Maybe old Buck was expecting something a lot worse," Freddie said.

Traffic opened up a bit, and we cruised down Seventh toward Madison Square Garden. We were at the corner of Thirty-fifth, and the early commuters were streaming down Seventh toward Penn Station.

I looked over at Freddie and said, "You may be onto something."

"Don't need to sound so surprised," he said.

Chapter 33

Susan's desk outside Daniels's office was empty. The gatekeeper had been given a reprieve for the night, or so I thought.

"Don't even think of trying to go in there without going through me," she said from behind me.

I turned to see her approaching with a coffee mug.

"Don't you ever go home?" I asked.

"No. Not until the boss man dismisses me," she said.

I looked at the mug.

"Green tea," she said. "He's concerned about his health all of a sudden."

"It's stressful being the king."

"Please tell me you came over to shoot the breeze with me, you good-looking pain in the ass."

"If only."

"Damn. I knew it. It's always Cal, Cal, Cal with everyone. I'm just the pretty face at the door."

"Eye candy, as they say in the biz," I said.

It was almost seven, and I was delivering on a promise to Daniels. I was to fill him in on what happened with McConnell.

"What do I have to do to get an audience?" I asked.

"Thought you'd never ask," she said.

She winked, went to the door, and poked her head in.

"Prince Charming is here, shall I send him in?" She turned back to me and said, "Enter at your own risk."

I walked in, and Daniels was staring at the wall of monitors, watching Liberty and all the cable competition.

"I saw McConnell," I said as I sat down.

"I know."

"He dismissed the photos."

Daniels eyes finally left the TVs and landed on me.

"I got a call," he said, taking a drink of his green tea.

The evening sky in the windows behind him was a brown haze, one of those unhealthy mixes of humidity and stagnant air.

"From McConnell?" I asked.

He shook his head.

"Ripley?"

Another shake of the head.

"How many more guesses do I get?" I asked.

"Try the Feds," he said.

"My tax dollars at work."

"I wish I could have a sense of humor about it," he said.

"What'd they want?"

He sat back and glanced at the TVs. One of our junior flamethrowers, a Jack Steele in training, was opening his show. Rick Applebaum was no more than forty and well on his way to cable-news stardom, or at least he thought so. He had the thick, it-might-be-fake it-might-be-real hair and a very strong sense of self-importance. Both were big pluses in the business.

Daniels looked back at me. "Where are the pictures?" he asked.

"I have them."

"Yes, I assumed as much. Where?"

"Why?"

"How about, being that I'm your boss, you answer my question." he said. He was sitting forward now, leaning over the desk.

"I'm a little nervous."

"You should be," he said.

"Why do you want the pictures?"

He gave me the stare that was essentially asking me to reconsider my answer and save myself. It was a nice gesture, but one I ignored.

"Cal, I have only one copy of these things. As far as I know they are the only copies, at least according to my source."

"Your source is a goddamned extortionist," he yelled.

"One, we don't know that for sure. And two, he'd probably prefer entrepreneur."

Daniels took a slug of green tea, looked at me, and shook his head. "You got some balls. I want those pictures in here," he said, taping his desk, "on this desk, in thirty minutes."

The pictures were resting securely in a locked drawer in my desk downstairs in the newsroom.

"Why do you need them?" I asked.

"Because I do."

"You want to turn them over to the Feds?"

"I do," he said.

"Then I'm not giving them up," I said.

"Then they'll issue a subpoena for them. Following that, I'll fire you."

"I dug to find them. I get to keep them. If the Feds were so vigilant and so concerned, how come they didn't find them?"

He said nothing for a few moments, and I used the time to come up with some semblance of a game plan.

"Give me a day to verify them. If I do, I get to go on the air with the story. If I don't, I hand them to you, and you give them to the Feds."

"You're mistaking this for a negotiation; it's not. I issued you an order," he said.

"And I defied it."

"You realize I can throw your ass out the door right now and have you escorted from the building for good," he said.

"I do. But you won't."

"No?"

"I'll take the photos and walk into CNBC, CNN, or some other newsroom, and they'll be on the air in a few hours."

He sipped his tea and looked at me with a face that was flushed red but gave no hint of emotion. After a few seconds he was ready.

"Here is my one and only offer," he said. "You have twenty-four hours from right now, seven ten p.m., to verify that yes, the guy in the pictures is or was an IT&E employee."

I was about to speak but he kept going.

"With an admission that yes, he was bribing some foreign official on behalf of IT&E," he said.

"I can live with that," I said.

"You get to go on the air, use the photos, and break the story," he said.

"So long as we agree that I give you the pictures only after I'm off the air," I said.

"Thanks for the trust," he said.

"Got to cover myself."

"You don't pin it down by this time tomorrow night, you hand me the photos," he said.

I made a mental note to make copies of these things as soon as I walked out the door tonight. "I'll confirm it," I said.

"Must be nice to be confident," he said.

Five minutes later I was down at my desk with the phone pressed to my ear. "Detective Pep Rinaldi," I said when the desk sergeant picked up.

Chapter 34

"Let me introduce you to William S. Hunter, better known as Billy," Rinaldi said, sliding a sheet of paper across a desk in a dreary, gray office in the back of the Thirteenth Precinct. It was nine thirty Wednesday morning. I now had about nine and a half hours to verify Hunter and confirm the bribe photos.

"Last known address 137 Ridgeview Lane, New Paltz, New York," Rinaldi said.

"And you're sure this is the Billy Hunter I'm looking for?" I asked.

"You forget I do this for a living," he said, gesturing to the gunmetal-gray desk and battered gray filing cabinets along the wall. "Or you think maybe I just like to come in here to take advantage of the luxurious office space?"

"What's a world traveler doing in a little college town upstate?"

"Tending bar, apparently," he said. "He's lived all over: Tucson ... Austin, Texas. Was born in Newburgh, New York, so maybe this is his idea of returning home to settle down."

"His work done for IT&E," I said.

I looked at the sheet and saw the line for present employment. P&G's, Main Street, New Paltz, New York. "How long has he been back in the good old U.S. of A.?"

"Passport hasn't been stamped since April. Looks like he came home end of March and hasn't left since. Maybe he's pursuing a degree at that fine academic institution up there," he said.

"Yes, international studies," I said.

"You going to tell me why you need this information now?" he asked.

"Can't. It's top secret. Part of a special investigative series," I said.

"I see. Is it anything the authorities should be aware of?" he said.

"Not at all."

"Why don't I believe any of this?"

"Because you've known me for thirty-some-odd years?"

"Yes, that's it," he said. "You've never been a good liar."

"I'll try to improve."

"You'll keep me informed if this gets a little tricky?" he said.

"I will," I said.

"Is this little investigation a solo effort?"

"No, I have a very competent and able cameraman, enforcer, and a regular man-about-town looking after me."

"That makes me feel better."

"Me, too."

Forty-five minutes later we were riding up the New York State Thruway past the Harriman Exit, where the road opened up and everyone instinctively stated driving faster, like they had been freed from the constraints of the stop and go around the city and could let loose.

Frequent checks in the side-view mirror indicated that we making this trip unescorted. "What if we can't find Billy?" Freddie asked.

"Must you always be the pessimist?"

"Long way to go for me to shoot an empty house," he said.

"You can go walk the campus, see if any of the summer students think you're a professor."

"Professor Freddie," he said. "Maybe meet a cute co-ed."

"Tell her about your class. Introduction to BS."

"I also teach the advanced BS course," he said.

"I've noticed."

"Okay, so let's say Billy's around," he said.

"That's my hope."

"You think he's gonna say, 'Yeah, sure, I'll go on camera and tell you everything'?"

"A man can dream, can't he?" I asked.

Freddie shook his head. "Absolutely no clue," he muttered.

"Don't take away my dream," I said.

"Pathetic," he said.

P&G's had the look and feel of a college bar. It was nestled on a corner of Main Street, which wound downhill with little stores, a bakery, and other bars lining both sides. The area had the funky, progressive feel of a college town and was framed against the backdrop of the Shawangunk Mountains off in the distance.

It was noon when we walked in and took two seats at the nearly empty bar. And there at the end of the bar, counting cash, was our very own Billy Hunter.

"Appropriate," Freddie said when he spotted Hunter with the money.

"At home anywhere there's cash, apparently," I said.

Hunter was oblivious to his two new customers and went on counting the cash drawer. Only when he was done did he look up and spot us. He made his way down the bar and tossed two coasters in front of us.

"Drink, guys?" he asked.

I ordered a glass of something called New Paltz Crimson Lager brewed by Gilded Otter while Freddie ordered a bottle of Heineken. I waited for Hunter to go down to the other end of the bar to pour my beer, then opened my folder and selected a copy of the shot of Hunter and the guy in the Middle Eastern attire.

I put the photo on the bar between Freddie and me.

"Here goes," I said.

"Pin out of grenade. Grenade tossed," Freddie said.

We watched Hunter make his way back to us with a drink in each hand. He was putting them on the old wooden bar when he froze, my glass an inch off the surface of the bar. It was like someone had unplugged him for a moment; he just stood there staring at the shot.

After a long moment he placed the drinks on the bar and glared at me. "What the fuck is this?"

"Whaaaaat?" I said. "What are ya talking about, Billy?"

He snatched up the picture, examined it, then peered at me.

"No way you two are cops," he said.

"Obviously not a viewer," Freddie said.

I extended a hand across the bar, but Billy didn't shake it.

"Sam North, with Liberty News. This here is Freddie. You don't need to know his last name. Heck, I'm not even sure he has one," I said.

Hunter flipped the picture back on the bar like it was a coaster and glanced down to where an older guy sat reading the paper and drinking from a coffee mug. His gaze then shifted past us and out into the dining room and toward the windows and door that looked out onto Main Street.

"You want to tell me what this is all about?" he asked.

"I was hoping you could do the same," I said.

I sampled my lager. It was clean and refreshing and quite good for a local brew.

"You need to tell me where you got this," he said, leaning over the bar and trying to be intimidating.

He was a pretty big guy, and the intimidation thing seemed to come easily to him. I had some more of the lager, savored it for a second, then put the glass down.

"So worldly, yet so naive," I said.

Freddie chuckled and looked straight ahead at the mirror behind the bar. Hunter stared at me like he wanted to come across the bar and hit me, maybe more than once.

"Billy, you were handing a foreign government official a sack of cash," I said. "We got a shot of it and are about to air it live, on national TV. Billy Hunter, bagman for Buck McConnell and IT&E. And you're copping an attitude with me?"

His face tightened up, and I assumed this was where he'd punch someone causing trouble for him about his past.

"Look," I said. "You've been overseas so much, immersed in different cultures, so you're probably a little rusty on how this works here in the U.S."

That got another snicker from Freddie as he took a pull on his beer.

"See, I have pictures of you breaking U.S. laws," I said. "I happen to be a TV reporter, which means I go on TV and say things. Later today, I am going to go on national TV and say Billy Hunter was delivering bribes for Buck McConnell, the CEO of IT&E."

"I'll sue your ass," he said.

"I'm sorry you feel that way."

"Sue you until you have nothing left," he said.

"Don't have too far to go," Freddie said.

I shot him a glance. "Thanks, friend."

"Ain't no friend," he said.

"Apparently," I said, "but let's not bicker in front of our new bud Billy."

I turned back to Hunter and heard the door open behind me. Hunter's eyes scanned the new arrivals then came back to me.

"What I need, Billy, is a yes or no from you."

"You ain't getting shit."

"Let me try this again," I said. "I have photos—plural—of you delivering money in big sacks. Hell, I even know the story of the car stuffed with cash, so I got you dead to rights. Now, the question is, were you authorized to do all this by Buck McConnell?"

"Like I talk to the CEO," he said.

I looked at Freddie, who was turned around in his seat and looking at the two young women who had taken a table out in the dining room.

"Am I not being clear?" I asked Freddie.

"About what?"

"Never mind. Billy, I probably should tell you that the Feds want the photos now," I said and watched his face for reaction.

There was a hint of tension, but not a lot.

"I'll just deny everything," he said.

"So ... what? That's like a body double or something in the picture?"

He hesitated, knowing he had no leverage.

He stood up straight, took a moment, and looked at me. He was used to dealing with thugs and local customs, and now he was using those very skills to get a handle on what his options were here. I knew he didn't have any. That finally dawned on him, too, a few second later.

"What do you want?" he asked.

Chapter 35

It was close to two, and we were on our way back down the thruway. I had five hours to be in Daniels's office with confirmation and proof that Buck McConnell and IT&E routinely bribed foreign government officials to win contracts.

I had it.

Hunter had said so, I had it recorded, and I was feeling pretty good.

"Remember when these were tapes?" I asked, waving the little memory card that held the interview with Billy Hunter.

"You sound like my grandfather when I was ten. I remember when ..."

"You saying I'm old?"

"No, I'm saying you sound like my grandfather. You losing your hearing now, too?"

It was hard not to be giddy. I was the proud owner of an interview with Billy Hunter, in which he had admitted to making more than a dozen bribes to various government officials—everywhere from Nigeria to Brazil—for IT&E.

He went on record saying that on two specific occasions he was told to pay whatever he had to pay per orders of the "man in charge."

He had been fired by IT&E six months ago, and once he was warmed up, he had no qualms about trashing McConnell and the company.

"So Billy says he was senior VP for bribes," Freddie said.

"Appears that way."

"You go on with his story and now you're really all over McConnell."

"I am."

"What's McConnell going to do next?"

"That's what I'm hoping to find out. I got a damn good story here. Let's see how he pushes back," I said.

"You think there's enough there to derail a presidential bid?" he asked.

"Maybe. Depends on where it goes after I break it."

"He'll probably blame it on an underling," he said. "That's what all these assholes do. CEOs, they know how to survive shit."

"It is always the peons who pay for this stuff," I said.

The thruway traffic was light up here; we were far enough north of the city that even with only two lanes in both directions we were still cruising along.

"There is something that bugs me," I said.

"Feel free to keep it to yourself."

"This whole thing with Herman."

"The blackmailer," Freddie said.

"We don't know if that was him. If it was, and he got nailed, why would he try it again?"

"Exceedingly dumb?"

"I don't think so. Hunter copped to everything, so Herman's pictures were legit."

"You call him to tell him you found Hunter?"

"Tried before. No one picked up. Just rang and rang."

"Maybe he went out for some fresh air, turned over a new leaf."

"I don't know ..." I said.

We were quiet for a moment before Freddie spoke up.

"I know where you're heading with this, and I don't like it," he said.

"Come on. It will just take a moment. We're already on this side of the Hudson."

"Got me visiting shut-ins now," Freddie said. "My social life is really suffering, hanging around with you."

"Maybe you can come inside this time," I said. "You know, see the place."

"No, thank you," he said.

"I'll tell Daniels we're on our way back. We'll be back by four, latest; that'll give me three hours before I make my triumphant return to his office with my award-winning interview nailing McConnell."

We continued down the thruway and made our way onto the Palisades Parkway south to the GWB, then headed once again out to Teaneck. A little after two thirty we were driving down Sherman Lane and parking in front of the Bindagi residence.

The street was quiet. People at work or inside to beat the heat. We walked up the front steps, I rang the doorbell, and we stood there in silence waiting for some sign of life. There was none.

"No one's home," Freddie said. "Let's go."

"This happened the other night. Herm's a little slow to the door. He'll probably peer out in a second."

"Place gives me the creeps," he said.

I tried the bell, then knocked, and still nothing. We had been standing there for probably five minutes now.

"Okay, I'm a little concerned," I said.

"I'm a lot concerned," Freddie said, looking down the street.

I pressed my face to the window where Herman had peered out of the other night but couldn't see a thing inside.

"Let's go around back, see what we find," I said.

"Don't want to be finding a pit bull," Freddie said.

"C'mon, you're supposed to be a big tough Rican from the Bronx."

"And you're supposed to be a semicompetent TV reporter," he said.

We walked around the side of the house on a narrow, beat-up concrete pathway between Herman's house and his neighbor's.

Around back there was a door with a few glass panes in the top half, and there were windows on either side of the door.

I tried the door, and it was locked. I peered in through a pane of glass.

"Anything?" Freddie asked.

"Nope. Kitchen is clean. No sign of the rottweiler."

"There's a dog?"

"There was. Was kept in the kitchen, but he's not in there now, I think."

I stepped back from the door and looked at the window to the immediate left.

"Oh, no, no," Freddie said.

"C'mon, it's not like it's breaking and entering," I said.

"You mind telling me how it's not?"

"I know Herman," I said. "I'm a concerned friend. We stopped by and didn't see him and, given his state of mind the other night, I grew concerned."

"And decided to break into his house?" he said.

"Yes, to check on him. I'm a do-gooder—what can I say?"

Freddie was shaking his head. "Don't like it. Not at all."

The window was about five feet off the ground. It was going to be pain in the butt to get in through there.

"You know, let's bag the whole window thing," I said.

"Thank God."

"I don't want to rip my pants or shirt."

"Don't blame you. Let's go," he said.

I looked around, spotted a baseball-size rock, and picked it up.

"Got a better idea," I said.

Before Freddie could say a word, I smashed the small glass pane in the door just above the knob. There was a quick burst of breaking glass.

I turned to see Freddie standing there shaking his head.

"That was easy," I said.

"Sometimes you seem to get stupider by the minute."

I used a stick to clear away the jagged glass, reached my arm in, and boom, we were stepping into the kitchen a few seconds later.

The place was quiet and clean and eerie.

"Herman," I called, standing in the middle of the room. I looked around for the Rot, but there was no trace of him.

"We're not going to go looking around the house, are we?" Freddie asked.

"How about you take the upstairs and I look down here?"

"Anything to get us out of here faster," he said, and he set off down the hall to the front of the house and the stairway.

I wandered through the downstairs to the little living room where Herman had been sitting in his recliner the other night. The chair was still there, but all the snack wrappers and soda cans and garbage were gone. It was like the place had been professionally cleaned.

I returned to the kitchen and checked the little office off of it, and that was the same. All of the scattered files were gone. The piles of papers were cleaned up. It was like the house had been empty for months.

"No sign of anyone or anything up there," Freddie said, coming back to the kitchen.

"Even the smell of the dog is gone." I said.

"There's no sign that anyone even lived here," he said.

"That's what worries me."

Chapter 36

The car door slammed shut as soon as we hit the stairs down to the street. I turned and saw a man walking quickly along the sidewalk toward us.

Up the street in the other direction another door slammed shut as a man got out of an SUV. They were making their way on the sidewalk coming from opposite directions, walking briskly and with purpose.

We both noticed them at the same time.

"Maybe they're real estate agents," I said. "Here to look at Herm's house."

"Crap, and my piece is in the Jeep," Freddie said.

"You've been carrying a gun? You never said you were carrying a gun. This is a no-gun operation," I said.

Freddie nodded toward the guy closing in from our left. "Tell him that."

I turned to get a look at the guy. In his hand was a small black handgun. The other guy was closing in as well, and I assumed he was armed, too.

There was only one way out, and that was back up the steps to

Herman's house. They had us cut off on both sides of the sidewalk; the Jeep was directly in front of us but wedged in between two cars. It would take some maneuvering to get out of the spot.

"Back door?" I asked.

"Sounds good," Freddie said.

The men were fifty yards away on either side now.

"Let's turn and run on three," I said.

"Three," he said, and we took off.

We took the steps two at a time and I could hear the sound of shoes on pavement behind us as we hit the little pathway alongside the house. We were at the back door again, reached in, opened it, and raced into the house.

"I'll take upstairs," Freddie said. "I'll make some noise to pull one up. You're on your own with the other guy."

"Not a problem," I said.

We ran down the hall, and I ducked into the living room; Freddie bolted up the stairs. I heard the back door smash open in the kitchen, then I heard Freddie stomping around above me.

I could hear each guy trying to play boss. It was another smooth-running operation.

"They're upstairs."

"How the hell you know they're both up there? Could be a trick."

"Then you go up, and I'll look down here."

"Why the fuck I have to go up?"

I half expected them to raid the fridge and discuss this further when Freddie made a huge commotion right above me.

"Holy shit, they might be going out the window."

"I'm going up."

I stood with my back to the wall right next to the opening to the hallway as one guy stormed past me and raced up the stairs. Freddie hit him as he got to the top, and he yelled, "Awwwwwww."

The guy in the kitchen yelled, "Hey, Pete ... you okay?"

I heard him bolt from the kitchen and race down the hall. I was going to have to move fast. I had boxed a bit as a kid and had studied karate throughout my thirties, but it had been a long time since I had thrown a punch. Morning-feature reporters usually aren't mixing it up all that much in pursuit of the next fluffy story.

Upstairs there were the sounds of a struggle and then a tremendous thrashing. It sounded like bodies were flying into walls and furniture.

My guy was coming hard down the hallway, and it sounded like a bull was loose in the house. I balled up my fist karate style and reminded myself to lead with the knuckles. I jumped out and hoped to hell my timing was good. The guy was wide and fat and moving too fast for his size. His eyes bugged out in surprise, and I saw his right arm start to rise; I assumed a gun was attached to the end of it.

I twisted to my right to load my punch then snapped it off. My knuckles sailed into his nose, and pain shot through my hand as his body stopped cold. His feet went sailing out from under him, and he was horizontal in midair for a split second. He landed with a thud, and his head snapped back and cracked against the floor. I stood over him, my fist cocked and ready to follow up, but he was down. His eyes looked past me, straight up to the ceiling.

I kicked the gun from his hand as I heard someone race down the stairs. I spun around ready to strike again.

It was Freddie.

"What happened to him?" he asked, looking at the load on the floor.

"Slipped and hit his head," I said. "Your guy?"

"Same," Freddie said, grabbing the gun.

Upstairs there was a commotion, Freddie's guy was getting up.

We ran from the house and leaped into the Cherokee. Freddie jockeyed the car out of the spot, and we pulled out just as the guy from upstairs came flying out the front door, his gun drawn.

"Go," I yelled.

There was a flash from the gun, and I heard a pop. I ducked but there was no sound of a bullet hitting anything.

"Thank God he's a lousy shot," I said.

We were speeding down the street, and I heard the slow pinging of something inside the Jeep.

"What the hell is that," I said. "You out of gas or something?"

Freddie glanced at the dashboard, then adjusted the rearview mirror and looked into the backseat.

"A door's not shut all the way," he said.

"Oh, crap," I said, spinning around and looking in the back seat.

"Sons of bitches broke in. Probably looking for the camera," Freddie said.

The camera was still on the backseat but the little door to the compartment where the memory card goes was broken off.

"Oh, no," I said. "They went for the memory card."

"Please tell me you took it out," he said.

"I did," I said. I patted down my shirt pocket, but it wasn't there. "I just don't know where the hell it is."

"It fall out in Herm's house?" Freddie asked.

"Don't know."

"When was the last time you saw it?" he said.

"I think, I think," I said, trying to remember.

"Stop thinking. That's the damn problem," Freddie said.

"Last time I remembered seeing it was when I called Daniels," I said. "It was in my hand."

The console. I had put it on the console between the seats. I looked down and saw everything that had been on the console—the papers and pens, the change and the other odds and ends that seem to fill up those things—was scattered on the floor at my feet.

"Look at this mess," I said. "What a bunch of animals."

"Anything spill on the floor?" Freddie asked.

"I got bigger things to worry about, like my career."

"Like I said, anything spill on the floor?" he said.

I leaned over and grabbed the bits and pieces and scrambled to sort through it all. There was no sign of the card.

I slumped back in the seat and exhaled.

"Gone?" Freddie said.

"Long gone. My exclusive with Billy Hunter."

It was just after three in the afternoon. I had four hours to meet the deadline Daniels set to prove Billy Hunter was bribing people for McConnell and IT&E. And the interview where he admits everything was gone.

"They got it," I said.

Chapter 37

"I don't know if I can take this anymore," Liz said.

It was a little after six and we were standing in the kitchen of my place. I had told Liz about the two guys at Herman's house and she left work early and came over. She was upset and in retrospect, telling her may not have been the most prudent decision I had ever made, but I felt she deserved to know.

"Can I make you some tea maybe, something for the nerves?" I said.

"I'm serious, Sam," she said. "The other stuff, the guy warning you to back off, then someone shooting at you in the car, those were bad enough."

"They were."

"But now it's getting crazy, with people chasing you and trying to ... to ..."

"Believe me, I'm not thrilled with the idea of someone trying to shoot me either."

I moved to her and put my arms around her waist and went to pull her close but she backed away.

"Was that interview with this Hunter guy that valuable to someone?" she asked. Her face was flushed and her eyes soft with a tear or two. "So valuable that they'd try and ..."

"Must have been," I said. "Someone sent two guys to get it, and to try to shut us up in the process"

She edged even farther away and at this rate she'd be it the living room in a minute.

"Do you think it was McConnell?" she said.

"Don't know. What I do know is that every time we turn over a rock close to Buck McConnell, we get shot at. First Herman, now Hunter. Every time we get a little closer, someone gets pissed."

"So he, or whoever, wanted the interview with this Hunter guy so you couldn't put it on the air?" she said.

"One would think so."

"And they got it?" she said.

"They did. But I scribbled down every detail and quote I could remember from Hunter."

"Is it enough to put on the air?" she said.

"Don't know. I'm going to have to sell Daniels on it, and the lawyers, probably."

She broke the embrace and stepped back and crossed her arms and looked at me.

"I can put an end to this, you know," I said.

She didn't respond.

"I can go to Pep and tell him everything. I'm sure he'd be happy to take over," I said.

The offer was met by another moment of silence before she spoke up. "Can you?"

"Sure," I said.

"No, I don't think you can," she said. "Things are already in motion, Sam. You provoked this guy, now he's reacting. You're in the middle of this."

"I'm sure Pep could have someone keep an eye on me. Maybe it'll make you feel better," I said.

Her back stiffened and for the first time in our relationship she glared at me.

"Let's not pretend this is about me," she said.

There was an edge to her voice and she was angry, which was another first in our relationship.

"You're right," I said.

"This is about you and your career and your needing to get this guy to make a name for yourself," she said.

"You say that like it's a bad thing."

"It is if it gets you killed," she said.

The exchange was sharp and probably would have become sharper if it weren't for the buzzer from the front desk sounding. I looked at her and thought it best to keep my mouth shut. I went and answered the front desk and was told a "Mr. Freddie" was here for me. I gave permission for him to be sent up.

"I'm close," I said, while we waited. "Real close."

"How do you know?" she asked.

"I think there's something else behind, or underneath this bribery story. If I can get on the air with this one, then I can dig out the bigger one. And if I keep pushing, he'll make a mistake. I know it. I just need to get on the air with this one."

Liz had softened just a bit, but she wasn't entirely with me, at least not yet.

"It's not as easy, or as safe, as you make it sound," she said. "Especially when people are trying to shoot you."

"I know."

"And if you keep closing in on him, or them, they're only going to come after you harder," she said.

"Which is why I have Freddie," I said.

There was a knock at the door and Freddie strolled in.

"Ah, right on cue," I said.

He walked in with a black backpack in one hand and looked at Liz, then at me, then back to her. Then he shook his head.

"How the hell?" he said. "I mean, this gorgeous young lady with ... you?"

I looked at Liz.

"My wit, right?"

"Maybe," she said, actually smiling.

"Let me introduce you two," I said.

"Boggles the mind," Freddie said as he took Liz's hand. "You have my sympathy. You have to put up with him more than I do."

"And thank you for keeping an eye on him," she said, looking in my direction.

"Lord knows he needs all the help he can get," he said.

"Yes, he does," she said.

"Hello," I said, "I'm standing here, you know. I'm in the room. A little respect, maybe?"

Liz was less angry and tense than a few moments ago. It was like meeting Freddie reassured her that someone did indeed have my back.

"This story salvageable?" Freddie asked. "Even without the interview?"

"Don't know. Going to be up to Daniels," I said. "But I still got the pictures, the ones from Herm. That's something."

"But is it enough to get the green light?" Liz asked.

"Hard to say. Daniels is going to want to go through legal, I'm sure."

"Sure that always speeds things up," Liz said.

"Pretty and a sense of humor," Freddie said.

Liz smiled at him. "On that note, I'm leaving," she said.

"Always leave them wanting more," Freddie said.

"Unfortunately, I need to be back at work," she said.

She turned to Freddie and expressed her delight in meeting him and thanked him for taking care of her significant other, and then I walked her to the door. We kissed, and she placed her hands on my chest and spoke in a whisper.

"Be careful," she said.

"I have Mr. Freddie watching out over me."

"Sounds like a gun-toting, cameraman hairdresser," Liz said.

"A whole new meaning to the term *shooter*," I said. "I'll be fine."

"That's not going to stop me from worrying."

"I know."

We kissed again, and I watched her walk to the elevator. I went back into apartment and Freddie was in the living room with the backpack on the coffee table.

"Some things I'm never, I mean, never, going to understand," he said.

"Math, right? The advanced stuff. With all the equations. Those things always killed me too."

"Talking about her with you," he said as he unzipped the backpack.

He reached in and pulled out a small black handgun, and I threw my hands in the air.

"Please, take whatever you want, just leave the flat-screen TV."

Freddie ignored the remark and offered me the gun.

"This is yours, starting now. It needs to stay on you."

I shook my head. "Actually, it needs to stay in your backpack," I said.

"We can get you a shoulder or ankle holster," he said.

"Nope," I said. "Put it back in the bag."

"You're not going to like being dead," he said.

I started to say something, stopped, then started again. "I don't even know where to go with that one," I said.

He again offered the gun. "Don't be stubborn," he said.

"But it comes so easily."

Freddie exhaled and shook his head. "You got a good reason for not wanting to protect yourself?" he asked.

"Yes, guns attract bullets," I said. "Now put it away."

"You seem to be doing just fine in that department even without a gun."

"Then think of how much worse it will be with a gun," I said.

He stared at me, and I stared back at him.

"I'm not touching it," I said.

Chapter 38

I stood standing alone in Daniels's office, staring at the monitors on the wall, specifically the one in the center. It was tuned to Liberty, and right now, at seven o'clock, there was a very attractive blonde woman reading the headlines at the news desk in the studio a floor below.

She looked as though she had just come straight from her high school class to work at the TV network. She was new, and I realized how out of touch I had been with life in the newsroom while I chased this story.

"She's a looker, huh?" Daniels asked as he walked in and closed the door behind him.

He was carrying a coffee mug, which I liked to think was filled with coffee, but knowing him, there was a good possibility it was something else.

"She probably wasn't even born when I had my first TV job," I said.

"Yeah, but look at her now."

"Probably in, like, eighth grade when I started here."

She had shiny blonde hair that Mary Anne down in makeup had blown out so she'd look like all the other blondes we had on the air. I sat down in one of the guest chairs in front of his desk, knowing without stories like this IT&E thing, my days were numbered in this business.

"Script," Daniels said, wagging his fingers at the papers I was holding.

"I'm fifteen minutes ahead of schedule. That should buy me some goodwill," I said.

"It doesn't," he said.

"Give me a deadline, and I meet it easily." I looked over at the blonde. "I bet she can't do that."

"Look like that, who cares?" he said.

"My point exactly."

"You got reaction from IT&E? The Feds?"

"Like I said, I'm a professional."

"I don't want to waste my time reading something that I'm going to have to hold," he said.

"You're not going to want to hold this," I said.

He slipped on a pair of reading glasses and started reading. I scanned my copy of the script, pretty damn proud of how I had pulled it all together, despite the boneheaded move of letting the Hunter interview get stolen.

I looked at the words and knew I had McConnell nailed. And once he was nailed I knew he was going to strike back, and that's when I'd discover something else that would tie him to Steele's death.

I read the script to myself while Daniels read his copy and worked on what words I wanted to emphasize.

Tonight ... evidence of a culture of corruption at energy giant IT&E. Proof that CEO and rumored presidential candidate Buck McConnell personally okayed hundreds of thousands of dollar in bribes to dangerous foreign governments to win contracts.

Bribes that are believed to be breaking U.S laws under the Foreign Corrupt Practices Act and punishable by massive fines.

One of McConnell's former executives, Billy Hunter, has come clean about the scheme, saying he personally delivered hundreds of thousands of dollars, in cash, to operatives of the governments in Nigeria, Brazil, and Yemen. In return, IT&E was awarded lucrative contracts to build energy plants and supply oil- and gas-drilling equipment to those countries.

In photos obtained exclusively by Liberty News, Hunter is seen hand delivering the cash, so much money that on one occasion he had to stuff the currency into the backseat of a Mercedes and deliver it to a government operative in Nigeria.

There was a lot more, including reaction from Stuart Ripley, saying everything was false and IT&E would vigorously defend itself and legally punish anyone spreading these malicious rumors. In some neighborhoods they would just say, "We'll sue your ass."

I had called the SEC and the FBI to get the usual no comment. But I had gotten a nice sentence from the FBI, saying they take every instance of corporate corruption, here or overseas, very, very seriously.

Daniels tossed my soon-to-be-award-winning script on his desk, ripped off his reading glasses, and tossed them on top. I took all this to mean that he was not happy.

"You're fucking kidding me, right?" he asked.

That was confirmation of my gut feeling, and I again complimented myself on my instincts.

"So you're good with it? I should get on the set?"

"You take all this time and hand me this pile of stinking horseshit you call a script?"

"I'm okay with criticism," I said.

"Where are the sound bites from the interview with this bagman Hunter?"

"About that," I said.

"I thought you found this clown."

"I did."

"And you interviewed him?"

"You're two for two."

"Then where on earth are the sound bites? What are you waiting for, your own special, maybe?"

"Not a bad idea."

He grabbed his mug a bit too fast, and the liquid, which did look like coffee, sloshed over the lip and onto my script. "Son of a bitch," he said.

"The Hunter interview was stolen," I said.

He swallowed and looked at me. I kept going to save him the trouble of telling me to.

"Right out of the car. That was before the two men came after my cameraman and me and tried to either do us bodily harm or ask for the time. I'm not sure which. But considering they had guns drawn, I think bodily harm was probably the goal," I said.

"You mean to tell me you track down and find this guy, your so-called smoking gun, and the interview gets stolen?"

"Yes."

He picked up the script and dropped it back on the desk for emphasis.

"And that's why I get you paraphrasing him in here."

"Yes."

"You know you can't go on the air with this," he said.

"We've put less on."

"Don't insult me," he said.

"I have pictures. I have confirmation from the man in the pictures as to his illegal activity," I said.

"You don't have shit without him on camera admitting that," he said.

"He did admit it."

"But you lost it," he said.

"Someone took it. There's a difference."

"Whatever. You can't go on the air and say, Trust me, I talked to this guy," he said.

"But I did talk to him."

"Can't you interview him again? Get him in here and interview him on the set?" he asked.

"He's not exactly close by," I said. I didn't mention the fact that Hunter hadn't returned the three calls I had placed to him since I discovered the recording of the interview had been stolen.

"Cal," I said, "let's talk bigger picture. We go on with this, and it serves two purposes. One, we get ourselves a nice scoop and Liberty looks great. We got the CEO of a major company—the guy who some think is going to run for president and save the country—breaking the law of the country he's supposed to save. Ironic, no?"

"If you had the story locked down, it would be. Yes," he said.

"The second purpose relates to the bigger picture of trying to figure out who killed Jack."

"Go on."

"Every time I tweak McConnell, bad things happen. I start asking about Jack's death, and a guy tells me to stop asking about it. I keep up with it and find this guy in Jersey with pictures implicating McConnell, and someone takes a shot at me."

"What?" he said.

"I'll explain in a minute. Then I find the guy in the pictures who confirms the illegal activity, and someone steals the interview. Every time I get a little closer the heat gets turned up. Mere coincidence?"

"Or conspiracy theory?" he said.

"Not all conspiracy theories are wrong."

"Only one I'm concerned about is this one," he said.

"You got to let me get on the air with this, Cal."

"I can't."

"It's accurate."

"I need more than your word. This blows up on us and guess who's going to get nailed?"

"I'm willing to take that risk," I said.

"I'm not talking about you, Sam. I'm the president of Liberty, I got a bit more to lose. You know how long and hard I worked to build this place?" He put his reading glasses on and looked at the script again. "At the very least, legal is going to need to look at this," he said.

"Well, that should take no more than, what, six months maybe?"

"They're not that bad," he said.

"They are."

"We need to cover ourselves."

"We're covered," I said. "Have I ever steered you wrong?"

"How much time do we have?" he said.

"Funny. Kind of," I said. "Look, who put his balls on the line and put up his own money to get you the footage of Jack being pulled out of the East River?"

"I paid you back."

"You did. But imagine if that had shown up on Fox or CNN or somewhere else that morning. How stupid would we look?"

He looked at me with no trace of emotion, which told me I had scored a point.

"I got pretty good instincts," I said.

"No one says otherwise," he said.

"Cal," I said. "Think about this. I take a call from Robbie Steele. My gut tells me maybe she's got something. I start sniffing around and turning over rocks, and people start shooting at me. What's that tell you?"

"That you're an easy guy to dislike," he said.

"All I'm asking is for you to trust me."

"Not with this script, I can't," he said. He looked away, toward the monitors. It was twenty after seven, and we were in commercial. Getting on the air tonight was now a long shot.

"You don't have this pinned down," he said.

I looked around his office at all the shelves of awards and celebrity photos and other crap and felt my patience slipping away.

"You know," I said, "You sit up here surrounded by all this … this shit. Making your decisions and covering you ass."

I looked across the desk and saw his cheeks redden.

"You probably want to stop right there," he said.

"No, I don't, Cal. You know I got something on Buck McConnell but you won't pull the trigger."

"You don't have shit," he said, picking up the scrip and dropping it on his desk. "You have a bunch of accusations with nothing to back them up."

"That's not the problem," I yelled, "And you know it."

"You need to shut up, Sam," he yelled back.

"You don't have the balls to go after Buck McConnell."

His eyes narrowed, and his face was a deep red. "Who the fuck do you think—"

The phone rang and he glanced at the incoming number, leaned forward, and punched the Speaker button hard enough to dent it.

"Daniels," he said. His tone was loud and sharp.

A man spoke on the other end and sounded like he was on speakerphone also.

"This is Drew Bradshaw, senior VP and corporate counsel for IT&E. I have Stuart Ripley, VP of corporate communications, here with me."

I looked at Daniels, and he was looking at me. I wondered if my face gave away the fact that I felt like I was going to throw up.

"We have something you may want to know," Bradshaw said.

Chapter 39

"Go on," Daniels said.

He didn't mention I was in the room while McConnell's mouthpiece Bradshaw started babbling.

"Stuart informed me of the seemingly personal vendetta one of your reporters, a Sam North, has against Terrance McConnell and IT&E. Stuart has also informed me of a story Mr. North has been working on that allegedly shows one of IT&E's employees paying what are described as bribes to people overseas."

Daniels reached over and hit the Mute button.

"Harvard Law," he said. "Got to be. I can feel the pompousness seeping through the phone."

Whatever anger Daniels had toward me a moment ago had faded, at least for now.

"Think this windbag is going to get to the point?" I said.

Bradshaw rattled on about the pictures of Billy Hunter and how he hadn't seen them and how he really needed to review them before a grave mistake was made by Mr. North. I could picture Ripley sitting in the room looking smug and self-satisfied.

Daniels took the call off mute and interrupted him.

"Drew," he said, and Bradshaw hesitated. "Do me a favor—things

move pretty fast around here, being TV and all. I'm going to ask you
to get to the point for me."

There was silence on the other end, and I assumed that was from
the collective shock in the room that someone had dared offend so
highly regarded a professional as Drew Bradshaw.

"Well, yes, of course," Bradshaw said when the shock wore off.
"My point, as you referred to it, is this. If Liberty News or any of its
affiliates dares run this so-called bribery story without my legal team
and me here at IT&E having an opportunity to review the photos of
this alleged employee, I am prepared to file a large-scale lawsuit that
not only will shed light on the irresponsible reporting of Mr. North,
but also seek a substantial monetary award for the damage the story
would inflict on our reputation."

Daniels was looking at me as Bradshaw added an exclamation
point.

"That, Mr. Daniels, is my point?" he said.

I looked at Daniels, and he tried to wave me off from speaking,
but it was too late, my mouth was open.

"Hey, Drew," I said, "your boy Buck looked at the photos the other
day, at the Sheraton. Ask Stu, he was there."

It was like a gas bomb had gone off. There was some coughing
from someone in the room and what sounded like a gag. Then Ripley
spoke up.

"It's proper to identify yourself when listening in on a call," he
said.

"Right, like all the other people in the room over there with you
have done," I said.

"Mr. North," Bradshaw said.

"Mr. Bradshaw," I said. "Please, call me Sam. Like I said, Buck saw
the photos. Stu saw the photos. You may be the only guy in the
company who *hasn't* seen the photos."

"And Mr. McConnell indicated to you that he did not know
anything about the photos, I believe," Bradshaw said.

"Yes, and I personally am choosing not to believe Buck."

"That would be a costly mistake," he said.

"How about this, Drew? I located the man in the photos," I said.

That quieted the lawyer and the flack down, and I rolled on, spreading information to my new, powerful friends.

"William—Billy—Hunter lives in upstate New York. I sat down with him on camera, and he admitted to handing out the cash. 'Cash for contracts' he called it," I said.

"And you have this ... this Hunter person admitting that?" Bradshaw asked.

I looked at Daniels, who was leaning forward over the desk, motionless.

"I do," I said.

I didn't consider it a lie. I mean, I had Hunter admitting everything; unfortunately, that particular piece of evidence had been misplaced at the moment.

"I would like to see that before it airs," Bradshaw said.

"Do I ask to see your legal papers before you file a lawsuit, Drew?" I asked.

"This is hardly a similar case, Mr. North," he said.

"Buck had his chance. He saw the photos and pretended he didn't know anything about anything," I said.

"That is simply not—" Ripley started, then was interrupted by the sound of someone entering the room over there.

An exchange took place that was hard to make out. I heard Bradshaw, but his voice was muffled, and my guess was he had a hand over the phone mic. He spoke after a few seconds.

"All of this may be moot in a moment," he said.

"Of course it will be," I said.

I stood, leaned over Daniels's desk, and hit Mute.

"Maybe they're ready to admit everything. Say that, thanks to us, they've uncovered a trail of corruption and are ready to go to the Feds and turn themselves in."

"Yes, and I'm a good dancer," Daniels said.

Bradshaw's voice boomed through the speaker. "Well, this certainly changes everything," he said.

Before Daniels or I could speak, he was on his way to nailing me.

"It seems this Hunter, William S. Hunter, to be exact, is not now, nor ever was, an employee of IT&E."

I looked across the desk at Daniels, who was looking back at me.

"Mr. Hunter at one time, and this is almost three years ago, was employed in the energy industry by a small Houston-based exploration company with no ties to IT&E whatsoever," he said. "But alas, William was asked to leave the firm after, and I quote, 'a series of incidents in which he was abusive and gave indications of a substance-abuse issue,' end quote."

"He expect us to believe that shit?" I said, not realizing Daniels had taken us off Mute.

"Yes, I do, Mr. North," Bradshaw said. "Being that this report comes from the city of Houston's official police report regarding one particular incident."

"What was the name of the firm he was with?" I asked.

There was silence while Bradshaw shuffled through papers to find my answer.

"Mr. Hunter was," he said, letting the "was" linger there, "an employee of Gulfway Energy."

Chapter 40

"So this Hunter cat was getting paid by Gulfway?" Freddie said.

I was back at my desk in the newsroom and on the phone with him, scrambling to connect the dots.

"Looks that way," I said. "Same place that employed Charles Bulger and his Bergen Security Services also was paying Billy Hunter."

It had to be owned by IT&E. If I could prove that, I'd be right back on track.

At the other end of the room I saw Daniels coming down the stairs from the executive level. It was late, the newsroom was near empty, and he weaved his way through it at a good clip. He was heading straight toward me.

"Let me go," I said to Freddie and ended the call.

Daniels had his suit jacket on and was on his way out. His car was waiting, and he'd be home at his nice Central Park West apartment in time to enjoy what was left of the evening.

"Boss," I said, getting up. "You're going to love me. This is why you pay me the big money. Wait until I share my latest little reporting coup."

I would tell him about the Gulfway Energy connection with him. Tell him both Hunter and the guy following me a few days ago were being paid by the same entity, an obscure little unit of IT&E.

Daniels face was rigid and serious. "You need to pack up your things," he said.

"What?"

"You heard me. Clean out your desk."

I looked at him, waiting for him to go on, but he didn't.

"You want to tell me what's going on?" I said.

"I just got off the phone with Drew Bradshaw, and Buck McConnell."

"Lucky you."

"This isn't a joke, Sam. IT&E is preparing a lawsuit to be filed against Liberty News," he said. "It's charging harassment, libel, and a half-dozen other things related to your pursuit of Buck McConnell and this bribe story."

"But I never got on the air with it."

"You're lucky."

"So what's their beef?"

"For starters, the way you stormed into the Sheraton the other day and bullied your way into seeing him."

"Only way to get results."

"Then this fiasco," he said.

"Funny, I was just coming to find you with the latest on that."

"There is no latest. It's over."

"Cal, what's going on?"

"You're taking some time off. Starting now. Sort yourself out," he said.

"I don't need sorting."

"Ever since you got tangled up with Robbie Steele, you've been a loose cannon, and I can't afford to jeopardize this network's reputation," he said.

"This has nothing to do with her."

"It has everything to do with her," he said. "Guys don't think straight around her."

"Are you firing me?"

"That remains to be seen," he said. "Right now you're off the air, effective immediately."

"You're suspending me?"

"You're lucky. They demanded I fire you now. Tonight."

"At least you didn't cave entirely."

"Your contract is up at the end of October. I want you out of here and off this story now. A week or two before your deal expires, you, me, and your agent can sit down and talk. We'll reevaluate where you are," he said.

From over by the hallway leading to reception, I saw one of the security guards heading our way.

"You called security?"

"It's HR bullshit. You know how it goes, Sam."

"You're going to have me escorted from the building?" I said.

I saw Glover crossing at the far end of the newsroom. He looked over, saw the guard, Daniels, and me, and stopped to watch. A handful of others stood up to watch as well.

Daniels had his hand out. "I need your ID, Sam."

"You're throwing me out?"

He didn't respond.

"Because Buck McConnell threatened you?"

His face reddened. "Do you understand that you wanted to go on the air with a story accusing someone of corruption and you didn't even have fact one nailed down?" he asked.

"Not true."

"This isn't some game, Sam. These are real people, and if you went on and got that wrong, this network would pay. I can't afford to screw around with this stuff. You need a break to pull yourself together. Get your priorities straightened out."

"I don't need a break."

The guard had arrived. It was a guy I saw almost every day in and around the building, and now he stood there as if we had never met.

Daniels snapped his fingers. "The ID."

I reached into my shirt pocket, took it out, and slapped it into his hand.

Chapter 41

"Look at this crap," I said as I swept a stack of books and papers off Jack's desk. Some of it slid off the side of the desk and landed on the floor of his home office.

"Hey," Robbie yelled. "Would you take it easy?"

I grabbed a folder and started rifling through it. "There have to be some personal papers of Jack's in here somewhere. Maybe notes or something."

There was nothing, just research notes for an interview, and I tossed the folder on the floor. "Useless," I said and Robbie yelled again as it hit the floor.

"Sam, enough. Stop it."

I had left Liberty and come uptown to Jack's apartment, calling Robbie on the way. She had cleared me with the doorman and now I was sure she was sorry she did. I was tired and irritable and not thrilled that the story that was supposed to save my career may have wrecked it.

"What the hell are you looking for anyway?" she said.

"I don't know. But there has to be something in here," I said, surveying the office. It was a small, windowless room off the hallway;

much like his office at Liberty, this place was a mess, too. There were stacks of books and papers and clutter everywhere.

"Somewhere buried in this pile of crap there has to be something about why Jack went out that night, and who he went to meet," I said.

Robbie scanned the mess on the floor. She was dressed in a kind of casual workout chic. Skintight workout pants with a button-down dress shirt.

"I don't think you're going to find it by creating even a bigger mess," she said. "And besides, the detectives went through everything in here."

"They weren't looking for what I'm looking for," I said. "They had no idea Buck McConnell was involved in this."

"Tearing up the place isn't going to help you find something," she said.

I was behind the desk and stepped back and Robbie left the room. I stood there by myself and took a few deep breaths that did me little to no good. She was back with two glasses of water and handed me one.

"They went through everything in here. I went through everything in here. I just don't think there's anything you're going to find, especially if you don't know what it is you're looking for," she said.

I had some of the water and it went down nice and cool and I actually felt better.

"I just got suspended," I said.

"What?" she said.

"From Liberty."

I explained the whole mess of an evening. I explained everything that had happened and every conversation I had had since our last meeting. I explained getting shot at. Twice. I explained how the oddest things seemed to happen to people when they started digging into things around Buck McConnell. Like people such as Herman Bindagi, who had been there one day but had disappeared the next.

"That guy contacted Jack, you know?" she said.

"He told me."

"Jack said it was amazing how once you took a shot at McConnell people would come out of the woodwork with dirt on him," she said.

I started to say something but stopped short. That was the same thing Doug Lee has said. There was no shortage of people eager to help take McConnell down.

"So you were about to go on the air with the bribery story?" she said.

"Yes. I wanted to take a swing at McConnell. See how he would swing back."

"But you didn't have the chance?" she said.

"No."

I explained how the Billy Hunter interview was stolen and how McConnell's lawyer had threatened Liberty.

"I was close," I said. "Real close to something. I know it. And I'm sure Jack was closing in on something. He had to be. Something McConnell just couldn't let him discover."

"Not the bribes?" she said.

"No. At least I don't think so. McConnell and his lawyers seemed perfectly well equipped to handle that story. There's no doubt they're guilty, but they've got an answer for everything. It's almost like they know McConnell can survive that."

"Jack said McConnell was dirty, whatever that meant," she said.

"That's what I need to find out. The bribes are bad enough. The Feds have been cracking down, but I can see what I T and E will say. It was a rogue subcontractor. They'll have enough layers between the guy doing the bribing and McConnell so he's protected. Then they'll justify it by saying that's the way things operate in those countries. Ultimately, they're prepared to pay the fines if caught and move on," I said.

"And if anyone pursues the story, they'll turn up the heat with lawyers," she said.

"Which is what they're doing with me. McConnell wants to make sure I stop right here, that I don't go any farther. He's got to be worried that I'll do down the same trail Jack did."

I looked around the office and all the piles.

"Somewhere in here there has to be a clue as to who Jack was going to meet," I said.

"Sam," she said, "Everything in here has been looked over."

"There's no personal notes, no names scribbled anywhere?"

She shook her head.

"And you've gone through everything in here?" I asked.

"Not one hundred percent of everything, but most of the folders. I even went through the stuff in the safe."

I looked at her.

"The safe?"

"Yes. Jack had a small one," she said, answering like everyone had one and pointing toward the floor in far corner.

She went over and pushed aside a pile of books and folders. And there on the floor was a small, gray safe, tucked in amid the clutter of the office.

"And why'd he have a safe?" I said.

She reached down and turned the combination lock as she spoke.

"He kept a few things in here, including his gun," she said.

I put the glass of water on the desk for fear of it slipping out of my hand.

"Whoa, a gun?" I said. "Jack had a gun?"

"Yes. He bought it about six, maybe seven years ago, when the show really started taking off. The threats increased, and somebody recommended he get it," she said.

It made sense, I guess.

"It was fully licensed and all," Robbie said. "But he only carried it every now and again, when he felt it really necessary. Manny carried a gun Jack said he didn't see the need for the both of them to be walking around armed."

She pulled on the black handle of the safe, and inside was a small silver handgun. The barrel was flat and it had a black handgrip. I looked in over her shoulder and saw the make. It was a Smith & Wesson.

"And the cops know he had this in here?" I said.

"Yes," she said, standing up. "They said it wasn't surprising that it was left behind."

"Because?"

Robbie took a breath and her eyes softened with tears.

"Well, if he had planned on jumping in the river, he wouldn't exactly need it, would he?" she said, her tone just short of mocking the police.

"That would be one theory," I said.

"You have a different one?" she said.

"Yes."

She looked at me and waited.

"Maybe he didn't feel like he needed it," I said.

Robbie frowned and I gave her a second and it hit her. The frown disappeared and her face relaxed with relief, like it was stating to make sense.

"I can see where you going with this," she said.

"Jack was going to meet someone he knew," I said.

Chapter 42

I was out on the sidewalk in front of the Steeles' building. It was ten thirty at night, and the air was hot and damp even at this hour. A few empty cabs cruised down Fifth. I scrolled through the contacts in my phone and called Lee, hoping it wasn't too late.

He answered on the third ring.

"Whattya want?" he asked.

"Good evening to you, too."

"It's night, my friend."

"I'm picturing you in a smoking jacket with a nice evening drink in the study at the Lee compound. Relaxing, maybe counting your money."

"Hah. Try again," he said. "You ever hear of some outfit called Trim Waist Inc.?"

"No."

"Makes sense, you're in shape," he said.

"Thank you."

"It's a competitor to Weight Watchers. A fast-growing competitor. They need money."

"And you have money."

"The question is, Do I want ShorePoint to own a piece of a diet company? You know how fast these fads come and go."

"Buy, profit, and get out."

"Yes, that's generally the rule, but it's the profit part with these guys that worries me."

"I need a piece of information," I said.

"Yes, I should have known. And I thought you were calling to say hello," Lee said.

A bus groaned past on its way down Fifth.

"Remember the other day when you said you had people calling you, offering you dirt on Buck McConnell?"

"How could I forget your visit to ShorePoint? It counted as a celebrity sighting in our humble little office. Maybe next time you bring a few glossy publicity photos."

"You said you heard from guys who went to Harvard with him. Guys who said they saw him buying his way out of trouble back then."

"I did say that," he said.

"You also said you had one guy tell you that he could help you take McConnell down if you wanted to," I said.

"Correct again. I did say that."

"But you didn't want to."

"I had made my money off IT&E."

"Can you connect me with him? This specific gentleman?" I asked.

Lee hesitated. I looked up Fifth and saw a woman walking a very small, furry dog. Behind her a few headlights shone as a handful of cars came down Fifth.

"He's a private man, a very successful fund manager. I'm not sure he'd appreciate being contacted by a member of the media, even an esteemed one," he said.

"How about you tell me where I could find him, and he'll never know you were involved?" I asked.

"And this is all in a quest to pin something on the sleazy Buck McConnell?"

"Yes. The same man who felt it was okay to spy on you and your children."

"And this is something big?" he asked.

"Possibly very big."

"Wrongdoing?"

"Of the worst kind," I said.

"Then I would merely be doing my duty as an upstanding citizen of our great republic?"

"Yes."

"Then how can I possibly not get involved?"

Chapter 43

I stood in the back of St. Pat's at 7:27 the next morning watching a couple of dozen people make their way back to their pews after communion. I spotted the man that best fit Lee's description of Anthony Edmunds, and kept an eye on him as he returned to his pew and knelt in prayer.

He was dressed in a gray suit, and I assumed he was on his way to work at the office of Edmunds & Associates, two blocks up Fifth Avenue. One of the bits of information Lee had told me about Edmunds was that he had made it a point to attend daily mass at St. Pat's on his way to the office.

I had searched the Web for a few hours last night, looking for every article I could find on Edmunds, and finally came up with one from the *Journal* that mentioned he was religious. And a nice feature spread on him in *Westchester* magazine showed him and his wife at home in their Mount Kisco estate and also mentioned he attended daily mass at St. Pat's. With that I had enough to approach him and not have to give away Lee as my source.

Mass ended, and everyone made their way back through the cavernous cathedral as tourists trickled in, staring up at the ceiling and stained glass. It was peaceful and quiet, and I watched Edmunds leave through one of the side doors at the rear of the church.

I followed him out onto the plaza that faced the corner of Fifth and Fifty-first.

"Mr. Edmunds," I said as I came up on him.

He turned and looked puzzled as I extended my hand.

"Sam North. With Liberty News."

We shook, but he wasn't quite sure why I was there.

"I read that you attended mass here and was hoping to run into you."

"You have. I'm Tony Edmunds."

"You went to Harvard," I said.

"You moonlight with alumni relations?" he asked.

"No. But I'm chasing a story related to one of your classmates. High-profile guy."

"It was Harvard. Most of the class was high profile," he said.

"This one may run for president."

Edmunds turned to leave and waved a hand.

"I have no interest in—"

"And he may have committed a horrible crime," I said, and it slowed him down on his way out. "Can I talk to you? It will take five minutes."

"I really don't think it's a good idea," he said.

Lee said Edmunds had called him, offering information on McConnell. So there was something there, something he wanted to unload. He just wasn't comfortable with it being to a member of the media.

"I saw you hesitate just now," I said. "You could have kept on walking."

I got a look that said he was worried, like maybe I was unstable. I figured I had ten seconds left before he waved over one of the cops stationed outside the cathedral.

"Anthony, I need some help here. I'm working on something about Buck McConnell that, if true, is pretty bad."

He shook his head. "I'm sorry, but I'm late for—"

"I know something happened years ago, back when he was in—"

"As I said, I can't help you, Mr. North." He turned and started to walk away.

I went after him. I put a hand on his arm to try to stop him, and he turned with a look that said that was a bad idea.

"Please take your hand off of me," he said.

"I read where you scrapped your way into Harvard, working through high school in the Bronx, hustling to get good grades," I said.

I kept talking and removed my hand from his arm.

"You busted your butt to get in. Then you came out and busted your butt to build Edmunds and Associates."

He looked at me and I thought he was going to say something but he stayed quiet.

"But I'm guessing you saw how McConnell operated at Harvard. How he seemed to have his own set of rules."

I was pretty sure I had him. He would open up and tell me what a jerk McConnell was. It was one of those instinctive things. I knew that he knew something; I could tell he had a piece of info, but he didn't want to let it go. I looked at him, and he looked at me, and I waited for it.

Instead, I got a shake of the head.

"Mr. North, I really don't think I can help you. And I need to be going," he said.

This was as close to desperate as I had ever been. I was unofficially out of a job. I was chasing a story that was going to be either gigantic or nothing; this guy knew something that could help decide which way it would go, but he didn't want to share at the moment.

"Anthony," I said, loud enough to startle him and draw the attention of the few people walking by on Fifty-first Street.

"Mr. North, really," he shot back.

"You know something," I said. "Something that's damaging to McConnell. Why do you want to protect him?"

"I'm not protecting him," he said.

"You keep hanging on to what you know, and you are protecting him."

Edmunds stared at me, and I expected him to turn to walk away again. But he didn't. His eyes scanned the people walking by, then came back to me.

"Let's go somewhere where we can talk," he said.

Chapter 44

"I think this suspension thing may have bought us some more time," I said.

"Here's the funny thing with that," Freddie said. "It's your ass that's been fired, and I don't care about this buying-more-time crap."

"I wasn't fired, I was suspended. Let's be semantically correct."

"I was," he said.

We were in the Jeep, driving up the west side with the towers of the GWB off in the distance. The humidity had lifted, and the sky was a clear blue over the dark waters of the Hudson to our left.

"I got a career to think about, a life to live," Freddie said. "I got clients lined up and waiting for me, personally, to train them and whip their asses into shape."

"Not nearly as exciting as this," I said.

"Far more exciting than this," he said.

"I have a plan, okay?" I said. "I just need you for another shoot or two, then that's it. You're cut loose. Back to training the beautiful things of the Upper West Side."

"Care to share this plan?" Freddie said.

"Let's assume Ripley called Daniels to follow up and was told the good news that I had been suspended."

"Fired."

"Right, suspended. I'm sure that news was then relayed to Buck McConnell."

"All smiles over there this morning," he said.

"Exactly. They think I've been defeated, that I'm going to crawl away quietly."

"I know I did."

"Yes, thank you for your unwavering faith in me," I said.

"You got nothing to go on here, bro. You're on fumes now with this story."

"And that is exactly what I want McConnell and Ripley to think. If they think they won and that I'm flat-out defeated, chances are they're going to call off the dogs, in this case that guy with Gulfway Energy. My gut tells me we can probably operate in relative peace while I push forward."

"How about you push forward without me?" he said.

"Who am I supposed to bounce ideas off of? Have witty exchanges with? You know, trade quips."

"Billions of people in the world, you'll find someone," he said.

"Boy, you really are in a sour mood. And despite my big win this morning."

I swept my hand across the dashboard in a grand motion.

"How can you be in a bad mood on a glorious day like this?"

"Maybe because you won't tell me where we're going," he said.

"I told you, Norwalk. Got to talk to a someone up along the sound."

Four hours ago I sat down in the empty office of Anthony Edmunds, and he told me of a long-ago incident with Buck McConnell while the two of them were undergrads at Harvard. He wasn't with McConnell when it happened, but he knew someone who was. He refused to give me the specifics, but told me where I could the other party. He said he'd leave it up to this guy as to what to disclose and what to keep buried.

We drove up the Henry Hudson Parkway and crossed the bridge over the Spuyten Duyvil Creek. The bridge felt like it was a mile high in the air, and off to the left the Hudson opened up, framed by the Palisades.

"Are we going out on a boat?" Freddie asked.

I looked at Freddie, and it hit me. "Aha," I said. "Now I get it."

"Nothing to get," he said.

"The big, tough cameraman gets seasick, doesn't he?"

"Do not."

"Come on. That's what's been bugging you. You're afraid of boats. Now it all makes sense. The cranky mood. The anger."

Freddie said nothing and took the curve took fast as we came around onto the Saw Mill River Parkway and drove north into Westchester.

"It's not a sign of weakness, my friend," I said. "I'm sure there are plenty of big, tough guys who get a little woozy out on the high seas."

"Keep it up and I'm throwing your ass out the car."

I looked over at the narrow shoulder, which was moving by at an unsafe speed.

"I'll hitch a ride," I said. "How do you like that? I'm calling your bluff."

"Throw your ass out and then call the *Post*. Say I saw you on the side of the road. Can see the headline now, 'Fired TV Reporter Wanders the Highway,'" he said.

"Yes, that will be the story next to, 'Tough-Guy Cameraman Afraid of Boats,'" I said.

"They'll come get a picture of you sitting on the guardrail looking lost," he said. "Caption say you looking for a ride back to your career. How you like that?"

We flew onto the exit ramp that led to the Cross County Parkway and cut across Westchester. Twenty minutes later we were on I-95 and cruising into Connecticut. Inlets and channels and little rivers feeding into the Long Island Sound were visible on our right as we sped through Hedge Fund Heaven, officially called Greenwich.

We exited I-95 in Norwalk and wound our way down to the

sound. Norwalk was a little city on the water with a revitalized downtown. All the old industrial buildings had been turned into apartments, shops, bars, and restaurants.

We drove along a street that ran parallel to the Norwalk River, which emptied into the Long Island Sound. It was picture-postcard-perfect weather, and small pleasure boats and sailboats cruised back and forth on the river. Little marinas were on the left, small unpretentious buildings with docks out back. On the right were small boat shops.

I watched the address numbers get lower as we drove closer to the sound and spotted our building.

"There she be," I said, "number seventeen."

It was a long, flat, gray, weather-beaten building that ran right up to the bank of the river out back.

"What a dump," Freddie said as he pulled into a little gravel parking area in front.

"It's a nonprofit—give 'em a break," I said. "You try living on donations."

"May have to if I keep working with you."

White gravel pieces crunched under our tires as he pulled the Cherokee up to a little sign on a grassy path by the door to the building: "SoundSafe. Keeping the Long Island Sound Clean. Est. 1983."

"We going in guns blazing and camera rolling?" he asked.

"No, no, no. Geez, this is my last shot to pull this together; you freak these people out, and I'm done."

"Don't give me any ideas," he said.

"You stay back and work on your attitude; a little introspection about your anger issues would be good. I'll go in and see what we got."

I walked to the front door, which was wide open. The place had a laid-back feel to it, the way places by the shore usually do. Like life slowed down when you were around large bodies of water. I stepped inside, and it took my eyes a few seconds to adjust from the brilliant sunlight to the darkness within the long shack of a building.

The place appeared empty. On my right was a desk and on my left were two others facing it. Farther down on the left was an old couch and a few chairs around a coffee table in kind of a loosely defined sitting area. A radio was on somewhere, the announcer talking about a blowout sale at a furniture store. The rear of the building was open, like a big garage door was up.

"Hello?" I called as I walked toward the open back door.

No answer.

The back opened out onto a little grass patch with an old wooden bench where you could sit and watch the boat traffic on the river, which was maybe forty feet away. The sound was off in the distance down to the right, with the cluster of the rocky Norwalk Islands right in front.

There was an ancient, weather-beaten boat up on cinder blocks not far from the back door, and I walked across the grass and then a gravel stretch to the boat. It looked like something out of the dark ages: a large wooden hulk, like an old-time fishing boat, with a small square cabin in the middle by the wheel and the controls.

It was painted light blue with the word *SoundSafe* in white in a swirling cursive like a wave. A local phone number was painted behind the tail of the wave.

I spotted a pair of Top-Sider-clad feet on the other side as I approached, and so I went around. There was a guy with his back to me inspecting a hole in the hull. He was dressed in shorts and a faded red T-shirt. He had a thick head of light brown hair and maybe a matching beard from what I could see. Sunglasses rested on top of his head.

"I'm looking for Michael Barnes," I said.

His eyes never left the boat.

"You found him," he said.

He was turned sideways to me now and I could see the full beard, and I walked closer. "What happened to the boat?" I asked.

He looked at me and appeared to be very, very pissed off. "Some fucking clown in his little water chariot clipped me down there," he said, nodding toward the long wooden dock that jutted out into the river. There were two smaller and equally beat-up boats by the dock.

"Quite a fleet," I said.

"Thanks. I guess that means you're here with a check so I can replace them all," he said.

"Not really."

"You look like a banker," he said.

I was dressed professionally, pressed dress slacks and a pressed white dress shirt, sleeves rolled up to the elbows. It was nice he noticed.

"Thanks."

"That wasn't a compliment," he said.

His face was round, red, and weathered, and his hair looked as though it had been a while since it had seen a brush. "What are you here for?" he asked.

"Drugs," I said.

He looked at me like he was trying to keep from throwing a punch. "You're a funny guy," he said.

"I like to think so."

"Comedian, I guess," he said.

"Nope. Oh for two. TV reporter."

"That's considered lowest of the bunch in some places," he said.

"What about around here?" I asked. I introduced myself and put out my hand, and I thought he took it only because he felt he had to.

"I'm not a big TV watcher," he said. He started to walk to the back of the boat. "You doing another one of those nice features on the former druggie turned environmental watchdog? Someone probably does one a year on me, used to be twice."

"Dropping off in popularity. Can't imagine why," I said.

"If you're younger than thirty, you probably have no idea how crappy the sound used to be."

We were walking now and at the back of the boat. He was inspecting it for additional damage.

"I'm working on a story on an old friend of yours ... Buck McConnell," I said.

His hand was on the back of the boat, scratching at a piece of rotting wood. He kept at it like he hadn't heard me. But I knew he had. In a moment he stopped what he was doing and turned to me. "What the hell do you want?"

If a question could be a threat, this was it.

"I need to know what happened at Harvard on the night of October 21, 1971," I said.

Chapter 45

The idea of going out in a boat with Barnes didn't exactly thrill me. But that was the offer he made. Just him and me. No Freddie and no camera.

I walked back inside the building on my way out to the Jeep but saw that I didn't need to go that far. There, standing at the other end by the front door, was Freddie, chatting up the young gal who sat behind the desk.

Typical, I thought. *I'm doing all the heavy lifting and he's getting another phone number.*

She was young, with long, tangled, stringy brown hair. She wore a sundress, and in another era she could have easily have passed for a follower of the Grateful Dead. And Freddie had her entertained, laughing like he was doing a stand-up act.

"Shhhhh," he said as I walked toward them. "Here comes the boss."

He introduced me to Jennifer, and she was quite pleasant, with a nice smile on a face that I guessed didn't see a lot of makeup. We exchanged greetings, and I asked to see Freddie outside for a moment.

When we were at the Jeep, I laid it out for him.

"Okay, here's the deal," I said.

"We're not going out on a boat, are we?"

"No, you big baby, we're not. You're safe. *I'm* going out on a boat."

"With Mike?" he asked.

"Yeah, how'd you know?"

"Jen told me all about him. Used to have a pretty bad heroin jones. Apparently, was not a nice guy."

"Why doesn't that surprise me?"

"I'll stay back with Jen," he said.

"I assumed as much. But she doesn't seem like your type."

"Need to keep an open mind with these things, my friend."

"Of course. Look, I'm not all that comfortable with this guy. He's a little edgy, kind of nasty. I get in any situation out there, I'm going to text you, understand?"

"And what, I'm supposed to swim out to you or something?"

"Good point."

"Like I'm a damn Labrador."

"Okay, okay, I get it. Well, just stay awake with this stuff while I'm out there. If, like, a half hour passes and you don't see or hear from me, call me. How's that?"

We went back inside, and Freddie pulled up a chair next to Jen while I walked through the place and out the back to Barnes. He was down on the little dock, looking at both of SoundSafe's other two boats.

"I'm ready for the high seas," I said as I reached him.

His eyes went from one to the other. "Trying to pick the least bad one. Both of these things need work," he said.

He gave them another look and finally started for the beat-up faded red one.

"We'll go with this one," he said. "The engine is in slightly better shape."

It was another wooden hulk from the same era as the one up on blocks. Another relic from a long-ago commercial fishing fleet.

A few minutes later we were pushing off from the dock under the power of a whining and wheezing engine. The engine groaned as we moved down the Norwalk River and out into the Long Island Sound.

It occurred to me that this was one heck of a way to spend a day at work, even if the boat felt like it was going to fall apart. Here I was, under a beautiful blue sky with a bit of a breeze, cruising out on the water.

The water was full of boats, with people taking advantage of a day made for being outdoors. We moved slowly past Sheffield Island and out into the sound. An occasional boat passed and waved to Barnes as he piloted.

The shoreline of Long Island was a shadow off in the distance now. Barnes cut the engine, and we walked to the back of the boat. He was a big guy but surefooted. I, on the other hand, took each step carefully, my nice Italian loafers sliding on the deck of the boat like it was ice.

"It's somewhere right out around here," he said, as he scanned the water.

"Buried treasure?" I asked.

"Funny," he said, in a tone that indicated it was anything but. "Try tires."

"Really?"

"Some clown has been making a dump run at night. Mostly tires, but you can figure he's probably not stopping there. If he's an auto shop, might be batteries and other crap."

"Geez."

"No kidding. I catch the guy, I'm going to beat the living shit out of him, then turn him over to the cops," he said.

It occurred to me being turned over would probably seem like a relief to the dumper.

Barnes moved to a little red Igloo cooler, and took out two bottles of water, and threw one across to me. He sat down across from me on the little bench that ran along the inside of the back of the boat and pushed his shades up onto his head.

"Why are you trying to dig up dirt on McConnell?" he asked.

I took a drink of water before answering. "Because he's a bad guy, but I just can't prove it yet."

"You want to be the reporter who takes him out? Knocks his ass right out of the race for the White House?"

"Rather it be me than someone else."

"You think you can handle him?"

"So far, so good. I've gotten close and been shot at for my effort," I said.

"And you're still here," he said.

"I am."

"And your buddy who's back there flirting with Jen, he knows what he's doing?" he said.

I smiled. Barnes didn't miss a thing.

"He does."

We both had some water, and I pressed him.

"October, sophomore year at Harvard. What happened?" I asked.

His eyes locked on mine from across the boat and stayed on them even as he had another drink of water. When he was good and ready he started.

"How'd you find out about this?" he said.

"From someone who doesn't think Buck McConnell should be allowed anywhere near the White House," I said.

"I tell you about this, you need to be real careful. This isn't about beating some parking ticket," he said.

"Understood."

He took another long pull on the water like he was still thinking about it, then started.

"There were three of us there," he said. "Middle of October. Not sure what happened over the summer with Buck and his father, but there was some issue and Daddy cut off the plentiful supply of money to teach Buck a lesson."

Out on the sound a motorboat zipped along, pulling a laughing teenager in a tire tube. She yelled as she bounced along, and it seemed like a perfectly good way to spend a day.

"Buck was, and I guess still is, a pigheaded, stubborn son of a bitch," he said. "So he's going to show Daddy McConnell he can make his own money."

"His way."

"The illegal way," Barnes said.

He paused and looked at me to see if it had sunk in. It had.

"Drugs," I said.

"Yup. Buck decides to use the McConnell entrepreneurial gene to distribute cocaine to the stressed-out undergrads," he said.

"Holy shit," was all I could manage.

"You got it. You ever get on the air with this and you'll be bigger shit than you could have ever imagined," he said.

"What happened up there?" I said. "He was going to buy wholesale and sell retail?"

"He arranges to meet some dirt bag dealer on the big night."

"You were with him?"

"Uh-huh," he said. "I was supposed to be the muscle."

The boat rocked on the rolling water and the sun beat down on us, and Barnes just sat and looked at me. Neither of us said anything for a moment.

"How much do you know?" he asked.

"Enough to know you got the short end of things."

"'Screwed' is how I like to refer to it," he said.

"So, you're with Buck."

He shook his head. "Stupidest thing I ever did. Got to remember, back then everybody was flipping out about heroin. Guys were coming back from Vietnam as junkies. Coke was just reappearing and seemed a like a fun, recreational drug. Until you got busted for it."

"So, you go to make a buy."

"About five kilos," he said.

"What happens?"

"Walk in to find the dealer and some other guys."

"Who weren't dealers."

"Cops. Two of them. African American guy and a white guy. Remember it like it was this morning. It was over in a flash."

"Harvard?"

"Also over in a flash. Got a degree from the state penitentiary system of Massachusetts."

"Buck?"

"I thought we were going away. I was wrong," he said.

"The best lawyers money can buy?"

"Some Houston hotshot flew in that night and had him out the next morning before I woke up from the twenty minutes of sleep I got. Never heard from him again," he said.

"At least he's loyal."

"To Buck," he said.

"Quite a start to the college business."

"Possession with intent to distribute. Was good for six years of my life. Could have been three times as much if it weren't for my uncle's help."

"In the legal business as well?"

"Yeah, deceased now, but a New York heavyweight back in the day. Did what he could to get it reduced from twelve years to six. I served almost six."

"And Buck?"

"Was back at Harvard a week later. Heard he was telling people he had to go home to say good-bye to his dying grandmother," he said.

"And get his butt kicked by Daddy."

"He moved on without missing a beat," he said. "Not sure how his dad's guy did it, but seemed like he got Buck's name erased from anything to do with that night."

The boat drifted a bit and Barnes stood up and put his shades down and went to the wheel. I got up and joined him.

"Let me ask you," I said, "he's been hiding this thing for decades. How'd he do it?"

"Got to remember, he was a snotty rich kid but so was most of the rest of the class. Wasn't Buck McConnell yet," he said.

"This gets out, he's done," I said.

He laughed and shook his head.

"Crap, guys drop out of presidential campaigns because they lied on their taxes or cheated on their wife," he said.

"And fact is, he wasn't looking to dabble as a recreational user. He was looking to make a hard-core, dealer buy," I said.

"That's right. As good as he is, no way you spin that. Buck McConnell was looking to go into business as a coke dealer? Not a lot of ways of reframing, as they say, that one," he said.

"You ever get any pressure to keep quiet?" I asked.

He had both hands on the boat's wheel now and was staring out into the sound.

"About six months after I got out, someone came by and offered me money. Some big guy," he said. "I figured he was a hired hand for Buck."

He stood still and stared. I kept my mouth closed because there was no reason to open it and speak.

"I was a mess. Living in New Orleans. Had a drug habit all my own and it was years before I cleaned up. Told the guy to screw off and he left. Think old Buck probably figured I'd help him out and self-destruct on my own."

A couple of gulls squawked overhead and swooped past us.

"There's something you need to understand," he said.

"Which is?"

"So long as Buck McConnell is running IT&E, really no reason for anyone to say boo. But if the man is running for president, hell, that's another story. He's a dishonest sleazebag."

"Either makes him highly qualified for the job, or disqualifies him. Can't decide which," I said.

"Either way, the voters should know. They need to know," he said. Barnes started the engine up, and it rumbled to life. It was way too loud to speak over, and I got the feeling he was well aware of that and had told me all he wanted to, or all he knew.

I tried yelling a question. "You ever share this story with anybody else?" I asked.

He looked straight ahead, never taking his eye off the water and the boats passing in front of us.

Chapter 46

We were sitting at one of the picnic tables on the deck of Sono Seafood overlooking Norwalk harbor. I was working on a fried clam sandwich. Freddie was just about done with his New York strip steak sandwich. The large seagull sitting on the post three feet away was getting antsy at the prospect of there not being a thing leftover.

"Don't throw him anything," I said. "You feed him, and you just encourage him and his buddies."

"Poor guy looks emaciated," Freddie said.

"Don't be an enabler," I said.

We had stopped for lunch on our way back out to I-95. The place sat right on the harbor, and you looked down onto boats coming in from and going out to the sound. We were just a few blocks from the plush offices of SoundSafe, and I was still trying to figure out if there was a connection between Jack and Barnes.

"You believe him?" Freddie asked.

"Barnes?"

"Yeah."

I took a bite of the clam roll and thought about his story of the drug deal gone haywire.

"Yes," I said.

"Going to be hard to verify," he said. "Be easy enough to check out if Barnes went away to prison, but old Buck got his record wiped clean, I'm sure."

"Scrubbed and tidied up," I said. "But there has to be some way of proving it. Some record of it somewhere, don't you think?"

Freddie finished a bite of the steak sandwich before answering.

"Happened decades ago," he said. "You'd think if it was going to come out, it would have before now."

"A rich guy's family lawyer can be a powerful tool," I said.

A couple of gulls circled overhead hoping to get lucky, then glided lazily back over toward the water.

"I don't understand why Barnes didn't nail McConnell with this before," Freddie said. "He had the goods on him for all these years."

"But Buck was just a CEO. He probably knew McConnell had sky high ambitions and was biding his time," I said. "Probably plotted this out while sitting in prison."

"Experience like that can make you bitter," Freddie said.

"And patient."

"Guess so," he said.

"Plus, he knew he couldn't just hand it to anybody. Needed to make sure it was going to someone who could put it together and someone with a big enough platform to make a splash with it."

"Jack Steele," he said.

"Yup."

A small motorboat buzzed past the dock on its way out to the sound. A guy in a baseball cap piloted it while a yellow Lab stood at the nose of the boat, head help up and enjoying the breeze on its face.

"So, you convinced he told this all to Jack?" Freddie said.

"Don't know for sure," I said. "It was like he refused to say anything after a certain point. He just shut down. Said he needed to get back and take his other boat out on the water to see how it was running. Sounded like an excuse."

"Maybe he got tired of your questions," Freddie said.

"Maybe."

"You can get annoying," he said.

"I'm just persistent."

"Obnoxious is more like it," he said.

There was a low rumbling of an engine somewhere behind me, and I turned to see the third boat in the SoundSafe fleet coming down the river and heading out toward the sound. This one was smaller than the other two, its hull painted in a light blue.

"How the hell does he expect to catch polluters in those piece-of-crap boats?" Freddie asked. "Needs some speedboats."

"Maybe you and your environmentalist friends can kick in a few dollars to make that happen," I said.

"Maybe not," he said.

We watched the slow progress of the boat as it cruised past, and I could make out the figure of Barnes at the wheel. He was too far away to recognize us, but we could see his silhouette piloting the boat.

"Here's what I think," I said.

"Always a revelation."

"I think he was going to tell Jack this story. But I'm not sure if he made the first move to do it," I said.

"Probably not. There's no way Jack would have sat on this if he'd had it," Freddie said.

"Unless he wasn't sure of it, or didn't have all the details for something this big. But yes, there'd be no way Jack would not have run this if he'd had it."

"He wanted to nail McConnell," Freddie said.

"They both did," I said. "Barnes is saying the voters need to know, but it's really all about payback."

"Always is," Freddie said.

In the water below us a small motorboat cruised by at harbor speed with a blonde woman sunbathing in the front. Some guy wearing a baseball cap was piloting and gave us a wave when he saw us watching their progress.

"How do I trade places with that guy?" Freddie asked.

"What, and give up our quality time? Who's going to help me solve this?"

"Someone else," he said.

I poked around at the clams that had fallen off my sandwich. "Barnes said he didn't watch much TV, but I think he's lying. I bet you he saw Jack going after McConnell as part as Operation Outrage."

"If he didn't see it, he probably read about it somewhere," Freddie said. "Sure he was keeping tabs on McConnell, being that the man had a part in his winding up on the inside for six years."

"So lets say Barnes sees or reads about Jack going after McConnell and the corporate corruption. Now he knows Jack and *Steele Yourself* would be the perfect platform to nail McConnell for good. Once and for all. Even the score," I said.

"Payback," Freddie said.

There was a burst of squawking as some guy at the other end of the deck decided it would be smart to feed the seagulls. Dozens of them, some big, swooped in from nowhere and circled the food donator and his date. Hopefully, he would think twice about such behavior in the future.

I downed a bit of my iced tea and glanced across the deck to the inside of the restaurant. I could see the dark bar area, and off in the distance a TV that was on above the bar. It was an all-news channel, but not Liberty. On screen was video of Buck McConnell. He was getting out of a car and walking across the sidewalk, standard B-roll shots.

When the anchor reappeared, there was a graphic behind her of McConnell superimposed over the White House.

"Hang on," I said, getting up.

I went inside and stood at the corner of the bar. The sound was down on the TV, but it didn't matter. Across the bottom of the screen a banner ran with two lines:

"IT&E CEO Buck McConnell to enter presidential race"
"Official announcement expected within days"

I read it and reread it then went back outside. Freddie was leaning back with his eyes closed and face tilted up to the sky, soaking in the sun.

"It's official. McConnell is going for the White House," I said.

"Wake me when there's something important to talk about," he said, "other than Buck McConnell."

Freddie was right, Buck McConnell could wait for the moment. I sat down and looked out toward the sound and took in view. Sheffield Island felt so close you could touch it, and sailboats with colorful sails glided across the deep blue water. I spotted the back of the SoundSafe boat chugging out into the open expanse of the sound, and it occurred to me that Michael Barnes had the best job in the world on days like this.

I closed my eyes, leaned back, and lifted my face toward the sky. I breathed in the salt air and heard gulls squawking out over the water. It was peaceful and I felt myself relax for the first time in days.

Then a boom shook the deck, a loud, violent explosion that jerked me from my rest. People gasped and screamed and jumped up from the benches of the picnic tables. Overhead, hundreds of gulls filled the sky screeching and adding to the chaos. People stood pointing toward the sound. I jumped up on the bench and saw Freddie already up, his camera on his shoulder, racing to the other end of the deck and pushing people out of the way to get there.

Off in the distance out on the sound, just to the left of Sheffield Island, a large fireball floated to the sky. Below it flames and thick, black smoke rose from the remains of a sinking boat. The nose of the vessel rose up and out of the water as it sank. I could see the color of the boat as it disappeared underwater. It was light blue.

It was the SoundSafe boat.

Chapter 47

Michael Barnes was dead. Killed less than an hour after I had left him. Herman Bindagi had disappeared, and possibly the same for Billy Hunter. The common denominator was they all had something on Buck McConnell. All three had also spoken to me. It was enough to give me a complex.

"Let's play a game," I said.

I was sitting across from Liz at a table for four at a little Mexican restaurant in the West Village. Freddie was next to her. It was a low-key place and the dining room was full and the noise of a dozen conversations gave us enough cover to talk.

"A game?" Liz said.

"Yes."

"I knew he was going to crack," Freddie said. "Pressure is just too much for some people."

"I just didn't think it would be right before our eyes," Liz said, before enjoying some more of her margarita.

I was having a tough time getting rid of the images of this afternoon, of the fireball rising from boat of Michael Barnes. A tough time getting rid of the thought that if Barnes had decided to take me out in that light blue boat, I wouldn't be sitting here, or anywhere for that matter. I needed to figure this out, and soon.

"I was twenty-two," I said. "My first job. Back at the *Bangor Citizen*."

"Thought you were a TV reporter in Bangor," Freddie said.

"That's what he told me, too," Liz said.

"Might be some secret past," Freddie said.

"No," I said. "Same guy owned the TV station and the newspaper. I had to report for both. Actually had no choice."

"A multitasker before there was multitasking," Freddie said.

"Talented," Liz said.

"A guy named Mel Henry was the city editor," I said. "And old Mel pounded the five Ws and the H into me."

"The five Ws and the H?" Freddie said.

"Is this a children's story?" Liz said.

"Who, what, when, where, why, and how," I said. "It's an old journalism rule. Answer all those, and you have your story."

I grabbed one of the paper menus from the side of the table and started writing in the margin.

"Jack's death," I said. "Let's start with who. Who did it?"

"Buck McConnell," Freddie said.

"Or someone he hired," Liz said.

I scribbled it in the white space at the margin.

"What," I said. "What happened?"

"We're not exactly positive," Liz said.

"But he wound up in the East River," Freddie said.

"Right," I said and circled the word what. "We'll come back to that. Next is when."

"Sometime after midnight, or maybe one a.m.," Freddie said.

"Close enough for now," I said.

I continued writing as I talked.

"Where?" I said.

"Thirty-fourth Street," Liz said. "He gets in a cab and gets dropped off at Thirty-fourth and First, right?"

"Right," I said. "The cops have a cabbie saying he picked him up outside his building, then took him down there, so we know that."

I read through what we had so far.

"Okay kids, why?" I said.

"Trying to prevent a story on IT&E equipment in Syria, or bribes overseas," Freddie said.

"I think he was afraid a story on the drug bust from forty years ago would kill his presidential hopes," Liz said.

"Right, maybe even both. It seems like we got enough of a motive," I said. "But the one we really got to figure out is, how. How the hell did this happen to Jack?"

"All we know for sure is that he went out without his fully licensed and legal-to-carry handgun," Liz said.

"Yes," I said. "Which I'm going to interpret as meaning he was going to meet someone he didn't think would pose a threat to him."

"Guy like Steele going out in the middle of the night, unarmed, with no security, you got to believe he was going to meet someone he felt pretty safe with," Freddie said.

We thought about it for a moment while the waitress paid us a visit and cleared the plates and took orders for coffee.

"There has to be some clues somewhere," Liz said.

"But where?" Freddie said. "All we know is the man was sitting at his desk then gets up and leaves his apartment to go meet someone, if you believe us."

"Or goes jumps in the river, if you believe the police," Liz said.

"And they got the note which makes their version look better than ours," Freddie said.

I looked at Liz, then at Freddie.

"What?" Freddie said.

"The note," I said.

"What about it?" he said.

"There has to be something there," I said.

"It is puzzling," Liz said.

"When was it written? How'd it get on Jack's desk? Where on Jack's desk was it found?" I said.

"So many questions," Liz said.

"He's got no problem with questions," Freddie said. "It's the answer thing he struggles with."

Chapter 48

"Where exactly was it?" I asked.

It was an hour later and I was back in the cluttered home office of Jack Steele, I was standing close enough to Robbie to get a whiff of a bath soap or body cream. Whatever it was, it was soft and pleasing to the nose.

"Right here," she said, tapping the pile of folders and papers. "There was a bigger pile here that night, but this is where it was."

"Jack had piles of papers and books everywhere," I said. "Why right here?"

"It was just here, right in the top folder. The one with his research and background for upcoming shows and guests," she said. "Does that mean anything?"

"Maybe," I said. "But I need to figure it out. And this note, you said you didn't find it, right?"

She shook her head.

"No, it was one of the detectives. Think his name was Vickers," she said. "I have his card if you need it."

"How'd he wind up in this room? The cop."

"I ... don't remember," she said. "He just came in here."

Her eyes were beginning to moisten, and she looked down at the desk.

"I was sitting out on the couch. He and his partner were asking about what Jack had been doing before he went out that night." She paused and tried to gather herself.

"And what was he doing that night?" I asked.

"We've gone over this," she said.

"We have. And we need to keep going over it until I figure it out."

"He either got a call or made a call. I heard him talking to someone. I told them that," she said.

"And that's what the police report said."

"But they didn't believe me," she said.

"And there's no record of it?"

"No," she said.

The police had checked Jack and Robbie's cell phone account and the apartment phone, but there was no sign of a call during the time frame she specified, incoming or outgoing.

"He had made a few other calls earlier in the night," she said.

"To?"

"He called Dr. Webber to cancel his session. And he called Manny and told him he was in for the night and to go home," Robbie said.

"But you're certain there was another call, later?"

"Yes," she said.

"What time?"

"Between eleven and eleven thirty," she said.

"Did you overhear anything at all? Anything specific?"

She shook her head. "No. We converted a room to a yoga studio on the other side of the apartment, and I was in there. There's a long hallway that separates that side of the apartment from this side. But I heard his voice. I know I did."

"And you're sure it wasn't one of these other calls? The Webber or Manny call?"

"Positive. This was later, much later," she said.

"What happened after the detective found the note?"

"The one guy came out and got his partner. They came back here, then they came out to talk to me and show me the note." She stopped to pull her thoughts together. "I remember he hesitated in showing it to me, and I yelled at him to just give it to me."

"You read it?" I asked.

"Yes, a couple of times," she said.

"And?"

"I knew right away it was fake," she said.

"And you told them so?"

"Yes," she said. "But they didn't believe me about the note and didn't believe me about the call."

"They thought you were just the emotional, distraught widow."

"Right," she said.

"I believed you on the note."

"Not at first you didn't," she said.

"You're right," I said. "But I quickly realized the error of my ways and came around."

A thin smile creased her face, and she was a different person.

"And I believe you on the call," I said.

"Okay," she said.

"There's something with the note, but I don't know what," I said. "At least just yet."

"But you'll figure it out," Robbie said.

"I hope. In the meantime, what I need is every phone bill you have: yours, Jack's, anything and everything. I know the police looked at them, but I want to see them."

"I can get those," she said.

"And I want a copy of all your credit card bills for the last three months," I said.

"Okay, but why?" she said.

"I have a hunch."

Chapter 49

"You realize they're going to come after you again," Freddie said.

We were sitting in the Cherokee, parked on Sixth Avenue out in front of Liberty. I had a stack of phone bills and credit card statements I was examining. It was just before eleven on Friday morning, and Freddie had WBGO on, listening to jazz.

"Must we focus on such unpleasantness?" I asked.

"If they had been watching Barnes up in SoundSafe, they saw you and him talking," he said.

"That boat had to have been rigged well before we got there."

"Yeah, but someone was probably watching, just to follow through," he said.

"So what are you saying?"

"I'm saying, if you're going to attract the same type of attention, I don't want to be too close to you."

"It's okay," I said. "I don't own a boat."

Freddie shook his head. "Man, how you got this far in life is a mystery to me."

I scanned the pages of credit card charges that Robbie had given me but was coming up empty.

"Nothing," I said, looking at the pages of American Express charges. "Although Robbie does a fair amount of shopping in Madison Avenue boutiques."

"Any lingerie purchases?"

"Easy."

There was a tapping at the window by Freddie and I looked over to see Susan.

"You know this gal?" he asked.

"I do," I said, and motioned for her to get in the back.

Susan climbed in and shut the door and Freddie locked them.

"Freddie was worried you were a stalker," I said.

"Well, I'd have two very attractive candidates for stalkees here, wouldn't I?" she asked.

Freddie smiled and looked at her in the rearview mirror.

"We miss you up there, big guy," Susan said.

"Talk to your boss, he's the one who suspended me," I said.

"He's telling people that you needed to take some time off. Get yourself together. That type of thing," she said.

"People buying it?" I asked.

Susan hesitated, and I turned and looked at her. She was attractive and feisty and not one to sugarcoat the truth.

"Yeah, I think they are, Sam. I mean, people are saying you've been acting pretty strange. Talk is that you're involved with Jack's wife."

"I'm not. I mean, I am, but not involved in the way people think."

"Doesn't matter to me," she said. "You do what you have to do."

I knew she doubted me as well but was still holding out hope that I hadn't taken up with Robbie Steele.

"I have the bills," she said, waving a manila folder.

"Hand 'em over," I said.

"No questions asked," she said, "but it would be nice to know what you're looking for."

"I'll know it when I see it."

I opened the folder and saw copies of Jack's Liberty News corporate American Express card statements. Susan had gone back and printed out six months' worth of transactions. She settled into the back while I started going over the paperwork.

"So, Mr. Freddie, what is it that you do?" she asked. "Besides sitting here listening to John Coltrane all day?"

It occurred to me that almost everything Susan said sounded flirty.

Freddie looked at her in the rearview mirror.

"Jazz fan?"

"Not my number one music, but I dabble."

I scanned the transactions, starting with the latest statement, and saw plenty of lunches from the expense account restaurants right around this neighborhood. And there were a few charges from Amazon.com. But nothing that jumped out at me.

The previous month started with more of the same, until I got toward the end of the billing cycle.

"What's this?" I asked.

"Might have to be a little more specific," Freddie said.

"Ohhh, and sarcastic, too," Susan said. "A man after my heart."

"This charge for something at Forty-sixth Street Electronics?" I said.

"That was me," Susan said. "In one of my roles as executive assistant to big egos at Liberty. Jack asked me to pick up something for him. Karen was out, and he asked if I could run out to an electronics store and pick up a phone."

"A phone?" I asked.

"Yes, you make calls with them," she said.

"What kind?"

"Rotary," Freddie said.

"Giving straight answers has become a lost art," I said.

"Thank God," Susan said.

I looked back at her. "Anyone ever tell you you're a joy?" I asked.

"Yes, thank you," she said.

"Tell me about this phone."

"Jack said he needed a phone for a story and wanted it right away.

He said he didn't want the hassle of setting up an account and all that crap," she said.

"And curses like a sailor," Freddie said. "What a find."

"What'd you do?" I asked.

"I explained all of his options to him," she said.

"And?"

"And he sent me on my way," Susan said.

"What'd he buy, or rather, what'd you buy, on his credit card?"

"One of those prepaid types. No credit checks or paperwork or all that other stuff," she said.

"He never said what story or anything specific about why he wanted it?" I asked.

"Sammy ..." she said, "do you think I bought the I-need-a-new-phone-for-a-story line? I mean, I nodded and smiled like I understood when he asked, but—"

"But you think it was for something else?"

Susan leaned forward in the direction of Freddie. "Is he always this naive, Mr. Freddie?"

Freddie chuckled, and she turned back to me. "What's the number one reason a guy would want a phone where there would be no record of his calls?"

Chapter 50

"No way in hell," Freddie said as he pulled up next to a hydrant in front of the Manhattan Yoga Project on Prince Street in Soho. "Absolutely no way in hell Jack Steele was cheating on Robbie Steele," he said.

"I'm not saying he was," I said. "But he gets a prepaid phone so no one knows who he's talking to. Now, my guess is, it's related to his digging up dirt on McConnell, or—"

"Or something else," he said. "Man would have to be nuts to run around on someone like her."

I opened the door and stepped out as two women in terrific shape and dressed for a workout walked past. Freddie watched them go to the door that led upstairs to the yoga studio on the second and third floors.

"If you're not out in sixty seconds, I'm coming in," he said.

A minute later I climbed the stairs up to the studio. Robbie had returned to teaching here a few days ago. When I called and said there was something I needed to speak to her about in person, she suggested I stop by.

I walked into a small reception area and was greeted by a young gal behind the counter. Her brown hair was pulled back in a ponytail, and she wore a gray tank top with enough signs of sweat on it and her forehead to tell me she had just worked out.

I told her I was here to see Robbie, and she pointed to a class under way in a studio on the other side of a glass partition.

"The class will be over in a few minutes," she said, with a helpful, eager tone.

I thanked her, and she offered something to drink.

"We have green or black tea, and water, of course."

"Of course."

"So ... water?" she said.

"Why not?" I said.

She got up and went into a little side room behind her desk, then emerged with a plastic bottle of water. The label on it appeared to be in French. I didn't see an English translation. I thanked her and glanced in at the studio to see Robbie leading the group in a stretch that looked both painful and illegal in some states.

"She's been through so much," the young receptionist said, watching me watch Robbie.

I opened my bottle of French water and took a drink. I found the English translation. It said it was from a spring in the mountains. "She certainly has," I said. "How's she holding up?"

"Pretty good, I mean, let's face it, her husband wasn't universally loved," she said.

"No, he wasn't."

I went over and sat down on a small couch in the corner that felt like it was filled with straw. I was willing to bet it was made with organically grown hemp from the Andes or somewhere.

"Did you know him?" she asked. "Jack Steele."

"I did. Worked with him, as a matter of fact."

Her eyes widened, and her little smile broadened. "Oh my God. You're that guy," she said. She was very excited now.

"Yes. Yes, I am, that guy," I said.

"The guy, you know ..."

"Yes, I do know."

"The guy on TV. On Liberty. You had the story on Jack's death," she said.

"I did."

I had more French mountain water while she tried unsuccessfully to compose herself. "Oh my gosh, what was that like?" she asked.

She had been flirty and fun when I walked in, but now she was dangerously close to crossing over to scary.

"Not the most enjoyable story I've covered."

"Oh, I can imagine," she said.

Something told me if this conversation continued, I was going to be called "poor thing" at some point. It needed to stop, and thankfully it did when Robbie walked into the reception area. She was drenched in sweat but still managed to look great.

"Manhattan's female elite adequately stretched out for the day?" I asked.

Robbie smiled at my new fan. "Heather, I'll be in the office if anyone is looking for me."

She led me into the little room behind reception and closed the door. She sat down on a low chair across the room, and I took a matching one by the door. The room was quiet and filled with little vases of bamboo plants. I expected we were either going to talk or mediate.

"What do you need to know?" she asked. She was all business.

"I may have partially solved the question of the phone call that night," I said. "The one there's no record of."

"Was never a question to me," she said.

"Jack had someone at Liberty run out and buy him a prepaid phone about six weeks ago. He ever mention it?"

She shook her head.

"You have any idea it existed?"

Another shake of the head.

"It would explain why there was no trace, no record of a call, on any of the other phones," I said.

"Can we find it, the phone?" she asked.

"I'll try," I said, knowing full well that was likely never going to be happen. For all I knew, it could be sitting on the bottom of the East River.

Now that I had given Robbie the good news, I needed to get a question cleared up. What if Jack *had* been having an affair? Hell, what if he was actually going out to meet her that night, and maybe a jealous boyfriend or husband showed up?

It was a whole other direction, but I needed to make sure there was nothing there. I had a plan, a strategy, for bringing it up. Now, I'm not saying it was a good plan, but it was the only one I had.

"Robbie, the YouTube video," I said, of the embarrassing reminder of his slip with the production assistant.

She nodded. So far, so good.

"Were there any other ..." I stalled and hemmed and hawed and was unable to finish the sentence. I was uncomfortable, and it was like my command of the language had slipped away.

"Any other what?" she asked.

"Any other ... incidents?" I said, blurting it out.

"You mean other incidents of my husband making out with someone a third his age, like he was a drunken frat boy?"

"Yes, that's where I was going."

She glared and said nothing, and after a few moments it became even more uncomfortable. "May I ask why you want to know if he was screwing somebody on the side? That is what you're hinting at, correct?"

There was something about the conversation that was upsetting the balance and calm in the room.

"Why don't we call it 'having relations'?" I asked.

"If you prefer the biblical," she said.

"I need to know because if Jack bought a phone so no one would know who he was calling, well ..."

I let it hang there, and she let it hang there too, allowing me to twist in the wind. The room was silent, and oh how I longed for some distraction to end this little session of pain. Finally, Robbie took mercy on me.

"No," she said, "as far as I know, Jack was not having an affair. Does that answer your question?"

"Yes."

Chapter 51

"Maybe Jack had strayed in the past," Liz said.

"Could be. Would explain the hostility from her," I said.

"You were flat-out asking her if her dead husband had been sleeping with anybody behind her back," Freddie said.

We were sitting in a booth of the Old Town Bar on Eighteenth Street. It was after eleven, and the place was quiet. We had the first booth by the door and kept the conversation low enough to not be overheard.

"So we know he wasn't using this phone for extracurriculars," I said.

"And Robbie says she's certain he spoke to someone that night," Liz said.

"Someone we think he was going to meet at Thirty-fourth Street," Freddie said.

"And someone he was unthreatened by, being that he left the gun at home," I said.

"But without phone records it's all guesswork," Freddie said.

And it was. But it felt like guessing was all we could do at the moment.

I took a long drink of my Guinness and glanced at the TV above the bar. It was tuned to CNN. The host of the ten o'clock show was sitting in the studio interviewing some guy on a subject neither seemed to be excited about. More "must-see" TV.

"Why Thirty-fourth Street?" Liz asked. She was sipping a glass of pinot noir from a winery out on the Island.

"What do you have over there?" Freddie asked.

"The heliport," I said. "Bet you Jack was familiar with that."

"But that's long closed for the day by the time he got there," Freddie said. "So it's not like someone choppered in, pushed him in the river, and choppered back out."

"So maybe Jack didn't pick the spot," Liz said.

Freddie was sitting opposite us, with his back to the door and looking at the TV at the other end of the bar.

"There's your boy," he said.

I looked up and saw more footage of Buck McConnell. It was new stuff: McConnell getting out of the back door of his car and walking into the IT&E headquarters in Houston. He had the confident stride of someone who actually believed he should be running the country.

On the banner along the bottom was the latest news:

"Buck McConnell expected to announce White House run in NY speech next week"

It was Friday night, and according to that, sometime soon the man I was sure was behind Jack Steele's death was going to tell us all he was running for president.

"Water," Liz said.

We both looked at her. She looked at me, then Freddie.

"Water," she said again, like it was a major revelation.

"You thirsty?" I asked.

"Maybe access to water had something to do with the location," she said.

I looked at Freddie, and he was already staring at me.

"Barnes," he said. "The man was a boater."

"The SoundSafe guy," Liz said. "Maybe that's who Jack was going out to meet."

"The guy knew the waterways," I said. "But it's hard for me to believe one of his beat-up old boats would handle coming all the way down the sound, through Hell Gate, and into the East River."

"You think that guy was going to shy away from a challenge?" Freddie asked. "Especially if he had a chance to nail Buck McConnell?"

I looked up at the TV again. The newsreader was talking, and a box over her shoulder displayed McConnell's grinning mug. I stared it and wondered about the secrets the man had, thanks to his thirst for power and desire to be the leader of the free world.

I felt Liz's arm wrap around mine, and she pulled me toward her. "What are you thinking about?" she asked.

I glanced toward the TV. "That guy," I said.

If he had gone to the lengths of killing Jack Steele because his secret was about to be exposed, and if he had gone to the lengths of killing Michael Barnes because he feared Barnes was about to open up about the drug arrest, then he was not going to just stop suddenly.

"When I was on the boat with Barnes, he said something," I said.

Freddie was looking at me, and Liz had her head on my shoulder.

"He said something like, the voters need to know what kind of person McConnell is."

"He's the kind of guy who sells his equipment all over the world, making bribes for contracts," Freddie said. "Real upstanding, by-the-book kind of guy."

"Would that be enough for Barnes to try and come all the way down here in the middle of the night?" Liz asked.

"I think Barnes knew he had to act," I said. "I think he realized now was time to even the score with Buck McConnell."

"So, that's a yes?" Freddie said.

"It is," I said.

Chapter 52

"You think she's going to show up?" I asked as we drove down Water Street in Norwalk.

"Ladies always show up when I call," Freddie said.

"Attracted by your modesty, I guess."

It was just before eight on Saturday morning when we pulled into the parking area in front of the SoundSafe building. The gravel crunched as Freddie pulled into the parking spot closest to the door.

We were the only vehicle in the lot.

"We still have a few minutes," Freddie said, reading my mind.

"Before you get stood up."

"Before *we* get stood up," he said.

"Oh, sure. Now it's we."

We sat and waited for Jennifer, Freddie's new crunchy granola friend, to show up and give us access to Barnes's phone records to see if he had placed a call to Jack the night was killed.

"You think she's going to show?" I asked again.

"What, you're thinking in the three minutes since you last asked me that I changed my mind?" he said.

"Is that your way of telling me to stop bugging you about it?"

"No, this is my way. Stop bugging me," he said.

"How'd she sound, you know, when you spoke to her?"

"She was a mess," he said.

"Lost a boss, maybe more," I said.

"Don't think so. Don't think they were lovers. But that's just a hunch," he said.

We had the windows down, and I pulled in a deep breath of the saltwater air. Freddie turned and watched the handful of cars pass by.

"That's the third time," he said.

I looked over. "For?"

"That white van, one with the ladder on top."

I spotted it at the light, heading away from the sound. "Like a painter's van or something," I said.

"I prefer the 'or something.' Guy was behind us on Ninety-five on the way up."

"Where'd you pick him up?"

"Back around New Rochelle," he said.

"Got Connecticut plates," I said.

"I know. Must have had some business in New York early, then comes back up to Connecticut and happens to get off the same exit we do," he said.

"And just so happens to need to come down here to Water Street by the sound," I said.

"What a coincidence," Freddie said.

"Or not."

The light changed, and the van drove slowly away.

"So ... follows us down," I said, "sees where we're parking, turns around, and heads on his way?"

"If you're paranoid, that'd be what you're thinking," he said.

A tan Prius slowed at the entrance with its blinker on and took a left into the lot to join us.

"Here comes your gal," I said.

"Our gal."

The Prius pulled in next to us. We got out, and Freddie went over to greet Jen. She stepped out dressed in a sundress that was damn near the same as the one she'd had on the other day. Maybe it had been a buy-one-get-one-free promo or something.

They hugged, and Freddie comforted her like they went way back. He was good that way, making people feel relaxed around him, and you would have thought they had known each other for years, not days.

I went around to give my condolences and kept an eye on the street for the painter's van. "Thanks for meeting us," I said.

"I needed to get in here and go though the mail and sort through the messages that came in," she said, wiping away a tear. "The funeral is Monday, you know."

She seemed like a sweet kid.

She unlocked the door and we all walked in. She flipped on the lights and got settled at her desk and took out an Apple MacBook Air notebook computer for herself, then unlocked the lower desk drawer and took out another one for us. A minute later we were set up at one of the desks across from her, logged on to Barnes's e-mail and accessing his Verizon Wireless account.

She asked if we'd like coffee and went back to a little table to get the coffee things together, and a moment later Freddie and I joined her there as the coffee brewed.

"The police found a leak in the fuel line," she said.

"And what, something triggered the explosion?" Freddie asked.

She poured a cup as soon as the coffee finished brewing and went about adding a little sugar and milk. When she looked up I saw tears in her eyes.

"Mike liked to sneak cigarettes when he was out on the water," she said.

I thought back to when I was out with him. I hadn't seen any sign he was a smoker. No cigarette pack tucked in a cubbyhole anywhere. No ground-out butts anywhere.

"They think he may have been smoking and the cigarette fell on the deck, or somehow landed somewhere and sparked the explosion."

She seemed to take comfort in the theory, like it all made sense. I had a strong suspicion it *didn't* all make sense, but I was not going to share that with her. I had no idea what, if anything, she knew about Barnes and his past and his connection to McConnell, and I was not about to volunteer any details.

We went back to our seats, but this time Freddie pulled up a chair next to her. I had an idea that it was partly to comfort her out of genuine sympathy, but I also knew he figured that if he distracted her, she would ask fewer questions about why I needed to see e-mail and phone records. We had told her only that it concerned a story on dumping in the sound, and I needed to see when he had contacted the suspected dumper. She seemed to buy it.

I started back in July and scanned the e-mails. Barnes was not a big user of e-mail, which didn't surprise me. He was an old-school kind of guy. But there were a number of correspondences with people who had e-mailed him with sightings of dumpers. They all had a theme of, "I caught 'em red-handed."

An e-mail from some woman in Stamford, who swore she had seen a pickup truck dumping steel drums into the water. A guy up the Connecticut coast in Stratford, who wrote that his neighbor the painter routinely pours excess paint into a tributary down at the end of their street that runs to the sound.

To all of them Barnes responded with businesslike politeness, thanking them for their tip and vigilance, and saying he would mark their info down on his list of places to check. The e-mail traffic was light during early July, and I checked the Save and then the Sent folders for anything of interest.

It was when I was scanning the Sent folder that I saw the message.

To: Jack.Steele@Libertynews.com
    Subject: B. McConnell

Barnes had sent it on July 14, a few nights after Jack's first report on IT&E and their equipment winding up where it shouldn't be. I wanted to jump up and shout but decided against it. I lifted my eyes and looked across at Freddie, and we made eye contact, then I opened the e-mail.

No way Buck McConnell makes it to the White House. Forget your story on that IT&E junk. I got something that that will really nail him.

I reread it, and it answered one question for me. Yes, Michael Barnes had contacted Jack Steele to tell him about the drug bust. But that was it. There were no other e-mails at least in the Save folder, that were related to this. No reply from Jack, no back and forth. Just a copy of the one sitting in the Sent folder, a folder that I'm sure Barnes had forgotten to clean out.

I looked across at Freddie.

"Hey, look at this," I said, "an e-mail to Liberty News. How about that?"

Freddie looked at me like I was mad, but Jen spoke up before he could say anything. "Yeah, Mr. Left Wing Environmentalist Mike Barnes actually watched Liberty. He would never admit it to anyone but me," she said. "I mean, no offense to you guys, you seem real nice, but it's not for me."

"No need to apologize," I said. "I get that all the time. Who'd he like?"

"Jack Steele. And that other guy, the younger guy on before him," she said.

I nodded, and Freddie chatted her up while I went back to work. But I had confirmation of what I had suspected. Barnes was a closet Liberty watcher. There were a lot more out there than anyone thought.

I brought up the window with the Verizon account info and clicked on the page listing all the calls to and from Barnes's phone and scrolled back to July. None of these numbers jumped out at me. They were all just phone numbers I didn't recognize.

It was on July 26 that I saw the number of an outgoing call from Barnes. It was a number that belonged to Liberty: 212-555-0133. It was called at 9:35 p.m. that night and then showed up again on July 30, around the same time, and then August 2 at just before ten p.m. It was called again at 9:47 p.m. on August 8, the day before Jack was found dead in the river.

It was the only sign of contact between Barnes and Liberty, and I stared at it and tried to place it: 555-0100 was the switchboard; 555-0140 was the assignment desk.

I looked across at Freddie, who was thumbing though a copy of the *Times*. I picked up the phone on the desk, and Freddie gave me a passing glance. Jen was tapping away at her keyboard. I punched in the numbers and it rang. Once. Then twice. Then a third time. I recognized the voice that answered right away.

"You've reached the desk of Marty Glover, executive producer of ..."

Chapter 53

I scrambled to print out all the pages of calls from the phone and wanted to get outside as soon as possible to tell Freddie that Barnes had called Glover. The printer, on a small table behind me, was in no great hurry to perform. I grabbed the pages as they came out, closed out of all the open windows, and almost knocked the desk over as I got up.

My flurry of activity had caught Freddie's attention, and he got up and came toward me. "You okay?"

"Yeah, yeah. Just totally forgot I have that interview at ten in Midtown," I said.

"What inter—" He saw my eyes widen, and he got the message. "Oh, okay, I can get you back in time."

"Jen," I said, "I can't thank you enough for letting us do this. It was a huge help."

"Did you find what you needed to know about Buck McConnell?" she asked with a slight smile.

I stared at her and was speechless for a moment, which is a pretty rare occurrence.

She looked up at me with innocence and just a touch of knowing in her eyes. "Mike said he had something that could 'take that bastard out.'"

I smiled at her. She had been onto us the whole time, and while I wasn't sure how much she knew about Barnes and McConnell, it was clear she knew something.

I thanked her again and headed for the door, leaving Freddie to say good-bye. A minute later he was next to me, and we walked out into the bright sunshine.

"What the hell you got?" he asked.

"Marty is—"

There was the screech of tires and the sound of a vehicle accelerating, and simultaneously we both looked to our left, down Water Street. The white van was speeding toward us with the window on the passenger's side down.

"Back inside," he yelled as the van flew closer.

I turned, grabbed the doorknob, and pushed in with my shoulder; Freddie tumbled in behind me. We both crashed to the floor, and the door swung closed behind us as two loud blasts sounded. I heard a dull thud as a bullet caught wood around the door. The gravel out front crunched, and I heard it ping off the Jeep as the van sped away.

Jen screamed, and Freddie scrambled across the room, crouching down and staying low. Tires screeched outside, and I pictured the van turning around to take another crack at us. I stayed low and went for the door and heard Jen yell to me.

"Mike kept a pistol in the bottom desk drawer."

I looked back across the room. "Really?" I asked.

"Get the freaking thing," Freddie yelled.

Outside it was quiet. I was closer to the door than the desk, so I decided to take a peek. I stood up nice and slow by the window to the right of the door. I felt like one of the cowboys in an old western, checking to see of the black hats were gone. I stayed to the side of the window and moved a little bit at a time until I could see outside.

The van was gone.

Chapter 54

"I'm really getting tired of living like this," I said.

We were driving back into the city, coming down I-95, or the New England Thruway, as it's known on this stretch passing Larchmont.

"Me, too," Freddie said. "Having to be chauffeuring your ass all over the place: New York, New Jersey, Connecticut."

"I was talking about this living-in-fear thing. Now I got to worry about violent painters."

"I'm talking about driving your sorry ass all over the tristate region. And I'm not thrilled with being shot at either."

"My big fear is eventually one of these guys is going to get it right and hit me," I said.

"Might as well call myself Freddie's Tristate Car Service. Specializing in driving round lame TV reporters who can't put a damn story together but endanger others while they try," he said.

"I'm close," I said.

"Better step on it, 'cause old Buck's gonna be in the White House before you figure this all out."

"Marty's involved somehow," I said.

"You told me that already. Didn't tell me how," Freddie said.

"Mid-July Barnes sends Jack an e-mail saying he's got something on McConnell."

"Saw Jack's rant about McConnell's crap overseas," he said.

"Right. So, what does Jack do with the e-mail?"

"Like any good anchor he hands it to his producer and says, follow up," he said.

"Right. And Marty might have even been the one monitoring the viewer comments to begin with."

"Either way, it's on Marty to talk to Barnes," he said.

"Yes. And less than two weeks later, Barnes is calling Marty."

"They probably had some back and forth already," he said. "Marty finding out what Barnes had, then telling Jack."

"Probably, but Barnes cleared out his e-mails and there's no trace of that. But let's assume they talked or connected via e-mail between July 14 and July 26. Then the phone calls from Barnes to Marty heat up. Every couple of days right up to, and into, the night Jack went out."

"Like they were arranging something," Freddie said. "What time did Barnes call him that night?"

"Nine forty-seven."

"That's after the show," he said.

"Yes. You're quite good at this figuring-it-out thing," I said.

"Someone's got to be. We wait for you, we'll have a coke dealer as president. Be inviting all kinds of riffraff over to the White House," he said.

We were on the Bruckner now, and traffic was moving. The Midtown skyline was up ahead in the haze.

"So Jack's show is over, and Barnes the environmentalist calls Marty," I said.

"The big question is, why?" Freddie said.

"Don't know."

"You got a plan on how to find out?" he asked.

"Working on it," I said. "Thinking about one even as we speak."

"Means you got no plan."

"How about you drive and I think."

"Sure, Freddie's Tristate Car Service," he said.

"Known for its cheerful and friendly drivers. Exceptional service with a smile."

"My ass."

We crossed over the RFK Bridge and went down the FDR, got off at Forty-ninth Street and drove west toward Sixth Avenue.

"I got it," I said.

"Uh-oh."

"We think Marty knows more than he's letting on about that night, right?"

"Now it looks like he be downright mixed up in it," he said.

"Right, so what's the best way to get the info we think he's holding back?"

"Beat it out of him," he said.

"Okay, the second-best way?"

"Beat it out of him," he said.

"Last time I use Freddie's Angry Rican Car Service."

"Don't make me kick your ass."

"Here's the plan. I lure Marty in by telling him all I know, never letting on that I wonder if he's mixed up in this, and then boom, he lets his guard done and tells me something without even realizing it. Get it?"

"No," Freddie said.

"Maybe I didn't articulate that well."

"Sounds like you're going to tell Marty *everything* you know and hope he tells you *something* he knows," he said.

"Yes. Look at that, you did understand it."

"Dumb plan," he said.

"You disapprove?"

"You going to show you're hand—"

"Please, think of it as our hand. Take a little ownership in the plan. After all, you've been shot at, too."

"Thanks for reminding me. So you going to show your hand to a guy who could possibly be mixed up in this and then just hope he gives you a little something back?" he said.

"Yes, there you have it. You were paying attention."

"You thought this out by any chance?" he said.

"Meaning?"

"Meaning, what if Marty *is* involved? Hell, what if Marty even pushed Jack in the river? Then what? You tell him everything you know, and then you going to stand there smiling, waiting for him to give you something in return?" he said.

"I don't know that I'll be smiling."

We sat in silence for a moment, until Freddie sighed and shook his head.

"Dumb-ass plan, is all I'm saying," he said.

"Trust me," I said. "I'm a skilled professional."

"Damn good thing you don't need to be licensed to be a reporter," he said.

"And thank God for that, huh?"

Chapter 55

It was Monday morning just before noon and I was ready to confront Glover, knowing I would probably find him at work. I explained how I had left my ID at home to get past the reception desk in the lobby and walked into the newsroom a few minutes later.

I spotted Marty at his desk in a rear corner, his head down as he pecked away at his keyboard. The newsroom was busy, the day-side shows in full swing, and as I cut across, Marty looked up and did a double take.

"I thought you were exiled," he said as I got to his desk.

"I think I figured out what happened to Jack," I said. I was all business.

"What do you mean?" he asked.

I stepped closer and lowered my voice. "I mean, I think I figured out who killed him."

"Oh, please," he said. "Not that again. You're not still chasing that nutty thing for Robbie Steele, are you? I thought you gave that up."

I looked around the newsroom. "Let's go somewhere and talk. I'll tell you what I found."

Marty got up fast, or as fast as someone his size could, and

suggested Steele's office. A minute later we were upstairs and inside
with the door closed. All of Jack's belongings had been boxed up, and
a stack of file-size boxes stood in the corner.

"Sam, listen, I'm worried about you. Seriously. Cal said you were
really consumed by this thing and—"

"Marty, hear me out."

"Cal said you're blowing up your career with this," he said.

"Marty, just listen," I said, snapping at him for effect.

He put up his hands like he was stopping traffic. "Okay, okay. I'll
listen. I'm just trying to help."

"I don't have this all locked down yet," I said, "but here's what
I got."

Marty took a seat on the couch, and it took great effort for him to
lower himself down onto it. I took a spot on the corner of the desk.

"I think Buck McConnell killed Jack," I said.

"What on earth—"

"Or he may have had Jack killed."

I let it sit there, and he waited to see if I was done. When he was
satisfied that I was, he gave a little shake of his head as if he didn't
understand.

"You're talking about the IT&E guy? Buck McConnell. The guy
who's about to run for president?" he asked.

"Yes."

"Excuse me, Sam, but I just don't follow." His tone indicated that
he thought I was crazy and quite possibly dangerous.

"McConnell went to Harvard," I said.

"Okay, so far."

"I had a source tell me he was busted for coke, and not just for
carrying. The guy was going to deal it out of his dorm room. He was
about to launch a career as an Ivy League drug dealer, and guess
what? He gets busted. But Daddy and his big Houston lawyers make
it go away."

He took it all in then said, "Let's just pretend this is true."

"It is."

"And you think it's something McConnell would kill Jack over?"

he said.

"Last time I checked, we hadn't had a president who had attempted to go into the drug trade."

"People are willing to forgive a lot of candidates, Sam," he said.

"You think McConnell would want to chance that?"

"Maybe."

"Doubt it," I said. "He's obsessed with the White House. Can't have this get in his way."

"And your ... your theory ... has Jack figuring this out?" he asked.

"Yes. He stumbled across it after he started reporting on IT&E back in July. I think someone saw his IT&E pieces and then e-mailed him with info."

"Funny, he never said anything to me, and I was his executive producer," he said.

I hesitated and said nothing for a moment, giving Glover a chance to backtrack. I knew he had some knowledge of Barnes and a bigger IT&E story, but he wasn't letting on.

"I'm not sure he had it all figured out, even up until that night," I said. "Jack knew he was onto something, he just didn't know how big it was."

Marty was shaking his head like it was the craziest thing he had ever heard.

"Sam, I'm not sure where you got this from, but there's no way this happened."

"I tracked down a guy who I know was with McConnell that night in Cambridge," I said.

"Really?" he asked, a bit more interested now.

"Guy by the name of Michael Barnes. He apparently served time while McConnell—the guy whose idea the whole drug buy was—walked free."

I watched Glover for a reaction to my mention of Barnes. All he did was shake his head and offer a slight shrug to indicate he was unfamiliar with the name.

He turned and looked out the windows to his right, like he was trying to make sense of it all. He stared off into the distance, looking at the office building across the street. After a few moments, he looked back at me.

"The cops ruled Jack a suicide, right?"

"They were wrong," I said.

"If you say so," he said. "But what about the note? Seems to make it clear the pressure was too much."

"I haven't figured that out yet," I said. "But I will."

"Of course," he said.

"Marty, think about it. The man is the host of the number one-rated cable-news show in the country. He has a beautiful wife and more money than he could possibly spend."

"Doesn't make him happy," he said. "I can attest to that."

"You're right, it doesn't make him happy," I said.

I had already determined I was going to have to break my promise to Robbie Steele about keeping her pregnancy a secret. If I was going to try to convince Marty or anyone else I wasn't truly nuts, and that Jack hadn't, in fact, killed himself, they were going to need to know why I was so convinced.

"But there's something else that no one knows," I said. "Something that proves there is no way Jack killed himself."

He looked at me, waiting for me to go on.

"Robbie is pregnant," I said.

His face reddened and his eyes narrowed; he shook his head like he didn't understand.

"She's ..."

"Pregnant," I said. "She told me early on and asked me to keep it quiet. I'm asking you to do the same."

"Oh my ..."

"She's probably somewhere around three months is my guess," I said.

"Jack had been talking about how they had been trying to ..."

"I know. She said he really wanted to be a father," I said.

"He did." He took a few seconds to digest it. "Wow," he said. "So maybe he didn't kill himself."

"That's the assumption I've been working under."

"And if he didn't, that means someone did," he said.

"Yes."

Glover closed his eyes, put his head back and rested it on the top of the couch, and exhaled. He rubbed his temples like it would help him find the answers he needed. After a few seconds he opened his eyes and looked at me.

"This is huge, Sam," he said.

"I know."

"Now I see why you've been acting like this," he said.

"I think something happened to him, Marty. I really do."

"Crap," he said. "And I had dismissed all the IT&E stuff as just the usual pissed-off PR people, but maybe there was something there."

"There was," I said.

"You know, after we aired that first IT&E piece, I told Jack to be careful with these guys. The way they reacted, that little PR dweeb—"

"Ripley?"

"Yeah, that guy. He was nuts. Said Buck McConnell doesn't forget who his enemies are in the media and always gets even," he said.

"Nice," I said.

"A real asshole," he said.

"McConnell is a mean SOB," I said. "But I don't think Jack realized it. I don't think he knew what he was onto. I think he went out that night to meet someone to get info on McConnell, and it was a setup."

"He told me he was working a story, but I had no idea it had to do with McConnell or that ..." Glover's voice trailed of, and he shook his head. "It's so pointless, Sam. I even remember telling Jack that night to call me if anything interesting came up."

"But he never did?"

"No, I went down to Malloy's for a drink after the show and never heard from him," he said.

I looked at Marty and didn't say anything. There was no need to.

"I'm sitting downstairs having a beer, and Jack is out there trying to work a story." His eyes began to well up. "All he had to do was call and I could have gone with him," he said.

Chapter 56

Jason Malloy owned and ran Malloy's Irish Pub downstairs on Forty-ninth Street, next to the Redwood Diner. It was the establishment closest to the revolving doors of the building that served liquor, which made it the bar of choice for Liberty staffers.

It was a little after three when I walked in. I saw Teddy Wells, a cameraman, working on a burger with a draft close by. He waved and went back to the copy of the *Post* spread out on the bar.

I headed straight to the far end, where a woman in her forties with strawberry-blonde hair stood at the register by the wait station. Rebecca was her first name, and I was willing to bet a paycheck no one at Liberty knew her last name. She was Rebecca, the barmaid/waitress.

"Have you given up drinking?" she asked, with just the last faint traces of a brogue. "It's been weeks."

"Been tied up on a special project," I said.

"Yes, I've heard all about your special project," she said, making the little air quotes around the words *special project*.

"Don't believe anything anyone tells you."

"I'd prefer not to in this case," she said.

"Is the man of the house in?" I asked.

"He is, but you're better off dealing with me. He's a cranky SOB this afternoon," she said.

"And that's different than any other afternoon?" I asked.

She smiled and said, "His office. But consider yourself warned."

I made my way back through the mostly empty dining room to a little office in the hallway off of which the bathrooms were located. I rapped on the door, and Malloy barked from the other side.

"Leave me alone."

I opened the door and steeped inside, and he was behind his desk looking rumpled and like a bar owner who needed higher receipts.

"Thanks for respecting my wishes," he snapped.

"You didn't say go away. That tells me you really wanted company," I said.

"Pushy reporter. The Fourth Estate used to be a respectful profession," he said.

"The problem is, now it is a respectful profession."

"Which is why my damn sales are in the crapper. These younger reporters don't have the same constitution of you and those before you."

"I'll buy a beer on my way out, if that will help."

"Be the first in a month," he shot back.

Malloy was in his mid-sixties, maybe older. He was an old-time bar owner, knowing everything about everyone, which is why I was here.

"You remember the night Jack died?"

"Was early morning, and yes, I remember it like it was today," he said.

"Who was in that night?"

"The usual group," he said. "Guys not wanting to go home to their wives. The single guys with no wives to go home to."

He started ticking off names of cameramen and control room guys, reporters and writers in a rambling rundown of a usual night at Malloy's.

"Bobby P. was in; Maxine and Frank, who I swear is going to get into trouble with her before the month is out. I can see it a mile away. Then we'll see more of him when his wife finds out, and they always do. Grace was here that night. Marty and Phil. It was a regular Who's Who of Liberty. With the exception of you, of course," he said.

"For the record, I work the morning shift. You're deep into your REM cycle when I'm walking into work at four a.m."

"Always an excuse," he said.

"Jack ever come in anymore?"

"Not really, and certainly not that night," he said.

"There was the whole drinking issue with him," I said.

"Like I said, always an excuse."

"And Marty?"

"Old reliable," he said. "Every night after the show."

"Dealing with Jack every day was pretty damn stressful."

"Well, it's not like he could get away from him here. The bastard would call him here just to chew him out. Or Marty would call to check in and act like he was a big shot with access to the great Jack Steele. They spoke that very night, as a matter of fact."

Bingo. I looked at Malloy and tired not to give away what I was thinking, that Marty had lied about talking to Jack. "What a lousy last memory to have of the man," I said.

He waved a hand to dismiss the comment. "Marty reveled in it most nights, Sam. Having someone important call him. He would take the call and talk to Jack and then tell us what big name was coming on the show. Marty could drop names like a pro."

"What about that night? He say anything about that call?"

"Not much. Marty came back here and asked me if he could use the office. Said he needed to call Jack to check in and he wanted some privacy. I think Jack was probably ripping him a new one that night and Marty didn't want to grovel in public."

"Just needed a place to hide, huh?"

"Sometimes you just want a place to go to keep your dignity," he said.

"You remember what time this was?"

Malloy squinted and tried to remember. "Wasn't too late. A bit after eleven, maybe eleven fifteen, or so."

"And Marty didn't say anything when he came out of here?"

"Nope. Just looked like his usual stressed out self," he said.

Chapter 57

"So Marty's lying?" Liz asked.

"Yes. Malloy says he took a call from Jack that night. And even used his office for privacy."

"But Marty told you he never spoke to Jack that night," she said.

"Right. He said he wished Jack had called him."

We were in the kitchen, unpacking a bag of Chinese food. There was a shrimp dish for Liz. I had sesame chicken. We'd ordered from Hunan Upscale Gourmet No. 1. I looked at the dish. It looked neither gourmet or very upscale.

"And this call from Marty to Jack fits smack in the time frame Robbie gave me for when she overheard Jack talking to someone," I said. "Between eleven and eleven thirty."

"You think Marty could have forgotten he spoke to Jack?" she asked.

"Possibly, but not likely," I said. "We were sitting in Jack's office reliving that night. I can't imagine he would have forgotten that he had spoken to Jack just hours before the man died. You tend to remember things surrounding those earth-shattering events."

We moved to the small table outside the kitchen. It was close to eight and already dark outside.

"And the only reason he would lie would be to protect himself," Liz said before slipping a piece of shrimp into her mouth with her chopsticks.

"Exactly."

"Or, he's protecting someone else," she said when she was finished.

"Hadn't really thought about that," I said.

"Maybe he's mixed up in this, or maybe he knows someone else who is," she said.

"Marty also never let on that he was familiar with Michael Barnes," I said. "I mentioned that Barnes was with McConnell at Harvard when the drug bust went down and he never flinched, even though Barnes called him that night."

"Does the time frame for that call make sense?" she asked.

"Barnes called Marty's number about ten to ten. Show is over at nine. They do their postmortem for maybe a half hour. Marty could easily be back at his desk when the call came in, especially if he was expecting it."

"Then what?" Liz asked, digging some rice out of the container onto her plate.

"Then Marty goes downstairs, has a few pops and calls Jack about an hour later."

Liz looked up as she put the pieces together. "You think that Marty ..." she let the thought trail off.

"Set Jack up?" I said. "He could have. He gets the call from Barnes that a meeting is on, then he calls Jack to tell him it's a go."

"Jack gets there a few hours later and ..." again Liz didn't want to finish the sentence or thought.

"It's a set up," I said.

We sat quiet for a minute until Liz spoke up.

"But what happened to Barnes?" she said. "He doesn't show up?"

"No, I'm not sure why. And unfortunately, he's not around to ask."

"He didn't give away anything at all about a meeting when you spoke with him?" she said.

"Nothing. He was pretty cagey. He never even let on that he was in contact with Jack, or Marty. Don't think he quite trusted me just yet."

"I trusted you when I met you," she said.

"Yes, which proves you have solid judgment and a keen sense of character."

Liz smiled and said, "That's one question that needs answering. If you think Jack was lured over there to meet Barnes, did Barnes show up? If not, why?"

"Another question is Marty," I said.

"What could Marty Glover, executive producer at Liberty News, gain from being involved?" she said.

"That's where I get stuck," I said. "Marty had a pretty prestigious job. EP of *Steele Yourself*. Number one rated show on a cable-news network. Great cocktail party currency and a way to impress the ladies."

"Life doesn't revolve around that," she said.

"What?"

"Impressing the ladies and all that may or may not follow said impressions."

"Fine time for me to find all this out," I said.

She smiled and picked up another shrimp with her chopsticks.

"He's got a great gig, paid well and seemed to be enjoying life to the degree that he allowed himself to," I said.

"He's a bit of a downer?" she asked.

"Can be. Always seems to have the weight of the world on his shoulders. I assumed it was the pressure of trying to keep Jack's show number one," I said. "If those numbers start to slide, things can get pretty intense."

I moved in for a piece of Liz's shrimp, and we sat eating in silence for a few seconds. We were both trying to find something we were overlooking that would link Marty to the events of that night.

"If Marty was involved," I said, "it would explain Jack's leaving the gun at home. He wasn't threatened by Marty, that's for sure."

Liz put her chopsticks down, picked up her wineglass, and took a drink of her wine.

"Where was Marty before this?" she asked. She had her legs crossed under the table and one foot was brushing my leg.

"That's very distracting," I said.

"Focus. Come on, you can do it," she said.

"He was with Jack at some radio station in Hartford all those years ago," I said. "See, I can focus."

Liz smiled, had another drink of wine and looked across the table at me. "Maybe there was something more going on behind the scenes in the life of Marty Glover," she said.

Chapter 58

I was walking up Third Avenue about a half block away when I saw Victor leaving the Lyric Diner on the corner of Twenty-second. He looked like an advertisement for a luau dressed in a shirt with swirls of blue and yellow and wearing knee-length maroon cargo shorts and sandals. He hailed a cab that sped off as I got to the door of the coffee shop.

It was after breakfast and before lunch and the place was quiet. I found Freddie sitting in the back at the very last booth, facing the door and looking through a few sheets of paper as I approached.

"Hey, tough guy," I said as I got to the table. "Supposed to be alert if you're in the seat facing the door."

"Saw you the whole way in," he said without looking up. "Saw you give that waitress over by the counter a smile."

"She's ten years older than me. I was being polite."

"That would make her, what, just short of ancient?" he said.

"I saw Victor leaving," I said, sitting down across from him with my back to the door, which made me uncomfortable.

"He's hard to miss," he said.

"He even tops you in the Life of the Party category."

"He's all show. All style, no substance," he said.

My friendly and older waitress appeared, poured me coffee, topped cup Freddie's off, and took my order for an omelet.

"No egg whites?" Freddie asked.

"Excuse me, Dr. Freddie?"

"Got enough people shooting at you, last thing you need is to survive them and get nailed by cholesterol," he said.

"Look, can we talk about what Victor the Walking Neon Sign found out?"

Freddie slid the sheets of paper across the table. Included was a recent credit check on one Martin J. Glover, as well as his financial history. I scanned the personal information, and it was accurate. Marty lived on West Eighty-first Street. He had mentioned one time that he had been born in Florida, and this listed Fort Lauderdale as his birthplace.

I scanned the lines of info and tried to take it all in.

"Crap," I said. "This is ugly."

"No kidding," he said. "Personal BK while he was in Hartford. Then promptly got himself right back in debt."

I checked the dates of the major events.

"The bankruptcy matches up with the period when he and Jack were on the radio in Hartford. Must have been two years or so before they made the move to Liberty."

"Son of a bitch is right back up to his eyeballs in debt," he said.

I looked on the second page and saw the news it held. Tossing the sheets of paper on the table, I sat back and looked at Freddie.

"Oh, man," I said.

"Didn't want to ruin the surprise for you," he said.

"This poor guy is getting crushed."

"Foreclosure's an ugly thing," he said.

I grabbed the papers and looked again at the second page. The mortgage was in his name, along with a Jane S. Glover. I checked the birth dates. Jane was thirty-three years older than Marty. Mother Glover.

"He buys a house for his mom," I said.

"At the top of the real estate market," Freddie said.

"Then can't make the payments," I said.

"But why can't he make the payments?" Freddie asked. "I mean, he was at Liberty when he bought the place and still is. I doubt his salary has dropped."

I scanned the rest of the items on the reports and saw a reference to something called MG Productions Inc.

"MG Productions," I said.

"Marty Glover Productions," Freddie said.

"There's an end date to it. Like a life span."

"Out of business. Another failed production company," he said.

"Probably."

"Look at the bank balances and credit card info," he said.

There was a Citibank checking account with $1,118.63 in it. A Bank of America checking account had $531.09 in it. He owed $37,641 on a Visa card. His Amex card was three months past due, with a balance of $31,634. And there was a Discover card with a balance of $17,289.

I scanned the rest of the info. His present salary was $195,000, according to this, but between his mortgage and credit card debt, the man was drowning.

"He's got to be spending this money somewhere," I said. "I mean, it takes effort to get this far in debt."

"Maybe his crummy production company hammered him, or was being used for something not on this side of the law," Freddie said.

"Or maybe someone was blackmailing him," I said.

"Drug habit?" Freddie asked.

"Who knows? But there has to be some reason money is pouring out of him," I said.

"Next thing you know, he'll be facedown in the river with a note blaming Amex," Freddie said.

I was about to pick up my coffee when Freddie spoke, and his words stopped me cold.

"Holy ..." I said.

"Got to give me more than that," he said.

"The note," I said. "That's it."

Chapter 59

"I know we've been through this before," I said to Robbie. "But this is it. One last time, I promise."

"How many times do I need to show you?" she asked.

"I'm slow, what can I say? It's why I went into reporting."

She huffed in exasperation but said nothing.

"I just need to make sure of something, okay?" I said. "Just show me again exactly where the cops found the note."

We were standing in the home office of the Steele apartment, and Robbie tapped the pile of folders and papers that sat on top of Jack's desk.

"Right here," she said, with impatience creeping in, "but I told you all this already."

"One last time. What happened?" I snapped.

Robbie was startled by the sharpness of the command and looked at me.

"Just tell me, okay?" I said.

She spoke slowly, like she was going to be precise in explaining things.

"One of the detectives was in here. He came across it and then spoke to his partner. Then they came to me with it."

"Where was the note originally?" I asked. "Just sitting out on the top of his desk?"

"No, like I said before, in a folder," she said.

"Which was on top of this pile?"

"Yes," she said.

"What else was in the folder?"

"Guest research for the next day's show. Ratings news. Stories on the business. That type of stuff."

"And Jack pulled all that together, the research?"

"No, Marty did," she said. "He called it the Take Home folder. Marty put it together every day and gave it to Jack after the show for the following day."

"Jack was known for not reading any research on guests, for mostly winging the interviews or relying on whatever questions Marty gave him to get started," I said.

"I know," she said.

"So, you have any idea if he ever read any of this stuff Marty gave him?"

"Never," she said, answering without hesitation. "He actually told Marty to stop wasting his time putting it together a while back. But it was like Marty had to check a box or something on his job description. It was habit."

"How specifically did the file get from Jack's office to here?" I asked. "Tell me every step."

"Marty would give it to Jack, who would put it into the briefcase he carried, or sometimes Marty would even stick it in there if Jack was showing less enthusiasm that usual for the material," she said.

I looked at Robbie, exhaled, and tried to keep my mind from racing to the conclusion it was headed toward.

"Do you think—" she started to say, but I cut her off by raising a hand.

"Hold on," I said. "Do you have those credit card statements? The ones I asked for?"

She stepped behind the desk, picked up a manila folder from the far side, and handed it to me.

"These go back six months," she said.

I opened the file and started flipping through the months until I came to the statement for May, then the one for April. I took the two of them and looked at the charges then turned to Robbie.

"Any idea what MG Productions Inc. is?"

"That was Marty's pro ..." Her voice trailed off as she put it together.

"Marty's production company?" I asked.

"Yes," she said.

"There are two charges here, one for four-thousand seven hundred dollars in May and one for three-thousand five hundred dollars in April," I said.

"Both were bogus," she said.

I looked at her, and she explained.

"Jack was helping him out. Marty started this little company on the side to bring in extra cash. Jack said he wanted to be a media mogul, plus he needed extra money."

"And these charges?"

"Jack agreed to back a documentary Marty was going to make on some court case in the Bronx or something. Something about a guy who was wrongly convicted," she said.

"It ever get made?"

"It never got talked about after that first conversation," she said. "That's what worried Jack."

"That MG Productions was becoming a charity for Marty Glover?"

She nodded.

"He also gave Marty a check for eighteen-hundred more in late June. Brought the total to ten thousand dollars. That was the agreement, that Jack would fund this project with ten thousand dollars," she said.

"But Marty came back looking for more?" I asked.

"Yes," she said.

"And Jack told him the checkbook was closed?"

"He said he was really worried about Marty's finances. He wanted to help him, but ..."

"Didn't want to enable him?"

"Marty was always trying to get rich," she said. "He'd waste money on whatever investment fad he heard about. He was always trying to get Jack to go in on things with him."

"The next investment was always going to be the big winner," I said.

She gave me a slight nod as all this was sinking in. "Sam," she said. "Please tell me that Marty couldn't ... couldn't do something like ..." Her eyes filled with tears as she struggled to continue then gave up.

Chapter 60

"Going to use the I-left-my-ID-at-home excuse again?" Freddie asked.

We were parked on Sixth Avenue by a fire hydrant, and I was trying to figure out how to get back into Liberty to confront Glover. I was going to drop the bomb on him, tell him I knew he was involved in Jack's death. Tell him that maybe he even wrote the suicide note. Then I was going to make him a deal, tell me what happened and I'll work with Pep to see he gets the best deal possible.

"You again underestimate my ability to charm," I said to Freddie.

"Means you ain't getting in," he said.

"Watch and be amazed, oh ye of little faith."

"Say you do get in," he said. "You know, on that slight chance, then what? Just walk up to Marty and say, 'By the way, did you write Jack's suicide note for him?' That's the plan?"

A fire truck wailed from a block behind us and edged its way through the thick traffic, giving me a moment to think about my plan. It passed, and I was still at a loss. Sometimes a moment just isn't enough.

"No plan, huh?" Freddie asked.

"I prefer not to share it just yet."

"Like I said, no plan."

"I have to make sure I have all my ducks in a row," I said.

"That some kind of hunting expression, or something?" he said.

"Don't know, not a hunter."

"Then why you trotting it out?" he said.

"Never mind."

I had every reason to believe Marty Glover placed the suicide note in Jack's folder. He had access to the folder and probably played the percentages, knowing Jack didn't check the folder. Ever.

But still, I tried to talk myself out of that idea that Marty was involved.

"I'm still having a hard time believing Marty could be tied up in this," I said.

"Man had enough issues," Freddie said. "Money, for one. Probably got promised a nice big pay day."

"But enough to make him help set Jack up to be killed?"

"Could be. Maybe he tells Jack that Barnes wants to meet over at Thirty-fourth Street. Jack gets there expecting to see Marty and meet Barnes, but finds a setup instead," he said.

"I know Marty, or thought I did. It's hard to believe."

"Maybe you don't want to believe," he said.

"Maybe."

"But you got to consider it," Freddie said. "You got to consider at least the possibility that he set Jack up, or maybe even did the pushing into the river, who the hell knows."

"Maybe he was the guy who got Jack over there, then handed him off to someone else."

"That's bad enough," Freddie said.

"But could be worse," I said.

I sat there and looked at the sea of people walking along Sixth Avenue. A guy on a bike sliced through a small mob crossing the street.

"What if we're wrong?" I asked.

"Ain't no 'we' if you're wrong. It's all you. If you're right, then we got a 'we.'"

"That's what I suspected."

My phone rang, and I saw the incoming number was blocked. I answered and Rinaldi cut me off before I could finish with hello.

"I'm losing count of the favors you owe me," he said.

"Would a tour of the Liberty News studios even it out?"

"No. Maybe a date with that blonde newsreader would," he said.

"Sure, I'll call and ask Lisa when you're available," I said.

"Never mind. The tour will be fine, thanks," he said. "You got a pen and paper?"

"Yes," I said, grabbing my pad from the pocket inside my suit jacket.

"Your coworker has quite the checkered history," he said.

"Criminal?"

"No, academic. Of course criminal. Let's start with a D and D at Foxwoods two years ago."

"Drunk and disorderly at a casino, is that even a crime?"

"It is if you're wandering the grounds screaming at the guests," Rinaldi said.

"Next."

"Disturbing the peace way back when. Hell, it was fifteen years ago. That one was in Atlanta."

"Okay. I knew he worked in Atlanta. Was in radio, I think."

"Whatever it was, they're weren't paying enough. He picked up an arrest for forgery there, too."

I smacked Freddie's arm, and he looked over.

"Forgery?" I said.

"Yes, when you sign someone else's name," Rinaldi said.

"Thanks for the clarification."

"In this case it was a deed to the Florida beach house his dear old dad had intended go to his stepmom," he said.

"How'd he get caught?"

"Apparently, by shooting off his mouth. Said something stupid to the stepmom, who had a lawyer look into it. Low and behold, he confesses," he said.

"Almost pulled it off."

"Good enough to get away with it but dumb enough to get caught," Rinaldi said. "Actually became a guest of the state for a while down there."

I looked at Freddie and knew we were having the same thought: that Glover wrote the note.

"You need to tell me what's going on," Rinaldi said.

"I can't. At least not just yet."

"You might want to bring in the professionals, Sam," he said.

"Give me another few hours, maybe a day."

"That's quite a wide range," he said.

"I'm not sure how fast I can pull it all together."

"I understand," he said.

"Thanks."

"Just don't let that range to be the difference between life and death."

Chapter 61

A minute later I called up to the newsroom. I was going to have to confront Glover now. I'd tell him I was downstairs and that we needed to talk. If he balked, I'd tell him I knew he was involved.

Freddie shook his head as I called.

"You actually think he's going to tell you anything?" he said.

"Don't know."

"He's going to deny everything, then call Buck McConnell and figure out how to get rid of you, too," he said.

"Always so negative."

"How does a smart guy come up with such dumb plans?" he asked.

"Years of training," I said as the phone rang on the assignment desk. A second later Blake Jennings answered.

"Blake, it's Sam."

He was full of late-afternoon nastiness.

"You back to your senses and ready to work again?" he asked.

"No. Not yet."

"Didn't think so," he said.

It sounded busy, with phones ringing and people talking in the background.

"Marty around?" I asked. "I tried his line, but he didn't answer."

"That's because he's not in," he said.

"Where is he?" I said, and Freddie turned and looked at me.

"Don't know, Sam. I generally don't check in on someone after they call in sick."

"What's the matter with him?" I asked.

"I didn't take the call. Why you so concerned with Marty's health?"

"Want to make sure he's not contagious. That's all," I said, and got off the phone.

"Let me guess," Freddie said.

"No need to."

Freddie started the Jeep.

"West Eighty-first, right?" he said.

I checked the info from Victor for the exact address. Glover lived on West Eighty-first Street and a few minutes later were out front of a six-story mustard-colored apartment building just off the corner of Amsterdam.

We double-parked in front, and I went up and opened the outer door and stepped into the little vestibule between doors. There was a board on my left with the buzzers for the apartments. I saw "Glover 4D" and pressed the buzzer next to it. I stood and waited to hear Marty's voice but got nothing.

I looked through the glass door into the lobby and saw a young guy heading across the lobby toward the door. He opened the door to leave and I stepped inside as he passed. I climbed the steps to the fourth floor and walked down the hallway looking for 4D.

The hallway was open and light, with a window at the end that looked out onto Amsterdam. It seemed like the type of place where young professionals lived, those without the safety net of Mom and Dad's money and unable to afford a nicer building. It definitely wasn't a high-end doorman building, but I had seen far worse. But for a guy making about two hundred thou, you'd expect something a little nicer. Unless, of course, he was under a mountain of debt.

Glover's apartment was on the right toward the end of the hall. I pressed the little button for the bell and then knocked.

Nothing.

It was three in the afternoon, and the building was quiet. Those with jobs were probably at them. I knocked again and waited, then heard a door open at the other end of the hall.

A young woman emerged and spent thirty seconds locking the various locks in the hopes of keeping her belongings safe for another afternoon. She was wearing a short sundress and flip-flops and had a bag slung over her shoulder; it looked like she was off to the park.

She glanced in my direction and smiled. "Hey, you're on Liberty. You work with Marty?" she said.

"I do," I said, smiling back.

"Marty left already," she said, like I knew where he was going.

"Oh, I thought the trip was tomorrow," I said.

"No, I saw him leaving this morning, around eleven. He was grabbing a cab, said it was for work," she said.

"Oh, right, right," I said. "I guess it was today."

She smiled again and turned to leave and I pulled out my phone.

"Let me give him a call," I said and thanked her.

I listened as she went down the stairs and when I was satisfied that she had reached the first floor I grabbed the knob on the door and turned. It was locked. I gave the door a shot with my shoulder but nothing. There were three locks, including the deadbolt. A minute later I was getting back in the car.

"He's running," I said to Freddie, as I slid inside and closed the door.

Chapter 62

At seven thirty I was handed a temporary ID at the security desk in the lobby after explaining I had misplaced my permanent one. At five after eight I was pacing in front of the closed door to Daniels's office, waiting for him to get off the phone. I had called him earlier to tell him I had it all figured out, and he agreed to hear me out.

The place was quiet, and Susan's desk outside his office was neat and clean. A small, flat-screen TV monitor sat on the table next to the desk, with the sound down low. I stopped pacing when I heard Tim Casey, one of the newsreaders, doing his update of top stories.

"And just moments ago, word that Buck McConnell will make it official tomorrow when he announces his candidacy for president at an event in New York. McConnell has been rumored to be entering the race for the White House for months, and it will all be official tomorrow. Liberty News, of course, will carry the announcement live, beginning at twelve noon."

I was going to need to get on the air and break this news before then. Convincing Daniels I wasn't nuts was going to be the toughest part.

I resumed my pacing and tried calling Liz. The call went to her voice mail, again.

"Liz, it's me. There's a lot going on and want to make sure you're at home or work. Call when you can and let me know where you are," I said.

The door opened as I finished and Daniels looked out.

"Let's go," he said.

He was all business. His suit jacket was off, and he was dressed in a white shirt with his tie loosened and the knot off to one side. His face was red and ruddy and showed all the signs of the stress the guy in charge usually shows. He led me into the office, shut the door, and sat behind his desk. I took my usual spot in one of the chairs facing him.

"I'm done," I said.

"With?"

"With chasing this Robbie Steele thing," I said.

"About time. Not really sure I have a spot for you at this point. Morning show is doing fine without you," he said.

"Sure we'll work something out."

"You said you had something figured out," he said.

"I do. I know what happened that night," I said. "The night Jack died."

He sighed like he was indulging me.

"For Christsakes, Sam," he said. He sat back in his chair and rocked a bit. "You realize what you say here is largely going to determine whether or not I think you're insane and need to be locked up?"

"I do."

"Then go ahead. Let's hear it," he said.

He gave me his full attention. There was no glancing at the monitors, no fiddling with the golf tee paperweight. Just his eyes on me as I spoke.

"There's two parts to this," I said.

"Go on," he said.

"First part, Buck McConnell killed Jack Steele."

His eyes never moved. His gaze stayed fixed right on me. "Second part?" he asked.

"Marty is involved."

He was still sitting back, staring at me.

"Start at the top," he said. "McConnell first."

I explained about the whole thing. I explained how at first I thought McConnell had Jack killed over the bribes story. Then I explained how I found a source who told me about that night at Harvard. Then I explained how I found Mike Barnes who gave me the details of that night.

When I was done, Daniels nodded. "And you're going to believe the word of a convicted felon and admitted one-time heroin addict?" he asked.

"Yes."

"You're willing to risk your career on the story of this guy Barnes?" he said.

"Yes. I've already risked my life."

I explained the encounters with the thugs sent to frighten, silence, or kill me.

"And this ... this Barnes person," he said. "He'd be willing to come on and tell his story on TV?" he asked.

"No."

"I see," he said. "A little uncomfortable on camera? Or does he prefer not to be quoted as he takes down someone who wants to run for president?"

"Neither," I said. "He's dead."

Daniels squinted and blinked as he tried to follow.

"Go on," he said.

"He died in an explosion on one of his boats about an hour after I left him. I saw it."

Daniels closed his eyes, sighed and rubbed his temples. When he opened his eyes, I was still there.

"Marty?" he asked.

Now I wanted to close my eyes and try and make it all go away.

"I think he set Jack up."

"There's no way—"

I held up a hand. "Hear me out."

"Go on," he said.

"Marty is in a financial hole the size of the Grand Canyon. Jack had been helping him out. Then recently stopped helping him out," I said.

"So he gets involved with Buck McConnell to get money or something? I don't get it," he said.

"I think he either knowingly or unknowingly set Jack up."

"How the hell do you unknowingly set someone up?" he asked.

"I'm trying to give him the benefit of the doubt," I said. "Maybe McConnell gave him a pile of cash to provide info on Jack. Maybe he set up a meeting with Jack under a false pretense. He may not have known he was setting him up to be pushed into the river."

"It still doesn't add up for me," he said.

"You put Marty in the picture and it explains two things."

"Such as?" he said.

"Jack owns a gun."

"I knew that," he said.

"But he didn't take it with him that night when he went out."

"Being that he was going to jump in the East River maybe he felt he didn't need it," he said.

"Or maybe he didn't think he needed it for another reason."

"Meaning?" he said.

"He was going to meet someone he knew and trusted."

"And you think that was Marty?" he said.

"Possibly."

"You have a lot of possibly and maybe in here. You need something definite," he said.

"I definitely know Marty lied to me and tried to cover up his involvement," I said.

"It's a start," he said.

"He told me he didn't speak to Jack that night. Says they never talked."

"But you don't buy it?" he said.

"Jason Malloy told me Marty spoke to Jack sometime after eleven that night. Even went into his office for privacy."

His body language said he was growing irritated. His shoulders were stiffening and he was shaking his head more now, both of which told me he was losing patience. "So, we have the dead heroin addict and now the alcoholic that we're basing this ... this theory on," he said.

"Recovering alcoholic," I said of Jason.

He glanced at the monitors and took a break from staring at me.

"I've been in this business for almost forty years," he said, looking back to me.

"A legend."

"And this may be the stupidest fucking episode I've ever encountered, Sam."

I started to speak, then stopped. There was no harm in letting him have his say. I knew what I knew and he wasn't going to change my mind.

"I got an all-star reporter who has thrown his career away chasing some conspiracy theory," he said. "You're hell bent on taking down a man about to run for president and somehow convinced he killed one of the biggest names in TV. It's the goddamned craziest shit I've ever heard."

"Not if it's true."

Daniels exploded. "It's not true, Sam" he said. He slammed his fist on the desk. "Shit, would you get real? I mean, what about Jack's note? How the hell do you explain that?"

"It's a fake."

"Right, of course it is. And let me guess, you're taking Robbie Steele's word on that?" he said.

"Did you know she's pregnant?"

It stopped him cold.

"What?"

"Robbie is pregnant."

He was at a loss. The whole equation had just changed on him.

"Robbie Steele is pregnant?" he said.

"Yes. That's why she knew the note was a fake right away. She told me the first time I met her but asked me to keep it quiet."

He sat back. "Holy crap," he said.

"She said Jack was fired up about being a father."

He said nothing. He was still trying to process it.

"I think Marty wrote the note," I said.

He was still quiet and I continued.

"Marty was convicted of forgery a long time ago," I said. "The note was found in the folder he put together for Jack every night. He knew Jack never looked at the folder after it left here."

Daniels sat forward, put his elbows on his desk and rubbed his forehead. After a moment he looked up.

"How does Buck McConnell connect to Marty Glover?"

"I don't have the direct line, yet. But McConnell must have discovered Jack got wind of Mike Barnes and figured the drug bust story was going to come out eventually," I said. "Then they probably figure the way to get to Jack is go through Marty. They do a little digging, find Marty is a financial mess, has a rap sheet, and offer him a payday for a little info on Jack."

Daniels exhaled like he was trying to relax.

"You want me to believe that Marty Glover ..." he said as his voice trailed off.

"Cal," I said. "I just went to his apartment. He's gone."

"To where?" he said.

"I don't know. He left this morning with a suitcase. Told a neighbor he was traveling for work."

"Not going anywhere that I'm aware of," he said.

"So no work trip?"

"No," he said.

"I didn't think so."

He picked up a pen and rotated it slowly in his hands, stared at it and thought about things.

"If what you told me is true," he said when he was done thinking.

"It is," I said.

"Then we need to bring the police in," he said.

I shook my head. "Not yet."

He face grew redder and he pointed at me. "This is about people dying, Sam. This isn't something you have a vote in, goddammit."

"I'm working with a detective already."

"And we need to get our lawyers involved. You know how many levels of approvals we're going to need to go through to get something like this on the air? Could take weeks," he said.

I shook my head. "No. No one else is going to know about this. If McConnell knows we're closing in on him, he'll find some way to make it all go away. Just like he did at Harvard. That's been his MO his whole life."

He slumped back in his chair and his shoulders sagged. He yanked at his tie knot and took in a long, deep breath before speaking. "I'm guessing you have your own plan, not that I'm going to agree with it."

"I do. A surprise attack."

"A surprise attack?" he said.

"During his presser tomorrow," I said.

"You're telling me you want to break this as he announces that he's running for president?"

"That's the plan," I said.

Chapter 63

At nine thirty I was at my desk. The newsroom was quiet, which meant there were fewer people around to ask me what I was working on. That was a good thing.

I stared at the computer screen and the script I had started. The file was locked and I was the only one with access to it. I started to read it in a low tone to see how the words flowed: *"Liberty News has uncovered evidence that Terrance 'Buck' McConnell was responsible for and involved in the death of Liberty anchor Jack Steele."*

It was too flat. It needed more drama and I played around with it.

Shocking evidence tying Buck McConnell to the death of Jack Steele.

I needed a stronger opening line.

Liberty News has learned that Jack Steele was killed ... by presidential hopeful Terrance "Buck" McConnell.

Better, but I wasn't there yet.

I stood and turned my head slowly from side to side, trying to stretch the tension out of my neck. I looked out across the big room and the empty desks. The little TV monitors scattered around the room flickered. Outside, the lights of the office towers on Sixth Avenue shone through the darkness.

I glanced at my phone. No new calls.

Where the hell was Liz?

I hadn't spoken to her since lunchtime, but it wasn't for lack of trying. I had called her four times—mobile, office, mobile, apartment—but nothing. I told myself there was some rational and probably mundane reason that she hadn't gotten back to me.

But it was getting tougher for me to believe that. There was a very good chance she was in danger, and if that was the case, what the hell was I doing sitting here?

My phone vibrated and I grabbed it from the desk. It was a number I didn't recognize.

"Sam North," I said.

There was a lot of street noise and no one spoke for a second. Then I heard a male voice. "Hey, remember me?"

"No," I said.

A horn honked and a siren yelped in the background.

"Shit, I'm the guy that made your career," he said.

"Then you're definitely not my agent."

"It's Wade."

"Wade, how are you?" I asked, wondering why this guy was bothering me.

"You got your money's worth on that Jack Steele footage, huh?" he said.

"I did."

I looked at the clock: 9:33:42 p.m. The workday had just begun for Wade.

"What can I do for you, Wade?" I asked.

"Got a little something that may be of interest to you," he said.

"Go on."

"Heard a call go out for a druggie an hour or so ago. Cops found some guy who was a heroin OD in a rat hole way down on Lower East Side, down under the Williamsburg Bridge. Guy was dead as a doornail."

"I'm listening."

"You know I only call you with the top-tier stuff," he said.

"Only the best."

"Well, we got ourselves another little Liberty News connection. How do you like that?" he said.

"Probably better once I understand it," I said. "Can you spell it out for me?"

"Absolutely. So, they're wheeling the body out, right? And I see a Liberty News ID hanging off the guy," he said.

I stood still with the phone pressed against my ear.

"You know some guy named Marty Glover?" Wade said.

My knees buckled and I put my hand on my desk for balance and opened my mouth to speak but nothing came out.

"Sam, you there?" Wade said.

I was having trouble breathing and felt dizzy.

"Hello? Hello? Hey, Sam, you there?" he said.

I sucked in a long deep breath and looked up and tried to pull myself together.

"Yeah, I do know him, Wade," I said.

"Oh, shit, Sam," he said. "Sorry, man. But he's dead."

Chapter 64

I needed to find Liz. Now. Three people were dead and McConnell was stopping at nothing to make sure this story didn't get out.

I rode the elevator down to the lobby and bolted as soon as the door opened. I crossed the lobby and looked outside for the Jeep and saw it parked on the corner of Forty-ninth. I was a few steps away from the revolving door when someone came up behind me.

"Remember me, asshole?"

I turned and saw a short, fat guy; the same guy I had leveled out at Herman Bindagi's house. Before I could speak he shoved me hard into the revolving door and my face crashed into the glass. He jammed himself in behind me and was pressed against my back, pushing me into the glass. It was like we were five pounds of crap shoved in a four-pound bag.

"Not a hotshot now, are you?" he said as he shoved me again into the glass door.

His partner was standing outside waiting and I was going to run into him as soon as the door opened to the sidewalk. I had one second, maybe two, before something bad would happen.

The door rotated open and I was pushed outside. I was face-to-face with the other guy now. I stopped short and in one motion rammed my right elbow back into the guy behind me. It was a clean elbow strike and he groaned. And with the same arm I snapped off a face punch to the guy in front of me. My knuckles crunched into his nose, pushing it up and back and snapping his head back and blood shot out.

I spun around and rammed my knee into the groin of the guy behind me and he yelled and pitched forward. I sidestepped him and he fell into his partner, who took a hand off his face and shoved him aside and came at me.

"I'm going to fucking kill you," he screamed.

I raised my knee high and snapped off a kick to his groin, and he fell forward. I snapped off another one, this one to his face, and he crumbled to the sidewalk.

"Ohhhhhhh," was all I heard.

Arms wrapped around me from behind as the other guy had gotten to his feet. He squeezed my chest like a vise and tried to lift me off the ground and it felt like all the air was being forced up and out of my lungs. He tightened the grip and the pressure built and my ribs screamed in pain. I tried to inhale and pull some air into my lungs. I got a little bit of air, held it for a second and tried to draw strength from it. I moved my elbows forward and loaded as much energy into them as I could and then rammed them backward, letting them go with every ounce of force I had. They smashed into his gut and I felt ribs and tried to drive the elbows in as deeply as I could.

He groaned loud and air shot out of his mouth like I had done the Heimlich. His arms fell away and I was free. With him still behind me I snapped my right hand back with a reverse wrist strike hoping to hit his face. The back of my hand smashed against something that felt solid like a block of wood, which I guessed was his forehead; he yelped.

Someone yelled and I looked over to the sidewalk and saw Freddie streaking toward me. I took off and raced away from the building toward him.

"Get back in the car. Let's go," I said.

"Why didn't you yell or something?" he said as he turned and ran with me.

There were footsteps coming behind us as the thugs crossed the plaza and raced toward the Jeep. We got in and Freddie had the thing started before I got the door closed. He slammed it into drive, cut the wheel and punched the accelerator. We lurched forward and jerked out into the traffic of Sixth Avenue.

Chapter 65

"She hasn't called?" Freddie asked.

"No."

"Where you want to go first?" he said.

"Not sure."

"When was the last time you spoke to her?" he said.

"About twelve thirty."

"And no texts? No voice mails?"

"Nothing."

It was almost ten and I was sure something had happened to her.

"Let's go by her place," I said. "See if her doorman has seen her."

Ten minutes later we pulled up in front of her apartment building on Fifty-fifth Street between First and Second Avenue. I walked in and saw Gene behind the counter. I made every attempt not to sound panicked and asked if he could call up to her apartment.

"No answer," he said, hanging up. "Everything all right, Sam?"

"I hope so."

I went back outside and sat in the Jeep.

"You want to swing by her office?" Freddie asked.

"No way I'm going to clear security there, especially at this hour."

Freddie started the engine and we drove and it felt better than sitting still. We went down Second Avenue in silence, staying in the middle of the avenue and catching most of the lights. We passed the strip of restaurants and the big theater complex just below Thirty-fourth Street in Kips Bay. Couples were out. People were going places and doing things.

I heard Rinaldi's words in my head. The warning about waiting too long to call in the professionals. I looked out at the passing buildings and prayed I hadn't pushed this too far.

Chapter 66

We had driven around awhile longer, just moving for the sake of moving. We went back to my apartment and made coffee and waited to hear from Liz. We never did. Now, just before one a.m., we drove up Sixth Avenue. We sat in silence, and outside the streets were near empty.

"McConnell, or someone connected to him, has Liz," I said.

Freddie said nothing for a moment, keeping his eyes on the street in front of him as he drove. We pulled to a stop at a red light at Twenty-eighth Street.

"I know," he said.

"It's more than twelve hours since I talked to her," I said.

"And he knows you got it figured out. And that you know something has happened to her," he said.

"I need to make a move. To do something," I said.

"He's making you twist. You done everything you could. Called. Texted. Went by her place. Called her friends. He's going to come to you when he wants to," he said. "He's playing with you now."

"He's going to try and strike a deal," I said.

"Probably try and use Liz as a bargaining chip," he said. "You for her."

"Unless he doesn't see any reason for either one of us to live."

The light changed and we moved on, passed by cabs and a handful of cars heading up Sixth.

"But McConnell still needs you," Freddie said. "Still has to find out exactly what you know, and who else you've told it to. He's scrambling too. About to run for president and you're going to blow it up on him."

Freddie pulled the Jeep to the curb in front of Liberty. The same place I was attacked a few hours ago. I scanned the plaza and the sidewalk and didn't see any sign of the thugs.

"There's nothing else you can do right now," Freddie said. "Except wait."

"I don't do that well," I said, as I opened the door and got out.

Chapter 67

Daniels had returned my ID and I used it to get back inside. Upstairs in the newsroom, the lights were down and it was as close to empty as it ever got. The room was filled by the eerie flickering of screen savers and the glow from all the TV monitors that were on with the sound down.

I took a right when I walked in and went to the far corner to a hallway lined with four edit suites, each the size of a walk-in closet. I would work while I waited. And I would have the taped piece ready to go to nail McConnell at his big announcement at noon.

I slid open the sliding glass door to the first suite, stepped inside and slid the door closed behind me. I sat down at the console with my back to the door and logged onto the computer, then clicked on the icon for the editing software and opened up my script. I leaned over the desktop microphone used to track voiceovers for our taped packages and read out loud, practicing to see how it sounded. I read the script once, then twice and neither sounded right.

Sitting back, I stared at the words on the screen and tried to concentrate, but all I could think of was Liz. Where was she? What had happened to her? I sat forward and tried to focus and played with the script some more, trying to find the right combination of words. I leaned closer to the mic and read it again: *"When Jack Steele was found dead, his body floating in the East River, police ruled it a suicide. But—"*

There was a noise behind me and I jerked my head around in fear. I saw the door sliding open and Daniels stepping into the suite. I exhaled in relief and sat back.

"You scared the hell out of me, Cal," I said. "Maybe you knock next time."

Daniels didn't say anything. He just stood there in his navy-blue suit and white shirt, its collar unbuttoned and tie knot off to the side, and stared at me.

"I didn't think you were still here," I said. "Give me a half hour and I'll have this McConnell piece done for you."

Still, he said nothing. He just stood there at the door, silent and staring down at me like he was in a trance. His face was hard with tension and his eyes locked on me and I wondered if maybe he had just heard about Marty.

"Cal, I don't know if you know this, but Marty ..." I said. I had trouble finishing the sentence. "Marty is dead."

His expression never changed.

"They found him in some drug den down by the Williamsburg Bridge."

His face grew red and hard and his eyes angry.

"I know," he said.

"You do?"

He stared down at me and said nothing for a moment. The room felt even smaller now. Finally, he broke the silence.

"I was there," he said.

My body snapped back in the chair as if I had been shoved.

"It was horrible," he said, his voice sounding like a low growl. "Horrible."

I watched his hand move as he reached behind him. He was going for the door. He slid it closed I shot out of the chair. He stepped to me and stuck a pistol to my forehead and I froze.

"Sit down," he said.

I hesitated and he jabbed the barrel of the gun into my forehead. "Sit the fuck down," he said.

His eyes were wild and his face grew a deeper red and I sat down. "You were there?" I said.

He started talking without acknowledging the question.

"Marty was a loser, Sam," he said. "But he was easy to deal with. Promise him a payoff, in this case twenty Gs, and he'd do anything. Even write a suicide note."

"Nice to know I got it right."

He shook his head. "You, you present a whole other set of problems."

I stared at the barrel of the gun and kept quiet.

"You know what you're problem is, Sam?" he said. "You find out there's something much bigger going on and you just can't leave it alone, can you?"

He yanked at his tie knot like it was bothering him.

"You just had to keep pushing and pushing and persisting, didn't you?" he said. "Bothering everyone with this crazy Robbie Steele shit."

"I'm stubborn, what can I say?"

He looked at me and shook his head. "Well, now you're going to be dead," he said. "Get up."

Chapter 68

"Where's Liz?" I asked, as we crossed the lobby.

"You'll see her soon enough," Daniels said. "Maybe."

He walked alongside me with the gun stuck in my ribs. I looked over at the guard. His head was back and mouth open, and he was snoring like he was in a competition.

A lot of help.

"Does this mean no new contract?" I said.

He rammed the gun farther into my ribs, and I figured my spleen was the next stop.

"How can someone so smart be so dumb?" he asked.

"I get that a lot."

"Not for much longer," he said.

We stepped outside into the warm, musty air and I scanned the cars at the curb looking for Freddie and the Jeep. There was no sign of either. But there was a black Mercedes at the corner and Daniels was steering me toward it. We crossed the plaza on an angle and headed for the car.

"So it was you," I said.

"Stop talking," he said.

"You were the connection between McConnell and Marty. I was trying to figure out how he got to Marty. It was you."

"Shut up," he said.

"You're connected to McConnell," I said. "I don't know how, but you knew Jack was about to find out about that drug bust."

Daniels picked up the pace and jammed the gun deeper into my side.

"You really can be annoying," he said.

"And you used Marty as the go between," I said. "Maybe offered him a payoff to keep you updated on what Jack knew about McConnell? Then when things got worse and Jack wouldn't back off, what'd you do? Up the payoff and have him write the suicide note?"

"Marty did what I told him to do," he said.

"You used him."

"He was a fucking mess. He had more debt than the U.S. government. He needed me," he said.

"And you used him."

"Shut up. You have no idea of how much I helped that man. You think he could have gotten a job anywhere else in this business? He was weak and dependent. He needed me, Sam."

"Marty talked to Jack that night," I said. "Found out Jack was going to meet Barnes. Then what?"

Daniels said nothing, just pushed me along toward the waiting Mercedes.

"He called you, right?" I said, as we closed in on the Mercedes. "Said everything was a go. But what I can't figure out is what happened to Barnes. Did he come in to meet Jack? That's where I get stuck."

Daniels spoke up as we reached the car.

"Jack was an arrogant and stupid man," he said. "All he had to do was sit down and talk to McConnell and this could have been solved. But he was as stubborn as you. He became hell bent on exposing Buck and trying to make an even bigger name for himself."

"And you knew he was going to be killed?"

"Jack knew full well what the consequences were. You want to fuck with someone as powerful and driven as McConnell, you're asking for trouble, as you're about to find out," he said.

"You going to kill every reporter who tries to expose McConnell?"

"Enough of the self-righteous reporter bullshit, okay?" he said. "Jack was trying to stay relevant. His numbers slip and he panics and thinks he needs to be some crusading journalist. The man was as much a journalist as I am."

"He was trying to show people what a dirt bag McConnell is," I said.

"No, he was trying to get his numbers up with a sensational story," he said. "If he had listened to me none of this would have happened. Hell, I made him and I could have fixed the numbers if he would have shut up long enough to listen to me."

Daniels was grinding the gun into me now, getting angrier as we stood there.

"Jack was a drunk fucking DJ when I pulled his ass out of radio," he said. "You think he would have the tens of millions of dollars, the books, the billboards all over the country, the Fifth Avenue apartment, without me? You think he marries a piece like Robbie Steele without me?"

"What the hell did McConnell promise you, Cal?" I said. "Money? A job in the White House if he gets there? What?"

Daniels had the gun in my chest now.

"Get in the car," he said.

"Why the hell are you protecting McConnell? There has to be something," I said.

He pushed me toward the back door of the Mercedes. "Let's just say we go back a ways," he said.

I turned and we were face-to-face. Close enough for me to see the lines that creased his forehead and wrinkles by the corners of his eyes. A thin coat of sweat lined his brow and his face was rigid with a scowl.

"Son of a bitch," I said. "You went to Harvard."

His face tightened even more and he smashed the gun into my ribs and I doubled over as my breath rushed up and out of my lungs.

"Shut your fucking mouth," he said.

I straightened up and looked at him. "The article on the wall of your office," I said. "You didn't drop out to support your mother. You got thrown out."

He shoved me into the side of the car and the door flew open and Bulger jumped out.

"Cal, not here," he said, moving to the rear of the car.

"That's it," I said. "You were there that night. Barnes said there was a third guy at the drug buy. It was you."

He stepped to me and jammed the gun under my chin and pushed up.

"You need to stop talking," he said.

"You got booted out of Harvard because of the drug bust, didn't you?" I said. "McConnell got Daddy's lawyers to make the criminal charges disappear, but Harvard was done with you."

He turned to Bulger. "Get him in the backseat before I shoot his ass right here," he said.

"It all makes sense," I said. "There was a chance to make a quick score dealing drugs. Things go wrong, and suddenly you're thrown out of Harvard, Michael Barnes goes to jail, and Buck McConnell skates through no worse for the experience."

Bulger opened the back door, grabbed a fistful of my suit at the shoulder and shoved me inside. "You stupid son of a bitch," he said. "You couldn't take a hint from me, could you?"

Daniels piled into the backseat next to me and yanked the door shut and I heard the locks click.

"You're so interested in Jack's last hours," he said, "we'll show you exactly what it was like."

Chapter 69

It didn't take a whole lot of genius to figure out where we were headed.

We cruised along Thirty-fourth Street, with Bulger driving carefully so as not to attract attention. The streets were quiet and we moved at a leisurely pace, like we were just out for a drive. No one said anything.

We crossed through the intersection of First Avenue and continued east to the end of Thirty-fourth. Bulger slowed the Mercedes as we went under the elevated FDR Drive and pulled in between two trailers underneath the roadway. I looked around for another car or any sign of Liz, but there was nothing.

We sat in the dark between the two trailers. There was a sign on the one on the right that said "New York Helicopter," and welcomed us to the helipad. The one on the left was unmarked. Straight ahead, set out like a stage, was the helipad. It was a rectangular asphalt strip marked with bright yellow paint that divided it into landing squares. It seemed to be no more than forty or fifty feet across to the other side, where low red-and-white caution barriers lined the edge. Beyond the barriers I saw the small yellow light of a tug pushing a barge downriver.

"Lovely, isn't it?" Bulger asked, looking straight ahead to the river. "So peaceful."

"Enough," Daniels said. "Let's go."

Bulger opened his door, got out, crossed in front of the car, and came around to my door. He opened it and reached in and grabbed me by my suit.

"Hey, easy," I said. "That's twice with wrinkling the suit."

"Believe me, you're not going to have to worry about dry cleaning anymore," he said.

Daniels gave me a push from the other side and forced me out of the car. Then he got out and came around to us.

"This all worked so well the first time," he said, "except Jack floated to the side."

"Probably because he was so goddamned fat," Bulger said.

"Or the tides," Daniels said. "There's a different moon tonight, so hopefully he'll get pulled right out into the river."

"Then it's a straight shot down into the harbor, and hey, maybe right down under the Verrazano-Narrows," Bulger said. "And who knows, maybe on to the Jersey shore. How about that? That's not a bad way to go, huh?" he asked, poking me with his own gun.

"Move," Daniels said, shoving me, and the three of us started across the helipad.

I didn't know where Liz was. I didn't know where Freddie was. What I did know was I needed a miracle. McConnell needed to be exposed, and now Daniels needed to be exposed. And I'd like to be around to see it all happen.

"So you get kicked out of Harvard," I said, turning to Daniels as we walked. "And you spin it as the story of a hardworking guy from modest means who had to leave school because his family couldn't afford the tuition."

"Got it all figured out, don't you?" he asked.

"But the real story is, you were a drug dealer. A low-level dirt bag."

Daniels stopped walking, and when he did, we all stopped. Bulger was behind me with his gun jammed in the small of my back. Daniels turned and glared at me. An occasional car rattled by up on the FDR over his shoulder.

"What a story," I said. "The big TV exec whom everybody admires and fears was a coke dealer."

Daniels rammed his gun under my chin, and the metal pushed my head back.

"You need to shut up," he said.

"Just a common criminal," I said.

He pushed the gun even harder into my chin. "You have any idea what it's like to have someone hand you a ticket out, and then find out you can't afford it? Huh, you have any idea what that's like?"

"Ticket out of where?"

"Out of the shit-hole town I grew up in, you idiot," he said. His voice was deeper and gravelly, like an ugly, perverted version of Daniels. "You think I'm going back home to dig ditches for forty years? No way. I worked my tail off to get into Harvard, and I was going to stay there. I deserved it."

"Even if it meant selling drugs?"

"I could give a shit how I got the money. I was doing what I had to do," he said.

I realized I had been wrong about something.

"You were the leader," I said. "You were the guy who arranged the drug buy. I thought it was McConnell, but it was you."

He stared back and said nothing, and I knew I was right.

"So how the hell did McConnell get mixed up in it?" I asked.

We stood there for a moment, and he exhaled and relaxed and then lowered the gun. "Buck McConnell was, and remains, a spoiled rich kid," he said.

"I've gathered as much."

"He comes back in the fall of sophomore year pissed off at Daddy for something and ready to show the old man that he can make his own fortune. That he doesn't need the family money," he said.

Bulger ground his gun into my spine and spoke up from behind me. "We're wasting too much time," he said.

Daniels ignored him. "Buck wants in on the drug buy. Saw me

making money in freshman year, so he knows it's real," Daniels said. "And he's going to be his own man and make his own money."

"And you figure with his money backing you that you can buy even larger quantities and make even more money," I said.

"And keep paying my tuition," he said. "Everybody wins."

"Until the cops show up," I said.

"Buck buys his way out of trouble, again. I get thrown out of school, but Buck convinces his old man to have his lawyers get me off. I got lucky and go into broadcasting and manage to do okay, as you may have noticed."

"What about Barnes? How come no one took care of him?" I said.

"He was a drug-using loser to begin with," he said.

"Recreational or addict?"

"There any difference?" he asked. "He was a customer of mine. A punk kid who liked snorting coke and was so smart that he could manage to stay in school while he did."

"You assumed he'd self-destruct," I said.

"We figured he'd be dead within a year in prison," he said.

"Just the three of you knew what happened that night?"

"Others heard rumors, but nobody knew the truth," he said.

"And it was fine for all these years," I said.

"Until Jack starts going after IT&E and beating the hell out of McConnell, repeating all the crap about IT&E's equipment," he said. "And now Buck has it in his head that he needs to run for president. I wouldn't trust the man running a coffee shop, let alone the damned country."

"And then Barnes e-mails Jack saying he has something that can destroy McConnell?" I asked.

"Piece of crap," Daniels said. "For almost forty years, we all kept our mouths shut. We had it good. Barnes cleaned himself up and was saving the Long Island Sound from tire dumpers. I'm sitting on top of Liberty News. Then the asshole gets so incensed about Buck wanting to be president that he's going to stop him. He's going to see to it that Buck McConnell doesn't get what he wants for the first time in his life."

"And Marty sees the e-mail from Barnes?" I asked.

"Jack never read a viewer e-mail in his life," he said. "Marty comes to me in July after Barnes contacted the show. He says there's some nut promising to take Buck McConnell down."

"And he has no idea you and McConnell have a history?"

"How would he? I play along, tell him it sounds big, and to let me know every time you hear from him," Daniels said. "The whole time Marty is hassling me for more money. Just gave him a contract a year ago, but apparently that wasn't rich enough. I gave him a few bullshit bonuses to make him feel good, and he's bending over backward to make sure he's keeping me in the loop on everything, including Barnes."

Bulger was antsy. "Cal, really, we can't wait any longer."

I looked over my shoulder. "Do you mind?" I asked, and he ground his gun in deeper into my back.

Daniels kept going. "I tell McConnell that Barnes has resurfaced. He says I need to get control of the situation. He's talking to me like I'm one of his fucking employees."

"Did Jack ever find out about the arrest?"

"He was close. Barnes wanted to meet Jack, and Marty was stringing Barnes along. Then Barnes gets aggressive. Apparently didn't trust e-mail entirely, so he sends Jack a letter referencing McConnell and a drug arrest forty years ago," he said. "Jack shows it to Marty, who shows it to me."

"McConnell know about it?" I asked.

"I told him. I said he needed to get some of his corporate goons to pay a visit to Barnes. Maybe buy him off. If not, then beat the crap out of him to get him to shut up. But instead Buck panics, says it's too late. He wants Jack silenced for good. And guess who he says is in charge of it?"

"You," I said.

"He says, take care of this guy. If Jack exposes me, I expose you. No way he was going to lose his shot at the White House over this."

"Barnes called Marty that night," I said.

"He called Marty a bunch of times. He was pushing Marty to set up a meeting with Jack. Give him the story in person. Wanted to do it in secret. Suggested taking one of his piece-of-shit boats down here to meet on the East Side."

"And you knew Marty could only put Barnes off for so long," I said.

"McConnell is ready to announce he's running," he said. "Barnes knows I run Liberty. At some point he's going to realize I'm blocking him. The man served time in prison while we walked. He's been carrying this grudge around for decades. He was going to figure out a way to even the score."

"Cal," Bulger snapped, "we need to move. Now."

"So it was you Jack met over there that night? Not Barnes?" I asked.

Daniels turned and stared out at the blackness over the river and didn't answer.

"You ... you killed Jack," I said.

Daniels turned back to me and pointed his gun at my chest, and my body tensed.

"Shut up," he snapped. "Buck ordered me to. He sat in the car and watched the whole thing to make sure I did."

"Was Barnes here?"

"No. It was a setup," he said. "We had a separate plan for Barnes."

Bulger took a step to Daniels and tried a new tact, speaking to him in a low voice.

"Cal, look, we really need to finish this, now," he said.

Daniels looked at Bulger, then at me. "Where's the girl?" he asked. "I want them going in together."

"They were supposed to be here by now," Bulger said. "That's what I'm worried about."

Daniels grabbed my arm and shoved me toward the edge.

"Let's go. Enough bullshitting. We're out of time, and that means you're out of time."

"Cal," I said, "this isn't going to solve anything."

He laughed. "Right. And you'll keep quiet about all this."

"I can," I said.

"Let me ask you something," he said. "You're a reporter: you get wind of the McConnell story, and a story about one of the top execs in the TV business having been a coke dealer in college, you think all that's going to stay quiet? I don't think so."

"No one has to know," I said.

"Once people find out I got kicked out of Harvard for dealing drugs, I'd be lucky to get a job in public television," he said.

He pushed me forward, and Bulger shoved me from behind at the same time. I took a step, then another, and then saw a flash of light from somewhere behind us, back by the entrance to the helipad.

Bulger stuck the gun against the back of my neck like he thought someone was coming to free me. "You're not moving," he said.

A car raced straight onto the asphalt of the helipad and parked sideways. The back door opened, and one of the guys who had jumped me at Liberty stepped out. He reached in the car and grabbed someone.

It was Liz.

Chapter 70

Liz struggled with the pair of goons as they hustled her across the helipad toward us. She slapped one in the face as he pushed and shoved her, and he slapped her back. I bolted for them, and Bulger came after me, grabbing me from behind as I got to her.

I took a swing at the shorter, fatter guy, and as I did something hit me from behind in the back of the head. It was the hard, sharp blow of a gun. My legs buckled, and I collapsed to my knees from the force of it.

Bulger grabbed me by the shoulder and yanked me up.

"Enough," he said.

I got up slowly and looked at Liz. Her eyes were wide with terror. I wanted to tell her just to hang on, but there was no way I could without these guys hearing me.

Daniels was waiting back by the edge of the helipad by the river and snapping off directions. "Let's go, get them over here. Everyone in the water," he said, a weird hint of glee in his voice.

Bulger and the two goons had us surrounded and were pushing and prodding. Liz leaned close to me and whispered in my ear. "Sam, where are they?"

She was worried the plan had fallen apart. At this point, so was I. I reached down and grabbed her hand and squeezed.

Daniels noticed it. "That's sweet. You two want to jump in together holding hands?"

We were at the edge now, and Daniels cleared out of the way. Liz and I were facing the river, and I knew we were out of time. I checked the sky uptown and saw the yellow light of a helicopter against the black sky. It was moving slowly, like it was waiting for a signal. For the first time, I wondered if something was wrong, if there had been a breakdown in communications.

The goons stepped behind us, one taking a spot behind me, the other behind Liz.

"It's like walking the plank," one said.

The guy behind me snapped off a punch that landed on the side of my head behind my ear and made my head ring.

"That's for the punch in Jersey," he said.

Daniels was to my left and waved his gun toward Liz. "I want her in the water first," he said.

I squeezed Liz's hand tight. Freddie was around here somewhere recording this, but I couldn't understand what he was waiting for. This was a lot closer than it was supposed to be. Liz and I were staring at the blackness of the East River and were about to be pushed in. I pulled in a deep breath and was about to yell for Freddie when I heard the screeching of tires behind us. Then a police siren yelped. Then immediately there were the sounds of more sirens and cars. I glanced to my left and saw Daniels snap his head around and look behind us.

"Now," I yelled. "Run, Liz."

Liz turned and spun around and raced past the guy behind her. I turned and punched the one behind me in the face and tried not to fall backward into the river. He yelled as I hit him, and the other guy lunged at me ready to swing. I ducked, and his momentum carried him past me. He flew over the edge, screaming as he hit the water.

Daniels was five feet from me, and he raised his gun at me and fired. I dove to the pavement to get out of the way and heard a series of rapid pops as more shots rang out. Daniels screamed, and his gun dropped to the ground. He crumbled in a heap, screaming in pain and grabbing his leg. Bulger took off running south across the long landing area. The helipad filled with cops running and yelling. There were more sirens, and the rapid flickering of police lights flooded the area. The thumping of a helicopter grew louder as the chopper sped toward us.

I got up in a panic and looked around for Liz, then saw her with a cop over by the helicopter company's trailer. I saw Freddie, too; he had the camera on his shoulder and was moving around and shooting the cops handcuffing Bulger, who was facedown on the pavement.

There were police everywhere, a bunch of them over Daniels, guns drawn while he clutched his leg and writhed in pain. Two cops had handcuffed one of the goons and yanked him to his feet. Another group was leaning over the edge and looking into the river, yelling instructions to the thug who had gone into the water.

Overhead in the sky, the helicopter's floodlight shone down on the helipad. Through all the movement and activity, Pep walked toward me.

"You guys get stuck in traffic or something?" I asked.

"How about a little gratitude?" he said. "Maybe a 'thank you.'"

"Thank you," I said.

"Better," Rinaldi said. "I'll see you in a few hours."

I looked around through the clusters of cops for Liz. She was still over by the trailer. I got to her, and she stepped to me and we hugged. Her hair was a tangled mess, and her shirt was ripped at the shoulder. The police lights flickered off her face, and her eyes were tired and moist.

"I'm sorry," I said, and hugged her. Her head rested on my chest, and her shoulders rose and then fell as she exhaled in relief. Neither one of us said anything. After a moment she stepped back and looked at me.

"It could have been a lot worse," she said.

"This was bad enough," I said.

In the flashing lights I could see a bruise under her eye. I touched it lightly with the back of my hand.

"A couple of slaps, but I'll live," she said.

I pulled her close and hugged her again.

"One more stop and it's over," I said.

Chapter 71

I got out of the cab at the corner of Forty-ninth and Park just before noon. The block in front of the Waldorf Astoria was jammed from corner to corner with TV vans and satellite trucks, all awaiting the official word from Buck McConnell on his presidential aspirations.

I found Liberty's live truck halfway down the block. I stepped up onto the little metal step, opened the door, and found Charlie Morris inside in a chair at the console. In front of him were the control board and a wall of tiny monitors. Some of the monitors showed the scene inside, from the Grand Ballroom, where a stage draped in red-and-white bunting was prepared for Buck McConnell to make his big announcement. Behind the stage large video panels were set up where striking, larger-than-life photos of the Grand Canyon, a bald eagle, and other iconic American images appeared on a slow-moving loop, one dissolving into the next.

Charlie was on the phone when I walked in, and he turned to me.

"Hang on. He just walked in," he said, and handed me the phone. "It's Blake."

Jennings was at the assignment desk in Liberty's newsroom.

"Anyone know about Cal?" I asked, before he could speak.

"No. No one seems to have noticed that he hasn't been in yet. If anyone asks, I'm just saying he'll be in later," Jennings said. His voice was serious, and he was tense.

"And Kelly and Dan, how much do they know?" I asked.

I was near panic with the thought that word of this would get out and I'd get scooped. Jack Steele was dead. Marty Glover, his executive producer, was dead. Cal Daniels, the president of Liberty News, was in Bellevue under police guard, nursing a bullet wound and expected to be arrested any minute on murder and conspiracy charges, and probably other charges as well. The thugs, including Bulger, had all been arrested on various charges; a police Zodiac craft had fished the one guy out of the East River shortly after we left, according to Pep.

"Kelly and Dan have no idea," Jennings said. "I told them that Cal wanted them to stay on and handle the announcement from McConnell. That it was a big deal and Cal wanted to see how they would do with political stuff. That maybe there was a role for them on election night."

"Brilliant."

"I thought so," he said.

I stood and looked at the monitors and the scene from inside the ballroom. There were aides scurrying about and technicians checking things. No one seemed to have a clue as to the death and chaos Buck McConnell and his obsession with being president had caused.

"The only people who know anything about this are you, me, and Charlie," Jennings said.

I glanced at Charlie. I trusted him.

"All right, I'm going inside," I said. "You go into the control room."

"On my way," Jennings said.

"Give me five minutes and then talk to me in my ear."

I ended the call and Charlie handed me my equipment, a mic, and an earpiece so that he, Blake, and I could communicate.

"You have everything Freddie shot this morning, right? The stuff at the helipad?"

"All of it. Some of it's a little dark, and the audio is weak in spots, but he did a nice job," he said.

Charlie looked at me; he was nervous and shaken. "Sam," he said.

I nodded.

"Jack ... and Marty ... it was all because ..." His voice trailed off.

"Because of Cal," I said. "And McConnell."

Charlie shook his head and looked at me.

"Let's nail the bastard," I said, and walked out of the truck.

Chapter 72

I saw Ripley standing in a group of people outside the closed doors to the ballroom. He spotted me a second later as I walked toward those very doors a few feet away.

Stepping away from the suits, he raced toward me with his hand up. "I'm sorry, the ballroom is now closed and no more press is being allowed inside," he said, louder than necessary. "And besides, Liberty is represented by Julie Parker, from your Washington bureau, a real political reporter."

We were face-to-face now, and the little minions had followed him over and were behind him, watching the drama and eager to see him banish me once and for all.

"Stu, buddy," I said. "You need to step aside and get out of the way."

He smirked and chuckled. "Oh, really? And you need to—"

Before he could finish a voice boomed from behind me.

"Hey, get out of the way and let him do his job."

It was Rinaldi, and he was yelling as he approached us with his badge out. There were two uniforms walking with Rinaldi, and what looked like a battalion right behind them. Police radios crackled as they approached.

"He's an accredited member of the press, and he's going inside the ballroom," Rinaldi said as he got to us. "We all on the same page now?"

Ripley tried to respond. "I ... I, uh ..."

"Good, I thought so," Rinaldi said.

I opened the door and went inside knowing Rinaldi and the other cops had the outside of the ballroom locked down. No one was getting in or out from this point on.

Inside, it was dark. The gigantic screens around the stage were filled with the image of an American flag rippling slowly in a breeze. From the speakers the voice of Ray Charles boomed, as he sang his emotional version of America the Beautiful. The song ended and the room stayed dark, then a deep voice came over the speakers.

"Ladies and gentlemen, Terrance McConnell."

I stayed in the back as the room lights came up and McConnell strode onto the stage from the right. He walked with confidence and smiled a big, wide smile and went to the podium. He was dressed in a navy suit, crisp white shirt and red tie. A walking American flag. He thanked us all for coming and began.

"Decades ago, in the oil fields of Texas, a little boy accompanied his grandfather as the man made the rounds checking on his wells, or holes in the ground as he called them. The little boy took it all in as his grandfather, and later his father, worked from sun up to sun down to build something lasting. A company that a family, a town, and a country could be proud of," he said.

I felt nauseous, or maybe it was just nerves and fatigue, as he went on, speaking of country and the work ethic his father and grandfather had instilled in him and the importance of integrity. He went on for five, then ten minutes, and then sometime around the twelve-minute mark he made a declaration.

"That is why I, Terrance, Buck, McConnell officially declare my candidacy," he said, his voice rising and cheers from supporters beginning. "For the presidency," he said and paused just a beat to let the cheers build. "Of this great country, the United States of America," he yelled as bombastic music blared and supporters cheered.

He stepped to the side of the podium and grinned and waved and it all felt very staged. I expected an attractive wife and clean scrubbed children, maybe even a golden retriever, to appear and join him.

I went over to the riser to my left where the control board and the audio and video engineers sat making sure everything went smoothly and spotted Wade seated among them. He got up and came over to me and handed me a mic.

"Give me a wave when you're ready. I can't wait," he said and then went back to his spot in the row of technicians.

On the stage, McConnell stepped back to the podium. "Thank you. Thank you," he said. He grinned and pointed to a few of the people who refused to quiet down. "Oh, gosh," he said. "This is just great." A few more seconds passed before everyone quieted.

"I know we have some of our friends from the media here," he said. "So I'll take a few questions. But folks, please, let's keep the questions geared to the important issues facing our great country, okay?"

He looked out to the crowd and pointed to a reporter. She stood and waited for an event worker to bring her a mic, then identified herself as Sally Marks with *The New York Times*. She asked about his reputation as a bare knuckles fighter as a CEO and just how that would translate to Washington politics.

He gave a little grin like he was flattered to be called combative. "You know, I also have a reputation as something of a bridge builder," he said, and I couldn't argue. He was the bridge between money and foreign governments on occasion. "I've learned it's often in everyone's best interest when both side learn to give a little," he said.

He was asked about the hostile and divisive tone of politics and he said all the right things.

"This president has shown a blatant disregard for opposing view points and is more concerned with pushing an agenda, an agenda that has damaged this country. That needs to stop," he said, his voice rising. "It needs to stop now. With this next election before the damage is too great to repair."

That brought a smattering of applause. The next reporter asked what his number one priority would be if elected. He gripped the sides of the podium and exhaled like and it seemed all too smooth, like he had practiced for this or a similar question.

"Boy," he said. "That is a tough one. There are a lot of things that need fixing."

The images behind him had cycled through a few times and the rippling flag was dissolving into a panoramic shot of the Grand Canyon. It was filled with golden sunshine and rich colors and at this particular moment Buck McConnell may have had the luckiest timing of anyone, anywhere.

"We need to restore the spirit of America. From day one. Now, I know there are big, important issues that need fixing, but so does this. For far too long we have walked around with our heads down and that has to stop." There were a few claps that grew to cheers and McConnell slapped the podium. "And it has to stop now."

When it quieted down McConnell looked out and said, "We have time for one more question."

I looked over at Wade and he flashed a thumbs-up. I flipped on the mic and started walking down the center aisle from the back of the ballroom. I thought of Jack and Michael Barnes and Marty, and I thought of Robbie as I began to speak.

Chapter 73

"Mr. McConnell," I said.

McConnell squinted and looked out at the crowd, searching for the person attached to the voice. I had stopped halfway to the stage and was smack in the middle of the room. McConnell found me and his face tightened. He recognized me and tried to strike first.

"We are only taking questions on—"

"What was your role in the killing of Jack Steele?" I said, cutting him off.

There were murmurs and talk and the room buzzed. People twisted in their seats and heads turned to look at me. I continued on, confident that Wade was on the job and was making sure my mic wouldn't be cut off.

"Mr. McConnell," I said in a loud, clear voice. "Please tell us about your role in the killing of Jack Steele. And while you're at it, tell us why you also had Michael Barnes killed."

McConnell shook his head and waved a hand to try and dismiss me. "Look, I'm not sure who you are, or what you're talking about, but you are—"

I took a few more steps toward him and cut him off again. "And can you explain your arrest on drug charges while you were an undergrad at Harvard," I said.

There were gasps now and every head was turned to me. People seated on the far left and far right stood to get a better view and hands holding phones were raised to record the confrontation.

McConnell looked to the wings of the stage, where a half-dozen security guards stood. "Could we please have this individual removed?" he said.

The bodyguards sprang into action, leaving the stage and crossing in front of it on their way to the center aisle.

"One last chance, Buck," I said. "Either you explain your role in these deaths, or I will."

McConnell slammed a fist down onto the podium and exploded, his face red with rage.

"Somebody remove him," he yelled. "I will not have this disrupted by a nut job."

The first security guard hustled to the center aisle and turned down it toward me. He was ten feet from me when a uniformed cop pushed past me from behind and confronted him, putting his hands on his chest and pushing him back. The room erupted with activity. Cameramen sprang from the riser and hustled to the front with cameras on their shoulders to get better shots.

A group of cops moved onto the stage and surrounded McConnell as I spoke. "You had your chance, Buck," I said.

I turned around and waved to Wade, and the large screens flanking McConnell went black. They stayed that way for five seconds and the room went quiet. Then the screens sprang to life with the grainy, dark video of Jack's body being pulled from the East River. My voice boomed from the speakers.

"In the early morning hours of August 9, the body of Liberty News anchor Jack Steele was pulled from the East River. His death was ruled a suicide. But Liberty News has learned that Steele and two other men, environmen-

talist Michael Barnes and Liberty News producer Martin Glover, were ordered to be killed by Terrance 'Buck' McConnell."

The room exploded in talking and shouting; McConnell's mic was still open, and he could be heard yelling in the chaos. "Someone stop this. Stop this now."

Reporters were up and yelling questions at him, and cameramen raced to the stage to get shots of him surrounded by cops. His mic was cut off and he tried to yell but no one heard him above my voice.

"The murders were part of a wide-ranging cover-up of a drug charge against McConnell almost forty years ago. Liberty News president Calvin Daniels, a former classmate of McConnell's at Harvard, took part in the cover-up and has already been arrested in connection with the three deaths. Early this morning Daniels was recorded confessing to the killing of Steele and implicating McConnell in the murders."

The video Freddie shot from the helipad was played, and the audio, picked up with the camera mic, had been enhanced so you could hear the voice of Daniels first, and then mine.

"But instead Buck panics, he says it's too late. He wants Jack dead. And guess who he says is in charge of it?"

"You."

"He says, take care of this guy. If Jack exposes me, I expose you. No way he was going to lose his shot at the White House over this."

"So it was you Jack met over there that night? Not Barnes? You killed Jack."

"Buck ordered me to. He sat in the car and watched the whole thing to make sure I did."

I watched McConnell's reaction on stage. He was surrounded by cops, and they, like everyone else, were watching my piece on the big video screens. But McConnell was twitchy, I could see if from here. He had tried to fight me and had lost and now it was time for flight. He glanced at the screens as more shots from the helipad played and then he looked back around the room.

I could see he was going to try something, and then he did. He spun and burst into action, shoving a cop with two hands and blasting through the opening that created. He took off down the steps of the stage and there was an uproar and commotion as people yelled and cameramen ran toward him. I started toward him and as I did Rinaldi sprinted past me from behind with more uniforms. Chairs were knocked over as cameramen and reporters raced over to where the action was on the left side of the ballroom.

McConnell made a run for the very far side of the ballroom, trying to get to the outer aisle, but two uniformed cops pushed through the crowd and when they got close enough one dove for him and tackled him from behind. There was more screaming and yelling and a crowd formed around the men on the floor of the ballroom. I arrived and pushed my way through with Rinaldi next to me.

"This really is no way to start a presidential campaign," Rinaldi said as the cops handcuffed McConnell and pulled him to his feet.

McConnell stood and glared at me. The sound of my voice filling the room as the taped piece played on, laying out McConnell's role in the deaths of Steele, Barnes, and Glover.

"I will sue Liberty News out of existence," he said to me. "Then I'll come after you."

"You're done, Buck," I said. "And no one is going to come save you this time."

Chapter 74

I was walking up Irving Place toward Gramercy Park hand in hand with Liz. It was almost eleven at night and the streets were quiet, with people out of town for the weekend.

"Kenny the Wonder Agent called," I said as we crossed Eighteenth Street and passed Pete's Tavern.

"Again?" Liz said.

"Yes, that makes at least a dozen times since the McConnell press conference the other day."

"Maybe he feels guilty for ignoring you for all those years and is making up for lost time," she said.

"Or maybe he's afraid I'm going to bolt for a real agent," I said.

We walked along, enjoying the feeling of not having to look over our shoulders and worried about who may or may not be following us.

"Speaking of feeling guilty," I said.

Liz squeezed my hand.

"I told you, I'm fine with everything," she said.

"Fine with your boyfriend of six months putting you in harm's way?"

"Fine with my boyfriend's plan working like a charm," she said. "I did exactly as you suggested that day. I called your friend Pep at the first sign of trouble."

"When the two thick necks followed you out of work," I said.

"Yes. They looked like a matching set of thugs," she said. "They weren't too hard to spot."

Rinaldi had assigned two cops to follow Liz, knowing sooner or later McConnell was going to go after her to get to me. She was never in danger, but the fact that one of the Neanderthals had slapped her upset me greatly.

I turned to her and looked at her cheek in the faint yellow of the streetlights.

"It's okay, really," she said. "It doesn't hurt, and you can hardly notice it with makeup."

It was a small bruise on her cheek.

"It could have been worse," she said.

I knew she was right. It could have turned out far worse.

"How was Robbie Steele?" she asked.

"It was odd," I said. "She was relieved that the person responsible for Jack's dying has been caught, and shocked that Daniels and Marty were involved. But with this solved now, it was like she now had nothing left to do but grieve."

"That probably got pushed aside. She was preoccupied with getting it all figured out," she said.

"And now she's alone in her big apartment, and their other houses, with a child on the way."

"You believed her," she said. "She probably saw you as one of her only allies."

"At the end, as I was leaving, she hugged me," I said.

"Doesn't everyone want to?"

"But it was like she didn't want to let go."

"She's not going to have it easy," Liz said.

"I know."

"So, now what?" she asked.

I looked at her and smiled. "Thought you'd never ask."

"I mean professionally," she said.

"Damn," I said. "I guess I go back to work in the next day or two and see what Blake has in store for me. He's been put in charge until a new president is named," I said.

"Is that a good or a bad thing?" she asked.

"Hard to say. In a way it doesn't matter. Kenny says he has three solid contract offers from the networks, for money I thought I would never see," I said. "Plus, he thinks whoever is named president of Liberty is going to offer me a new deal immediately. Says I should be able to name my price."

We walked on, crossing Twentieth Street. A breeze floated through the trees of Gramercy Park up ahead and cooled us.

"Why'd you stay with Kenny all these years?" Liz asked.

I shrugged.

"Some odd sense of loyalty. He was there when no one else would take me on. And he needed clients at the time."

"But now that he has plenty of clients, you get less attention," she said.

"I'd describe it as zero attention."

"Until this story," she said.

"Yes, now I'm popular," I said.

"Would it be a good time to consider new representation?" she asked.

"You mean, make a move while I'm hot, that sort of thing?"

"Yes."

"It's occurred to me," I said.

"But?"

"But I'm okay staying with Kenny."

She leaned in to me and wrapped her arm around mine.

"I knew you were going to say that," she said.

I pulled her tight, and we walked home.

ACKNOWLEDGMENTS

To Rani Clarkin, Regina Clarkin, and Tom Riley, a group of early readers any writer would envy. Your ability to let me know what worked and what didn't work was invaluable. Thank you for your time in reading the early drafts, and your patience in pushing me through the writing process. To Nora Reichard, whose edits tightened and focused the manuscript more than I realized possible.

ABOUT THE AUTHOR

In more than twenty years as a business journalist, Greg Clarkin has covered Wall Street, the economy, and the housing-market boom and bust, and squeezed in stories on sports, whenever possible. He has worked as a reporter for CNN and the *New York Post* and was a correspondent for the nationally syndicated business show, *BusinessWeek Weekend*. He has written for dozens of publications, including *The New York Times* and *Men's Journal*. He lives in Connecticut, with his wife and three children.